P9-EMP-079

TOR BOOKS BY KEN SCHOLES

Lamentation

Canticle

Antiphon

Requiem

Hymn

HYMN

KEN SCHOLES

TOR

A TOM DOHERTY ASSOCIATES BOOK
NEW YORK

MORRILL MEMORIAL LIBRARY
NORWOOD, MASS 02062

Sci. Fict.
Scholes,
K.

This is a work of fiction. All of the characters, organizations, and events portrayed in this novel are either products of the author's imagination or are used fictitiously.

HYMN

Copyright © 2017 by Kenneth G. Scholes

All rights reserved.

A Tor Book
Published by Tom Doherty Associates
175 Fifth Avenue
New York, NY 10010

www.tor-forge.com

Tor® is a registered trademark of Macmillan Publishing Group, LLC.

The Library of Congress Cataloging-in-Publication Data is available upon request.

ISBN 978-0-7653-2131-2 (hardcover)
ISBN 978-1-4299-4958-3 (ebook)

Our books may be purchased in bulk for promotional, educational, or business use. Please contact your local bookseller or the Macmillan Corporate and Premium Sales Department at 1-800-221-7945, extension 5442, or by email at MacmillanSpecialMarkets@macmillan.com.

First Edition: December 2017

Printed in the United States of America

0 9 8 7 6 5 4 3 2 1

For Dr. Eugene Lipov

and

For Lizzy and Rae:

Thank you for turning my lamentation into a hymn

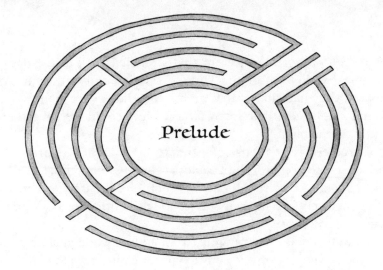

Prelude

The watchman, Cyril Thrall, waited beneath a moonless sky scattered with stars that he'd been able to name since childhood, though he'd not seen them until his twentieth year. He'd dreamed of them, of course, and when he'd reached adulthood, he'd stood beneath them for the first time here at Endicott Station, not far from where he now sat and in fact *had sat* for so many nights these past four decades. That canvas of space above him, until last week, had been more full of wonder than anything he'd ever seen. A million points of light that illuminated and enhanced the plain paper charts he'd studied on the ceiling of the observatory when he was a boy. He'd wept the first time he stood beneath them, his lungs full of the dry, dead air of the Barrens after spending the first two decades of his life hidden away.

And then last week, the dream had brought a new wonder to him.

Cyril had not fully understood the significance of it in the moment of the dream. But he had given himself to the experience, taking it all in, slack-jawed and rubbing his eyes. The massive tree white with seed, the multitudes stretched out across the plains and the loud voice of Winteria bat Mardic, a daughter of Shadrus, rising above the roaring wind to conclude two thousand years of dreaming with the proclamation that would allow the Firsthome Temple to be unsealed.

The path to the moon will now be open again, Cyril realized as he stood in that field and bore witness. It was the culmination of millennia spent waiting, watching and preparing carefully. It was the fulfillment of Frederico's Bargain—an event that stretched back to the days of the Under-Exodus, before the Time of Tending and Gathering. And somehow, they had shared that dream together, every man, woman and child. He'd seen them for as far as his eye could see, all gathered together on the plain.

It stirred everyone's sense of wonder, and launched a flurry of activity. Vessels to prepare, ambassadors to send out and now, most recently, guests to receive. His own two children, barely grown, had already been sent out in their service to the council for their part in the making of history.

Cyril watched as he always did, from a plain wooden chair facing south, just at the edge of the run-down stone buildings that made up Endicott Station. Most nights, all he saw were stars, or a field-worker returning home. Only once in forty years had there actually been an intruder at the station, and it had been dealt with quickly and efficiently. The grave wasn't marked, but Cyril knew just where it was. He blinked away the memory of violence, grateful that it had been done by hands other than his own. Still, he felt remorse from having any part in it and had dug the grave himself.

Guests were another thing altogether. He couldn't recall the last occurrence in their carefully recorded history. In the earliest years, they'd received a slow trickle of pilgrims and refugees seeking sanctuary, but that had evaporated over the course of a few hundred years. That trickle started again, according to historians, once the Y'Zirite blood cult sprang up. But eventually, that slow migration had stopped. Or, if people out there still attempted the journey, the harsh travel conditions—and the imperial Blood Scouts who hunted down any apostates that fled—prevented their arrival.

But now, guest cottages were being cleaned in the midst of everything else.

The hours slid by, and twice Cyril stood to take a slow stroll around the station. It was a quiet night with no wind, making it easy for him to hear the approach.

It was the softest hum at first, growing louder in the south. He stepped toward it, scanning the night sky as he reached into his pocket. He put his hand upon the stone there and focused his words through it.

"I have an approach from the south," he said in a quiet voice.

A small patch of sky shimmered and Cyril focused his eyes there, watching as the shimmering grew along with the hum of the engines that propelled it toward him. They'd made them as quiet as they could, but the noise seemed deafening to him against the backdrop of the night's stillness. It amazed him that these vessels could fly over cities and villages, unnoticed by the unsuspecting souls below. He felt it drawing near now—a fluctuation in the air that raised the hairs on his arm.

The reply came through, a tickle in his skull. *Escort them to the translation point.*

"Understood."

He'd seen the ships a few times—well, not exactly *seen*. The vessels were coated with an extract that rendered them nearly invisible, and they were never anchored too close to any of the access points for longer than was necessary to disembark passengers.

Now the entire sky above him warbled and shifted, and suddenly, ropes began to drop. Even as they fell, shadowy figures descended. Cyril stepped back as they pulled the airship down. A doorway opened and a gangplank was lowered.

"Disembarking," a voice said from the doorway.

Then, a stream of people exited. A large number of them—at least ten—were bound, with their faces hooded. Men and women in dark robes moved around them, guiding their sluggish steps. A woman wearing the uniform of a captain in the Council's Expeditionary Force stepped off the gangplank briskly and approached Cyril. "I believe we are expected."

He nodded, taking in the group. "I hadn't been told it would be so many."

Behind her, two more robed figures materialized. Each held a sleeping child—a boy and a girl. "There were complications," the captain said.

Cyril knew better than to ask. Instead, he turned. "Come on then."

Behind him, he heard the slightest whisper of the gangplank and ropes being pulled up.

He led the way, entering the first low building. In the back room, he moved the thick, ancient carpet to reveal the hatch and then spun it open. "You'll have to untie them," he said, pointing to their prisoners.

The captain nodded. "They're still recovering from the salva root. I don't expect they've much fight or flight left in them."

Despite the root, at least two put up brief struggles when they were untied, but the rest were peaceable enough. Guards before and behind, they started down the metal ladder. Cyril waited until everyone had descended, then followed, sealing the hatch behind him.

Another hatch waited at the bottom of the shaft, and beyond it a silver pond stretched out, lit dimly by lichen that scattered its high ceiling. At the edge of the pond, a white tree stood, its limbs heavy with purple fruit.

Cyril touched the stone in his pocket again, his eyes moving over the group of people gathered by the edge of the pond. "Endicott Station preparing for translation." Then he went to the tree and picked four large, purple globes.

They pulled off the hoods, revealing frightened but slack faces beneath, eyes rolled back from the power of the drugs they'd been given. All but one of the prisoners bore the cuttings of Y'Zir, though Cyril couldn't read the runes carved into their flesh. The other was a young, bearded man—one of the strugglers—with fierce, dark eyes. The look on the man's face was disconcerting enough that Cyril's hands shook as he tore into one of the globes. "Bite into this," he told each of them as he stood before them.

He watched as they chewed and swallowed the fruit; then he went to the children. He wasn't sure who the others were or what complications had led to them being brought along, but these two he'd expected. The boy and the girl were just past two years old, and while Cyril wasn't certain that they were the salvation of the world, they certainly were an important move in that direction. Important enough that the council was intervening in matters that it normally would not. Important enough that Grandmother had sent for them that she might give her blessing in the midst of everything else that transpired.

And that these two children might be safe from the insanity that produced them in the first place.

He sighed, then gently shook the little girl's shoulder, pressing the fruit against her lips. "Eat this," he whispered, though she certainly couldn't understand the words he used. But she licked at the juice he dribbled into her open mouth and finally stirred to nibble at the fruit. When he was satisfied, he did the same with the boy, then stepped back and touched the stone in his pocket again. "Endicott Station translation commencing."

Then, one by one, he watched as the men and women stepped into the pool, evaporating instantly with a flash of blue and green. The boy stirred and opened his mouth to cry out when the woman who carried him stepped into the pool. In that moment, his mouth and eyes open wide, Cyril saw terror. But the boy was gone before he could make a sound.

When the room was empty, Cyril left. He was halfway up the ladder when his scalp tickled again.

Translation complete.

He climbed out of the shaft and locked the metal hatch before moving the carpet back into place.

Then Cyril returned to the remainder of his watch, but the stars no longer held him. Instead, it was the look upon the boy's face.

Perhaps, he thought as the stars winked out and the sky went slowly gray, *we should all be frightened*.

But even as he thought it, Cyril Thrall felt more wonder—not fear—stirring to life within him.

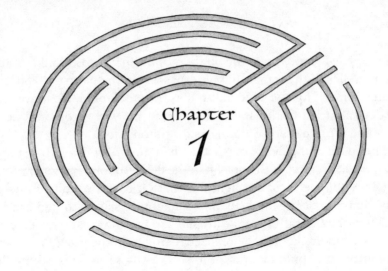

Chapter

1

Rudolfo

Lord Rudolfo of the Ninefold Forest Houses, General of the Wandering Army and Chancellor of the Named Lands, brought the glass of chilled peach wine to his lips to drink deeply.

Then watched his enemies do the same.

The effect was instantaneous and it caught him off guard, blinking for a moment before fastening his eyes onto Yazmeera's. Hers were wide now even as she dropped her wineglass. He smiled and kept his eyes locked onto hers, his hand straying to the pouch of magicks tucked within the bandage that wrapped his chest. The wound ached with each beat of his pounding heart, and an exhilaration washed through him. The Y'Zirite general collapsed, wheezing and thrashing about on the floor.

She was not alone. Her officers and her Blood Guard joined her there—a room full of people dying together in puddles of spilled peach wine in the midst of a half-eaten banquet. This—the sight of them kicking their last upon the floor—was the very future he'd drank to when she'd suggested it as a toast just moments before.

Rudolfo wanted to stay and watch, sipping this victory like the finest of his wines. He wanted to crouch next to Yazmeera and watch her breathe her last, maybe stroke her iron-gray hair and whisper to her how happy the moment made him, but he forced that desire aside and pulled out the pouch.

He opened it and threw the powders at his forehead, shoulders and feet, then licked the remaining bitterness from the palm of his hand, bracing himself for the sudden lurch as they took hold. He moved for the door that led to the stairwell, picking his way across a floor of thrashing limbs already quieting as death took hold.

The speed and efficacy of it astonished him. According to Renard, this was the first test of the poison in the field. Rudolfo knew very little in the way of specifics, but he knew that Orius—the Androfrancine Gray Guard general—and his own General Lysias both had armies hidden in the Beneath Places with plans to use the poison on a bigger scale. A weapon like this, he realized, could turn the tide of the war.

Not that he would be present to see it. All of this—his taking the mark, the poisoning of Yazmeera and her staff—was for Jakob. Rudolfo had been lost, overwhelmed by circumstance and uncertain of his path until recently, but it had become clear to him. His son was in more danger in the Empire of Y'Zir as that blood cult's Child of Promise than he could ever be in Rudolfo's care, even in the midst of an invasion.

And so now he fled the rooftop garden, feeling the strength gathering in his legs as the scout magicks flooded him. The spiced food from the banquet churned in his stomach, and he gritted his teeth against the nausea and vertigo that seized him. The powders had that effect, and he knew it would grow worse before too long. When he reached the doorway, he felt hands upon him.

We must flee, Ire Li Tam pressed into the soft skin of his upper arm.

She slipped a loop of thread around his wrist and pulled it taut as she moved ahead of him. She went slowly and he followed, taking the stairs down from the rooftop garden where Yazmeera's officers had dined. Behind him, he heard the first screams as the servants discovered his handiwork, and Rudolfo smiled again.

Twice, Ire pulled him aside as Blood Guard swept past, unmagicked but with knives held ready. When they reached the first floor, she led him out into a warm evening as the sounds of third alarm rose up around them.

Outside, soldiers assembled and Rudolfo saw the eddies of dust that betrayed magicked scouts as they moved in. It would take them time to determine exactly what had happened; and until they identified the dead, they wouldn't know that he and Ire were missing. And certainly the loss of the majority of their officers was going to work to Rudolfo's advantage, creating chaos in the Y'Zirite chain of command. Still, he could not afford to waste time. At some point, the enemy would find their footing, and by then Rudolfo needed to be at sea.

They ran for hours, and he was grateful for the running he'd come back to in recent weeks, though the little he'd managed had certainly not prepared him for this. Even with the magicks burning in him, he felt his legs growing heavy and his breath growing ragged as they put the leagues behind them. Still they ran, keeping to the fields and forests away from the roads. In the distance, Rudolfo saw the scattered farmhouses and villages of Merrique County slipping past, washed by the red-gold of evening.

The sun had set by the time they reached the small river that served as the border with neighboring Jessym County. There, Ire Li Tam turned them west to run downstream in the deepening shadows of cypress trees that lined the bank. She slowed them from a sprint to a jog, and Rudolfo felt gratitude for the change of pace in his ankles and knees.

They'd run alongside the river for perhaps five leagues when a low whistle brought them to a stop. A dark figure separated itself from the shadows.

"Hail, Rudolfo," a quiet voice called.

"Hail, Renard," he answered, settling into a crouch as he slipped his hand from Ire's guide-thread.

The tall man took shape in the dim light of evening, the simple garb of a farmer looking out of place on his angular frame. "You've kicked up the hornets," the Waste guide said with a grin.

Rudolfo smiled, though the magicks masked it. "I've set fire to their nest. Now you and Orius and Lysias will need to keep it burning."

"Aye," Renard said. "We will." His eyes wandered the gray landscape around them. "They'll likely realize it was you and be looking for you by morning, so keep moving. Stay magicked and off the roads."

Rudolfo silently counted the leagues before answering. "Yes." They were two days from the coast, and a quick sail to the mainland. There, he could get word to Philemus and arrange for a ship to bear him across the Ghosting Crests in search of Y'Zir.

To take back my son. He blinked, his memory suddenly flooded with the sight of the boy in the dream, calling to him and so real that Rudolfo could smell his hair. He pushed the memory away and turned his attention to Renard.

"There is a bridge house at the next crossing with fresh clothing, magicks and some supplies. Send what you're wearing down the river before the magicks burn out. Our friend in Talcroft Landing is Simmons. Ask for him at the docks and he'll see you to the mainland."

"Thank you," Rudolfo said. "And thank Orius for me as well."

Renard's face sobered at the mention of the Gray Guard general. "He bid me ask you reconsider, of course. I told him that if I had a son in the clutches of those bloodletters, nothing could keep me from taking him back. Still, with what's coming, I can't blame him. We'll need every soldier in the field and every general on the hill."

"Philemus and Lysias will serve well on my behalf," he said. But he also wondered exactly what was coming. Rudolfo had seen the poison do its work in one room with the element of surprise in his favor. It remained to be seen how they would deliver that poison in such a way as to make a difference in a war they were losing. But he knew better than to ask. "My son will need a home to return to; I trust you all to give him that."

Renard nodded. "We will do our utmost. You've given us a good start. Word of it will spread, and hope will spread with it." The man extended a hand toward him and Rudolfo took it, squeezing it. "Hunt well, Rudolfo."

"Aye," Rudolfo said. "You also."

The Waste guide paused, his face clouded as he looked around. "Your companion goes with you?"

Rudolfo hadn't asked but had assumed, given that Ire Li Tam had sworn allegiance to him the night she'd found him in his tent. He said nothing, waiting for her to answer for herself.

"I follow him to Y'Zir," she said. "I will help him reclaim my nephew."

Renard looked in the direction of her voice. "Good. Soon enough, it will not be safe for you or your kind in the Named Lands. Heed me carefully, Ire Li Tam: If you return with him, you will die."

She said nothing. Rudolfo opened his mouth to the threat but then closed it. There'd been no animosity in Renard's tone; he'd spoken the words as a matter of fact.

They've found a way to deliver the poison broadly. Curiosity pushed at him, but he knew inquiring was pointless. Renard had said what he would say, and Rudolfo knew the benefit of knowing less rather than more in the event of his capture.

"Now run," Renard said.

This time, no looped thread slipped over his hand. Instead, he felt strong fingers interlace his own as Ire Li Tam pulled him alongside her. They ran at a measured pace, Rudolfo's mind replaying every word of Renard's as he worked through the implications of what was coming. Somehow, he thought, the Androfrancines must have access to the Y'Zirite supply lines. Though he wasn't sure how that was possible, especially given the additional security their enemy would certainly implement after the massacre at Rudolfo's Markday Feast.

He continued to ponder it, even after they let themselves into the bridge house to change and remagick themselves. As the stars appeared overhead and they continued their run north through darkened fields, his mind kept at it like a hound to a rabbit. With each muffled footfall, the question echoed within him, and by the time the sky lightened, Rudolfo still had no answer.

What home will we return to?

His breath ragged and his companion's hand cold and firm in his own, Rudolfo kept running and hoped his feet could carry him past the fear that snuffled at his heels.

Jin Li Tam

Jin Li Tam danced the knives in utter darkness and let hatred fuel each move. She went from crouch to lunge, dodging deftly around the room's furniture, building speed as she went. The knives—gifts given to her by Rudolfo on their wedding day, though she'd already wet them in battle months earlier—were perfectly balanced in her hands, precise extensions of her rage.

And they went where she pointed them, the blades whistling up and down as she slashed and thrust at the air ahead of her.

She forced her awareness into the moment and gathered her focus toward the only objective that remained for her: vengeance upon the man who had taken everything from her.

She remembered the night she'd found her father's note beneath her pillow, bidding her to bear Rudolfo an heir as part of Vlad Li Tam's great, secret strategy in the Named Lands. She'd come to motherhood reluctantly under those conditions but had grown to love Rudolfo and the idea of giving him a family. Then, so soon after Jakob's birth, she'd found herself—and their son—at the center of the Y'Zirite blood cult as their Great Mother and Child of Promise. Most recently, they'd been carried to this place—an empire she'd had no knowledge of until recently—to meet the Crimson Empress, her son's betrothed based on the Gospels of Ahm Y'Zir.

She'd watched Jakob play with the little girl, Amara Y'Zir. And then, in a night filled with blood and fire, she'd watched her father murder both children before her eyes.

She flinched at the memory but kept her pace. Jin had chosen a larger room this time, one she was less familiar with. So much of the palace was empty now between the plagues and the uprising of disillusioned, despairing faithful who'd never imagined a world in which their faith could so easily shatter.

A part of her felt a deep connection to them, though she'd never embraced their religion.

Because, she realized, *I am shattered, too.*

Jakob's face flashed before her eyes, and she felt a sob tugging at her throat and shoulders. Jin missed a step, staggering as she clipped a chair with her thigh. She recovered quickly and conjured the one face that could drive her child's face away and give back her form and substance. She held it before her and danced toward it, knives carving at it as she moved.

Father, I am coming to end you.

She heard the door behind her whisper open. "Great Mother?"

I am no mother now, she thought with a flash of anger and bitterness even as she recognized the voice. Jin untied her blindfold and turned to face the older woman. "Sister Elsbet."

The woman closed the door behind her. She wore the dark robes of her office as Chief Mother of the Daughters of Ahm, her long white hair braided and hanging over her shoulder. "Lynnae told me you were here." She took in Jin's sweaty night shift and knives, and Jin was uncertain how to catalog the look upon her face. Of course, whatever emotion Sister Elsbet showed was quickly subdued and washed out with a look of strained, forced calm.

Jin inclined her head. "I'm sorry for my appearance, Sister Elsbet. I am training."

She returned the nod. "I see that you are. Should I come back at another time?"

"No," she said, sliding the knives into the sheaths at her hips.

Sister Elsbet gestured to a pair of sofas facing each other across a low table. "Shall we sit?"

By habit, Jin picked the sofa that offered the widest view of the room, including its two entrances and three windows. She'd not studied the room when she'd first selected it, and now she saw it was a meditation room of some kind—various paintings of a younger Ahm Y'Zir in different reflective poses, fixed to the wall within view of scattered chairs and sofas.

Jin's eyes went from the room to the woman before her. Sister Elsbet's signature calm still dominated the woman's face, but Jin could see the frayed edges. And deep in the woman's eyes, she saw something far more than disillusionment.

She is as lost as I am.

The realization was so intense that Jin broke eye contact. They were quiet, together, for a minute.

Finally, Elsbet leaned forward. "Are you sleeping?"

Jin shrugged. "Only a little."

"I could help you with that."

Jin shook her head. "No." She'd spent days asleep, kept under by their powders and medicines, after she'd watched her father murder her son. The memory of sluggish rage and nightmares, fueled by loss and chemicals, in which she could not run fast enough to save her child, made her shudder. "I don't want to sleep more. I have work to do."

The woman nodded. "You still intend to go through with it." It was a statement, not a question.

Jin met the woman's eyes. "I do. Yes."

Now Elsbet looked away. "Part of me," she said slowly, "wants to talk you out of it, wants to remind you that even if you succeed, you won't survive the blood magicks." She paused. "But I know you understand that already. And I can appreciate why that might not deter you." Jin followed the woman's gaze to the window. "Part of me wants to strap on knives and join you."

"Surviving is . . . irrelevant," Jin said. She knew the Imperial Blood Guard started ingesting the blood magicks in infancy, mixed with their milk, to prepare their bodies for the toll they took. When she'd first begun learning V'Ral, the Y'Zirite tongue, Elsbet had provided her with a dreamstone and a small phial of blood magicks to enhance her learning, but that limited exposure would do little to help her. At best, she'd have four days under the Y'Zirite scout magicks, and at the end of it, her body would give out from the strain. A sacrifice she would gladly make.

Elsbet sighed. "Yes. I had thought you might feel that way." She reached into the pocket of her robe and drew out a silver phial. Leaning forward, she placed it on the table. "Our own search for your father has yielded little fruit. Lately, he's been abducting magisters and Daughters. We're finding some of the bodies." She looked away. "Not all."

Jin reached out and touched the phial with a tentative finger. "He's looking for something."

"Yes," Elsbet agreed. "We think it's the spellbook, but we can't know for sure. Regardless, it's been relocated to a secure location."

Jin knew little about the book—only that like the staff her father now carried, it had once belonged to the Moon Wizard, Raj Y'Zir. The Imperial Archaeology Society had found it, and for centuries it had been kept hidden deep beneath the Temple of the Daughters of Ahm. But she knew that if her father found it, it couldn't bode well for the Y'Zirites. The Moon Wizard's staff had already given him power beyond anyone's wildest imaginings, and he'd used that power to desolate their faith with plague and fire, murdering anything that stood in his way.

Even children. Jin felt the sob take her shoulders and she wrestled it down, forcing calm to her face. "I will kill him before he finds it," she said. "He's done enough."

"Yes," Elsbet said. "He has."

The woman stood. "The regent has committed two squads of Blood Guard to aid you. He regrets that he cannot do more."

Jin blinked, surprised that he offered so many. Most of a squad had committed suicide after the children were killed, grief-struck and despondent over failing to protect their Crimson Empress and Child of Promise. And with so many military resources committed in the Named Lands, sparing any of the empire's most elite was significant. "Two squads is very generous. Please thank him for me."

Elsbet walked to the door and paused. "There is one more matter, before I leave," she said. She looked over her shoulder at Jin. "We've not been able to contain the news about . . ." The woman's composure nearly failed along with her words. Her eyes were furtive and dark, her face washed in sorrow and weariness. She took a deep breath, her hand steadying herself against the doorframe. "About the children. Word is spreading and will reach our forces overseas." She paused again, and Jin sensed this time that the woman was waiting for some kind of response. When none was offered, Sister Elsbet continued. "If you intend to inform Chancellor Rudolfo personally of all that's transpired, it should be soon."

Jin felt the ice in her stomach even as her face flushed. It was something she thought about every day and then tried hard not to think about again. How could she tell him that his son was dead? The child he'd never expected to show up in the middle of his life, the one she'd deceived him into having with her though it was a deception he'd welcomed despite her—and her family's—betrayal of him. "Yes," she agreed. "I do need to tell him."

Elsbet's composure returned, and she inclined her head as she opened the door. "I will tell the ravener to expect you. Thank you, Great Mother."

She felt the sting of the title again as the woman let herself out. Jin took up her blindfold and tied it over her eyes. Then she drew her knives and moved into the steps of the familiar dance.

But no matter how hard she tried to conjure the face of her father to focus her rage, all she found was the face of her husband, Rudolfo, General of the Wandering Army and Lord of the Ninefold Forest Houses. She owed him words, and she had no idea how she would speak them.

Rudolfo, my love. It was how she always began with him. It had started in the early days when there was new love between them and she'd kept it as her preferred salutation. This would be her last message to him, she suspected, and it was fitting to start as she always had. But the fractures in her heart deepened at the weight of what she needed to tell him after.

I brought our son here without your knowledge or consent, and the man who manipulated your life, killing your parents and your brother—the man who commanded me to marry you and bear you an heir—has murdered him.

Jin Li Tam faltered in her steps and, in a flash of anger, hurled her knives across the room. They clattered off the wall, and the sound of it didn't satisfy her. She ripped off the blindfold and kicked at a nearby chair, knocking it over.

Then, Jin Li Tam fell to the floor, sobbing and raging at the hole in her heart that threatened to swallow her utterly.

Vlad Li Tam

The warm evening air was heavy with the smell of smoke and decay as Vlad Li Tam forced his latest fish down deserted streets. He'd kept to the quarters of Ahm's Glory that had been most ravaged by the plague, slipping out only to catch another and drag the poor unfortunate into one of a network of abandoned buildings he'd found.

How many now? Five, he thought. Maybe six.

He glanced to the man beside him. He looked less impressive without his magister's robes and the silver markings upon them that had betrayed his rather high placement in that order's hierarchy. Those robes were tucked away neatly in an alley most of a league behind them now.

Vlad squeezed the staff. "Turn left here. Then we cross the street."

The magister moved with him, his eyes wide and bulging, his mouth twisted into a forced silence. Still, his step was steady and without hesitation. Vlad smiled despite the deep ache in his bones and the fever that burned his brain. For everything the staff gave him, it took as well. He knew that in the end, it would kill him. But he also knew that he would gladly be spent in such a way if it let him end this cult and find his lost grandson.

They turned, then crossed the street. Vlad led them to the end of the block to a blue door. "Open it and go inside."

The magister obeyed and Vlad followed, closing and barring the door behind him. He closed his eyes against a sudden spike of pain and flash of light as he pulled power from the staff. "There is a chair in the next room. Sit in it and fasten your ankles and wrists into the manacles."

As the man shuffled into the room, Vlad glanced quickly around them before closing the last door. Once the magister was secure, he stepped back, leaning upon the staff, and regarded his latest catch.

He tried to keep his voice warm and calm. "I think you know who I am," he said. "What is your name and position?"

Vlad moved his finger over the warm steel, giving the man back his tongue to answer. The magister said nothing.

He braced himself for the nausea that swept over him. "You will answer my questions," he said.

The man's eyes went wide and his nostrils flared. "I am Tamyr Aviz, arch-librarian of the Magister Holdings."

A librarian. That was new. And a favorable development, he hoped. The others he'd taken had known very little, mostly serving more bureaucratic roles, whether as Daughters of Ahm or the Magisters of the Knowledge of the Faithful.

Vlad reached into his pocket and drew out the round white stone, extending it before him in the palm of his hand. "What is this stone, Tamyr Aviz?"

The man squinted, and his face registered surprise. "It is a moon-stone."

Yes. The others had known that much at least. And Vlad had suspected as much. In the dream, the kin-raven had landed upon a similar, larger white stone. He put it away, then pulled out the small pamphlet he'd found with it, there in the empty warehouse where he'd expected to rendezvous with the others. He held the pamphlet closer than the stone. "And do you recognize this?"

"Yes. I do. It contains the prophetic utterances of a small, under-ground group called the Lost Children of Shadrus."

Vlad nodded. "They seem to have been expecting me."

"They are a variation on Lunarism cults that have existed for thou-sands and thousands of years. They were particularly focused on the notion of wrathful Younger Gods showing up at the end of time to make things right." Tamyr Aviz paused and his mouth twitched. "Of course, we know that you are not a Younger God, Lord Tam."

"Yes," he answered. "Some of you *do* know that. But some of you aren't sure anymore." He'd planned it that way, even setting out to ful-fill some of the prophecies. And it was as if they were waiting for him to do so, because even as the statue started bleeding and the plague began its brutal sweep of the city, there was a sudden outpouring—more and more of the tracts showing up. Vlad had been happy for the extra help in his carefully planned terror.

He put the tract away. "This is the last question." He waited until the man's dark eyes met his own. Then, he drew in a slow breath and released it. "Does the word *Endicott* mean anything to you?"

The man's eyebrows arched. "Endicott? That's an old word, one that's been long out of use. A place. A myth, really, though I suppose most myths start with a seed of truth."

"Where is it?"

Tamyr Aviz shook his head. "I don't know. Nowhere, I suspect. It was a legend spoken of in the early days of the empire, a place of refuge for those unwilling to be saved by the blood and the blade."

Vlad closed his eyes and saw the kin-raven again as it perched upon the stone. He watched its beak open and listened again to the single word it uttered. *Endicott.* "Surely there is more in the holdings about this so-called legend?"

"Some," the man said. "But it's largely myth and apocrypha. In two

thousand years, we've found no evidence to support that such a place
has ever existed."

Vlad nodded. "Is there anything else you can tell me about it?"

"No," Tamyr Aviz said. "Not anything specific." His eyes narrowed.
"Why are you asking me about Endicott?"

Vlad felt the weariness shifting in him as his hand twitched upon
the staff, ready to be done with it all. He regarded the man. "Because
I think it's a real place," he said. "And I think your Crimson Empress
and your Child of Promise have been taken there."

The man's face flooded with a dozen emotions—hope being one of
them even as his eyes filled with tears. He opened his mouth to speak,
but Vlad held his breath and squeezed the staff, crushing the magister's
heart as he did.

As Tamyr Aviz slumped forward in the chair with glassy eyes, Vlad
leaned back against the wall and forced himself to release the staff,
propping it into the corner. The weakness poured into him along with
the pain, and he gritted his teeth against it.

He would leave this one. He was too tired to dispose of the body,
and he made a point of never using the same space twice anyway. There
were plenty of other empty buildings and rooms, though he hoped this
part of the work was over. A lot depended, he realized, upon how co-
operative the Lost Children of Shadrus would be. Though he expected
that given his own role in their prophecies, cooperation was probably
not going to be a problem.

Vlad regarded the man he'd killed and thought about the hope he'd
seen on his face. It was transformative in the midst of so much grief.

He'd heard the wailing now for days as the Y'Zirites mourned their
lost. And as word spread slowly and as the group suicides and riots
had grown in frequency and number, he'd felt a growing satisfaction
laced with sorrow. Sorrow that his own daughter believed, with the
rest of them, that he'd murdered the children, and sorrow that he could
do nothing to change that belief without jeopardizing the work he
knew would save them all from this madness. Still, despite the grief,
the satisfaction was real. He'd traveled far from the days of his impris-
onment upon Ria's table, his suffering beneath her knife as he watched
her cut his family away from him, child by child, grandchild by grandchild. And now, he'd shaken that great tree of blind, bloody faith to
its roots. He would keep shaking it until he brought it down.

No, not me, he reminded himself. *The staff.* He'd accomplished
more in a few weeks with this terrible tool than he'd ever imagined

possible, and this from a man whose family had leveraged vast change over the course of its history in the Named Lands.

He couldn't think about the staff without thinking about the blue-green ghost who'd brought him to it. His first sight of her, twisting and writhing in the water, and his last sight of her, suspended above him in the basement of the Ladder, filling the room with her light. "Thank you, my love," he whispered.

Then Vlad Li Tam straightened, took up the slender silver rod, glanced once more at the dead magister, and let himself out into the darkening night.

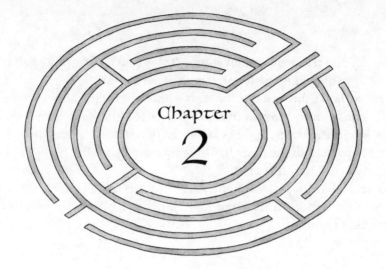

Chapter 2

Neb

A cold night wind moved over his silver skin and Neb's nostrils flared, taking in smells both familiar and unfamiliar, as he flew the skies above the Named Lands. Overhead, a scattering of stars pulsed, and the lights from occasional villages and farms marked the landscape below.

Ahead of him in the distance, the Dragon's Spine Mountains spread out across the horizon, and to his right, the Keeper's Wall made its steady march south from the Spine down to the tip of the Fargoer's Horn. Below him, the First River, wide and shining in the starlight, crept down from the mountains to meander slowly south to the Entrolusian Delta and waiting sea.

Neb twisted and turned in the air, dropping in altitude as he adjusted the speed of his secondary wings to compensate. He was still learning exactly how the kin-dragon worked, and he was confident that he'd barely scratched the surface of what the great metal beast was capable of. Still, he'd learned quite a bit beyond the fact that he could suddenly fly fast, as fast could be. His senses of smell, vision and hearing were enhanced to the point of becoming overwhelming, though along with it he found he also had the focus to filter the flood of stimuli. On his first morning, he'd narrowed down his sense of smell to the point of identifying baking bread from a chimney from a league above and fifty leagues south. And his eyes had followed his nose, picking out the cottage with relative ease.

Of course, the woman he sought—Amylé D'Anjite—likely knew far more than he did about what the kin-dragons were capable of. And as much as he hoped that he wouldn't need to find out, he was confident that the beasts had strong offensive and defensive capabilities. Petronus had even speculated that the kin-dragons were likely responsible for the attack on the antiphon, crashing them into the southern lunar sea.

Neb hung suspended in the air, savoring the dull roar of his beating wings. He'd spent a few days now with the kin-dragon, flying the skies of Lasthome but never bringing himself to land. Not for the first time, he was plagued with uncertainty.

Of course, the ground hadn't stopped shaking beneath his feet for over two years now. Not since the day Windwir fell. From then, he'd buried a city, fallen in love, joined the Foresters, been captured in the Churning Wastes by Y'Zirites and discovered that his adopted father wasn't dead after all . . . and that his real father was actually a Younger God.

And then I flew to the moon. At every point along the way, the uncertainty had plagued him. Now was no different. He needed a staff—the administrator's rod—to finish his work in the Firsthome Temple, whatever that work was, and he had no idea how to find it. And he was confident that Amylé D'Anjite sought the same staff, though he was equally convinced that her intentions for the artifact were dark.

And Winters. He felt the loss and shame. The last time he'd seen her, she'd been terrified of him. And not just because he'd been clothed in light and fresh from baptism into his heritage. No, she'd seen beyond the surface, into the deeper places. She'd seen in that moment how he'd changed, how he'd *been* changed, by everything that had transpired since he'd kissed her goodbye in the Ninefold Forest. In that look of a moment, Neb knew he'd lost her love and gained her fear.

He wasn't certain that showing up now in the form of a massive silver beast would help reverse that, even if he knew where to find the girl. He'd last seen her in the north, but that had been weeks ago.

The ache to find her, to somehow make things right, was a constant with him. As constant as the fear of what he would find in her eyes again when he did. Still, he was her Homeseeker, and she was the queen of his heart.

Neb hung in the sky, his mind racing as his wings beat time. He couldn't continue to just fly about and hope to find whatever clue he needed in order to chart his course. He turned his snout north and took in the scent of evergreen and snow, then turned it to the north-east to take in the smell of the Prairie Sea and its nine island forests.

Neb surged forward, dropping in altitude even as he built speed. He'd tested the beast over the past few days, pushing it to speeds that dizzied him. He did so now, speeding over the Western Steppes and across the wide expanse of snow-covered prairie. He found himself wishing he'd paid better attention to the geography of the Named Lands as he tried to remember exactly where Rachyle's Rest, the recently appointed capital of the Ninefold Forest, was located.

It took the better part of an hour to find it, and in the end it was the library that gave it away. Its windows stood lit against the night upon a hill that overlooked Rudolfo's Seventh Forest Manor. In the dim light it cast, Neb saw it had grown considerably since he'd left it for the Churning Wastes to chase down Sanctorum Lux.

Neb gave the library and the city that rose up around it a wide berth, circling twice before settling into the forest not far from the road into town. He wriggled about, still unsure of exactly what mechanism separated him from the beast. He only knew it when it clicked into place and he found himself spilled out into the snow and mud, suddenly aware of how cold it was. He stood and tugged at the strap of his leather satchel, yanking it free from the crowded interior.

"Stay nearby," he told the kin-dragon. "But stay hidden."

The beast lifted off and vanished, leaving Neb to shiver alone in the darkened forest. The thin clothes he'd been wearing when he'd been taken into the dragon were better suited for running the lunar jungles, and they were already worn.

"Clothe me," he whispered, and felt the blood of the earth moving up over his ankles, spreading over his body to form a snug layer between him and the cold. He slung his satchel from his shoulder and turned north for the road that would bear him up the backside of what was now called Library Hill. It took a few minutes of navigating the wet branches and muddy puddles of melting snow to find it, and when he did, he saw the lights of Rachyle's Rest to his right and made for it.

His hand fell to the battered satchel, and he opened it, digging around inside. His fingers found the cloth-wrapped dreamstone but moved past that artifact to the silver crescent. It no longer played the canticle that had ultimately taken him to the moon; now its mate rested with Petronus where he waited in the Firsthome Temple. He pulled it out and held it to the side of his head.

"Petronus, are you there?"

He waited, then heard an answer from far away. "Yes, I'm here. Where are you?" Neb still couldn't get used to the subtle change in the timbre of the man's voice after shedding nearly forty years of age.

"I'm in the Ninefold Forest," he said. "I'm hoping to learn what's happened in our absence. I don't think I'll be back tonight."

The last three nights, he'd flown back through the Seaway to continue his exploration of the Firsthome Temple, sleeping in a small room he'd set up there for himself near the library's grove of bejeweled trees. Still, his mind pulled constantly to whatever work it was the dreams had called him to, and he'd spent hours flying aimlessly, crisscrossing the oceans and continents of Lasthome. At first, he'd reveled in it, staggered by the wonder of the wind moving over him as he raced across the skies, testing the kin-dragon's speed and maneuverability. And then the uncertainty had returned.

"Be careful," Petronus said.

"I will," he said. "And I'll be back in the morning."

He slid the crescent back into the satchel and continued toward the light. He was half a league away when he heard the faintest of footfalls and paused.

"Hail, traveler," a muffled voice whispered in the dark.

Neb took hold of the fabric of his sleeve with his thumb and forefinger, pressing at it and feeling it yield to his intentions. "Hail, scout," he said. "I seek audience with Lord Rudolfo."

"Lord Rudolfo does not grant audience to strangers in the middle of the night." The voice had moved, and Neb turned to track it, squinting into the dark. He could feel the blood of the earth moving in him now, giving him strength and focus, opening his senses up to his surroundings. He caught the slightest hint of sweat from the man's shirt and the warm scent of his boot leather. "And the borders of the Ninefold Forest are closed."

"I assure you," Neb said, "I am no stranger to Lord Rudolfo. I am Nebios Whym. Captain of the gravediggers' army of Windwir and officer of the Forest Library. First Captain Aedric can attest to this, as can Lady Tam for that matter. I have a room in the manor." He stumbled over the words. "Or at least I did when I left."

The scout moved closer now. With his enhanced vision, Neb could see the slightest shimmer of the man's body heat. "The lad that was sweet on the young Marsh Queen? Vanished in the Wastes?"

Neb nodded. "The same. Send a watch-bird back; I'm certain they will want to see me."

The man's tone was sober. "There are no watch-birds, lad." Neb heard his feet now moving away. "But follow along. You've come calling in perilous times. The officer of the watch will want a word."

Neb didn't move. "Rudolfo will want to see me right away, I think."

He heard hesitation in the scout's silence. *He is uncertain of what to tell me,* Neb realized. Finally, the man cleared his voice. "General Rudolfo is on the Divided Isle, disbanding kin-clave and taking the mark of Y'Zir as our new chancellor. Captain Aedric is in Y'Zir with Lady Tam and Lord Jakob."

Neb heard bitterness and rage, tightly controlled, beneath the words. And for good reason, it seemed. What had happened in his absence? "Then the officer of the watch will suffice," he said.

The scout started walking again, and Neb matched his stride. When they broke from the forest, he saw the library and for a moment wished he'd simply landed, kin-dragon and all, upon its patio. But even as he thought it, he knew that moving gently through this place was in order. There was a darkness in the scout's words that he'd not heard before in one of Rudolfo's men—a hopelessness. But with good cause if indeed the Gypsy King was now a Y'Zirite collaborator, his family fled to Y'Zir . . . all while Neb was on the moon. And Rudolfo taking the mark?

It's simply not possible.

Of course, nothing he'd experienced since Windwir's fall seemed possible. So as he followed, he found his stomach aching as he wondered what other impossible things might have happened in the world he'd left behind.

Winters

Rain traced its way down the windowpanes, and Winters stared beyond the glass to the gray, choppy waters of Caldus Bay. The fire she'd laid to the cottage's small stove did its part to drive the cold and wet from her bones, but it did little to help the musty smell that permeated the one-room shack. She wrinkled her nose at it, not sure it was an improvement upon the strange, stale air of the Beneath Places. Certainly the fire was an improvement after two nights of pushing through rain and snow to reach the small town named for the bay she now studied.

She'd spent her life in the north, tucked away from the so-called civilized peoples of the Named Lands, only venturing as far south as Windwir after that dread day in which it fell and traveling only as far east as Rudolfo's Seventh Forest Manor so that her shadow, Hanric, could attend the Gypsy King's Firstborn Feast. Both journeys—and every journey since—had been filled with violence, and she felt suddenly out of place in this cozy shack by the bay.

She looked away from the window, glancing to the two mechoservitors that stood together. The metal men were silent, shutters opening and closing rapidly even as their amber eyes grew bright and then dim in sequences too fast for her to comprehend. She watched them for a moment and wondered what they discussed. When Enoch saw her watching, she looked away quickly to Tertius.

Her old tutor sat by the fire on one of the cottage's few unbroken chairs, his shoulders slouched from the weariness of too many leagues marched both above and below the ground, his bearded chin resting on his chest, eyes closed.

Hebda had left to scout the town shortly after ushering them into the abandoned home. They'd seen at least one unfamiliar ship at dock, and she suspected it was an Y'Zirite vessel, which meant a contingent of Y'Zirite soldiers were likely garrisoned nearby. But the Androfrancine arch-behaviorist was confident that the Order had friends hidden here as well, and had gone to find them and quietly pick up supplies.

The thought of Hebda brought back the anger she'd held at bay since the day they'd lost Charles. What was it that he had said? *We have reason to believe you will be unaffected.*

Something was coming, and though it would likely turn the tide of the war they now faced, it would also kill indiscriminately anyone who'd been exposed to blood magicks. And that, she feared, included a portion of her own people in the north. Along with Rudolfo's son, Jakob.

But not me.

The two men had refused to tell her why, and the weight of one more secret broke the dam that held back her anger. But she'd been clear: She would know before they left this place for their new home on the moon or they would not be coming. And for Tertius, who'd spent years studying the Book of Dreaming Kings and its promise of a soon-coming home, being left behind would mean missing the fruition of his life's work.

The door latch rattled, and the mechoservitors moved with such swiftness that her eyes were pulled back to them. They took up positions to either side of the door, only relaxing their posture when Hebda entered.

Hebda put the sack he carried onto the room's single table. "I've bread, cheese and smoked salmon," he said. The man's eyes were hollow, his face gaunt and pale from exhaustion. "I've also talked with some of the locals who are sympathetic to our cause. We are safe here for now . . . but not for long."

Winters nodded, feeling the growl rise from her stomach as the smell of fresh bread and salted fish did its best to force out the musty odor of a house that had been empty and unheated for too long in this wet place. "Then we won't be long here," she said.

He looked at her differently now, since the dream they'd all shared and since the confrontation two days ago. Even now, he regarded her with something akin to respect behind his eyes. "Where will we go?"

Her voice was cool. "I don't know where you will go, Hebda. I am going to gather my people and take them to the moon."

She'd had a lot of time to think as they made their way through the forest, and though she had no idea exactly how they would get there, she knew that everything else her people had slowly dreamed over the course of two millennia was coming to pass. The details of this last leap in faith were lost to her now, but she knew that somehow, she would know when she needed to know and they would find their way. Meanwhile, there was a more pressing matter to attend to. "You say that what's coming could harm my people. Steering them from harm's way before this happens is my highest priority."

"I'm not certain that is possible, Lady Winteria."

"What is and isn't possible is being redefined daily," she answered. "But we won't know which is which until you are more forthright with me." Then she repeated something that Jin Li Tam had told her in the Machtvolk Territories, something she'd told Tertius and Hebda two days before. "The time for secrets is past."

Hebda sighed and looked to Tertius. The old man nodded. "I agree, Hebda. It's time that she knows the truth."

Winters glanced from one to the other, then to the collection of metal men. "But first," she said, "we have something more pressing. Enoch?"

The leader of the mechoservitors opened its eye-shutters. "Yes, Lady Winteria."

"Can I count on you and your metal cohort to shepherd my people to safety?"

The eyes flashed. "We will escort them all the way to the moon, Lady, as the dream requires."

As the dream requires. She had not thought to ask them in their mad rush to flee the Beneath Places and make their way to Caldus Bay. But now, the question begged asking. "And how would you propose to do this, Enoch?"

"With ships, Lady Winteria. With the temple unsealed, the Moon Wizard's Ladder will be functional. We will return the House of Shadrus to its home in the same way that its advent Downunder began. By sea."

The idea that they might reach the moon by sea was yet another impossibility on a growing list, and she regarded the metal man for a moment. Going by sea meant bringing those people of hers in the Ninefold Forest south to the bay—that was the closest port—and she didn't see how they could possibly reach the shore, find ships and flee under the watchful eye of the Y'Zirites. And waiting until the fruition of Orius's plan meant the strong likelihood of losing some—if not all—of them.

Where can we go? She called up her memory of the maps she'd studied under Tertius's tutelage. An idea struck her and she locked eyes with Hebda. "How far and how fast will this weapon travel?"

"Fast," he said. "Under a week. And from the mountains to the sea."

From the mountains to the sea. She looked again to the metal men, then back to the arch-behaviorist. "Then the Churning Wastes are safe."

His eyes widened. "Safe from this but certainly not safe otherwise." He thought about it a moment. "But they could reach the Keeper's Gate ahead of the pathogen."

"Enoch, how long would it take you to reach the Ninefold Forest?"

"We can make the run in two days' time at top speed."

She closed her eyes, calculating the distance. "And you could have them past the gate and into the Wastes within ten days of that?"

The metal man inclined its head. "Yes. If we send word ahead and they are ready to leave when we arrive."

"We will still need ships," she said, "and a place for them to rendezvous. But that is secondary to getting them out of the Named

Lands." She pulled herself up to her full height and felt the weight of command in her voice. "Very well, Enoch. Send word ahead to Seamus to have them ready. And entreat Rudolfo's new steward to outfit them as necessary. See my people through the gate and to the nearest suitable landing; I will meet you there once I've gathered the others and secured vessels."

The eyes flashed amber, dull then bright, and the other eyes flashed as well. "Yes, Lady." The metal man drew a black stone from the pocket of its robe and held it in metal fingers. She recognized it, and it brought back the memory of her stretched out upon a much larger but similar stone, lying next to Isaak as they dreamed the Final Dream. "We will access the aether and inform our cousins once we are away."

She nodded. The Blood Guard and Daughters of Ahm also had access to the aether, but she trusted the metal man to take whatever precautions necessary. "Thank you, Enoch. Shepherd well and tell my people that home draws nigh. Bid them wash away the mud and markings of their sorrow."

The metal men said nothing. As one, they turned toward the door. Then the mechoservitors stepped out into the gray winter day, and were gone.

After they'd left, she gave a hard look at Hebda and then at Tertius but said nothing, waiting for them to speak.

Finally, it was the old man—the one who'd taught her much of what she knew of the world—who spoke while Hebda looked away.

"Nebios Whym," the old man began in a slow, measured voice, "is not the first of his kind that the Order has encountered."

Winteria bat Mardic sat and closed her eyes, letting the words wash over her like cold rain. "Explain," she said, with as much bravery as she could muster.

And then her world changed again as he did just that.

Petronus

Petronus paced the halls of the Firsthome Temple and marveled at what the Younger Gods had commanded.

No, he reminded himself again. Not the Younger Gods. The People. The ones who had fashioned this moon and the world it orbited, building into them everything they would need as a species.

He ran his hand along a pale wall, startled again by the fleshlike warmth of it. In the days since Petronus had unsealed the temple, it had sprung to life in unexpected ways. Water flowed throughout the structure through vines along the walls, hot and cold both, in addition to rooms where it bubbled up in bathing pools. And scattered throughout the varying levels of the tower were rooms given completely over to fruit orchards. He and the others had sampled them. He could've sworn that one of them had a taste and texture akin to rare beef beneath a skin much like a tomato's.

He spent his time wandering the temple and running the jungles around it while the last of their mechoservitors made maps and notes and Rafe fished the canal. There was little else to do while he waited for Neb to finish his work and return.

It wasn't a bad way to spend his last days.

Petronus had no idea how long he had left, but he knew from the spider, Aver-Tal-Ka, that his transformation would ultimately cost him his life. Weeks or months, the spider told him, and his new, younger body would fail. Still, it had taken forty years off his life and turned back time in even deeper places, restoring Petronus to a heritage that had been lost.

Because I am also of the People. They all were.

His breath caught again at the wonder of it all. He'd spent his life in service to the light, serving the Order in its role of digging the lost and fractured past from the ruins of the Churning Wastes. He could still remember the first time he'd seen the Great Library as a young acolyte, astonished at the vast sea of books. As he'd climbed the ranks within the Order, he'd seen even more—artifacts, leftover bits of magick, mechanical oddities like Isaak and the others. And now, he saw that all of that had merely been the leftovers of a people who had already forgotten themselves.

The light, he thought, *is far brighter and vaster than I ever imagined.* The temple evidenced a light that stretched back across the void to . . . He reached for the word. Firsthome, they called it. The place they'd sprung from as a species.

And these are the Last Days of Lasthome. Petronus couldn't remember where he'd heard the words. Perhaps it had been the spider or something he'd read during those days in the aether waiting for Aver-Tal-Ka's gift to finish its work in his body. He wasn't sure how many days he'd spent there, but that part of the aether looked and felt much like one of the quieter wings of the Great Library, though full of titles no Androfrancine had ever heard of. Between that and the library here,

Petronus saw more and more a vast bridge of light that spanned more years than he could imagine.

Back to where we came from. He suspected that the place he now wandered, a named testament to that first home, was designed to invoke the kind of holy awe he felt.

A distant hum tickled his ears, and Petronus turned in the direction it came from. It wasn't something he could've heard before: the slight creak of metal joints and whisper of metal feet upon the mossy floor. But now he could even hear the water bubbling through its steam pipes as the mechoservitor climbed the stairs at top speed.

"Father Petronus?"

He moved in the direction of the reedy voice. "I am here."

"The camp is at third alarm. Master Merrique requests your immediate presence at the portico."

Third alarm? He was on the stairs now and could see the metal man standing below. "What's happened?"

Petronus didn't wait for an answer. He moved past the mechoservitor, taking the stairs three and four at a time as he built speed. He'd run the tower with Neb several times, racing him to the top and managing to even win once; it gave his feet a sureness now made more confident because the moss beneath his feet seemed to sing as he ran over it.

He reached the bottom and moved across the wide open room toward a portico that opened upon the canals and jungles beyond. Rafe and the others stood waiting with the other mechoservitor, their faces turned toward the southern sky.

Petronus squinted out into the afternoon. "What in the hells is going on?"

Rafe glanced to him and then nodded southward. "We appear to have company."

Petronus stepped forward and shielded his eyes from the light. Something large and silver moved quietly toward them, cruising slowly just above the jungle's green canopy. "What is it?"

But he already knew it was a vessel of some kind. And as it drew closer, he realized it was larger than the golden ship the mechoservitors had built to bring them here. But this craft moved slowly through the air, a bright blue flag hanging from a large metal cabin fixed to its underside.

Even as he watched, another flag ran out to join the blue. This was green, and Petronus raised his eyebrows. "Blue for inquiry," he said.

Rafe finished the thought. "Green for peace."

The vessel slowed further, and its shadow swept around as it banked and circled the tower once. As it passed, Petronus could pick out faces pressed to portholes, and despite his better judgment, he raised a hand in greeting.

When the ship came around the other side, it stopped and descended until ropes snaked out and uniformed figures swarmed down them to pull the vessel farther down.

Rafe glanced at Petronus, then back to the vessel. "What now?"

Petronus shrugged. "They know the colors of kin-clave." He looked around at the ragged group left from their initial landing here. One sailor, two scouts and the old pirate captain were all that remained besides he and Neb. "And we'd be no match for them if they didn't come under a flag of peace." Still, he doubted whoever came could stand up to what Neb was now capable of, and the boy was just a shout away. He felt for the silver crescent in his robe, reassured by its cool metal surface. "I think," Petronus finally said, "we go and meet them."

A gangplank lowered as Petronus and the others left the shaded portico. He saw a small group of men and women gathered in what he assumed was the cargo bay of the ship. They wore blue uniforms and stood around a woman who wore a plain blue dress decorated with a long silver scarf. Her ginger hair was tied back, and at first glance Petronus thought she must be a Tam. She held a slender book in her hand and talked in low tones with an older man with silver piping on his uniform that spoke of rank.

Her eyes met Petronus's, and he saw a smile work at her mouth even as she blushed. He left the others and approached the foot of the gangplank even as she did the same.

Petronus saw the others shifting as she walked toward him but saw no evidence of weapons or malice.

"I am Ambassador Nadja Thrall of New Espira. Are you the Homeseeker, Nebios Whym?"

The words washed over him, and Petronus blinked. *Ambassador. Espira.* "Nebios? No, I'm not Neb. He is . . . unavailable." He extended a hand to grasp hers. "I am Petronus."

Her blush deepened. "The Pope?" There was the slightest stammer in her voice, and it raised his eyebrows further. "I didn't realize you were here. It is a great honor to meet you."

He squeezed her hand and noticed that she hesitated before releasing it. "You know of me?"

The ambassador nodded. "I've studied your speeches. Imagine my surprise when I learned you weren't dead after all." She smiled, and her teeth were even and white. "And now I'm actually meeting you," she said, glancing up at the planet that hung above them. "On the moon."

A hundred questions begged asking, and Petronus found himself holding his breath as he sorted through them. Finally, he released it. "And you are from New Espira?"

"Yes," she said. "We came through the Seaway." She thought for a moment. "The Moon Wizard's Ladder, you call it."

"I've not heard of New Espira." Of course, until recently he'd never heard of the Empire of Y'zir. He looked up at the ship that hung silently above them. "And I've not seen a vessel like this."

"It's an airship. This one is called *Frederico's Hope*." She took a breath and continued. "We typically take great care for them not to be seen."

He squinted up into the open cargo bay, taking in the uniformed men and women that held back, watching their young ambassador. "And you're looking for Nebios Whym."

She nodded. "But I'm very glad to meet you." She glanced away, her cheeks again red. "I've modeled my own career with the council on many of the principles that guided you into your papacy. Your last recorded speech—the one about the backward dream—was the subject of my philosophy dissertation."

Petronus felt heat rising to his own face. "I'm afraid you know much more about me than I do about you, Ambassador Thrall."

She laughed. "Yes," she said. "Also something we've taken great care about." She took a tentative step forward. "But the time of Sowing is at hand, and the time for secrets is past."

Yes. He wasn't certain why he trusted this woman with her gentle smile and her easy blush, but he knew that he did. And just as he had been for much of the last two years, Petronus found himself surprised at how very small he was and how very little he knew. The light, indeed, was vaster in its scope than he'd realized, and the world he and his Androfrancine Order had thought they understood so well was much larger than he'd ever imagined.

"I will let Neb know that you are here," he said, his hand brushing against the crescent in his robe's pocket. "I'm sure he will want to meet you at his earliest convenience."

"Good," Nadja said as she stepped off the gangplank and onto the surface of the moon. "We have a treaty to negotiate and saplings for the library."

The hundred questions had bred into a thousand, but this time Petronus asked none of them. Instead, he stood back and watched as the ambassador and her crewmates disembarked. And he realized as he did that if he'd needed to find any common ground with this woman and her people, it was the look of rapt wonder upon their faces as they took in the majesty of the Firsthome Temple and the brown, scarred planet that hung above it.

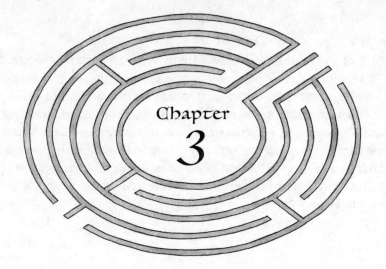

Chapter 3

Lysias

Eyes still running and stinging from smoke, Lysias gulped air and listened to the moans of the wounded around him.

He tried to slow his breathing, to slow his heartbeat, wondering how it was that after so many years of soldiering, he suddenly found himself shaking and afraid.

It's because you've never fought underground like a sewer rat. He'd trained as a young officer at the Delta's famed Academy and had been tested against minor Y'Zirite resurgences, Marshfolk incursions and the occasional trouble with neighboring Pylos back in his days in the Entrolusian military. It had all culminated in the War for Windwir, where he'd learned to respect the Gypsy King and his Wandering Army. He'd never imagined at that time that one day he would not only serve General Rudolfo, but also build him a standing army to protect his assets in the Ninefold Forest.

And certainly, he'd never imagined fighting underground. *In the dark.*

They'd moved largely undetected through the Beneath Places, escorting two of Orius's officers northward to an access point for the Named Lands' water tables deep beneath the ruins of the Papal summer palace. Along the way, they'd established a series of camps and couriers to keep lines of communication open with the Androfrancine Army.

It was quiet until the dream.

The memory of it still raised the hair on his arms. He'd experienced nothing like it before, finding himself and his men suddenly in a great field, surrounded by thousands and thousands of others, watching a massive tree gone white with seed. He'd been close enough to see the mechoservitor and the Marsh Queen, Winters, clearly, and thought he'd seen someone that looked like Pope Petronus, only the younger man Lysias had first met some forty years earlier, not the old man the Pope had grown into. He saw all of this and felt connected to everything and everyone in a way that he'd never experienced before. He had shared something with the people there that defied his capacity to articulate, and it dogged him like a hunting hound even now.

But in the midst of the dream, he'd also seen the others and knew them by their uniforms: Y'Zirites moving among them, and not caught off guard by the suddenness of the dream. They were counting men and measuring distances with shifting eyes.

Not long after, they'd lost contact with a courier. And then after, the ambush.

Lysias pressed himself against the wall of the cave. He felt hands pressing a canteen into his, recognizing the voice that whispered in his ear. It was Tybard. "Wash your eyes out, General. There's some kind of irritant in the smoke."

The Y'Zirites had struck hard and fast, carving through them with a squad of blood-magicked honor guard, then retreated as the caves filled with an acrid, burning smoke.

Lysias held back his head and forced his eyes open as he poured the canteen over them. He blinked in the dark. "We need to keep moving. Where's Royce?"

"We lost Royce."

"Lost or dead?"

"Dead, sir."

Lysias felt a stab of sorrow that quickly became the anger at having lost a good officer at the worst possible time. "And Blakely and Symeon? Are they safe? And their package?"

"We're here, General," Symeon whispered. "And the package is safe."

Good. Their enemy couldn't possibly know what they were up to, but now that they knew there was an army moving below them, just north of Windwir, they would have to wonder why.

And I can't afford for them to wonder. Or to wait around for the Y'Zirites to figure it out. Lysias turned in the direction of Tybard's voice. "How many have we lost?"

"Thirty, maybe forty. With twice that injured."

It was a significant loss, especially with Royce. All from what he estimated to be five or six blood-magicked Y'Zirites that had scouted them out. Lysias suspected they'd used the dream somehow to work out their general location, but at least three of the scouts had fled, laying the smoke beyond them. They would report back, and that would bring others down upon them.

Lysias had not been so naïve to think they might get to their destination unnoticed, but he'd hoped they'd get farther. Still, they'd considered the potential of being discovered and had worked out the best contingency they could. "It's time to split the army," he said. "Otherwise, they'll harry us down to nothing now that they know we're here."

"Aye."

"I want the walking wounded to make their way east and up. Give them to Lieutenant Drake. They're to retreat to the forest and once they're fit for duty, take up positions on the border." Lysias paused, closing his eyes and pulling up the maps from memory. "I want you to take the remaining half and head west. Meddle with the Y'Zirites and keep them busy while we run north."

"Where shall we meet up after, General?"

Lysias chuckled. "I'm not sure there will be an after, Captain."

He felt the man's hand settle on his shoulder, then felt the words his fingers pressed there, though the Gypsy hand-language was still new to him. *I've not asked what lies north or what comes, but I do need to ask, on behalf of my men, if it is worth the blood it will cost.*

No Delta officer would speak to him in such a way, and Lysias found the candor and concern for the men refreshing. Rudolfo expected his leaders to be forthright and even passionate when it came to the men they commanded. And true to the excellence of the Gypsy King's officers, Tybard had known to ask his question in a way that no others could hear.

Lysias felt for the man's arm and pressed his own words into the flesh he found there. *It may win us this war.* Then he followed it up with his voice. "If there happens to be an after, bring your men to the surface if you're not already there. Beyond that, you'll know what to do; it will be obvious. We'll rendezvous at the grave of Windwir."

"And the wounded who can't walk?"

He'd considered this as well, and had expected the question. Those few times that Lysias felt uncertain in his command of Rudolfo's men, he'd asked himself what he thought the Gypsy King would do and based his decisions on that measure. There were plenty of areas where Rudolfo was a brutal, methodical strategist. But his love for his men at times went too far. Still, Lysias hated the words he now formed carefully. "I will tend to them personally." He offered no further explanation, and Tybard's bicep stiffening beneath his hand told him that the captain understood. Lysias lowered his voice. "We can afford to have no prisoners taken, Captain."

The man's voice was controlled and cool. "Understood, General."

A hooded lamp guttered to life and cast its light over the group of huddled men. Lysias squinted into it, checking the faces of the soldiers around him. "Pass the word, Captain. I want everyone on their feet and on the march in fifteen minutes."

Lysias stood from his crouch and cinched the straps on his field pack. Then he checked the hilts of his knives. He'd preferred the saber of an Entrolusian Academy graduate but found that here in the Beneath Places the twin blades of a Gypsy Scout served him better. "I'll need kallacaine and scout magicks," he told his aide.

The young man moved down the line even as Tybard moved up it, passing Lysias's orders as he went. Next, Lysias took in Blakely and Symeon. Neither were actual soldiers; they both bore the soft edges of an Androfrancine scholar out of place in the midst of uniforms and violence. Still, these men were their best hope of taking back the Named Lands. He'd seen with his own eyes what the pathogen they carried had done to the Y'Zirite scout. Once it was delivered into the water, it would multiply rapidly and indiscriminately kill anyone exposed to Y'Zirite blood magicks of any kind.

If this could turn the war, it was worth the cost.

The aide was back now, his hands full of pouches and packets. Lysias took them by fistfuls, pushing them into his pockets. "Now," he said, "find Lieutenant Reynal and tell him he's a captain now. Have him ready our men." He nodded to the two Androfrancines. "Take them with you."

"Yes, General."

Then he moved his way down the line, and as he went, he touched the men here and there, spoke to them in a low and reassuring voice, even as they checked their equipment and prepared to move out. When he finally reached the end, he saw the medicos and the handful of men they sat with.

"Find your units," he told them as they climbed to their feet.

The medicos stared at him. One of them—the highest ranking, he noted—opened his mouth. Lysias didn't wait to learn if it was a challenge or a question.

"Find your units," he said again, this time his voice harder.

Then he watched as they moved off. He noticed the slouch in their shoulders and hated himself for adding to it.

Lysias crouched by the first man. He was young, maybe twenty, and he'd been one of the first carved up by the Blood Guard. He already slept under the kallacaine they'd administered for his pain. The field dressings were already soaked through again.

This one will be easy.

Lysias put a hand on the young man's head, tousling his hair. "I'm sorry, Son."

Then, he tipped two packets of kallacaine into the soldier's mouth, washing the powders down with water from his canteen. The man groaned but swallowed it down, and once Lysias was certain, he followed up with a pouch of scout magicks. Even as the man started convulsing and vanishing from view, Lysias was moving to the next fallen Forester.

This man—maybe in his thirties—regarded him with wide and frightened eyes.

This one will not be easy.

Then Lysias sighed and did the work that he could never order another of his men to do. And while he did it, he heard the music of the dream and saw the seeds borne upon the wind and wished he could go back to that meadow and stand before that great tree, as far from this dark place as he could possibly travel.

Rudolfo

Exhaustion rode Rudolfo as his feet pounded the ground. He felt it in his body—his ankles, his calves, his knees—and he felt it in his muddled mind and the constant roiling of his stomach. They'd run through a night and a day, stopping only for minutes at a time to gobble down the dry, flavorless Grey Guard rations Renard had provided, chasing it back with tepid water. Then they were on their feet and running again.

They'd magicked themselves once more and Rudolfo felt the effects of it. His nerves were stretched tightly, lending a hypervigilance to his heightened strength and enhanced senses. The scout powders weren't as effective in broad daylight when it came to rendering them invisible, but no one was working in the pastures as they ran, and he and Ire Li Tam steered wide enough of any towns and houses they encountered along the way. Still, now that the Imperial Blood Guard was in pursuit, the magicks they used weren't going to be enough.

Not now.

As if responding to him, the howling started up again somewhere leagues behind them. Ire had told him to expect the kin-wolves, but it had still jarred him. And each time the howls arose, he found his legs pushing harder, the mournful wrath of their cries driving them north to the Divided Isle's inner coastline.

The wolves meant that their hours were numbered. Their pursuit also told them that Rudolfo's absence—and likely his complicity in the assassination of Yazmeera and her officers and Blood Guard—had been discovered. It was easy enough to find something with his scent upon it and set the wolves to it. And doing that gave away the direction he fled, which meant more eyes to evade. Staying off the roads would help that, but it wouldn't keep the kin-wolves and the Blood Guard that surely ran with them at bay.

Rudolfo felt the slightest tug to the left on his guide-thread as Ire Li Tam adjusted their course. He squinted ahead of them and saw the distant lights of a small city. It was likely Collinsfort, the seat of Collin County, which put them just fifteen leagues southwest of Talcroft Landing.

More howls behind, and Rudolfo suspected there were fewer leagues now between them and the kin-wolves than there were between them and their destination.

And beyond that, he wasn't sure his body could handle much more. He'd spent his time under the powders off and on, though it was unseemly for a king to use them, but they took a toll on those who didn't use them on a more regular basis. He'd been magicked now for longer than was prudent. The days following even their briefest usage left him haggard, exhausted and aching from a thousand pulled muscles. And he didn't have the luxury of succumbing to that kind of misery. He'd need to stay sharp and intent upon the work at hand until they were safely aboard and underway.

They passed the city, angling their way between the widely scattered farms and manors that surrounded it. Once they were clear of the outskirts and had crossed their last river, Ire slowed them and dropped back to run beside him. She slipped his hand from the loop and then pressed her fingers into his shoulder as they ran.

Drink on the run. No more stops.

He didn't trust himself not to stumble and offered no reply. Instead, he heeded her and slipped the canteen from his belt and took a quick sip. Once it was tucked away, she slipped the silk thread around his wrist and moved ahead. This time, the tautness of the guideline pulled him forward at a faster pace that his knees and feet protested until, once again, the howling behind them filled the night.

They're even closer now.

The terrain around them changed as they climbed the low hills that served as a barrier from the inner seacoast. These were lightly forested, and the climb would slow them. But it wouldn't slow the kin-wolves. They were made for the rugged terrain of the Churning Wastes, and nothing short of the sea would stop their pursuit.

He felt the line pull right, and he willed his feet to take him where his guide led them. It startled him just how much she had his trust.

And my grace, he realized. More than that, he'd felt an instinctive and powerful attraction to this lost daughter of House Li Tam. It had surfaced in a noticeable and uncomfortable way the night they'd first met and then again in the hours leading up to the assassination of Yazmeera and her officers. And he knew that just as it was with her sister, Jin Li Tam, his attraction to Ire was a response to her efficient and focused formidability.

Her ruthlessness as well. Perhaps that, he thought, lent a near-feral quality to his unexpected desire. Not that it was something to explore beyond his own awareness of himself. But the timing amused him.

A kin-wolf howled, and this time the nearness of it caused him to stumble. When he did, he pulled his hand back. The guideline snapped. He heard a muttered curse and felt a firm hand seize hold of his wrist.

Rudolfo let her lead him, the branches and underbrush slapping at him as they crested the hill. Here, he could smell the salt air, and the scent of it drove his legs harder as they launched themselves down-hill. Ire took his renewed burst of speed and held him to it, pulling him forward as they angled themselves to the northeast and raced for the coast.

He could hear the underbrush crashing behind them and imagined the massive wolves loping their way uphill.

We're not going to make it.

He and Ire were climbing again and the trees were thinning as they went, though he barely noticed it as he ran with his eyes down. But when he did venture to look up, he saw a clear sky speckled with stars beyond the canopy of trees.

He could hear the snarls and the grass being torn up by massive paws now, and as they crested the hill, Rudolfo became aware of two things. First, below them the lights of a village—Talcroft Landing—cluttered the shore of a natural harbor.

The second thing he noticed was the wind that rose up around them.

With the wind came the softest whistle, and it stopped Rudolfo's heart, flooding him with a sudden joy that brought tears to his eyes. It was the first notes of the Ninth Hymn of the Wandering Army—a music-based strategy the Gypsies had used since their earliest days in the Named Lands. It had grown to three hundred and thirteen hymns, each designed for a specific military scenario and overwhelmingly successful when executed properly.

He felt Ire Li Tam pulling him around and he pulled back. "These are mine," he said, tugging free from her grip only to seize her wrist himself and pull her forward.

Behind them, already, the wolves were yelping and growling as a half-squad of Gypsy Scouts fell upon them, but Rudolfo knew that even his best and brightest couldn't stand for long against the kinwolves and the Blood Guard that no doubt followed after.

A ghost ran along his other side, and Rudolfo became aware of a strong and acrid odor that set his teeth on edge and turned his stomach. "Hail, General," a muffled voice whispered. "The Grey-Cloak, Renard, suggested you might be coming this direction and in need of assistance."

"Hail, Philemus," he answered, trying not to gag as he did. "Gods, what is that smell?"

"Urine," his acting first captain said, and Rudolfo heard disgust in the man's voice. "Now run. Simmons is readying the boat."

Philemus slipped a thread over Rudolfo's wrist as they entered the town, and Rudolfo let his acting first captain lead him and Ire Li Tam past the buildings down cobblestoned streets. As they ran, Philemus cut loose with an even louder whistle, and Rudolfo heard it returned from behind them. It meant his men were disengaging now to fall back on their commanding officer.

Somewhere behind them, the tone of the wolves' howling had changed in its pitch. It no longer had the same driven, focused quality. And it no longer induced terror.

As the scouts fell in at a run around them, the smell grew stronger, and he realized his men reeked of it. Whatever urine it was, it seemed to have had more of an effect upon the kin-wolves than their blades had.

They ran for the darkened docks now, and a shout rose up. Once more, the scouts whispered away as Rudolfo, Philemus and Ire ran out onto the wooden planks, slipping past moored fishing boats as they went. In the distance, in the direction the scouts had run, Rudolfo heard the sound of steel on steel.

Ahead, he saw a crouched figure on the deck of a small boat. As they approached, Philemus slipped the line from Rudolfo's wrist and whistled again. "Climb aboard, General."

He climbed into the boat and pulled Ire behind him. A middle-aged balding man wearing a rain cloak straightened. "Well-met, Lord Rudolfo."

"Master Simmons," Rudolfo said. He inclined his head as he did so, though he knew the man couldn't see him.

Philemus and the others were scrambling into the boat now as well, and once they were aboard, two young men cast them off. Rudolfo heard nails on the dock and looked up to see three large forms slouched at the shoreline, whining and growling as they raked the wood surface with their paws.

Rudolfo released a held breath and realized he was still holding Ire's hand. He squeezed it once and let go. "We're away."

"Not quite yet," Simmons said. "We've still got the Y'Zirite Navy to contend with."

They'd rowed far enough out to raise the sails and now angled the boat toward the mouth of the harbor. The night wind caught them and drew them along as Rudolfo lay back. The exhaustion from it all—the mad, magicked sprint from Merrique County to here, preceded by the stress and strain of both the Council of Kin-Clave and the feast to commemorate his taking of the mark—settled over him like a heavy quilt, and he found his eyes drooping more and more as he slowed his breathing.

He didn't realize he'd slipped into sleep until he was jarred awake by sudden activity on the deck. "We need to get you belowdecks, General," Philemus said as he shook him gently. "And you need to remagick."

Rudolfo's stomach twisted at the sudden awakening and the thought of taking the powders again so soon. He climbed to his feet and took in the sea around him in the gray light of predawn. Approaching fast from port was a long, dark vessel that he recognized as Y'Zirite.

He moved toward the hatch and stopped when a tremendous tearing sound reached his ears across the water. He looked toward the vessel that pursued them and blinked. Now, it was two vessels, but something seemed odd about how they moved. No, he realized: Something had split the Y'Zirite ship into two pieces that now rolled to the side and took on water.

A large object moved through the wreckage it had created, growing as it rose up from the sea before them. Rudolfo had no frame of reference for something like this, and he watched, slack-jawed, as it slowed. The beast was made of metal and something like a serpent; deep inside of it, he could hear gears spinning as it was propelled through the water. It came alongside the fishing vessel as Simmons and his men scrambled to the sails and rudder, but Rudolfo knew—and suspected they did as well—that it was not something they could outrun.

Still, whatever it might be, it was at least an enemy of their enemy. And it showed no signs of treating them in similar fashion.

The metal sea beast slowed further even as the fishing boat increased its speed and an impulse seized Rudolfo. "Bring us around," he said.

As the ship came around, slowing itself, the metal creature stopped entirely. A low whine started up from deep inside, and slowly, its large metal mouth began to open.

Standing in it, dwarfed by the size of the creature's gullet, a metal man waited. But this was like no metal man Rudolfo had ever seen. It looked more like his men's descriptions of the Watcher, only instead of dark and pitted and ancient, this looked brand-new and made of such a polished silver that it perfectly reflected its surroundings. Its red eyes cast a smudged and bloody glow.

"Lord Rudolfo," it said, "I would hold parley with you regarding a most urgent matter."

Then the metal man turned and limped back down the beast's throat.

Jin Li Tam

With the rising sun behind her, Jin Li Tam walked the ranks of her two squads with slow and measured steps, pausing before each woman to make—and hold—eye contact.

The Y'Zirite scouts stood at attention in their loose-fitting dark silk uniforms and running boots, their hands resting against the sides of their legs, not far from the two knives each wore—silver for ceremony and steel for combat. Each also stood with packs upon their backs, ready to mobilize at her word. And within those packs, she had no doubt she would find every part of a Blood Guard's kit, clean and in working order, ready for use. Still, for this inspection, Jin was unconcerned with their equipment or their appearance and the neatness thereof.

I need to see their eyes. Most were hollow and dark-circled. Some were red and bloodshot. But all of them so far held what it was she searched out: enraged resolve.

Satisfied, she returned to the front, where their captain waited with Sister Elsbet. She met the officer's eyes after a glance to the older woman and saw the sorrow and anger that danced there. "Your Blood Guard is impressive," she said as she inclined her head.

The captain returned the gesture. "Thank you, Great Mother."

The gardens around them were quiet with morning, the air heavy with the smell of smoke. Jin took in the surroundings, noticing the charred skeletons of trees torched on that horrific night her father and his followers had stormed the palace. Of course, those fires had gone out days ago. The smoke she smelled now came from the city that burned. In the distance, beyond the wall and gates, she saw the massive structure of the Temple of the Daughters of Ahm. Not long ago, a gigantic gold statue of Ahm Y'Zir had adorned the top of it. Now, it lay in broken pieces in the central courtyard. And though it was under constant guard, she'd heard tell of looters making off with bits of their cast-down messiah under the distant, unseeing eyes of disillusioned soldiers.

"I will see as many of them home to you as I can," she said.

The captain's eyes were hard. "If their blades find a home in that Deicide it will be enough for them."

Jin regarded the woman. "Still," she said, "enough has been lost us. I'd just as soon not lose more."

"They are yours to command, Great Mother, even unto death."

She had no reply and turned back to the scouts. Twenty-four women of varying age and height, all scarred with the marks of their faith and all craving recompense for the sudden, terrible negation of that gospel. "Stand easy," Jin called out to them.

As one, they relaxed into a resting posture as their hands slipped behind their backs.

"I am Jin Li Tam," she said in a loud voice. "I am the forty-second daughter of Vlad Li Tam, Queen of the Ninefold Forest." The next words broke her voice as she uttered them, but she forced them forward. "Great Mother of Jakob, the Child of Promise and Betrothed of the Crimson Empress." She paused again. "And I will be avenged upon this murderer of children. Will you hunt with me?"

They spoke with one voice. "Aye."

She raised her voice even louder. "Blood for blood," she shouted.

"Blood for blood," they echoed.

She opened her mouth to say more but closed it quickly when a shadow fell over them and a loud noise the likes of which she'd never heard filled the morning air.

It was a roaring initially, but a metallic, shrieking cry twisted out of that roaring with a force that hurt her ears, and Jin Li Tam looked up.

What she saw, hurtling down from the sky above them, defied explanation and brought with it a kind of fear that turned her legs to water and made her cry out. And whatever it was had similar effect upon the others; she was vaguely aware of the captain shouting out.

"Hold. Hold your ground."

It was large and long, with silver skin. Its thick neck supported an arrow-shaped head with dark offset eyes, a blunt snout and a wide mouth lined with jagged teeth. Two sets of wings moved at a blurring velocity as the creature landed heavily in the garden, its six legs bending as they absorbed the impact.

The beast shrieked again, and Jin heard gasps of terror among the Blood Guard.

A bright light burned at its core and grew until it left her eyes blinking and watering. The light built to an intensity that forced her to look away and then subsided. When she looked back, the large beast crouched silent and still and a woman clothed in silver stood beside it, a hand stretched out and laid across the creature's face the way one might touch a beloved pet.

An alarm now rose as the guards and scouts patrolling the garden ran for them. The captain beside Jin whistled, and several of the Blood Guard—already magicked—became a wind that moved across the grass.

The woman held up her other hand, her eyes fierce, and Jin understood the implied warning even as the beast's wings began to buzz and its mouth opened to unleash another shriek.

When the woman spoke, it was a voice like the roar of an ocean, and the words rolled out with power. "Stand clear, Downunders, and you will not be harmed."

Jin found her feet and bid them move her a step closer even as she studied the woman. She looked to be young—perhaps twenty—and her long blond hair hung in a single braid. She was tall and slender, and even as the Y'Zirites slowed in their advance, her robes moved and tightened over her body to form a silver skin that Jin Li Tam recognized.

When Neb had arrived in the north in search of Winters, he'd come in similar garb to do battle with that ancient mechoservitor, the Watcher. Jin had not understood exactly how or why he'd come into such power, but she'd seen that suit protect him and lend him a strength and speed impossibly beyond him and beyond even the scope of what blood magicks could do.

The woman regarded them with cool eyes, and when they found Jin's, they held. "I seek the administrator's rod," the woman said. "This place reeks of its handiwork. Bring it to me and I will leave you in peace." And even as she said the words, an image formed in Jin's mind. It was a long, slender, silver staff, and she recognized it instantly.

The staff of Y'Zir.

She glanced to her left and right, and when neither the captain nor Elsbet spoke, she took another step forward and raised her own voice. "We do not have the rod," she said. "But we seek the man who wields it." She paused, careful in the words and the feelings they might betray. "He has caused great harm with it."

The woman fastened her eyes on Jin's. "Yes. The tools of the parents are not toys for children." Her brow furrowed and her eyes narrowed. "You," she said to Jin. "Come forward."

Jin kept her hands clear of the knife hilts they itched to draw and walked toward the young woman. The others stood well clear, watching warily. As Jin approached, the creature growled, and she heard the woman hush it like she might hush a child stirring in its sleep. She hesitated, then continued forward until she was an arm's length away.

The woman's eyes were blue and clear but Jin sensed a kindred darkness in them, and behind that darkness, she saw something more. Something she'd seen in Sethbert so long ago.

This one sojourns in madness. And simultaneous with that realization, Jin knew that made the woman dangerous. As if reading her mind, the woman now smiled. "Do not be afraid, Downunder. I will not harm you."

Jin said nothing and wondered if her face betrayed the calm that reasserted herself. She waited for the woman to continue.

"Who is this man who wields the rod, and where can I find him?"

She hesitated, but only for a moment. "His name is Vlad Li Tam. He is in the city somewhere." She looked over her shoulder. "These women and I start our hunt for him today."

The woman took a step closer, and Jin caught a sweet and unfamiliar scent. The blue eyes narrowed again. "He has indeed caused great damage." Jin felt something pulling at her mind like fingers, opening it. *Show me,* a voice whispered beneath her scalp.

She tried to resist but couldn't. The fingers pried at her, and the memory was too close to the surface of her every waking thought. She closed her eyes against the fire and against the wind upon the rooftops as her father swung the sack.

The woman gasped, and her voice became a whisper. "Your own father did this," she said, her voice husky with horror.

"Yes," Jin said.

They both shuddered, and something about that shared and visceral reaction gave Jin an affinity for the woman despite the madness and danger she saw there.

"He will be easier to kill once I've taken back the rod," the woman said.

Uncertain of what to say and caught off guard by the sudden connection she felt, Jin repeated herself. "Yes."

Then the woman nodded once, slowly. "Very well," she said. "Hunt well, Downunder."

"And you," Jin replied. Then, instinctively, she stepped back as the woman laid her hands upon the beast that had borne her.

Jin continued her retreat, walking slowly backward, her eyes never leaving the woman before her. As the light built, she blinked at it, and when the next shriek was released onto the morning air, she did not flinch and did not feel afraid as the woman vanished and the beast launched itself into the air.

Instead, Jin Li Tam smiled and savored the thought of her father falling beneath her knives, stripped of his power by something larger and more fearsome than the monster he'd become.

Chapter 4

Neb

Neb chewed slowly, savoring food he'd not tasted in more months than he could remember. For the longest time, it seemed, he'd lived from rations or from what could be easily gathered. And with the exception of the fruits he'd sampled on the moon, most of it had been rather plain fare, nothing like this.

When he'd finished with the officer of the watch, they'd brought him to the manor. He'd not recognized the steward, and when he'd asked his escort about Kember, a shadow had crossed the man's face and he'd shaken his head. Still, the new steward—Waryn—welcomed him in the Gypsy fashion with food and drink. So now, Neb sat in the midst of a half-dozen platters. For his first plate, he'd settled on roast rabbit served over a wild rice thick with mushrooms and green onions, chased with a light, sweet beer.

He was considering a second plate when the door to the dining room opened. Neb heard the slightest whistle and the metallic clicking of the metal man as it entered.

"Lord Whym," it said as it inclined its head. "I am First Generation Mechoservitor Designation Two. I am called Hezekiah. I am the chief officer of the Forest Library."

Neb felt awkward eating in front of the mechoservitor and sat back in his chair, gesturing to the table. "Please join me, Hezekiah."

They are all taking names. The mechanicals had been changing ever since the canticle had given them their metal dream. *And ever since my true father gave me to them and to the Order.*

Hezekiah adjusted its robes and sat. "You have unsealed the tower."

Neb shook his head and swallowed the shame he felt. "No, I . . . couldn't. Petronus did it."

The metal man's eye-shutters flashed open and closed. "That is unexpected."

Neb nodded. "Yes." Unexpected had been the norm. He was also supposed to have had the Moon Wizard's staff—no, he corrected himself, the administrator's rod—so that he could access the Library of Elder Days and do whatever else this bargain of Frederico's required. But that had gone awry. Just as he'd missed the Final Dream, missed Winters, because he'd been trapped inside the tower unable to access the aether.

The mechoservitor released a gout of steam from its exhaust grate. "Much has happened since you left."

"Yes." He'd heard. Rudolfo becoming chancellor and taking the mark had been just some of it. The messenger birds were dead. Isaak was somehow still alive, though missing along with Charles and Winters. Jin Li Tam and Jakob were in the Empire of Y'Zir with Aedric. And then there was the matter of the dream. "Much has happened," he said, "and much more is coming, I think."

"It is the fulfillment of the dream," Hezekiah said, his reedy voice reverential in tone. "My brothers and cousins and I stand ready to serve."

Neb regarded the metal man and felt a sudden kinship. He'd lost count of how many of them had sacrificed themselves for the dream. And it was a constant weight upon him, knowing that he was a key part of that dream. *They have done this for me to do my part.* "You have served very well, Hezekiah."

The metal man inclined its head. "So have you, Lord Whym."

Neb flushed. "I . . . I am not so sure that I have."

"Perhaps it is not important that you be sure," the metal man said. "Especially with so many others sure of you."

But that is part of the problem. From the moment Winters had declared him as the Marshfolk's Homeseeker, others had believed too much of him. No, he realized. It had started with Petronus and the gravediggers' army. And it stretched back to his infancy when he'd been brought to the Order, in the heart of Windwir where the

Androfrancines could keep close watch on their found offspring of the Younger God Whym. "I wish it felt like enough," he said.

Now the food in his stomach felt heavy as the anxiety chewed him. Usually, it started at the top of his head, settled onto his shoulders, and slowly moved down his spine. The stomach was the last place he felt the weight of it all, and it usually meant that particular wave of fear was moving past him. He forced his eyes to the mechoservitor. "But I know that how I feel is irrelevant. The tower is open. The ladder is working. The path is clear for Winters and her people." He took a deep breath. "Now I need the staff."

"Lord Tam is in possession of the staff."

Neb cocked his head. "He is?"

"Yes. He is utilizing it to dismantle the Y'Zirite faith in their imperial capital." The mechoservitor paused, and Neb blinked at its matter-of-fact tone. "Father Isaak is seeking him now."

Father Isaak. "How do you know this?"

"We have been in communication with Father Isaak in the aether."

In the aether. He'd thought about using the tiny kin-raven but had learned firsthand how dangerous that could be when he'd accidentally used it to bring the Blood Guard upon him in the Wastes. Even now, baptized into his heritage, he didn't have the experience or training to use the device with any skill. And he knew that even if he did, others were listening. He'd have no way to effectively communicate without giving his enemies more help than they already had. Yet the mechoservitors had managed to. He thought about this. "Are you able to communicate with the other mechoservitors?"

"Not directly; we do not have enough of the smaller dreamstones. But Father Isaak is able to reach all of us." As if reading his mind, the mechanical continued. "We are cautious. Each message is meticulously coded, but the Y'Zirite Blood Guard monitor the aether and are able to track those who use it. We are not certain of their code-breaking capacity in the absence of the Watcher."

Neb nodded. It made sense that they would be careful how and when they used the aether. "I need to get word to Isaak and the others. And I need to find Winters."

"At last word, she was in Caldus Bay," Hezekiah said.

Neb hadn't been that far south in the Named Lands—at least not until he'd arrived with his kin-dragon—though he knew of the town. It was where Petronus had hailed from and retired to after faking his own assassination. He'd seen it and the other dozen scattered villages along the bay from far above. "Who is with her? And how is Isaak reaching Y'Zir?"

The mechanical released another gout of steam. "She is with Arch-Scholar Tertius and Arch-Behaviorist Hebda. I am unaware of how Father Isaak intends to reach Y'Zir. The aether is carefully monitored, so few details are shared."

Neb knew he could pull the tiny kin-raven from his pouch and attempt to reach Isaak directly. But too many things had gone wrong of late, and he didn't want to add the risk of revealing wherever they might be to that growing list of things gone awry. He had no doubt that he could protect himself from the Y'Zirites now, unlike when they'd traced him through the aether before. But he couldn't run the risk of exposing his friends. "When you report in next, tell Isaak I have returned and seek the staff."

The mechoservitor inclined his head. "A report is already being coded."

"Good. Have preparations been made for Winters's people to sail for the Seaway?"

"They've been storing supplies for the journey, and my brothers race toward the Ninefold Forest even now. We will escort them through the Keeper's Gate and to the horn."

Neb opened his mouth to ask why they were taking the less direct route through the Churning Wastes but was interrupted by a knock at the door. It swung open slowly, and a scout poked his head in. "Master Nebios," he said, "I have another visitor here for you that was most insistent he be admitted."

An old man moved past the guard, his eyes wide with wonder and his hair tangled in the mud and sticks of the Marshfolk tradition. "Homeseeker? Is it you?"

Neb stood and the mechoservitor stood with him. "Yes."

The old man stepped farther into the room. "Is it true then? Has the Time of Sojourn passed?"

Neb felt heat rising to his cheeks. The awe he heard in the man's creaking voice, the shine in his eyes as he asked it, made him feel uncomfortable. "Nearly," he said. "The way home is open." He paused, unsure of what else to say. Neb glanced to the metal man.

"This," the mechoservitor said, "is Seamus, first of the Council of Elders."

Neb had heard of Seamus. He had been captured by the Y'Zirites seeded among the Marshfolk and forced to take their mark. He'd come here with the first of the Marshfolk refugees. "It is an honor to meet you, Elder Seamus."

The man laughed. "Oh, the honor is mine. And there are many more who want to meet you." There was more light in the man's eyes now, and it took Neb a moment to understand what it was.

It is the moment that hope is fulfilled and becomes joy.

The power of that realization caught him off guard, and Neb wasn't sure of what to say. Seamus rescued him from that moment when he held up a hand and took a step back. "But I see you're eating now. I'm sorry for interrupting; I just had to know. We'll wait until you're finished."

The words connected for Neb. *There are many more who want to meet you. We'll wait until you're finished.* He swallowed. "You'll wait?"

"Yes." The old man nodded toward the window. "Just outside the manor."

Seamus left, and the scout pulled the door closed. Neb stared after him, then slowly turned to the metal man. "They're waiting outside?"

The mechoservitor nodded. "They started gathering before I arrived. They wanted to know if Home had been found."

Neb felt a pang of guilt, realizing how little he'd really regarded their investment in this. He'd been named their Homeseeker and from that time had been tossed about, pulled through circumstances and revelations he'd never conceived possible. And all the while, he'd really thought very little about the people whose mythology he'd seemingly been born to fulfill.

No, I've been thinking about their queen. Or about myself.

And now, in the predawn gray of a winter morning, they stood outside in the cold hoping for some word from him. For all of his uncertainty, Neb found something he could be sure of now. These people had spent thousands of years dreaming toward a new home and deserved to know what had been found for them.

"I need to see them," Neb said.

"Yes. Are you finished eating?"

He nodded. "I am."

The mechoservitor led him out and when they reached the manor gates, he saw the crowd gathered there. Some held candle stubs, but most just stood in the dark, waiting silently. Seamus stood at the head of them along with eleven others—a mix of elderly men and women.

Neb felt the hem of his sleeve and rubbed it, bringing the silver body sheath in close against his skin to keep in the heat. As he stepped up to the gate, he thought he heard his name called from far away, but just as he bent his ear toward the sound, Seamus raised his voice.

"Behold, O House of Shadrus," he shouted, "Homeseeker is now Homefinder and Home is now found. Wash ye away the vestments of your sorrow and gather ye now for Homecoming."

The quiet crowd came to life with a roar, and Seamus stepped back and joined them. Neb watched them and was surprised to note that some of them did not bear the dirt and mud of Marshfolk but instead, the scars of Y'Zirite cuttings. It puzzled him, and he turned to Hezekiah with a raised eyebrow.

"These are members of House Li Tam, cut during Lord Tam's kin-healing. They are converts as a result of the Final Dream."

Neb looked back to them and saw the same wonder and joy that he'd seen on Seamus's face. *And I am a part of this.* The idea of it staggered him.

They quieted, and he knew they were waiting for him to say something. And in that quiet, he realized it was Petronus's voice he'd heard, distant and far away, from the crescent in his pouch. But Petronus would have to wait.

Neb took a breath and raised his voice. "It is true," he said. "Home is found. I've seen it." A murmur washed over his audience, moving out like a ripple in a pond. "It is . . ." Neb called up memories of the jungles and the blue sky, the birdsong and monkey-chatter. "It is beautiful," he finally said. Now the murmur moved toward a roar, and Neb raised his hand to quiet them. "Even now the queen prepares your path home," he said. "It will not be long before you will set out for it."

The voice in his pouch was more urgent now, and he glanced to Seamus, his eyes asking if this was enough. The old man nodded and turned to the crowd. "The Homefinder has much work ahead of him. We must let him rest."

As the crowd began to disperse, Neb drew out the silver crescent and held it to his ear. "Petronus?"

The voice on the other end was excited. "Nebios? Can you hear me? We need you up here."

"I can hear you," he said. "What's happened?"

Petronus chuckled. "We have houseguests. And they know where your staff is."

"Houseguests?"

"Yes," Petronus said again. "*Houseguests.*"

Neb scanned the tree line just beyond the manor, calculating just how many leagues he could put behind him before he called down his kin-dragon. As much as it might add to the moment to have the beast come for him here, in front of these people, Neb just couldn't bring himself to do it.

"I'll be there in two hours," he said.

The officer of the watch took a step forward with a raised hand. The look on his face told Neb he wasn't keen on him leaving just yet. "I'm sorry," he told the officer. "I'm needed elsewhere."

As he said it, he pulled from the suit he wore and felt the strength surging into his body. A dull light built from it, casting a feeble glow about him that would guide his feet until he was a safe distance from town.

Neb started out at a walk then broke into a run, building speed as he made for the road that led south out of Rachyle's Rest. When he'd put five leagues behind him at a full run, he called the dragon down and held his breath as it folded him into itself and gave over control to Neb.

Houseguests. Who know where Lord Tam and the staff is.

Nebios Whym turned his snout south for the Seaway and willed his wings to carry him home, listening as his speed cracked the sky behind him.

Marta

Kings, Marta realized, are much shorter outside of one's imagination. That was her first thought when Rudolfo and his companion cautiously entered the room. Her second thought wasn't of the king at all but of the woman that walked beside him, her eyes wary like a cat's and her hand resting upon the hilt of a scout knife. Her exposed skin was a lattice of scars, much like Winters, but these marks were worn differently. Marta marked her instantly as dangerous.

The king himself looked haggard and worn, his eyes ringed and dark. He wore nondescript clothes with the exception of the low scout boots.

"You've called for parley," he said, "and I am here." His eyes found Marta where she sat in the corner. "Who do I hold parley with?"

Isaak chuckled. "Forgive me, Lord Rudolfo. You don't recognize me."

The man's eyes narrowed. "I recognize the limp, but I would be sure."

"I am Isaak; it is the name you chose for me when you found me in the ruins of Windwir."

"If so, the limp is the only thing recognizable about you."

"It is so, Lord Rudolfo. Recent events have . . . *changed* me."

Rudolfo's eyebrows arched. "You match the description of the Y'Zirite mechoservitor designated the Watcher. Though you are much newer in appearance, I'm told."

Isaak nodded. "I was reconstructed by the Bargaining Pool in keeping with the more robust template the Watcher provided. Aspects of the Watcher exist within my submemory."

Rudolfo's eyes met her own again. "And who are you?"

Surprised by his question, she hesitated before answering. "I am Martyna. Marta. Of Mayhap Falls." She wasn't sure what else to say, but his eyes held hers and were expectant. "I travel with Isaak."

Rudolfo seemed satisfied by her answer. His eyes left hers, and she shuddered at the fierceness she'd seen there. "If you are Isaak, you will remember the first words you spoke to me."

"Llew etiuq kaeps nac I," the metal man said.

She watched the man's eyes widen. "Isaak?"

The metal man inclined his head. "You saw me in the dream as well. With Winters." He paused. "And Jakob was there, too."

"Yes." The look on the Gypsy King's face at the mention of his son was a mixture of anguish and joy. But only for a moment, and then a look of resolved control returned to his face. "I believe you. So how is it that you come to me in dreams and in metal beasts rising up out of the ocean? What is happening, Isaak?"

Isaak's voice lowered, taking on a reverent tone, as if he was quoting something sacred. "The metal dream is fulfilled and the Book of Dreaming Kings finalized. The Firsthome Temple is unsealed, and the Seaway is open for the House of Shadrus to return." As he spoke, his eyes flickered red, casting shadows in the dim-lit room. "The terms of Frederico's Bargain are nearly complete and the People are nearly restored."

Most of the words were lost on her, and it seemed they were also mostly lost on Rudolfo. But Marta suspected that the woman that stood with Rudolfo understood some of it from the look on her face. Still, Isaak continued. "These events mark great change in the path, and they've arrived at terrible cost. The light is vaster than we ever knew, and many have been called to serve it with their lives."

Rudolfo cocked his head. "Why do you tell me this?"

Isaak offered what Marta knew was his closest approximation to a sigh. "Because the light requires service of you, Rudolfo."

She noted the absence of his title and knew that with Isaak, there were no accidents.

There was anger in Rudolfo's voice and eyes. "I've given your so-called light enough," he said. "My son is my light now; I serve only him."

"Your son," Isaak said slowly, "is the light of the world. The gospels of Ahm Y'Zir are not completely false in their promise. Lord Jakob and Lady Amara represent the last generation separated from their heritage. Their children will have full dominion restored to them."

She watched the words working their way into Rudolfo. When he spoke, impatience rode his voice. "You speak to me in riddles, metal man. If you are Isaak, then speak plainly with me."

"Do not go to Y'Zir, Lord Rudolfo. Stay in the Named Lands and lead your people. I will see Lord Jakob and Lady Tam home."

The surprise on the king's face was nearly violent. "Stay?"

The metal man continued. "General Orius cannot be trusted. A dark and terrible ending is coming for the Y'Zirites, and if he had his way, he'd add the spell to that darkness. The Named Lands needs someone not bent on revenge at the helm. Someone with clearer vision."

"You do not think I've an eye for revenge as well?"

Isaak shook his head. "Not like Orius. Lady Tam once observed that she found your interest in rebuilding the library at a time of war a trait that made you distinct from all others in her eyes. I concur. You think first of what you can build and restore, not what can be torn down or destroyed. You have vision, and the Named Lands will need that vision in the days ahead." He took a step forward and slowly raised his hand, settling it upon Rudolfo's shoulder. "Lord Jakob needs a home to return to, and I would only trust his father with that task."

But Marta knew the real issue wasn't Isaak's trust in Rudolfo, but the reverse. And she could imagine that being asked for the kind of trust Isaak requested—a trust that let someone else do a task that you knew in your very bones to be yours—was a defining moment for the man she saw before her. She watched his eyes narrow as he thought about it. "What assurance," he finally asked, "do I have that you will be successful?"

"There is no assurance I can give you. I can only ask for your trust in the dream and in me."

"The dream is impressive in its scope," Rudolfo said in a low voice. "But my trust will be in you if I offer it." He glanced at the woman beside him before looking back to Isaak. "I need a moment to discuss the matter."

Isaak nodded and moved toward the cabin's hatch, gesturing for Marta to follow. She left her place in the corner and joined him in the corridor as he pulled the hatch closed.

Isaak sighed, and his voice was heavy with grief. "I ask more of him than anyone should ever ask a father. And more than any should ask of him especially. He's paid a great price in all of this."

Marta reached out a hand, pressing it against his shoulder. "You have, too." She closed her eyes against the grief that threatened to become anger at the thought of Windwir. *He killed my mother there.* No, she realized, he'd been used as a weapon. In the same way that the Androfrancine general, blinded by his wrath, wanted to use the same spell against the Y'Zirites.

Isaak looked down at her, and she saw the silver tears leaking from his red jeweled eyes. "We have all paid too much," he said.

When the door opened and Rudolfo stood before them, his posture spoke of anger. But his eyes held resignation in them.

"I will stay," he said. He glanced to the woman beside him. "But Ire Li Tam has sworn her blades to my service, and she will go with you bearing my grace. With what Orius has coming it is not safe for her to stay in the Named Lands." His eyes were cool and level, meeting Isaak's directly. "Swear to me upon your dream that you will see my son home safely."

"I swear to do my utmost, Lord." Isaak's voice lowered. "But swear to me that no matter what you hear, you will not come."

Now, Marta noted the absence of the name and knew referencing only the role was every bit as intentional as earlier. And Rudolfo noticed it as well, his voice trembling as it rose in volume. "Of course I swear it. He is everything to me, Isaak. See him home."

There were no other words. Marta thought there would be. Or that they would embrace. Or that he would whisper words of farewell to the dangerous woman she now had to share the Behemoth—and Isaak—with for the voyage ahead.

No, Lord Rudolfo, King of the Ninefold Forest Houses and General of the Wandering Army said nothing as he strode deliberately to the hatch at the end of the corridor and ascended from the throat of the beast to walk his new path.

Winters

Winters walked the shoreline at low tide, slowly breathing in and out with the waves that licked at the rocks and sand. She'd tried to sleep after her conversation with Tertius, but in the end, she'd tossed and turned to the point of frustration, finally letting herself out into the cold night to walk the coast away from the town and its small Y'Zirite outpost.

As she put each foot in front of the other, she bid her breath go in and out as her mind worked at the knot it had been tangled into.

"Your mother came into the care of the Office for the Preservation of the Light from an undisclosed source," Tertius had told her. "She came speaking little Landlish and specifically seeking the lord of the House of Shadrus—Mardic, your father."

Those first words gave her little to work with, but the dread had started growing nonetheless. He'd gone on a bit before she'd interrupted.

"Came from where?" she asked.

Tertius had shrugged. "We don't know. Somewhere in the Beneath Places we think, not long after Neb came under our care."

"Tertius," she asked. "Who was my mother?"

He had sighed. "We believe she was a Younger God. Some of your very elders—your Whymer Seers—saw foreshadowings of her in the Book of Dreaming Kings, though they were never in full agreement."

"How is that possible?"

He shrugged. "How is Nebios Whym possible? And T'Erys and P'Andro before him?"

For the next several hours, she'd mined what she could from the old man, but his mind had wandered into detail that she had little interest in and glazed over the more important matters or lacked clear recollection of them. In the end, she'd learned very little.

I am the daughter of a Younger God.

And so she walked the beach and let the ocean teach her how to breathe.

The weight of this revelation surprised her. She'd felt different, set apart, her entire life as the daughter and heir of Mardic and as the first Dreaming Queen for her people. But this sense of difference was more alien to her, and it conjured up memories of that night with Neb.

He terrifies me. She shuddered as she remembered the fire in his eyes and the heat of him, burning white with light, as he laid his hands upon her wounded flesh.

What had Ria called him? Abomination. And she'd felt the sting of those words in him, cutting him like knives.

She'd not used that word, and she'd not had the same hate in her voice, but the fear of him upon her face was too closely related to not be another knife.

And now I am what I fear. I am Abomination as well.

Only there had been no explosion of light. Her hair had not turned white. No, instead, she felt more alone than she ever had before. She'd not known it was possible, and suddenly she found herself wishing Neb were with her here.

Her fear of him was gone now, swallowed by the guilt she felt over letting it drive her for too long. And now, her terror was replaced by a sense that he of all people would understand the sea of emotions she now swam as a result of what she'd learned about herself. In his case, he'd learned that Hebda wasn't actually even his father. At least for her, Mardic and Salome were actually her parents even if one of them was a Younger God in hiding and placed among her people by the Androfrancines. With those kinds of revelations in the offing, it didn't seem to take much deception to set one to questioning everything. She found herself, as she walked, full of sorrow, doubt and questions.

Tertius had been light on answers and seemed to find the mystery of it all to be akin to the awe he experienced regarding the Book of Dreaming Kings. For the old Androfrancine, it was a part of his sense of wonder regarding her people. And after that hour of trying to get answers out of him, she'd started to find his excitement over the mystery of it all the more infuriating than the secrecy leading up to him finally telling her. He'd known she was unhappy when she'd climbed up from her bedroll, strapped on her knives and left to walk the beach.

Winters checked the sky. The sun would be up soon, and being seen was not in her best interests. Her scars didn't allow for her to be incognito, and Hebda and Tertius had not wanted her to leave in the first place. But she couldn't stay there with them any longer in that cramped space—not with her head bursting with questions there were no answers for. She'd hoped the walk would help. It hadn't.

Sighing, she turned back and moved up into the tree line, away from the shore. As she went, a rumbling like distant thunder caught her ear and she looked up. It came from the north, but the sound grew steadily louder, and it was unusual enough that she stepped back onto the shore and craned her neck. Something large and dark moved quickly through the sky. It slowed as it approached the scattered lights of the town, and she noted that the thunder was more a whisper now as it climbed and then hovered.

It was too dark to see exactly what it was, but it was much larger than anything that had any business being in the sky. Whatever it was hung there for a full minute, nearly quiet now, and she watched it, less afraid than she thought she would be. She felt some apprehension, certainly, but alongside that caution, she felt an inexplicable curiosity. More than that, she realized. *I'm drawn to it.*

She walked toward it now, squinting up and seeing nothing but a massive dark patch against a darker sky. She'd left the tree line entirely and no longer watched her surroundings.

Winters couldn't take her eyes off whatever it was that hung there, and for all she couldn't see, she could sense. There was an ancient majesty about it blended with something familiar, and the sense of it all was so jumbled that she couldn't sort out exactly which senses were guiding her. Smell, she thought, and perhaps the sound of a quiet heartbeat somewhere buried amid the buzzing that she now thought could be wings. It was shifting now, and then slowly moving south out over the water. Once it was far enough to sea, she heard the thundering again and scanned the predawn sky for where it had vanished.

She was so intent upon it that she jumped at the words spoken quietly just to her left. "It was a kin-dragon, Lady Winteria. They are flying again."

She spun, her hands moving for the hilts of her scout blades. The man who had materialized beside her leapt back, his hands held up and out.

"I'm sorry I startled you," he said. He spoke the words with an accent.

The blades were out now, and her hands felt reassured as she moved into a crouch. "Who are you?" He wore plain clothes beneath a heavy cloak that ebbed and flowed around him more like the sea than any fabric she'd seen before.

"I am Captain Endrys Thrall of the New Espiran Council Expeditionary Force. I've had my people watching and waiting for you at every likely place you might turn up. We lost track of you when you joined the Androfrancines in the Beneath Places." He paused. "Until the dream, of course."

His words moved faster than she could comprehend them, but something in his tone and posture caused her to relax her grip upon the knives. "You're watching for me? Why? And what is this expeditionary force?" *And where,* she wondered, *is New Espira?*

The captain smiled. "There is a lot to explain. We're watching for you because you are Winteria bat Mardic, daughter of the Younger God Salome and the Dreaming Queen of the House of Shadrus. My ship bears an ambassador who is eager to meet you. On his behalf, I extend an offer of asylum for you and your companions. Caldus Bay is not presently safe. We can keep you out of Y'Zirite hands."

Winters looked out over the bay. "I don't see a ship."

He shook his head. "No, you don't. But return with the others after nightfall and we will provide you refuge and transportation." He turned away, toward the coast behind them. "Of course, you are under no obligation to accept our hospitality. But there is a squad of Blood Guard tracking you and a sizeable reward for the capture of your Androfrancine traveling companions. I'll wait for you here tomorrow." He started walking. "If I do not see you, I will assume you have made other plans for your safety."

Winters sheathed her knives and straightened. "And how do you know about my mother? I only just learned myself." She paused and scrutinized him again. "What is your part in all of this?"

He chuckled. "I've told you what is prudent to tell you. Come back and let the ambassador tell you more himself."

Ambassador. She was a queen, certainly, but ambassadors weren't something they used in the north. And New Espira—and this man and his strange cloak and accent—did not fit into her sense of things. He wasn't Y'Zirite; he bore no scars that she could see and did not wear their dark uniform. But he also was certainly not of the Named Lands.

She opened her mouth to ask another question, but he was gone with the slightest popping sound.

Blinking at where he'd been, she watched and pondered until the first of the sun began to rise behind her. Then, she turned quickly and made for the cottage.

Daughter of the Younger God Salome. Not even she had known that until earlier today, and he had not answered that question. How did this Captain Thrall know more about her than she herself had known?

Winters wasn't sure what exactly she felt, but in that moment, she chuckled. It was a dry laugh devoid of joy, with irony and resolve in equal measure.

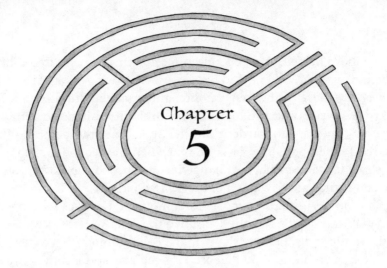

Chapter

5

Vlad Li Tam

Vlad squinted against afternoon sun and struggled to keep up with the Lunarist he followed. He'd started by watching for the places that the tracts were most frequently turning up. It had taken only a bit of patience, a willingness to sit and watch, for him to see the drops taking place. Now was the hard part of remaining unseen and keeping up as the young woman led him through various quarters of town, carefully leaving her leaflets behind her as she went.

He'd thought of confronting her and using the staff to make her take him to her people but knew that he would earn their trust faster if he came to them with an inclined head and opened hand, as an ally in their work. So instead, he used the staff to shield himself from unwanted eyes and moved his aching legs as fast as they would carry him.

"Halt!" Vlad actually stopped when he heard the shout, then realized it was not intended for him. He saw the girl ahead break into a run even as a Y'Zirite Blood Guard held up a dropped tract and whistled the alarm.

Growling, he drew from the staff and flooded his body with strength. As he increased his pace, he watched two more Blood Guard join the pursuit. This particular quarter was still well populated, the street markets active, and it made keeping the Lunarist in his field of vision more of a challenge. Still, the black uniformed backs of the

Blood Guard helped, and he found himself fixing his eyes upon them as he ran.

He drew close to the first Y'Zirite and stretched out the staff. He flicked his wrist, and the blow to her ankle lifted her and sent her careening into a wall harder than her speed merited before falling heavily. The Blood Guard lay still, and when the second looked over her shoulder to see what had happened, he shoved the staff into her face and smiled at the crunch of breaking bones.

The courier noticed now, and for a moment, her eyes locked with Vlad's. Whatever she saw there drained the color in her face. She ran all the harder now, her feet slapping the cobblestoned alleyway.

The last pursuing Blood Guard stopped and spun, knives drawn as she lunged at him. Vlad sidestepped her thrust, feeling one of her blades catch in his robes. Vertigo swept him as he stumbled against the alley's wall, and a moment of panic seized him when he realized the staff was slipping from his hands. His fingers scrambled for it even as the Blood Guard smiled and advanced.

He watched the staff tumble away and then the Y'Zirite fell upon him, dropping Vlad like a sack of bones. He felt the knife-tips at his throat and at his heart and stopped struggling against the woman who pinned him.

She grinned, and then her face went slack as the staff connected with the side of her head. As she fell to the side, he saw the courier regarding him with wide eyes, the silver rod clutched tightly in her hands.

"Who are you?" she asked.

Vlad met her eyes again. They were dark and frightened, lost in the spiderweb of markings that scarred her face. "You know who I am by what I do."

She looked back to the staff. "Yes."

"I'm looking for the Lost Children of Shadrus." He could hear bells and shouting now beyond their alley. "We have shared purpose," he said.

The Blood Guard stirred, and the courier hit her again. Then, she extended the staff to Vlad. "Follow me."

He groaned as he used it to pull himself up onto his feet, aching and trembling. He drew strength back into himself, a slow trickle, and nodded for her to lead.

The Lunarist set out at a jog, keeping her pace easy to follow. She led him through a Whymer Maze of narrow streets and alleys, the ringing of the bells growing fainter behind them. Finally, they reached a run-down building in an old, quiet corner of the city that stank of garbage and smoke. She drew him into the alcove to stand before a heavy wooden door.

"Wait here," she said. Then, she knocked twice and slipped through the door when it opened a crack.

Vlad watched the street as he waited and caught his breath. A stray cat worried at something dead in the street, its ears back and its tail up. Other than that, it was still. And nothing moved behind the few windows that weren't boarded up.

He heard muffled words behind the door. When it opened, Vlad saw that the woman had been joined by an old man in an orange robe, his face bearded and free of Y'Zirite cuttings. At the sight of Vlad, his mouth broke into a toothy smile, and his eyes lit up with delight. "It's *you*," he said. "Amen and amen, it's *you*."

The woman gestured Vlad in, and he stepped into the room as she closed and locked the door. The look upon the man's face captivated him; he could feel the force of the man's intense joy. Vlad didn't speak.

"Come with me," the old man said.

He moved off through a curtain on the other side of the room, then slipped down a corridor. He opened a door at the end of it and waited for Vlad to catch up.

The door opened onto a larger room, this one crowded with floor mats and blankets, a motley assortment of men, women and children stretched out upon them sleeping or meditating. A few families prayed together. The old man cleared his voice and raised his hands up in supplication. "Behold, O my people," he cried out. "A visitation is upon us in these last days of Lasthome!"

Every eye turned to Vlad, and despite the rein he kept upon his emotion, he felt heat rising to his cheeks at the wonder and adoration those eyes held for him. This, he thought, may be a mistake.

No. Not a mistake. Vlad smiled. "These," he said loudly, "are indeed the last days of Lasthome." The words were easy to find for him, as was the tone and fluctuation, the rhythm and cadence, to inspire. He continued. "And those who raised their fists to the moon and took it from its heirs—that thief Y'Zir and his house—now reap the violence they have sown. The blade of heaven now cuts its own mark upon their heart and the heart of the world." Vlad now raised his own hands. "And the path home is now open for all of Shadrus's children." He paused and lowered his voice. "We have seen it in the dream."

A murmuring passed through the room, and from there, Vlad moved now among them, squatting with the children to ask them questions and offering an encouraging word to their parents. He gave it two hours, and when he was finished, muscles and brain aching from the effort, he cast a look to the old man who was their priest. "I would have words with you in private, Father."

"Elder," he said. "Elder Reeve."

Vlad inclined his head. "Elder Reeve."

The priest led him through another door into a smaller room, this one with a table and chairs. He pointed to one while sitting in the other. "Thank you," he said. "I think your words meant a great deal to them. We are overjoyed that the day has arrived, but it is a day with great cost."

"Aye," Vlad answered as he sat. "They are the pains of a difficult birth."

Elder Reeve smiled. "And the pains of a difficult death as well."

Vlad leaned forward. "More pain is coming. And in the days ahead, I must know who I count as friend and ally in my chosen ministry."

"You have me, Lord. And all of the Lost Children of Shadrus. We are not many, but there are pockets of us throughout the empire."

"It does not take many," Vlad said. He regarded the man, once more noticing his lack of scars. "You are unmarked. How is that possible?"

The man shrugged. "It's very difficult. But I was set apart for the priesthood at birth and raised within my own faith, away from the bloodletting of Y'Zir."

"I've heard legends tell of a place of refuge from the knives of the Wizard King. A place called Endicott." Vlad studied the man's eyes as he spoke the word.

He saw the spark of recognition before the man spoke. "Yes. Endicott. It is an old, old story. From the days of the Last Weeping Czar and the Year of the Falling Moon. It was said that Frederico was the emperor who, after persecuting the Lunarists, became their ally." The elder closed his eyes, and when he spoke next, his voice took on the tone of a recitation. "'And Frederico arrived by way of Rufello's Behemoth before the First Lunarists of Espira and preached unto them a new way and called them forth to the Refuge of Endicott.'" He opened his eyes.

Rufello's Behemoth. His mind flooded with memories of the metal beast as it clanked and hummed through the depths of the sea. "Do you know where Endicott is?"

Elder Reeve laughed. "You would be more likely to know, Lord. It is one of the old places, after all."

Vlad sat back. He didn't need the staff to tell him that the priest was being honest. He noted the data, tucked it away in his mind for future use, and moved to the next subject. "And what of our other allies?"

Now the man's eyes betrayed a glimmer of something. Surprise, Vlad thought. "Our other allies?"

"You have other help," Vlad said. "You are a small group. But in the last several weeks, you've significantly increased your distribution, and I know it started before I arrived and launched my . . ." He paused, looking for the word he wanted. "My ministry," he finally said. "Some benefactor has assisted you. I need to know who my allies are."

The man was uncomfortable now, and Vlad saw the conflict playing out upon his face. *I could force him with the staff.* But he continued without resorting to that, willing the authority into his voice. "I want to meet them." He waited. "I require it."

Elder Reeve's eyes surrendered. "Yes, Lord," he said.

And Vlad Li Tam smiled at the blessing of his godhood, real or imagined, by way of the staff that hummed in his closed fist.

Ria

The wind rose beyond the rough plank walls of her hastily constructed command cabin, and Winteria the Elder stopped talking to let it have its own voice. Sister Gwendolyn and Magister Captain Onell exchanged a glance between them, and Ria wondered yet again what information they held back from her.

None of it had gone the way Regent Xhum had spelled it out upon his last visit. For the longest time, the Watcher and the Prophet Ezra had been her touchstone with the home she'd left behind, and since she'd taken her rightful place as Queen of the Machtvolk, she'd operated with a great deal of autonomy.

But not so now. The invasion had changed that with the arrival of these two officers—one from the Daughters of Ahm to provide mission oversight and another from the Magisters to take over the excavation of Windwir.

"As I was saying," Ria continued as the wind outside settled, "Captain Daenyr has already briefed me on troop movements. She is investigating Androfrancine sightings in the Beneath Places just north of us and will not be joining us." She leaned forward, and the Wicker Throne creaked beneath her. She'd wanted to leave it behind—leftovers of her people's past when they followed dreams instead of the true gospel of their heritage. But of course it had followed her.

At least the axe was useful. She glanced to it in the corner of the room near her armor. The magister clearing his voice brought her eyes back to him.

"I will be very curious to speak with any prisoners she might take," Onell said. "Something is afoot."

Ria leaned forward and caught another sideways glance between the two of them. "Plainly, it is," she said. "What has happened?"

Sister Gwendolyn opened her mouth, then paused and looked to the magister again. At his nod, she continued. "There's been an attack at our main command center on the Divided Isle. General Yazmeera and her senior staff, including visiting officers from elsewhere in the Named Lands, were poisoned at Chancellor Rudolfo's Markday Feast. The chancellor himself is missing and is likely responsible—with help from the Androfrancines or their sympathizers."

Ria felt her eyebrows furrow as she calculated the impact. Certainly, it would be noticeable. And it would take weeks to regain lost momentum, though Yazmeera's counterpart on the Emerald Coasts would likely have the savvy to assume full command. But it would take time for promotions and transfers to ripple through the occupation force, and that would slow things down. "That is a surprising development." She hadn't expected him to take the mark so easily, and until now, she'd regretted missing the event. "Do they have any idea where he is fled to?"

Sister Gwendolyn shook her head. "They believe he reached the mainland, but beyond that is anyone's guess."

Ria nodded. It was indeed anyone's guess. Would the Gypsy King flee back to his Ninefold Forest, or was something brewing with the Androfrancine remnant they'd discovered beneath them?

She had hoped her eastern neighbor would ultimately embrace his father's faith and his son's role in that faith. She'd hoped the same thing for his father-in-law, Vlad Li Tam, when she'd taken his kin-healing upon herself. It was bad enough that her unfinished work had somehow managed to lay hold of the staff and now used it to terrorize Ahm's Glory. Now, Rudolfo had surprised them all by somehow assassinating the woman responsible for the occupation of the Named

Lands . . . along with her senior officers and staff. "This is hopefully a minor setback," Ria finally said, raising her eyebrows to the two before her.

"We hope so," Sister Gwendolyn answered.

"Meanwhile," the magister said, "our excavation of Windwir continues. We are using the Beneath Places to catalog and store findings for now. The navy assures us that we'll have ships moving up and down the river soon and we can resume exports to Y'Zir."

Ria felt her face moving to a frown and hoped they didn't notice. Originally, the regent had assured her that the artifacts of Windwir would remain in the Named Lands. But it was just one of many changes that had left her suddenly feeling on the outside of an invasion she had been a careful part of since her first awareness. Xhum had been like a father to her in the absence of her own, and she'd trusted him. Even when he'd visited for the Mass of the Falling Moon, she'd trusted his words.

"Some plans may change," he had assured her, "but the gist remains the same: The Machtvolk and the Gypsies will govern with minimal interference from Y'Zir. The Child of Promise and Great Mother will be promptly returned once the dust clears. We will maintain a small presence in Pylos for the spiritual well-being of the Named Lands and leave the rest to you and the chancellor."

She wasn't sure if it was Tam's interference that had changed things or if it had always been part of the Y'Zirite plan, but Ria had felt more and more removed from decisions since her failure with Tam.

I was so close. If she'd finished, the Child of Promise would've been given a full lifespan and Vlad Li Tam would be dead. That truth had been kept carefully from the boy's mother and from all but the smallest handful of the faithful. The unfinished kin-healing left the boy with only forty years to fulfill his calling and an enraged Vlad Li Tam— now somehow in possession of the staff of Y'Zir—unleashing the army of his pain upon the city she grew up in.

"And last," the magister said, "we have the matter of the dream."

She looked up and met his eyes. Then, she swallowed. "Yes. What do we know?"

"We know from our experience with the Watcher that the mechoservitors can greatly enhance the range of a small dreamstone. And we believe the Androfrancines discovered a large-enough stone that, combined with the mechoservitor, could reach their party on the moon . . . along with the rest of us."

Yes. Ria remembered it well. She'd spent her life using a combination of blood magicks and meditation to resist the dreaming that was
in her bones by birth. They were ghosts of a time when her people
served the Abominations who had disdained their heritage and were a
distraction from the gospel, according to Sister Elsbet and the regent.
But none of that training had prepared her for the power of that Final
Dream.

She shuddered at the memory of it, her stomach turning as those
feelings of awe and curiosity and hope saturated once again. "Have you
had any luck locating the stone?"

He nodded. "We know where it is. But we do not know if it survived
the blast, and we do not know how far we'll need to tunnel to reach it.
The Androfrancines were thorough in collapsing that section of the
Beneath Places."

If it was intact—and if somehow the Watcher could be restored—
their best hope of reversing the damage of the dream was to counter it
somehow with a different dream. Because combined with Tam's work,
this dream of her little sister's was devastating. For the first time in
centuries, there were people abandoning the faith. In their last meeting,
Gwendolyn had told her about desertions in the navy and ships bound
for the Moon Wizard's Ladder.

Called home by my sister. She remembered one of her early conversations with Winters. She'd shared the gospel's truth with her, that the
Machtvolk home was not some place they would someday find but
was the place they had already found, deeded to them by Xhum Y'Zir.
Home was for taking, she'd told her, not for finding. And yet Winters
had found something—whether or not it was a home remained to be
seen—and she'd shown it to the world in some powerful way that
transcended mere dreaming using the machines and magicks of the
Abominations.

She shuddered at the blasphemy and forced her attention back to
the meeting. "I hope we can counter the Final Dream's effect."

Gwendolyn offered a weak smile. "The Daughters of Ahm are at
work on it. If the magisters find the stone intact, we will be ready to
use it."

Ria nodded. "Good. Is there more?"

"No," Onell said. "I believe that brings us current."

Gwendolyn nodded her agreement and the two of them stood. They
recovered their coats from pegs near the door and let themselves out
into the night.

Ria watched the lamplight and the shadows it cast, ignoring the stack of papers that awaited her attention. She felt uneasy and used one of Elsbet's mind-quieting techniques to trace the feeling back to the root.

The dream. No, more than that. *My sister.* Winters had been there, her voice strong and true, calling them home. *Calling me home,* Ria realized.

She shook it off and slipped out of her uniform and into a sleep shift. Then she knelt beside her bed and cut her left thumb for evening prayer. She closed with a long intercession on her sister's behalf and then crawled into bed.

She was nearly asleep when the scream rang out through the camp and Ria sat upright, drenched in a cold sweat and disoriented.

She heard shouting outside her door even as the camp went to third alarm and finally singled out one voice that boomed out over the shouting of the guards. "Oh my queen," the voice cried out, racked with grief. "Oh my queen."

Ria knew the voice and went to the door. "Ezra?"

She opened it to find him in the cold mud, held down by two guards. The old prophet wore his sleep shift, his long white hair tangled and his milky eyes wide. Tears wet his face and beard, and his sob was a gout of steam on the winter air. "Let him go," she told the guards. "It's Ezra."

The officer of the watch approached—a man she vaguely remembered was called Garyt. "Release him," he said.

The old man stood, his lower lip quivering. "Oh my queen," he said again.

Ria reached out and took his hand. "I'm here, Brother Ezra."

"I've had a most terrible dream."

She squeezed his hand. She'd known Ezra since girlhood, though his visits to Y'Zir were sporadic. He'd spent most of his life here in the north, planting seeds quietly among her people and preparing for their return to their service of House Y'Zir. "Tell me."

He took a ragged breath. "Only you, Lady."

She shot the guards an angry glance, then drew him into the cabin and closed the door. "Tell me," she said again.

Ezra took a deep breath. "We've lost them. We've lost them both."

She wasn't sure she heard him correctly. "Lost who?"

"The Child of Promise and the Crimson Empress," he said. "I saw fire. I saw Blood Guard taking their own lives in dishonor. I saw

Regent Xhum weeping in Sister Elsbet's arms." He paused. "I saw Tam laughing and the Great Mother dancing with her knives in grief and rage."

Ria wanted to assure him it was simply a nightmare, but she knew better. Ezra swam the aether like no other, and it had fed him the truth too many times for her to discount it. Still, she couldn't believe it was as it seemed. "Take heart, Ezra," she finally said. "You yourself have often told me that our dreams are not always what they seem upon the surface of them. Who knows what interpretation to attach to this?" She pulled him close to her and felt his body tremble in her strong arms. The old man wept openly now, and she found herself soothing him the way she thought a mother might soothe her child. "This dream may be a warning. Or it may be revealing a fear to shine the light of your faith upon. It need not be true in its simplest sense."

Not this dream. Nor my sister's dream.

But the sobbing old prophet in her arms and the memory of that massive white tree whispered to her that she might be wrong. Winteria the Elder, Queen of the Machtvolk, closed her ears against it and bent her will toward blind faith.

Petronus

Petronus watched the young man, Nebios, and felt what he imagined must be like a father's pride. He'd studied him for most of the morning, sitting in a corner of the room while they talked, and he marveled at how Neb had grown.

He remembered the boy he'd found, made mute by the Desolation of Windwir and plotting Sethbert's murder—an act of foolishness that Petronus had saved him from. Those had been among the darker days, the bones of Windwir scattered in a charred forest marked with rubble and craters while the armies of the Named Lands gathered for war.

Neb had proven himself then, taking over command of the gravediggers' army when Petronus came out of hiding and took back his rejected papacy.

But now he is seasoned. Harder. He watched the line of Neb's jaw and read the intentions there as Neb discussed the terms of a treaty he'd had no idea possible until early that morning. Neb had asked pointed questions and gotten the same answers as Petronus. And Nadja Thrall was forthright as far as Petronus could tell, though she firmly but politely refused to discuss the location of New Espira. "Its location is irrelevant to the present dialogue," she repeated each time.

But the rest, she'd told them. A third player in a game of Queen's War. *And we only knew of the second player after Windwir fell.* Until Petronus had seen Vlad's notes, he'd never considered the possibility of an Y'Zirite Empire growing in a crèche of its own, deep in the southern hemisphere. He'd not even known of the crèches until he'd seen them from the moon and realized the tucked-away corner that he'd called home was one of four that could be seen on an otherwise scarred and empty world.

So it shouldn't surprise me that the others may be occupied. Still, it did. But more than that, the New Espirans themselves surprised him with their airships and their knowledge of the Named Lands.

"We've been among you for thousands of years," Nadja had told him over dinner on the day they'd met. And she'd been able to support the statement by listing a string of facts that he suspected were more accurate than some of the Order's own chronicles. "It is our version of your service to the light, observing and seeking to understand and document the world as it was and as it is now. It's called the Time of Tending and Gathering."

And they'd managed to stay hidden while they did it. But they'd been effective at the work. He'd actually blushed when she quoted one of his speeches that even he had been fond of during his papacy.

He heard his name across the room and brought his focus back to the moment. Neb was watching him, waiting for a reply.

"I'm sorry," Petronus said. "My mind wandered."

"I was letting Nadja know that you absolutely can speak on my behalf on matters going forward until I finish my work back . . ." Neb paused, and Petronus saw the hesitation pass over his face. "On Lasthome." The young man stood.

Nadja stood as well, inclining her head. "Thank you, Lord Whym."

Neb blushed. "Just Nebios," he said. "Or Neb."

Petronus noted it and then noted her smile and pursed lips. *No. She would not call him that. Not in public.*

It was, as far as he could tell, the boy's first mistake in the interaction, though it would cost him little. A bit of awkwardness was to be expected. Men like Rudolfo had their entire lives to learn their kinghood. Neb's office was much more convoluted, and it impacted the very core of his identity. He could be forgiven wanting to be treated as normal. Still, despite that, when it came to the terms of the New

Espirans' access to the temple, he'd been direct and matter-of-fact, asking for exactly what he needed in return. He'd been impressive.

Petronus stood as well and approached them as Nadja gathered her papers from the table. She smiled at him as he did, and he returned it. "Are you taking lunch?" she asked.

Petronus shook his head. "I need to speak with Neb—Lord Whym—before he leaves." He turned to the tall youth. "I'll see you to the roof then?"

Neb nodded and slung his pouch. "Thanks."

They left quickly and made for the winding circular stairway that took them up the levels of the temple. "It sounded like it went well," Petronus offered.

Neb chuckled. "I think so. Did you see the letters from Frederico?"

Petronus nodded. "They seem to be an impressive people. They've certainly followed his instructions. Quite carefully, it seems."

Somewhere below them, Petronus was certain they were already unloading the saplings for the library. It had been one of the first items discussed, and she'd shown them one of the slender white trees rooted into a clear glass orb. "All of our work, everything we've gathered and tended, is here," she said stroking the tree. "We have more Downunder."

They would integrate them into the library. According to Nadja, the library would take the information. But it would not dispense it without the administrator's approval. Of course, that would be easier to get now that Neb knew where the staff was.

If he can take it from Vlad. Nadja had shared some of what his old friend had done with the artifact, and none of it had surprised him but much of it had left him sick at heart. "So you'll go to Y'Zir, then?"

"Yes. I'll find Isaak and Lord Tam." He paused. "I also need to find Amylé D'Anjite." And then he sighed, and Petronus heard a resolved sorrow in his voice. "At some point, I need to meet with Winters, too, and talk about all of this."

"Yes," Petronus said. "You need to meet with Winters soon. You are her Homeseeker, after all." He saw uncertainty and fear wash over Neb's face and knew he was still shaken by his most recent encounter with the Marsh Queen. Still, he did not know the best way to reassure the awkward young man. "The meeting with Winters will be fine." Then he added, "But be careful of Vlad Li Tam."

Neb nodded. "I will."

They were silent now for a time, running the stairs like they'd run the jungle not so long ago. As they ran, Petronus noticed the little things. His breath was more ragged now, and he felt a dull ache in his joints. Still, he had no trouble keeping up. But he paid for it more than he had a week ago, and he knew this was the beginning of an end he wouldn't be able to escape a third time.

They reached the top, and both flopped down to lap water from the cool pool at the center of the temple's rooftop garden.

Neb stood and moved to the edge. He smiled. "I'll keep you informed through the crescent," he said. "Now you should go have lunch with our ambassador."

Petronus stood with a chuckle. "I'm sure she's busy enough without me."

Neb arched an eyebrow. "You do see it, don't you?"

Petronus blinked. "See what?"

Now it was Neb's turn to laugh, and he laughed long enough for Petronus to shift uncomfortably. Finally, he looked at Petronus. "You have to see it."

And in that moment, Petronus did, and the realization brought heat to his face. "I'm old enough to be her grandfather. She's just enamored of my place in history."

Neb smiled. "She's enamored of something."

"And that reminds me," Petronus said, gruffness entering his voice. "Let her call you Lord Whym. It's who you are."

"It feels . . . wrong." Neb met his eyes. "But yes. I know. Now go have lunch with her."

"I'll have lunch with her after you've spoken to Winters," Petronus growled, waving him off. When Neb grinned and made the call, it sent shivers down Petronus's back. But it was the reply that lifted the hair on his arms as something large cast its shadow over them.

"Be safe," Petronus said.

"I will," Neb said. And then he leaped.

Petronus watched the kin-dragon catch him and draw him into itself. Then he watched Neb fly south for the Ladder.

He thought of the woman below, Nadja Thrall, and for a moment considered finding her, sharing another meal with her.

But instead, Petronus went below and sat in the library, watching the New Espirans as they planted the seedlings into the soft loam of the massive room in the shadow of the much older trees. And as he watched, he wondered how much of what waited for him in this orchard of knowledge he'd have a chance to see before his time ran out.

Jin Li Tam

Jin Li Tam closed her eyes against a hundred aches and pains earned from a day spent hunting and cursed how close they'd come to finding her prey.

She looked at the body sprawled to the side of the alley, amazed by the amount of blood. The left foot was bent at the ankle, and there'd been enough force that the Blood Guard's head cracked open when she struck the wall. She'd likely died upon impact. "This was the first, then?"

The Y'Zirite officer nodded. "The other two are farther down the alley, Great Mother."

Jin saw that the woman clenched something white in her hand, and she bent to remove it. It was a crumpled bit of paper and she smoothed it out, reading the words printed upon it in V'Ral, the language of Y'Zir. She looked up. "This is one of the tracts they've been finding around the city."

The officer nodded. "Yes, Great Mother."

She looked at it again. He'd been tied to the tracts in some way, she'd suspected, and had been surprised to learn her father wasn't manufacturing and distributing them himself to lend power to the terror he wrought. These Lunarist prophecies had persisted in Y'Zir since the earliest days in one form or another, though there had certainly been a resurgence of literature strategically distributed to key parts of the city just before Vlad Li Tam's arrival.

No, she realized, he wasn't writing their prophecies.

He is fulfilling them. She shuddered at the thought, but it made perfect sense. Her father had trained her since childhood to look around her for the people she could use for whatever work he set her to. Some of those people were weapons, he'd taught her, and some were shelter or information or an opportunity for misdirection.

"He is involved with these Lunarists in some way," she said. "We'll find him by finding them, I think. Where are the witnesses?"

The officer nodded to a group of people standing under guard. "They reported that it was an old man with a silver staff. There was a young woman with him that they had seen in the area before."

"I'll want to question them tonight," she said.

He nodded. "Yes, Great Mother."

She studied the witnesses. "I will also want to question any of these

Lost Children of Shadrus that we can find. They are our best path to finding him." She whistled for her squad, and when they'd gathered around her, she launched into a gentle run, mindful of the ache in her legs.

The sun burned hot and low in the sky as she ran through the city of Ahm's Glory. They ran in formation, a dark wing that swept around her, always between her and whatever passersby they encountered. The city was far quieter now, though the bells and whistles of alarm still rang out from time to time. Of course, the city had buried or burned two-thirds of its population now because of the plague. Many others had already fled, and now, as she ran the streets, Jin Li Tam occasionally saw wagons being loaded or slowly making their way out of the city, weighed down with the lives of those who fled.

But where will they go? The plague had spread out from here—still spread even—to the other cities, and she suspected it wouldn't stop as long as her father held the staff.

But none of that bothered her. She loathed the loss of innocent life but had no love for this empire built on blood.

And they brought their bloody knives to my family. Though to be fair, her grandfather had been complicit in that. Regardless, it didn't grieve her to see Y'Zir fall.

She steered them toward the center of the city, where the palace and temple awaited, and as they crossed the massive central courtyard, the afternoon sun reflected off the golden statue that lay broken there.

They paused briefly at the gate, and once it opened Jin led her Blood Guard through the orchards and around back to their barracks, then dismissed them with a reminder to be ready for the next day's hunt. She let herself into the palace and walked its nearly empty halls until she reached the administrative offices.

A guard stood at Regent Xhum's door, and Jin Li Tam inclined her head. "Is the regent available?"

The Blood Guard, like so many of them, was hollow-eyed still with grief, but her face held the flat affect of military discipline. She returned the gesture. "I will check, Great Mother."

Jin waited as the guard slipped inside. When she returned, she motioned her into the room.

Regent Eliz Xhum stood from a desk covered in papers as she entered. Their eyes met for a moment before he looked away, and she saw quickly why. His own eyes were set in dark pockets of sleeplessness, and the worry lining his face gave the scars of his cuttings an ominous aspect. "Great Mother," he said, pointing to the chair across from his desk. "How goes the hunt?"

Jin sat. "He was seen in the market quarter and killed three Blood Guard."

The regent sat as well. "He also killed another magister. The chief librarian, actually."

Jin's brow furrowed. "How long ago?"

"Yesterday or the day before."

What is he up to? Her father was the most brilliant and ruthless man she'd ever known, though what he did now was far more forthright in its destruction than his past choices. House Li Tam preferred moving in the shadows, not in the light, using others to accomplish its work whenever possible. "Do you think he's still looking for the spellbook?"

The regent shook his head. "I do not pretend to know." He sighed. "I think more than anything, he's bent on undermining the empire at its core."

Jin forced her face into an expression of empathy and hoped he wouldn't see the falseness of it. "I concur."

Their eyes met again, and the regent's tone was sober. "Between him and that damnable Marsh girl's dream, it's working. Word is spreading both at home and to our forces abroad, with devastating results. I must bear these dark tidings to Lord Y'Zir."

The words struck her like a closed fist and Jin stared. "Lord Y'Zir?"

The regent pursed his lips. "Yes. Lord Ahm Y'Zir."

Ahm Y'Zir. She'd known that Amara, the Crimson Empress, was a Y'Zir, but she had assumed some kind of blood magick had brought that about. She'd not considered the possibility that the seventh son of Xhum Y'Zir had somehow survived these last two millennia. The notion of it staggered her, and more wonder crept into her voice than she wanted. "I don't see how that's possible."

"Our magisters have used what technical and magickal wonders they can to preserve his life. But . . ." He paused and looked away, to the window and the massive temple of the Daughters of Ahm beyond it. "He has not been well for over a thousand years now. The Daughters of Ahm take care of him as best they can, but it is most prudent to keep him safely out of sight, away from the public." He sighed, and she could hear the resignation and reluctance in his tone. "Preparing him for travel will be . . . a challenge. But we will be leaving within the week. If you've finished by then you're welcome to join us. Or I can arrange transport for you back to the Named Lands."

She wasn't sure how to answer him and chose instead to change the subject. "I have some witnesses to interview tonight. And I think Father's working with the Lunarists; I've recommended gathering as many of them up for questioning as possible."

Xhum nodded. "They're a very small thorn in a very large paw, but they've stepped up their efforts of late." He shuffled papers around on his desk until he found a pencil and bit of parchment. "I will order the Daughters to make an interrogator available to you."

Jin inclined her head. "Thank you, Regent Xhum."

"You're welcome, Great Mother. I am as eager as you are to see an end to the man."

She stood. "It will be soon."

He stood as well and walked her to the door. "Good. We will parade his corpse through the streets."

The thought of it jarred her and she wasn't sure why, but she kept the surprise from her face. It made sense that they would want to show their people justice drawn in stark and brutal lines. Still, she knew it wouldn't be enough. The work he'd started had unraveled thousands of years of careful plotting and strategy, and without the children their faith relied upon, she didn't see how the center of control could be restored. *Especially when this new dream beckoned.*

As Jin Li Tam moved through the palace into the deeper levels where the interrogation cells were kept, she found herself smiling. She knew it must seem a cold smile to those who saw her, and she didn't know which added most to it: the image of her father beneath her knives or the image of the blood cult of Y'Zir gasping its last in a fog of plague and blood and fire.

Chapter 6

Neb

Neb slowed his speed to pass through the Seaway, savoring the surreal transition between the moon's tropical climate and the cooler clime of Lasthome's deep Ghosting Crests. The name of that sea had always captured his imagination, and as a boy, he'd wondered if someday he might see the fabled d'jin who supposedly swam those waters.

But now the Ghosting Crests were empty.

By day, it was impossible to see it, but at night the oceans of Lasthome were dark now. And the lunar seas were alive with blue-green light. He'd noticed it earlier, and Rafe had encountered the same while sailing. When Neb mentioned it to Nadja Thrall, she'd nodded and her voice had been bright with enthusiasm.

"Yes," she said. "The temple summons them to the Time of Sowing. We are not certain of their role, but the light-bearers or d'jin are part of that process."

He'd asked more questions, and she'd furrowed her brow. "Frederico's Bargain," she said, "touches on the smallest point of a much larger tapestry, and we barely understand that smallest point." She sighed. "As much as I detest it, there is a measure of faith to the work we do."

Maybe, Neb thought, all work required a measure of it.

He built speed as he cleared the massive arches of the Moon Wizard's Ladder and turned south. The water returned his shadow, and he lowered himself to fly close enough to taste the salty spray as it moistened his snout.

The three ships on his horizon surprised him and he threw his wings forward, casting himself back and up to hover. They bore Y'Zirite markings and were bound for the Seaway, moving fast across the water under broad, dark sails.

Neb twisted himself, climbing higher as he did, to gauge the distance between them and the Ladder. If that was their destination, he could only assume they were bound for the moon, and that was not a complication they needed right now.

He turned back to the ships. They were small now beneath him, but he could see that they had altered their course, scattering now in three different directions.

They have seen me.

Certainly he'd been seen before since returning, despite doing most of his flights by night. But this was the first time the idea of it pleased him.

A beast in the sky. *Let them be terrified.*

But what came next didn't please him. Still, he didn't see another viable choice.

Neb beat his wings against the sky, feeling the sun upon his silver back, and studied the scene below. He couldn't let them pass. Petronus and the others did not have the military resources to deal with an Y'Zirite force. Not unless their new allies had some hidden armory Neb was unaware of. During his day of talks with the New Espirans, he'd not seen a single weapon. But it was more than them not having the resources.

I do not want them there. And I have the power to stop them.

He remembered Grymlis, the old Gray Guard captain who had asked him as a boy if he could kill for the light. Dying for the light was easy, he'd said.

Neb took in a deep breath. Then he pitched himself forward into a dive. He stretched himself out as he dropped, aiming for the nearest ship and watching as it grew larger.

Even this far above, his eyes could make out the figures scrambling on its deck. A roar built up in his ears as he fell faster and faster, and at the last minute, Neb closed his eyes and tucked his head into his wings, pulled in his legs, and crashed through the wooden deck of the vessel.

Then, he felt the cold water engulf him as he tore through the hull and plummeted into the deeps. He unfurled his wings to slow him, and he worked them against the water to guide his trajectory upward. When he broke the surface, he threw back the wings to catch the wind and climbed back into the air.

Beneath him, the vessel was broken apart at the middle and sinking fast. Its crew was scattered in the water or scrambling over the wreckage.

Neb drew in another breath and gained altitude. The remaining ships were changing direction yet again, having seen what he'd done to their companion, but here on the wide-open sea, there was nothing they could do to escape him.

He hit the second ship off center, rolling it as he ripped through it, and felt a brief moment of panic when found himself scrambling and tearing to open the hull for his escape. But ultimately, he saw the same results.

The third ship was sinking behind him when he finally turned south again. Early in his talks with the New Espiran ambassador, he'd learned that Vlad Li Tam had the staff in the Y'Zirite empire's capital, Ahm's Glory. What little she'd shared of Lord Tam's exploits there had Neb uncertain if the kin-dragon would be enough. But after seeing what it had done to the ships, he felt more confident.

The wastelands she had shown him on her maps broke the horizon ahead of him now, and as the sun set behind him and to his right, he crossed over that dark continent, charred still from the Wizard Wars that had destroyed the world of Frederico and his empire and brought about the Age of the Wizard Kings.

Neb inhaled the ancient smell of scorched stone and ozone mingled into something like—but far worse—the air above the Churning Wastes. Nothing grew here. Nothing survived here, not this far out.

Flying low, he moved past the darkening mounds that had once been cities and across mountains that wept for snow, black and cold. When he reached the canal, he turned west to follow it. Here and there, he now saw scattered villages dug into the more forgiving soil near the water. By the time it was fully dark, he had passed over the locks and into the crèche that sheltered Y'Zir.

The air here smelled of citrus orchards and smoke.

And something else.

It was a powerful smell, warm and musky, and the impact it had upon him was instant. His heart began to race, and a dull euphoria mixed with longing tingled through his snout and into the rest of his body.

Neb twisted and turned in the air, trying to ascertain the direction of the smell. He turned northwest and deviated from his course, a wave of desire washing over him as he tracked the scent.

The force of the blow was sudden enough that his wings stopped beating, and when he tried to make them work, he found they were pinned to his body by the massive form that clung to him.

He felt teeth at the nape of his neck.

Nebios.

He knew the voice, though it caught him off guard to hear it tickling the inside of his skull. The sound of it, and the pressure of the teeth on his skin, sent another aching wave over him. *Amylé.*

They were falling now, slowly, her wings bearing his weight as he struggled against her. *Fly the skies with me like we swam the light.*

This was the calling. He remembered it well, though the scent of her—and her dragon—was greatly enhanced by his dragon's acute sense of smell. *No. Return with me to the temple.*

The claws raked his hip and reached under to his stomach as the teeth moved along his neck. *I will not.*

Now he struggled harder, and instinctively he used his own claws and momentum to twist around. As he did, his own teeth moved along her throat, and something like ecstasy made the world around them suddenly silent and far away. *We might be able to help you.*

Ending this, she said, *will help me.*

Then he felt a claw poking at something near the base of his neck and in between his first set of wings. There was a jarring, snapping sound and a moment of intense vertigo as he was expelled from the dragon and cast into the night air. The power of being severed physically from the beast before whatever joined their minds was completely withdrawn sent a sharp, pounding pain through his temples, and he cried out.

He was dimly aware of his dragon being shaken and tossed aside as he plummeted toward the dark lands below.

Do not pursue me, Nebios Whym.

But Neb no longer listened to her. Instead, he bent his voice into a call even as his thumb and forefinger worked the hem of his billowing robes, pulling them into a sheath of light that enwrapped him.

He braced himself for impact, holding his breath against it as he watched the kin-dragon dive for him. Neb felt the branches of the lemon trees catch at his back as the dragon caught him and took him in.

He floundered into the trees, rolling and kicking as he went, his wings tearing up limbs and foliage as he found his feet. Then Neb launched himself back into the air, sniffing for her scent on the wind.

Once he'd regained his altitude, he caught the scent, but he also now saw the lights of a vast city stretching out before him.

Ahm's Glory.

From that direction, he smelled death and smoke. And something else, he realized, but this was not her scent. *Fear.* Widespread fear.

Now what he'd done at sea caught up to him. How many Y'Zirites had he killed? He felt the knot in his stomach and chose a different path for his memory to follow. The memory of those knives upon him, the sight of the scars upon Winters, and every other cut upon them all—going back to that razing blade of blood magicks, the Seven Cacophonic Deaths, that felled Windwir—massaged any guilt out of his soul.

They earned their ending, he thought. And he realized as he thought it that it applied not just to those he'd killed at sea earlier but to all of them. Even those now under Vlad Li Tam's knife.

For the first time, he wondered if taking the staff now wasn't premature.

Then Neb took in a great lungful of the air above Ahm's Glory and shuddered at the taste of death and smoke and lemons upon the wind.

Winters

They waited, huddled in the cottage with their belongings packed and ready to flee once the night deepened. Winters sat in the corner and listened to the pounding rain outside. She'd said very little since returning, sharing the information with Hebda and Tertius along with her decision to join the New Espirans.

They were more suspicious, and their questions had reflected their lack of trust. It hadn't helped that she really couldn't answer their questions. But in the end, they agreed that waiting here was as untenable as fleeing.

And it is time for trust. She felt the weight of a burden growing within her, and she recognized that it slowly alchemized into a calling that she must respond to. When she'd first left the Beneath Places, what came next had seemed so clear there in the face of Enoch's words. *Maybe my people are only those within my reach, not those beyond it.* She'd had clearer vision in that moment, so fresh from the Final Dream. But that had faded, grown foggy since arriving at Caldus Bay.

So she would go with the New Espiran captain and meet his ambassador. But the sense of calling that grew within her told her that their offer of safety and asylum might indeed be the opposite of what she actually needed. Still, they knew more about her than she'd known about herself until recently. And they were also aware of Y'Zirite military movements. Getting answers from them couldn't hurt. And if these new allies could provide transportation as well, discreetly, that could be useful.

A sharp knock at the door startled her, and Winters's breath caught in her throat. She looked to Hebda and Tertius. Hebda stood, drawing a knife from his belt, and she did the same, slowly. Tertius watched the door with wide eyes. They said nothing.

There was another knock. "Winteria bat Mardic, we know that you and your companions are within," a woman's voice said.

Winters glanced furtively around the room, taking in the small windows. But there wouldn't be time for anyone to get through them and to safety. Sheathing her knife, she walked to the door and unbolted it.

It swung open slowly, and the Y'Zirite Blood Guard stepped inside, dripping from the rain. Her black uniform was soaked, her boots caked in mud, and she pushed back the hood of her rain cloak to reveal a hawk-like face beneath short-cropped black hair. The officer had dark circles beneath her eyes, and her demeanor was more resigned than threatening. Three other Blood Guard stood behind her, and Winters suspected that the remainder of the half-squad watched the cottage from various points of cover.

The woman looked at them and their packs. "Gather up your things," she said, "and follow me." She raised her hood and turned back into the rain.

Something is amiss. She had faced the Y'Zirite Blood Guard before; they were ruthless hunters. But these women looked lost, sleepless and nothing at all like the others she'd encountered. She took up her pack, not bothering to wait for Hebda or Tertius. As she slipped out of the cottage, she felt hands drawing the knives from her belt and she let them do so, her mind spinning to grasp this new development.

The other Blood Guard fell in around and behind them as they set out through the town. It was already dark, the rain turning the streets to mud where it wasn't rushing toward the waterfront in ditches. The streets were empty, but people watched, faces blurred behind curtained windows.

And the others watched as well. If Captain Thrall had known to find her on the coast, he'd also known where she was staying in town. That meant being watched now was a fair wager. She looked from left to right, to the alleys between buildings, half expecting magicked scouts to sweep in and spirit them away to an invisible ship. But as they moved through town, nothing like that occurred. Instead, they moved silently and she watched the woman that walked ahead of her. She moved with none of that dangerous grace Winters would expect from the empire's elite, and her shoulders were slumped.

These women are broken in some way.

Winters struggled with the straps of her pack and quickened her pace, trying to catch up. "What has happened?"

The officer glanced at her. "It is of no concern to you."

Winters said nothing but noted the firmness in the woman's jaw and the way she averted her eyes when she spoke. She fell back and glanced to Tertius. He regarded her soberly. Beside him, Hebda walked, his face perplexed and his eyes moving from guard to guard.

They stopped in front of the gate to a manor on the west end of town with a view of the bay. Two soldiers opened it for them as they passed through into an abandoned courtyard. Smoke poured from four chimneys on a large three-story house, and lights beckoned from a dozen windows. Winters felt her stomach rumble at the smell of roasting meat from the kitchen entrance they approached.

The Blood Guard separated them as they entered there, stripping away their packs and searching their prisoners quickly before ushering them deeper into the house. Winters tried to count the soldiers and Blood Guard she saw but lost track quickly as they were rushed through and up the stairs. They paused at a door, opened it and gestured Hebda and Tertius inside. Two of the guard stayed back, and the rest followed Winters and their lieutenant, taking up positions and opening a set of double doors at the end of the hall.

The woman strode into the den and sat at its single desk, waving to the chair across from it. Winters heard the doors close behind her and she sat, glancing quickly around the room. It was lined with books and decorated with antlers, lit with lamps that gave it a warm tone.

That combined with their rather anticlimactic capture painted a surreal contrast against her earlier dealings with the Y'Zirites.

The woman folded her hands on the oak desktop. She glanced at a sheet of paper and then looked Winteria in the eye. "You were taken with two fugitives of the Androfrancine Order thought to be killed in Windwir." Her voice was matter-of-fact, as if going through the motions. "We know there is a remnant of the Order hiding in the Beneath Places, and we know that you have been in their camp." She paused. "I want to know everything you know about them."

Winters blinked. "I know very little. They are in the Beneath Places, and they wish you harm."

The woman scowled. "How strong are their numbers?"

"I do not know. Not very strong." Winters paused. "What has happened? I see it on your face and in your eyes."

The woman's face went hard and cold. "I told you it is not your concern." But the eyes that wouldn't meet Winters's revealed a chink in the woman's armor. "How many soldiers do the Androfrancines have hidden underground? What other armaments did you see while you were with them?"

Winters tried to hold the woman's eyes. "I do not know. They weren't plainly visible." She leaned forward. "It's something terrible," she said in a low voice.

The woman's resolve broke, and Winters saw anguish and despair when their eyes finally did meet. "Yes," she said. "It is terrible."

Winters saw the tears building and fought an unexpected panic that moved through her shoulders and into her stomach. With the woman's armor cracking now, she saw a mountain of grief upon her bent and breaking back. She was surprised to find that she wanted to suddenly reach across the table and take the woman's hands. Instead, she leaned forward and waited.

"We've lost them both," the woman finally said, stifling a sob. "We had the kin-raven just today. The Crimson Empress and her Betrothed are dead."

Her Betrothed. She didn't initially make the connection, but when she did, she felt the room spin and go gray with the wave of utter sorrow that rushed her, washing over her, pulling her into an ocean of cold, deep grief. *Oh Jakob.*

She heard the cry before she realized that it was her own and buried her face into her hands, the sobs shaking her shoulders as the memory of his skin, his smell, his laughter and his eyes flooded her. The woman across from her held back for as long as she could, and Winters heard her own sobs, quiet and guarded, given against her will.

The initial wave of grief subsided, and she sniffed as she looked up. "What happened to them?"

The woman's eyes were wet and no longer held any anger. "They were murdered by Vlad Li Tam."

The words and their meaning struck her and brought more tears. Jin's own father had murdered her son, and the thought of it was a knife twisting in her heart. She tried to fight this wave of grief but couldn't. She leaned forward in her chair and wept openly.

Finally, with shaking shoulders, she looked up. "What does this mean?"

The woman sniffed and tried to find her composure. "I do not know. We continue as planned." The words were hollow.

They sat in silence, and after a few minutes, the woman stood. "We will talk more tomorrow," she said. "You will be shown to quarters and brought food." She wrinkled her nose. "Water for bathing as well." Then the woman moved to the door and finally met Winters's eyes. "Your grief surprises me, Lady Winteria."

Winters stood and walked to the door. "It should not surprise you. It is a horrible loss in an ocean of horrible losses."

Then she surprised herself and the woman when she quickly embraced her captor before leaving.

A single guard escorted her down the hall to a small room—a guest chamber not unlike the one she'd used in Rudolfo's manor. The guard led her into the room and showed her the small bath chamber that connected it to three other rooms.

After the guard left to arrange food, Winters sat on the bed and stared, unblinking, at a spot on the carpet. Before this news, she'd felt the calling come upon her, and now, in the face of such loss, she was confounded by doubt.

Bring her to the dream.

The voice was a whisper but loud enough that she looked about the room.

Bring her home.

Her own voice was a whisper in the room. "Who is this?"

The voice was old and deep, low and distant. *I am . . .*

I am.

Winters waited.

I am awake. Bring them to the dream, Daughter of Shadrus, Daughter of Salome. The Time of Sowing is at hand.

She shook her head. "I don't understand."

But there was no answer. And when the plate of steaming food arrived, it went uneaten upon her table. The lure of the hot water held nothing for her either, and after an hour more of pondering and weeping, Winters fell into a deep sleep and dreamed of white forests and impossible light in dark places.

(D)arta

Marta felt the vibration of the Behemoth's engines through the warm metal wall that she leaned against, and she closed her eyes against it, willing it to lull her to sleep.

She had her own room, as did the Y'Zirite woman they now traveled with, but the room with its soft, sponge-like cot did not appeal to her. Neither did being away from Isaak.

The metal man sat beside her on the floor, his eyes dim though occasionally light sparked deep in those red jewels. He'd spent more time sleeping since boarding the Behemoth, though she knew it wasn't sleep in the same way that humans slept. He sat still, the fluid line of his mouth occasionally twitching, and she sat beside him with his metal hand held tightly in both of hers.

After a few days of slow meandering through the water to make their rendezvous with Rudolfo, they were now moving fast and, according to Isaak, southward. Still, he'd not talked much about what to expect when they arrived.

He's changed a lot since the Final Dream. Or maybe it was because of the death of his creator, Brother Charles. Or all of it. Regardless, he was quieter and more aloof. And there were times when he knew things that perplexed her, not the least of which was his claim to have seen her father weeping over the loss of her in the dream.

Of course, the weight of that knowledge made her choice to do her part that much more a worthy sacrifice in her eyes. And occasionally, she missed the man and her older brother. But not in the way she missed her mother. And not in the way that she would miss Isaak if she had turned back at his bidding and returned home.

She glanced at him and then back to the open hatch that spilled red light into their room. She'd seen the woman, Ire Li Tam, prowling the corridor and checking the rooms as she went. The Y'Zirite Blood Guard was quiet now and Marta thought she might get up and go looking for her.

But the metal hand twitched in hers as she started to move, and instead of standing, she squeezed the hand and settled back down.

She'd seen the other girls all moon-faced over boys before, and she'd never really given it much thought. Now she wondered about it all of the time and played back her experiences with Isaak, looking for the moment that curiosity and compassion sparked to become love.

I love him. She'd said it before, to Charles, and she said it to herself over and over again. *But I hate him, too.*

Isaak had killed her mother and thousands of others when he'd been bent and twisted into unleashing the dark magick that brought down Windwir. And doing so, he'd started the series of escalating conflicts that engulfed her world in war.

Still, her hatred of the Y'Zirites was greater. She knew that hating a sword made little sense when it was the hand and arm swinging it that truly were at fault. But she hated him a little; she could not help it. *Swords and arms and hands all kill together.*

But she hadn't hated him enough to leave him. The love, she knew, was stronger, and it bound her to him. She felt it in every aspect of her being, at times a comfortable fire to warm herself and at times a raging, heated conflict inside of her. And she'd felt other parts of herself awakening as well, but those feelings had frightened her and she'd left them unexplored.

I am no different than those other girls. But as soon as she thought it, the metal hand twitched again, and she looked over at the large, silver object of her deepest affection, towering above her even as they sat together against the wall. This, she realized as she squeezed the hand back, was definitely different.

The eyes flashed and flickered as she watched them, growing brighter. Silver shutters moved like liquid over them as he blinked himself awake. Isaak looked down at her. "Have you been here this entire time?"

She chuckled. "Of course I have."

"What about our guest?"

Marta shrugged. "She's wandering around. I prefer your company."

She felt the slightest pang of loss as he drew his hand away from hers, but she didn't resist. "Did you sleep well?"

His eyes flickered. "It is not really sleep," he said. "It is . . . a place of contemplation and reflection within the sub-aether. For purposes of internal processing, integration and restoration."

Marta wrinkled her nose. "It sounds like sleep." She paused, staring at her empty hands. "Do you still dream?"

It was odd to hear the metal man sigh. "I do. But it is murky in this place. The metal dream is gone. The Homeward dream is gone. A new dream emerges." A shudder took the metal man. "And beneath that dream, a voice whispers and I cannot hear it."

This was the most she'd gotten him to say in days, and Marta sat up. "What kind of voice?"

He blinked. "A very old voice." He blinked again and looked at her. "Little human—" He paused at her scowl and nodded. "Marta, when we reach Y'Zir it is going to be very dangerous. I could not stop you from coming because choice is the first gift given. But I am authorized by directive to take actions necessary to preserve life."

She felt a spark of anger. "What does that mean?"

"It means I will be leaving you on Behemoth until it is safe for you to join me."

She banked the anger, knowing it did nothing but confuse him. Instead, she changed tactics. "What will you do when we arrive?"

"I will meet Nebios Whym there, and we will seek Lord Tam. We will take the staff from him."

"And what will Ire Li Tam do?"

Isaak paused and cocked his head. "I do not know. She is sworn to aid us by her oath to Lord Rudolfo. It will be for her to determine."

"Because," she asked, "choice is the first gift given?"

Isaak nodded. "Yes."

Marta smiled. "Then my choice is to be at your side. Danger or not."

Isaak sighed again. "Lord Rudolfo would call you a formidable woman."

A voice from the other side of the room surprised her and she jumped. "Lord Rudolfo would be correct," Ire Li Tam said with a dry chuckle. She looked at Marta. "Formidable indeed."

Marta blushed, unsure of how much of the exchange the Blood Guard had overheard. She watched the woman watching her and finally looked away. But she discovered she liked the approval she saw in her scarred face, and if she was honest with herself, even Marta felt a bit of pride in that last bit of reasoning with her metal friend. "If what you say about choice is true," she said, "then leaving me here against my will violates the first gift given."

"That," Ire Li Tam said, "is why the second gift is so important."

Isaak's head swiveled quickly, his eyes meeting the Blood Guard's. "You know of the gifts?"

She nodded. "I studied aspects of Lunarism as a part of my training as a Daughter of Ahm, prior to selection for the Blood Guard. Both the elements suppressed in the populace and those that were adapted and integrated into the worship of the Wizard Kings."

The words meant little to Marta. "What is the second gift, then?"

Isaak said nothing. Ire Li Tam waited and then spoke. "Love."

Choice and love. These made sense to her. She looked at Isaak and felt her face growing red as she said the words. She wanted to stop herself, especially because of the woman that watched them now. But she couldn't stop. "I choose to go with you," she said, "and I choose the danger *because of* love."

Isaak studied her, then studied the woman. He stood, and Marta heard whispers and groans from deep inside him as he processed her words.

"And I," Isaak finally said, "may choose to stop you."

He didn't finish the sentence, but Marta did not need him to. And she knew because of that unfinished sentence that he would indeed try to leave her behind in Behemoth and she would find a way to follow. Both would do what they did for exactly the same reason, and she felt the words alive in her stomach as she finished the sentence on his behalf.

Because of love, Marta realized.

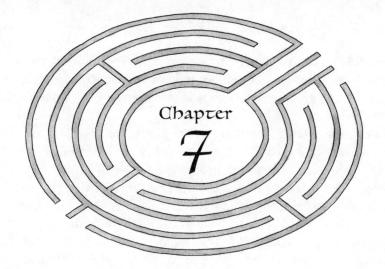

Chapter 7

Rudolfo

The floorboards overhead creaked with heavy footsteps as Rudolfo and his men sat around the basement's single table, sipping steaming hot chai.

They'd changed their clothes on the ship, dressing in the winter woolens of fishermen, just before landing at Calapia. There, at the dock, Simmons had turned them over to other friends of the Order who escorted the motley group of Gypsies down wet streets until they reached the safehouse.

"Word of what you did in Merrique is slowly getting out," the master of the house told them as he ushered the men into the basement. He had smiled and inclined his head. "We will do our part to spread that word, Lord Rudolfo."

The large open room was damp and cold, but old army blankets had been piled on the floor and the chai kettle had shown up along with a platter of bread, cheese and fruit not long after their arrival. Rudolfo nibbled at a bit of apple and looked at his men.

Seeing the scouts and his acting first captain was like sudden sun after a long stretch of rain, though they were a bedraggled, worn-down looking lot. Not that Rudolfo fared much better. And all of them stank of fish and were splattered in the mud of the city-state's rain-drenched streets. Still, this moment was a heaven he embraced as he warmed cold fingers on the hot tin mug, savoring the heat of the chai as it burned down to his stomach. Some of the men passed a flask of firespice between them, mixing it into their tins. Rudolfo licked his lips, suddenly craving the extra nudge of heat a few splashes would give his cup.

For a time, after the bombing of the library that nearly claimed his wife and son, he'd turned to the powerful spirit. It had fogged the anguish of knowing he couldn't protect his family until he'd found his way back to a better path. It was a time he never wished to return to. And those dark days were before his memory all of the time now since his meeting with Isaak in the belly of the metal Behemoth.

He looked away from the flask as it moved from scout to scout, took another sip of the chai and sighed. He'd been angry since that rendezvous despite the high trust he had for his metal friend. Rudolfo's faith, he knew, was well placed. Isaak had put himself in between Jin Li Tam and Jakob on the afternoon of the blast, and the explosion had nearly destroyed the mechoservitor.

No, Rudolfo realized, it eventually *did* destroy him, when the crack in the sunstone that fueled him finally went too far and he exploded deep in the Beneath Places. He didn't know exactly what had happened, but he knew from Charles's report that the metal man had been protecting Neb from the Y'Zirite's ancient mechoservitor. Isaak and the Watcher had both been destroyed, but Neb had supposedly been spared.

Because Isaak saved him, too, like he did my son and my wife. No, Rudolfo knew he could trust the limping mechoservitor. If Jakob could be found and returned, Isaak would do it.

Still, it angered Rudolfo to leave the path he'd chosen. He'd heard his men laud him, claiming he *always* knew the right path and *always* chose it, but the weight of fatherhood had changed him. There were right paths and best paths and wrong paths for good intentions, and he found himself changing directions too many times for his comfort. And the stakes had never been higher. The eyes of his son were ever before him, stronger now after the dream, and of everything in his life that he had lost or could lose, Rudolfo knew it was the one loss he could not sustain. Entrusting Jakob to Isaak enraged him because he was a father who should be able to protect his son.

Of course, there were other ways of protecting a son, and Rudolfo found more rage in that observation. *Like negotiating a treaty and arranging your son's chancellorship of a conquered Named Lands.*

He shuddered.

The door leading to the stairs opened and a tall form ducked into the room, his face obscured by the hood of a dripping rain cloak.

"Gods," he said. "This was a surprise." Rudolfo knew the voice even as the hands pushed back the hood. Renard smiled. "Albeit a welcome surprise. What changed your mind?"

He hesitated, looking for the right words. "A friend went in my place. I'm going to ensure instead that there's a home for my son to return to."

Renard came to the table and sat. "I will pass the word."

"I want to meet with Orius," Rudolfo said. "Esarov, too."

Renard blinked. "I don't think meeting with Orius is going to be possible. And why Esarov?"

Rudolfo's eye narrowed. "My resources are committed in this war, and I'm preparing to commit more. I'll have parley with the Androfrancine general." He paused while Renard poured a cup of chai, then splashed it with firespice. "And of course Esarov is involved. He used to be an Androfrancine before he took to the stage and to politics. I've no doubt he knew of Orius's hidden army long before the rest of us did."

Renard nodded slowly. "I will see what I can arrange. General Orius hasn't left the Beneath Places since Windwir."

"Good." He hadn't expected Renard specifically, but he was glad for the rangy Waste guide's presence. "I also require ongoing use of at least two of your moon sparrows."

Renard scowled. "Those are in short supply."

Rudolfo leaned forward. "Couriers are not fast enough to coordinate what we have coming, and there is much work to do. I need the birds."

"I'll see what I can do."

Rudolfo nodded. "Good. I have more."

Renard chuckled and sipped his chai. "I'm sure you do."

He nodded to Philemus. "I want my captain and half his men escorted from the city." Rudolfo looked at his officer as he said it and watched the man's jaw tense. "They'll need scout powders and magicked horses." Rudolfo met Philemus's eyes. "I'm going to need my army brought south."

The second captain nodded. "Aye, General."

Rudolfo sat back and turned to Renard. "My conversations with Esarov and Orius will determine exactly what I do with that army."

The Waste guide inclined his head. "I am glad you're here, General."

He uses my military title now. Rudolfo returned the gesture. "Those who aren't dead will be driven from our lands once your weapon's done its work. Until then the war must wage quietly."

Renard smiled. "You've won us a great victory in that quiet war. Esarov's employed bards to set your assassination of Yazmeera and her officers to music. The story's being told in taverns and markets all along the coast and creeping inward every day." The smile widened. "You are a hero of the people, Rudolfo. Or you will be once we've finished spreading the word."

And three days ago I was a collaborator in their eyes. But it would be a good weapon in that quiet war, the one that turned the people's hearts toward hope after so long under the cloud of war. And one he hoped would make his enemies all the more afraid, especially when the Androfrancines' weapon took a surgical knife to the Y'Zirite's military and spiritual leadership.

Rudolfo smiled. "Whatever serves our effort."

Renard drained off the last of his cup and pushed back from the table. "I will go and pass word. You will be moved sometime within the next few hours to more comfortable accommodations in a manor outside of the city."

Rudolfo stood as well. "Thank you, Renard."

Renard walked to the door and paused, looking back at Rudolfo. "You must really trust this friend of yours. Had I a son in similar straits, I'm not sure I could entrust him to any but myself."

Rudolfo felt the weight of his own words even as he said them. "I'm not sure of my path, Renard. But he is an extraordinary friend, and aye, he has my trust." He paused. "He has earned it."

Renard pulled his hood back up and opened the door. "Then I wish him well." He tipped his head forward. "You and your men, too." His smile was brief. "I'm glad you are here."

Renard closed the door behind him, and Rudolfo gave the table another glance before retreating to a corner. He couldn't remember when he'd slept last, and as uninviting as a blanket on the cold basement floor was, he would dream it to be his softest mattress on the summer balcony of his Third Forest Manor.

But as Rudolfo slipped into a light sleep, his dreams did not bring him comfort. Dark objects flew through darkened skies, and kin-wolves howled upon his heels. A dark-eyed boy wandered lost in a Whymer Maze of corpses, while a white tree the size of a world snowed seed upon the bloody ground.

Jin Li Tam

Jin Li Tam watched the building from the shadows of the alley and tried not to think about Rudolfo. But the news from Sister Elsbet kept intruding, even now as her Blood Guard took up their positions with knives drawn.

Rudolfo, my love, what have you done? He'd somehow poisoned the general responsible for overseeing the conquest of the Named Lands along with the senior staff and a half-squad of Blood Guard. And then escaped. If she knew the man, he was likely bound for Y'Zir, whether or not he had received her message. The idea of facing the man, meeting his eyes, being seen by him—it filled her with a dread that hurt her stomach.

Because I let my father kill our son.

She shuddered and forced her eyes back to the building. She called up her father's face and eyes, pushing Rudolfo's aside, and found her anger again. All night in the interrogation cell and they'd found their best lead. It was an old, abandoned building used by several Lunarist families along with their local elder, a man who had eluded the Y'Zirite authorities for decades. Her father was working with these people—it was exactly his kind of weapon—and they would know where he was. *If he isn't here hiding among them.*

She checked her people again. Half of her squad was already magicked and ready, positioned at each exit to apprehend anyone fleeing the building. The other half were in place now, and she touched her throat, feeling the chain that held her phial of blood magicks. Once she used them, she had three, maybe four days to finish her work before they killed her. But she couldn't bring herself to use them until she knew with certainty she was in reach of him.

She moved out of the alley and into the street, walking quickly toward the doors where three of her Blood Guard waited. She nodded as she approached, and one of the women brought the door down with a heavy kick. Then they were moving into the building as another three Blood Guard, these magicked and with knives drawn, swept in past them like a wind from the streets.

They entered a corridor lined with doors, and Jin paused as her ghosts slipped down it, opening each door carefully and checking within. Still, the only door that showed any light beneath it was at the end of the hall. Behind it, Jin heard quiet voices.

She stopped at the door and felt her magicked Blood Guard brush by. The others were close behind her now as well, and she paused to let them take the lead. At her nod, the door came down with a crash and they flooded the room with knives ready.

She followed after, her eyes sweeping the room for a familiar old man. Instead, she saw the slack-jawed, wide-eyed men, women and children huddled there. A few of the younger ones started to cry, and Jin felt the ache of it in her own body. Her hands went sweaty and she felt dizzy for a moment, fear tugging at her breath.

She'd not heard a child's cry since . . . Nausea washed through her, making her knees weak. She took a slow, deep breath and forced calm into her voice. "I'm looking for Elder Reeve."

Silence.

Jin looked around the room. "I'm also looking for an old man with a staff."

More silence, but with careful glances away. Two of the children had met her eyes, though, and those looks had told her what she needed to know.

"He's been here," she said. "Where did he go?" She looked around. "Where is Elder Reeve?"

Jin waited, her head throbbing at the idea of another night spent in the interrogation cell. "I would rather not have you all brought to the palace for questioning," she said. "I care nothing for your religious practices. I only care about finding the old man."

She looked from face to face, already calculating which would be the easiest to break, and waited for some kind of response. When none came she sighed. "You've left me no choice. Gather them up."

Jin turned her back to leave, and a child's voice rang out behind her. "You have a choice," he said.

She turned, her eyes narrowing. "What did you say?"

He was four or five, possibly, and clinging to his father. "You always have a choice. It's the first gift given."

She stared at the child, then the father, and opened her mouth.

The ground suddenly shuddered, and a massive roar shook the walls and rattled the glass, throwing Jin off balance. She moved for the wall as the floor shook again. Outside, alarm bells clanged, and shrill whistles pierced the air.

"See them to the palace," she said as she moved quickly down the corridor.

She let herself out into the street and saw a cloud of dust and debris rising from the edge of the city. She heard a roar from that direction that hurt her ears, and something massive leapt up from the cloud, hovered above it and dropped again. In the moment that it hovered, she recognized the beast.

She's found him. Jin smiled and didn't wait for her Blood Guard. She launched herself into a run, strength flowing through her. Certainly she wanted to end him herself. But watching someone else do it would be satisfactory if the outcome was the same. Still, if she was honest, she savored the idea of taking the magicks and finishing him, then being finished herself when they burned her out.

I would die strong, fast, avenged.

No, she realized. She would die invisible and alone. But he would be dead, too, and that was worth the price.

Jin Li Tam ran, stumbling and staggering as the ground continued to shake beneath her feet. The streets were littered with broken glass and scattered debris—some she suspected had landed here from elsewhere. Ahead of her, the dust cloud grew, and at the center of it, something silver flashed. She felt the sting of it now as the wind whipped at her eyes and she drew the phial from around her neck.

The wind became a roaring, and she realized it was the wings that stirred it up, blowing dirt and ash as the beast dropped again. Deep in the dust cloud, Jin saw lightning flash and heard a loud cry.

She lifted her voice against the wind. "Father?"

Jin pushed herself forward. She could see him now, the staff held in both hands as he swung it. The beast was on the ground, its wings tucked in, lunging forward with tooth and claw.

She cried out again. "Father?"

He looked at her this time, though he was too far away, too obscured by the dust, for her to read his expression. She heard a crack and saw another flash of lightning as the staff connected and the beast leaped back.

She slowed to a walk. *I should wait and see how she fares.* Still, her fingers tugged at the stopper.

The beast lunged again, and this time, her father leaped forward to bring the staff down hard upon its broad silver forehead. There was a flash and a loud cracking sound as the dragon split open and the woman inside of it fell out. A loud shriek drove Jin to her knees, and she forced her eyes open as her father swung the staff again and the massive silver beast threw itself into the sky, fleeing at top speed.

The girl lay still, and Vlad Li Tam's eyes went from her to Jin.

She could see his face now, and for the briefest moment, she saw some combination of sorrow and weariness before it became a mask of calm. She took another step forward and he raised the staff.

"Stay back, Daughter," he said.

Jin unstopped the phial and drained it, feeling the fire move from her throat to her belly, out into her fingertips and the tips of her hair. "Oh no, Father," the forty-second daughter of Vlad Li Tam answered. "I'll not stay back any longer."

And then, drawing her knives, she fell upon him.

Vlad Li Tam

Vlad Li Tam barely had time to lift the staff before the storm of his enraged daughter's blades was upon him. He felt his purchase on the silver steel grow slippery with sweat as he tightened his grip and parried her blows. All while stepping around the unconscious woman the creature had left at his feet.

It had all happened fast, too fast, and as he worked the staff to stay alive he tried to lay hold of exactly what had transpired. He'd been out with Elder Reeve, on his way to meet with the Lunarists' mysterious benefactor, when the giant metal beast had descended upon him with a roar from on high.

In all his years, he'd seen nothing like it, though he'd seen his share of mechanical wonders. This creature was different from Rufello's recreations. It was easily the size of a small house, with two pairs of wings and six legs. It had a short neck and a wide head set with large black eyes. Its mouth was lined with teeth like long knives. And yet the entire creature was made of a silver so bright it hurt his eyes.

Its landing had shaken the ground, tumbling Vlad from his feet, and even as he used the staff to find his balance, the long tail snaked out to drop him again.

Vlad felt fear flooding him, and the force of it was surprising. Still, he breathed that fear in and out, clutching the staff and begging it to give him strength.

He'd landed a few tentative blows before the staff began to sing in his hands, and as its song built, he sensed a release coming. It sparked now in a way that it hadn't before, hot within his hands, and he felt that heat moving through his body. Lunging forward, Vlad brought the staff down upon the base of the creature's skull and heard the cracking sound even as the lightning blinded him.

When he blinked at the ground before him, a woman lay unconscious there, and the beast that had carried her was gone.

But the end of one ambush was simply the beginning of another. He'd suspected that his daughter would come after him, but when he looked up and saw her watching him, her face twisted with open hatred, it was as surprising to him as the creature that had dropped from the sky. And when she'd unstopped the small phial and poured its contents into her mouth, he'd known exactly what she was doing, and it cut him deeper than her knives could have.

What have you done? He meant the question as much for himself as he did for her. After all, he was the one who'd brought her to this point. His actions had assured her hatred of him, and now she'd ingested Y'Zirite blood magicks . . . something she knew as well as he did would ultimately kill her just as they'd killed her sister, Rae Li Tam. The irony that Rae had taken the blood magicks to save Vlad's life and Jin had taken them to end it was not lost on him.

He wanted to talk to her, to lower his voice and speak in reassuring, fatherly tones to her, but Vlad found it was all he could do to keep her knives at bay. He felt them catching and cutting at his robes as she pressed him back and away from the fallen woman.

He squeezed the staff and was able to make out the blurred shape of her despite the magicks at work. He could see none of the detail of her face, but he'd sparred with her enough as a child to remember the way her eyes narrowed and her nostrils flared when she was in the heat of battle. And he knew that she would not stop until he was dead.

Or until I kill her.

Neither was an option for him, and the only other alternative was not something he was certain of. When he'd stormed the palace, he'd been able to pull the blood magicks out of the imperial guard, feeding those magicks to the staff. But he'd ripped the magicks free of them with no thought or concern about the impact it might have upon their bodies. Some he'd outright killed in the effort, and others he'd left writhing and shrieking upon the palace floor.

"Stop," he said, his voice a ragged gasp, the staff sparking against the steel in her invisible knives.

She pressed on and he parried again, this time testing the dark aura her magicks cast over her blurred image. He closed his eyes and used his mind to pull, his feet moving to the steps of her dance.

It was like lifting a wet and heavy sail; it resisted in ways that the others hadn't, and he opened his eyes. Then he tugged harder, feeling it give the tiniest amount.

Growling, he moved to the left and swung the staff, connecting with her leg. She buckled, and he pulled the magicks out of her, watching her blurred image take on definition and form as he did. And as he did it, the staff burned hot in his hands as it fed on those magicks. Wave after wave of euphoria pushed at him even as his legs threatened to give out.

Jin Li Tam fell to the ground, gasping and seizing, and his first impulse was to slide down beside her, take her into his arms and soothe her. But he knew better. Instead, he crouched and looked up and down the street, his breath ragged and his eyes wide. She flopped onto her stomach, hands still scrambling for her knives. He used the staff to move them out of her reach, then went back to watching.

He saw the magicked Blood Guard as she came around the corner, and he felt the heat once again as he ripped the magicks from her, sending the woman careening into the side of a building before she stumbled and fell still on the street.

There will be more.

A guttural noise at his feet brought his attention back to Jin. It was a despairing sound, part sob and part scream, as she stretched herself out upon the ground and crawled for her knives.

Watching her, something broke inside of him that he'd tried very hard to keep unbroken. It was worse than Ria's knives upon him or upon his family.

Because my blades had carved my children into this shape long before Windwir fell. The destruction of the Androfrancines and the rise of the Y'Zirites in the Named Lands had only taken those cuts and gashes deeper and farther.

Vlad slid his hand down the staff to kneel beside his forty-second daughter. He no longer saw the other woman, unmoving and nearby. And he no longer cared who might find them there. All he saw was this daughter of his that he had broken, and the weight of it now broke him.

He dropped the staff and pulled her to himself, resisting her fists and nails and feet as he did. "Oh my daughter," Vlad Li Tam said in a quiet and mournful voice, "things are not what they seem."

Then there were hands upon him, and he looked up into Elder Reeve's wonderstruck face. "The kin-dragons are flying again," the Lunarist said, his voice full of awe.

Others had joined the old man, and Vlad Li Tam resisted when two younger men pulled at Jin Li Tam. The priest's warm, reassuring hand on his shoulder made it easier to let her go. And when others came and took him by the elbows, raising him back to his feet, he let them guide him. He was dimly aware of them also carrying the girl from the kin-dragon, but it was a detached awareness.

Because Vlad had seen in his daughter's eyes and heard within her sobs and snarls something that had flooded him with a realization he'd never quite laid hold of before. And now he knew just what kind of darkness and pain he was responsible for in the world. And Vlad Li Tam knew he deserved something far worse than death because of it.

Neb

Neb watched from the shadows and calculated, startled that Vlad Li Tam had so simply separated Amylé from her kin-dragon and Jin Li Tam from her blood magicks.

No, not Vlad. The staff. He saw it in Vlad's hands and nearly raced out from the alley to grab it up when he saw the old man lay it down to take up his daughter.

But by then, he'd seen the people slipping out into the street to help them. And he'd seen something they had missed. When Vlad had pulled the magicks from Jin Li Tam, there'd been a sparking and popping in the air above them and the slightest shimmering of something large and invisible hovering over Ahm's Glory. Whatever Vlad had done with the staff, it had affected it, revealing for the briefest moment a vessel the approximate size and shape as the New Espiran airship anchored near the Firsthome Temple.

They're here and watching as well. He looked around the street and saw no other onlookers. Only the small group of people gathered around Vlad. And that group was beginning to move up the street now, away from the direction Jin and the Blood Guard had come from. Neb broke from the shadows once they were farther up the street and pressed his thumb and his forefinger together, feeling the slick, warm cloth.

Hide me, he willed the blood of the earth, and it complied. It flowed over his body and turned the light away from him as he moved into the street to follow.

Neb wanted to simply take what he'd come for, but if Amylé's ambush, a kin-dragon dropping from the sky, had failed to separate the old man from the staff, Neb wasn't certain he could do any better, even in this vulnerable moment.

And I'm not certain that I should take it from him now. The realization surprised him, but the ships earlier pressed at him, the memory of the wood breaking beneath his massive, plunging body. The Y'Zirite knives had marked them all with its gospel, and that violent blood cult already sailed for the moon. Vlad Li Tam's brutal work here reduced that threat. And it was work that wouldn't have to be done later by someone else.

Neb sighed. *Like me.*

He followed them as they moved down back alleys and deserted streets, entering abandoned buildings only to leave them through back entrances for another Whymer Maze of streets. As Neb went, he sensed others went with him, though he couldn't confirm it. He kept watch for scout-sign, but Renard had trained him in the Churning Wastes, and the only cities he'd run there had been the fused glass-and-metal ruins left deserted other than the occasional Androfrancine expedition for millennia. It was nearly impossible for him to pick up much in a living city, regardless of how little life actually showed.

So he continued and hoped that if his instincts were correct, it was the New Espirans and not the Blood Guard that shadowed them.

The shops and houses above them on this street were becoming increasingly of a higher class, and Neb realized they'd moved across several districts within the city. This section of Ahm's Glory was less run-down, though the shops themselves were closed and the streets were empty.

The small group moved down an alley and slipped into a door. Neb waited to a count of twenty, picking out the guards nearby within the shadows. He watched, then checked behind him before drawing a breath and slowly releasing it.

Reveal me. He pressed the hem of his sleeve as he said it, and the silver material loosened back into a robe. Then Neb approached the door, keeping his hands visible as he did.

He spoke slowly. "I seek audience with Vlad Li Tam, Lord of House Li Tam," he said in a low voice.

Startled, the first guard replied in a language that Neb didn't comprehend. Furrowing his brow, he tried again. *Peace. No fear. I seek the man you shelter. Vlad Li Tam.*

The guard's eyes went wide, but not wide enough. Sighing, Neb rubbed the hem again and felt the material heat up as the robe grew brighter, driving out the shadows in the alley. He felt the fear rising in the guard and tried again to reassure him. *Peace. No fear.*

The man's face was white—as was the face of his companion—when he slipped behind the door. He was back in a moment with an old man.

The man's Landlish was broken and accented, but his eyes were full of wonder. "You've come for Lord Tam?"

Neb nodded. "Tell him it is Nebios Whym." He swallowed before he said the next words, still uncomfortable with their taste in his mouth. "The Homeseeker."

The man said something to the guard and then motioned for Neb to come inside. He left Neb near the door, disappearing up a flight of stairs. When he returned, five minutes later, he motioned for Neb to follow. He led him up the carpeted stairs and deeper into the house until they reached a large dining room that had been turned into makeshift living quarters. Jin Li Tam and Amylé D'Anjite were both stretched out on sofas, still unconscious. Vlad sat slouched in a chair in the corner holding his staff.

He looked up as Neb entered, and their eyes met. The old man's were bloodshot and buried in dark hollows, his skin stretched out and yellow like ancient parchment. Tam had been old when Neb had last seen him back in the ruins of Windwir, but he'd not been frail.

He is dying. And Neb knew it was the silver rod clutched tightly in his fists that was slowly killing him.

"Nebios Whym, is it?" Vlad chuckled and then coughed.

Neb studied the room. "Father Petronus sends greetings from the moon."

The old man didn't laugh this time. His eyes narrowed. "How is that old wolf?"

"He is dying," Neb said. He nodded to the staff. "The tools of the parents are not toys for the children."

"We're all dying," Vlad said. "Some of us more slowly than others."

Neb said nothing.

Vlad's jaw was grim as he tried to sit up in the chair. "I suppose you've come for this," he said as he lifted the staff.

Neb nodded slowly. "I have. It is needed elsewhere."

Their eyes met again. "I'm not finished with it yet," Vlad said. "But I will be soon."

Neb had seen enough of the city to see what the enraged old man had already accomplished. He'd seen the bodies smoldering in piles outside the city, victims of the plague Tam had unleashed. And he'd seen the toppled statue in the courtyard, the look of loss and despair upon the faces of the Y'Zirite populace and soldiers.

Neb chose his words carefully. "With respect, Lord Tam, it was made for a higher work." But even as he said it, he wasn't certain. The desolation he'd seen here in this city was nothing compared to the massive grave of Windwir. He'd watched it fall and he'd buried its dead. And beyond that knife upon the world, their knives had also cut him and cut the woman he loved. The scarred old man before him was effectively taking the blade out of Y'Zirite hands.

Vlad smiled. "Who is to say that this work isn't as important as yours?" Despite his discomfort with all of it, Neb had been called to a work dreamed about and pointed to for thousands of years. Careful planning had gone into each step along the path of revelation, though from his present viewpoint it was clear that the planning and prophecy had not been enough. In the end, he'd not unsealed the temple; Petronus had. And in the end, the staff had not fallen into his hands but into the hands of Vlad Li Tam.

Vlad continued. "Not all of the work to be done was written into Frederico's Bargain or hidden within your Marsher dream," he said. "There could be no way of knowing exactly what that work would look like over so long a stretch of time." He sat up straighter in the chair, his eyes taking on a ferocious and intelligent light. "But my house and I were born and groomed for that work, and it will go faster if you aid me in it. When we've finished, I'll gladly give over the staff."

What Neb saw in the man's eyes told him already what his answer must be, but also told him that it was an answer best considered elsewhere and given at another time. "You would have me help you destroy the Y'Zirites?"

Vlad nodded. "At least the part that makes them dangerous. It is not far off now. Or did you intend to flee to the moon and leave us to contend with them?"

The question's edge cut him. *Because it's true. I've not thought at all about what is left behind.* He'd stopped three of their vessels, but he'd not be able to stop all of them, not unless he spent his days and nights patrolling the seas surrounding the Ladder.

"You have the power," Vlad Li Tam said, "to help me end this."

Neb blinked, surprised at the conviction he suddenly felt. "I'll not use my heritage in such a way."

Vlad shrugged. "Then I will give you your staff when I'm finished honoring my own heritage and the love that led me to it and placed it within my hands in the first place."

Neb knew there were no more words in this moment. He wouldn't interfere with Tam's work until he had to. But he knew better than to pretend that he wasn't complicit. He might not be crushing the Y'Zirite's backs himself, but he wasn't preventing it, either. And all of it brought a heaviness to him that pulled at his shoulders. *I need you, Petronus,* he prayed toward the moon. Then he looked to Amylé where she lay on the couch. "The girl is not well," he said. "I can take her with me and see to her."

Vlad smiled, though it was strained with pain. "No," he said. "You may not. But I will tend to her when she wakes."

Neb met the man's eyes once again, reading bemusement and re-solve there. More than resolve, he saw danger there. A kind of mad abandon to the exigencies of war that told him Vlad Li Tam would do anything, kill anyone, sacrifice everything to finish the work he'd undertaken. His daughter could not stand in the way; neither could a kin-dragon with the element of surprise. And though the man said he'd lay it down when he finished, Neb knew in that stare that he would likely have to take the staff. Because Vlad's work might be of the sort that could never be finished.

I should say something. He felt his jaw stiffening as he spoke. "Finish your work, Lord Tam. I will come back for the staff in one week's time, and when I do, you will lay it down."

Neb turned away and did not wait to be escorted out. And when he reached the street, he'd already determined his next steps. First, he would seek out the New Espirans here and parley with them. He would convince these new allies to help and to keep watch over the staff until his return.

Then he would rise to the heritage that had been his before the mantle of godhood settled upon his shoulders. The heritage he'd dis-covered in the wide, dark eyes of a Marsh girl and in the glossolalia that had rolled from her tongue as the dream had taken them together so long ago on the edge of Windwir's grave. He would find his queen, his love, and help lead her people homeward.

Then, when Vlad Li Tam's week was up, Nebios Whym would return to Ahm's Glory as a god and take back the staff of his office.

Winters

The dark basement of the house was a stark contrast with its bright, well-furnished upper stories, and Winters was surprised that her guards had brought her here.

She'd awakened after sleeping fitfully, bathing quickly before dressing and eating the breakfast that awaited her. The halls were crowded with Y'Zirite soldiers and Blood Guard now as another day of occupation began. Winters kept an eye out for Tertius and Hebda as they moved through the house, but she did not see them.

And when the guards had locked her into a cider cellar that had been converted into an Y'Zirite cutting chamber, she'd felt a sinking in her stomach. Still, she sat on the bench beside the table with its straps and buckles and blood-catchers, and waited.

The lieutenant did not make her wait long. When the woman entered, her uniform had been replaced by long dark robes. She laid her knives upon the table and took the other chair, facing Winters. The officer's face showed little evidence of any sleep. Her eyes were still hollow and dark, her skin pale and giving her Y'Zirite markings a pink glow in the dim-lit chamber.

"I am required," the lieutenant said, "to learn everything you know about the Androfrancine remnant."

Bring her to the dream. That's what the voice had bid her do as she lay grieving the loss of Jakob. And the memory of that voice brought a calm to Winters now. She opened her hands in her lap and offered a weak smile. "I've told you what I know." She paused. "What is your name?"

The woman blinked. "I am Lieutenant Erys of the Seventh Imperial Brigade."

Winters lowered her voice. "Erys," she said. "I've told you what I know." She nodded to the knife and table. "This won't get you any more from me. As you can see, I've been beneath your knives before."

Erys nodded. "You participated in the Mass of the Falling Moon. It is a great honor to take the sins of the people."

"It was a great honor to protect my people from that blade," Winters said. "We follow the dream, not the knife. Not the blood."

Recognition and surprise washed the woman's face. *She remembers the dream.* Erys glanced to the knives now before looking to Winters. "There have been a lot of cuttings."

And what has it brought you? Winters didn't ask the question. She knew she didn't need to. The woman had likely asked it of herself as soon as the news of her empress's death—and by it, the death of her faith—had settled in. "There has been too much bloodshed," Winters finally said. "It is time for a new way."

The lieutenant's shoulders slumped. "We need it." She regarded Winters a moment, her lips pursed. "I trust you've heard the news regarding Chancellor Rudolfo?"

She shook her head. "I've not."

The woman sighed. "He's poisoned General Yazmeera and her senior officers. He escaped the Divided Isle and is suspected to be en route to Y'Zir."

Does he know about Jakob? It was the first thing she wondered, and it started her heart to breaking yet again. She met the lieutenant's stare. "What does that mean for you and your people here?"

Erys shrugged. "I await orders from Y'Zir. My commanding officer was in attendance at Rudolfo's Markday Feast."

"So you are in command here now?"

The woman nodded. "I am. From the eastern borders of the Entrolusian Delta to the southern edge of the Prairie Sea."

Winters leaned forward. "You could let me go about my work."

The woman also leaned forward. "What work is that?"

"To bring my people home," Winters said, sitting back in the chair. "You were there. You saw the tree, Erys."

Yes, Daughter of Shadrus and Salome. Bring her to the dream.

Winters felt her breath catch at the whisper and felt the awe of that voice raising gooseflesh on her arms and legs. She'd spent her life in service to the metaphysics of her people's dream. She'd seen visions and spoken in unknown tongues, but none of those experiences prepared her for this voice in her head. The experience that had come the closest was the Final Dream, and she knew that somehow it was that dream that awakened this new voice. "You heard me there and felt the wind as it lifted the seeds and dropped them like snow upon us as we gathered in that place."

Erys blinked, and Winters saw her eyes were full of tears. "Yes," she said. "I saw it. We all saw it."

It suddenly struck Winters that not only had they seen it, but surely they'd talked about it. Especially in the light of recent developments. "And what do you make of it? You dreamed it. And I am here now."

"The Daughters of Ahm insist it is a product of the Abomination."

"The Daughters of Ahm also insist upon the shedding of blood." Winters wanted to push harder, to remind the woman that the Daughters of Ahm had also insisted that their Crimson Empress would heal the world, but she could not use that loss so directly. It violated the sanctity of Jakob's life to use his death to manipulate this woman.

But bringing her to the dream was another matter.

Winters took a breath and released it. "Erys," she said, "I do not pretend to know what this new dream means. But the old dream—my people's dream—brought it about, and we have all shared in it. The moon has been opened to us, and I am gathering my people to take them home."

The woman shook her head. "I cannot release you, Lady Winteria. It is not my choice to make."

"It is absolutely your choice to make," she answered. "But do not make that choice now. Instead, send me away under guard—manacle me if you must—but let me be about my work."

"You want me to provide you with an escort?"

Winters nodded. "Yes. Me and my friends."

Something flashed across the woman's face, and Winters wasn't certain what it was. Still, Erys sat quietly, her mouth firm in thought, before she spoke. "Why would I do this?"

"Because you remember the dream. It was like nothing you've ever experienced. The hope. The sense of history. The awe. I remember it, too, and I'm compelled by it to remind everyone that even if comprehending it fully lies beyond our current grasp, it still holds great meaning. And it is something we can all lay hold of—because it is something we have all shared." Her words tumbled out faster than she'd thought they would, and as they did, she saw the light growing in her captor's eyes. "The way to the moon is open. You've seen it your entire life, green with life in the sky above this dying place. The dream is the harbinger of Homecoming."

Yes, Daughter.

Erys stood, suddenly agitated. "I will take your request into consideration," she said in a terse voice. Her face showed frustration, but in her eyes, Winters saw more. *She is also compelled but does not wish to be.*

"I am grateful for your consideration," she said, inclining her head before standing herself.

Her guard was waiting, silent and hollow-eyed, and Winters followed her back up the stairs to her room. When the door closed behind her, she listened for the key in the lock and heard nothing. Sitting on the edge of her bed, she found her mind once more wandering back to Rudolfo and what he'd done.

More than that, she realized. *What had been done to him.* And to Lady Tam, of course.

And the thought of her friend and mentor, the woman who'd taught her to dance with the knives, brought back the tears that were never far from Winters now.

How was it possible that the little boy was gone? How could Jin's own father have done this? Winters had never contemplated motherhood until she'd met little Lord Jakob. That, combined with the blossoming love she'd experienced with Neb, had brought about those first stirrings, though she knew that path was distant if ever she were to walk it. And she no longer imagined Neb being the one she shared that path with, as badly as she wanted to. Or at least she hadn't when he was something alien to her, something different and frightening.

But knowing now that she was every bit as different stirred something in her, and she knew that her fears of that boy were unfounded. He'd charged to her rescue without a thought, even though Winters was a girl who needed no rescuing, and he'd done it for love. He'd even risked his role in the dream to seek her out, somehow knowing she was beneath the regent's careful blade.

And he was out there somewhere, doing his part for her and her people. "I must do mine," she said to the empty room. "And trust him to find me when it is time."

Outside, the rain was letting up and the first rays of sunshine burned their way through the low clouds, casting dirty light across her room.

They'd all done their part and had all paid high prices. Some of that cost now brought her shoulders to gently shaking again.

Do not despair, Daughter. All will be well.

It was the voice again, ancient and quiet and sure. Winters took a deep breath and held it, willing the comfort of that voice to drive out the sorrow of loss that weighed her heart.

When it couldn't, she let the loss wash over her and through her, and watched the waves outside, waiting for her captor to set her free.

Because despite everything that broke her heart and clouded her vision, Winteria bat Mardic knew that the shared dream would not only bring about her freedom but also the freedom of a scattered people she would soon be calling home.

Lysias

General Lysias of the Ninefold Forest Army lay on his belly in the dark, his head cocked and listening. Tybard lay beside him, their hands upon each other's shoulder.

He heard nothing, but that meant little down here. They'd lost men to cave-ins and sudden drops along with their casualties from the Y'Zirites they'd encountered along the way. It had been worse around the vicinity of Windwir, but once they'd had those initial contacts, their enemy had stepped up patrols.

Lysias hesitated, then pressed his words into the man's shoulder. *Blakely says this is the path.*

The others were at least a league behind them now. The forward scouts had brought them here without light, moving as silently as they could.

Lysias felt Tybard's fingers moving. *We are near the ruins of the palace.*

Lysias had visited the Papal Summer Palace a handful of times during his career, usually escorting Sethbert to visit his cousin there on matters of Order business. Now, it was a pile of snow-covered stones somewhere far above them, brought down by the Machtvolk Rebellion that tossed their young queen from her wicker throne and established her sister, Ria, instead. And deep below, he lay on his belly listening at the edge of a shaft, feeling the warm air from it as it tickled his hair and beard.

He pressed more words into Tybard's flesh. *Bring a platoon up. Send the scouts down. Tell Blakely and Symeon to be ready.*

Lysias lay still as Tybard crept back and passed his orders along. They were nearly done now if all went well. But what after? Keep to the Beneath Places and make his way south? Or bring his force up and out of the hole, a small but sharp knife at Ria and her Machtvolk's back. Most of her forces were near Windwir now, providing support to the Y'Zirites. If he and Orius had done their work well, the Y'Zirites had no way of knowing why Lysias and his men had ventured so far north. And ideally, splitting the army yet again had covered his tracks to this place.

A new hand on his back and Lysias rolled to the side, letting the scout move past and onto the iron rungs set into the side of this shaft. They'd been warm to the touch, and it had chilled him. He put his own hand out to touch the scout's magicked shoulder. *Eyes and ears open.*

The scout didn't reply. Lysias felt the slightest passing of five more and then waited. He wasn't sure how long he waited; time passed differently in darkness. But before long, he heard the slightest shuffle of boots moving in the corridor behind him.

Tybard's hand on his arm made him jump even though he expected it. *We're here.*

How long had it been? An hour at least, he figured. *If the first scout whistles clear, we descend quickly. Blakely and Symeon last.* He paused, then said what he knew Tybard already understood. *I go first.*

When the whistle came, it was soft and low, and Lysias was not sure if its softness was the distance it traveled or the scout's intended volume. But at its sound, he pushed his pack to the side. They'd learned fast to lower the packs by rope after, rather than lose men to something as unnecessary as falling off a ladder. Lysias turned and twisted himself, dangling over the edge of the shaft. He felt Tybard's strong hand on his arm, steadying him as his boots found the rung and he began his descent.

The warm air was disorienting; it seemed out of place, but so did the warmth in the metal rungs. They'd seen strange things—rooms with quicksilver lakes and lichen to give light, strange stones set in dark and pitted metal. And some of the other places had felt warm to the touch, but most of it was cold. *Cold and dark.*

He climbed past his first count of one hundred, his arms and legs feeling the strain as he moved. By two hundred, he knew there were others above him, but he couldn't hear them. His own heart, beating in his temples, drowned out any noise they made. His breath was ragged and his arms cramping when his foot hit the ground. Five hundred and sixty-three.

The scout met him and guided him to the side. Lysias leaned against the wall and caught his breath. Then he pulled his canteen and took a long drink. He ventured a whisper. "Have we found it?" It was sudden noise in hours of silence.

"Aye, General. We think so."

"Strike a lamp, then," he said.

The three sparks it took to light it cast strange shadows into the space around them, and as the mining lantern glowed to life, Lysias saw a large round room with a tunnel exiting across from where he waited, sloping down and lost in darkness.

When the others reached the bottom, he took the lamp and led them forward, leaving the scout behind to watch their flank. As they moved, he realized that the corridor wound its way downward in a spiral, the slope gradually increasing. Below, a dim light grew, and as it built, he shuttered the lantern and let it guide them.

This room was long and wide, its walls covered in a wet moss that also provided light. Moving along the edges and ceiling of the room, he saw white tubes that he at first mistook for bones. They joined something like the rough trunk of a black tree that ran from the top of the room to its bottom. Blakely paused and drew a small but old book from his pocket. Symeon leaned over his shoulder. "This is it," the Androfrancine said. The excitement in his voice seemed out of place, though Lysias himself understood a certain amount of awe. In their wanderings thus far, he'd not seen anything like it.

He stretched out a hand to touch the surface of one of the white tubes. "What are they?"

"Roots," Brother Symeon said. "They feed into the water supply for the Named Lands."

As the platoon spread out into the room before them, the two Androfrancines moved quickly to the center. Lysias followed closely, watching as their hands moved over the system of roots, following them to the larger trunk. "What do they do?" he asked.

"General Orius has not cleared you for that information. But suffice it to say, delivering the pathogen here will bring about our desired effect."

Blakely unslung his pack and began working the straps. Lysias watched him draw a large cloth-wrapped tube from it, then turned back to Symeon. "For how long?"

Symeon's eyebrows furrowed. "For how long?"

"How long does it poison the water for them?"

Blakely answered in Symeon's hesitation. "Forever," he said. "It isn't poison. It is a living organism released into the water. It will reproduce and remain there."

Blakely had unwrapped a metal cylinder and crouched with it now. Lysias crouched with him. "Has the Order done anything like this before? Is that how you know about this place?"

The man said nothing, glancing up to his partner. Symeon's voice was flat. "Again, General Orius hasn't authorized us to give you that information."

Lysias felt his anger spiking but set it aside as Blakey drew a leather satchel from his pack now and unrolled it. He lifted a wool bundle from it and unwrapped it, revealing a long, thick needle made of a bright silver Lysias instantly recognized.

Firstfall steel. The same metal Isaak was made of. And the Marsh Queen's axe. Rudolfo's arch-engineer, Charles, had even managed to turn that highly reflective metal into a device that could detect magicked scouts.

Symeon joined Blakely now, carefully holding the canister as Blakely fitted the needle to it. Then they stood, and together they put the needle against the largest of the white roots just above the place it joined the dark trunk. Nodding to each other, they pushed, putting the full weight of their bodies into it as the needle resisted, then penetrated the root.

Once it was in all the way, Blakely twisted the bottom of the canister, and Lysias heard the softest hiss.

Their silence told Lysias that he would need to have a conversation with Orius if and when they met again. The idea that the water supply of this entire corner of the continent was controlled through one point, deeply buried beneath the surface, raised his curiosity. And if the Androfrancines knew of it, they likely knew why as well.

The hissing had stopped, and the men looked to Lysias now expectantly. He stared at the canister. "That's all, then? We're done here?"

Blakey grinned. "Yes, General. The war will be over in a matter of days."

Could we really win it from here? He remembered the Blood Guard, kicking and choking her last from the water she'd sipped. Lysias and Orius had drank from the same canteen. The idea of what it might do to an army and leadership that relied heavily upon blood magicks made him want to smile as well. But he didn't. Something dark in all of it pushed at him, but he did not fully understand why. "Let's hope so," he said. "This victory's been a long time coming, paid for in blood."

They carefully removed the needle and its canister, wrapping it again carefully in the cloth. And when it was time to leave the room, Lysias sent the others ahead and followed after at a slower pace.

Could it be so easy?

Somewhere, above them and distant, a kin-wolf howled in the Beneath Places and assured Lysias that it could not.

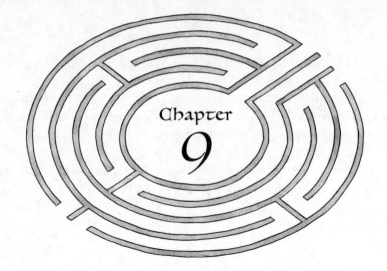

Chapter 9

Rudolfo

The thick carpet beneath his bare feet was welcome after days in his boots, and Rudolfo stretched before the dressing room's mirror. Several options had been laid out for him, clothing from the manor's owner gladly offered up to the hero of the Named Lands.

The wound upon his chest was angry and red but healing and itched more now than anything else. The hot water of the bath had soothed it, and now the cool air in the room brought the itching back.

Rudolfo resisted the urge to scratch and opted against the fresh dressing for the mark. Instead, he chose a dark cotton shirt and pulled it on, followed by a pair of trousers the color of buckskin. He found soft slippers by the dressing room's door and slid his feet into them, padding back into the bedchamber.

They'd been in this new location for just a few days now—a hunting manor tucked into the forests between the eastern edge of the City-States and the western shores of Caldus Bay. He'd spent his time learning what he could from his host about the war and about developments among the Y'Zirites. There were rumors of dark tidings back in Ahm's Glory, though there was limited intelligence available. Their host, Lord Carylin, had hoped Rudolfo would know more, having come fresh from the Y'Zirite command on the Divided Isle.

Something is afoot there. Vlad Li Tam was at the center of it, and it strained Rudolfo's judgment to give over those thoughts and turn instead to the image of his son in the shadow of that white tree.

I've seen so little of him these two years. He felt a stab—pain as real as a knife—when he contemplated their separation. And that pain gave him resolve to end that separation by making a home that his boy could return to. One more war as a general and then half of a life to spend as a father.

And librarian. Rudolfo chuckled at this.

There was a knock at the door, and it swung open before Rudolfo spoke. He opened his mouth and closed it as Esarov and Renard slipped into the room.

"We must be quick," Renard said as he pulled an ornate wooden box from beneath his cloak.

Esarov approached Rudolfo, wiping the rain from his spectacles. His long hair was tied back and damp from the rain. "Lord Rudolfo," he said, extending both his hands.

Rudolfo took the cold hands into his own and squeezed them. "Overseer Esarov."

It was obvious that the man didn't like his new title, but it had fallen to him in the manner he'd supported from the start—his council of governors, each elected to rule their particular city-state—had named him so, and since then, he'd been spearheading talks with the Y'Zirites.

The man's smile widened. "I had no idea of your plan. Renard was quite quiet about it. It was . . ." He paused, looking for the right word. "It was poetic."

Rudolfo inclined his head. "It was necessary."

"And effective," Renard added. "It's destabilized their command structure quickly."

Rudolfo gestured to the sitting area just off the bedchamber. After they were seated, Renard placed the box upon the small table between them and worked at its Rufello lock.

"General Orius cannot meet with you at this present time," Renard said. "But he sent these and told me to assure you that he will arrange a meeting soon."

He lifted the lid of the box and tipped it toward Rudolfo. Laying in a velvet bed were two still, silver sparrows, their wings folded closed and their bodies stretched out from beak to tail. Renard lifted one of the birds, his fingers gently pushing at its neck as he raised to his lips. "Activate. Voice authorization Renard. New authorization follows." He held it to Rudolfo as the tiny bird stirred to life. "Tell it your name."

Rudolfo leaned toward it, his mouth suddenly dry. "I am Rudolfo."

"Close authorization." Renard handed the bird over, and Rudolfo took it carefully, unprepared for how heavy it sat in his hand for something so delicate and old.

Renard did the same with the second moon sparrow, then showed Rudolfo the hidden switches beneath the silver feathers on its neck and beneath its wings. "It is oriented to place names and can be oriented to specific individuals by touch. If you send it to me, it will find me. And vice versa."

Rudolfo held the birds in one hand, amazed at how perfectly still they balanced there. He glanced up to Renard. "Thank you," he said. He stared at them for a moment, then passed them over to the Waste guide.

Renard deactivated the moon sparrows and tucked them back into the box. "Be careful with them," he said. "Kin-raven have been known to hunt them."

Rudolfo nodded. He remembered well the moon sparrow sent to Isaak—the one Jin Li Tam had rescued from one of the larger Y'Zirite messenger birds. "I will be careful," he said. Then he turned to Esarov. "How reliable are your lines of communication in the absence of the birds?"

The overseer shrugged. "We have the usual—couriers and codes and drops. Since the Watcher has been taken out of the equation our codes have lasted longer."

Rudolfo turned to Renard. "I'm assuming that Orius is in communication with the other houses and is aware of what resources he has available to him when the time is right?"

Renard nodded. "Aye. And he's working with Lysias as well."

"I've sent Philemus to gather the Wandering Army and bring it south. I will need to coordinate with Orius." He leaned forward. "Do you have any idea how long before this plan of his is executed?"

"We believe Lysias and our men should have it implemented within days if it hasn't already been. Last word was that they were close."

Rudolfo's eyes narrowed. "And am I allowed at this time to know exactly how the poison is being delivered?"

Renard and Esarov exchanged knowing glances before the Waste guide continued. "I think it is safe to tell you now. It is being administered through the water supply."

Now his eyes widened. "Gods," he said. "How are you accomplishing that? The Y'Zirite forces are scattered across the Named Lands. The amount of coordination necessary would—"

Renard shook his head. "Not camp by camp," he said. "We're putting it into the water supply of the entire Named Lands."

Rudolfo sat back in the chair. "You can do that?"

Renard nodded. "Yes. There is an access to the water tables in the Beneath Places."

The mention of the Beneath Places brought Rudolfo's eyes up. Yazmeera's words, hazy now in the fog of all that had happened since then, prodded at him. "How long have the Androfrancines had access to our water supply?" Rudolfo's eyes narrowed, and he leaned forward. "And have they taken advantage of that access in the past?"

Renard looked uncomfortable, and Rudolfo noted it. "It's really not a matter we're at liberty to discuss."

Rudolfo looked to Esarov. "Do you know about this?"

The overseer regarded him carefully and nodded once slowly. "The Office for the Preservation of the Light has been aware of it for about fifteen hundred years."

Rudolfo pursed his lips. What had she said on the day she'd told him about the Keeper's Crèches? Pockets of habitable land—more than just the one he and his people called home—set aside like life boats, she'd said. And the Y'Zirite general had hinted that these crèches controlled the population and that the Androfrancines were aware of it and could have prevented it. "What else have the Androfrancines put into our water, Esarov?"

The overseer blinked. "To my knowledge, they haven't."

Rudolfo nodded. "But there are other organisms in our water?"

"This," Renard said in a firm voice, "is a conversation for another time, General. I'm sure Orius will happily answer all of your questions once the Y'Zirite threat is contained." The Waste guide glanced at Esarov. "Continue, Overseer."

Esarov cleared his voice. "The organism will reproduce and spread quickly. As you've seen, it won't harm those who've not been exposed to blood magicks."

Rudolfo had seen what their pathogen could do. He had no doubt that if they could deliver it, it would bring the war to a quick end. But another question tickled at his brain, and initially, he tried to push it aside. When he spoke, his voice was low. "As you know," he said, "my son has been exposed to blood magicks. How long before he will be able to safely return to the Named Lands?"

But even as he asked it, something Renard had said earlier to Ire Li Tam came to mind. He'd told her she would need to leave, and he'd not mentioned her ever returning.

Now the two men looked at each other, their faces dark. Rudolfo waited, and when neither spoke, he asked again. "How long?"

Renard sighed. "It will become a permanent part of the water supply."

Rudolfo felt his scalp tingle with the anger that spiked. "So when my son returns, it is only to die the moment he has his first bath or his first drink?" He heard the edge creeping into his voice.

Their silence now had a weight to it that spoke of more dark news. "I think you should come with us," Esarov finally said.

They stood, and Rudolfo followed them from the room, walking quickly down the stairs to the main floor of the manor house. They took him down another set of stairs, where Esarov used a dark key to open a door. Behind it lay a cluttered workroom, its single table scattered with papers and pens. There, nailed to a plank by its wings, was a massive kin-raven, its body already decaying. As Rudolfo approached, its glassy eyes opened and its head twisted.

"This bird arrived last evening," Esarov said. "For you."

Rudolfo blinked. "It found me here?"

Renard nodded. His voice was grave. "Yes."

"Was it followed?"

"We don't believe so," Esarov said. "But we are moving you later today as a precaution." The man's face was grief-struck but resolved. "We will leave you to hear it."

Rudolfo waved away the man's words. "I don't require privacy."

But their eyes told him that he did, and he swallowed as they slipped from the workshop and closed the door behind them.

He stepped forward, and the bird's dark eyes fixed upon his own. Its beak snapped open, and the tinny voice that drifted out of it was heavy with a sorrow Rudolfo had not known possible.

"Rudolfo, my love," Jin Li Tam said, her voice cracking beneath the weight of that sorrow, "I bear unbearable news."

And as she continued, the room went gray and began to spin as Rudolfo heard a roar of wrath and grief the likes of which he'd never known possible. His knees went out from beneath him and he fell to the floor, bruising his fists upon anything he could strike. The roar was his, inconsolable and stretching beyond his sense of time; it chased him—a man carved by darkness—into a midnight of grief beyond his wildest imaginings.

Vlad Li Tam

The warm sea was full of light, and Vlad Li Tam swam the waters, dancing with the blue-green d'jin that surrounded him. He felt a vague, distant pull at his mind and wondered how it was he breathed beneath the water without his staff. Still, he did not question overmuch and focused his attention instead upon the single d'jin whose voice he heard most clearly, easily pulling it from the thousand, thousand others that sang around him.

He opened his mouth to sing and drew in a great lungful of the salt water. His voice warbled, rasping and ugly within the context of their song, and he stopped nearly as soon as he started, though the joy and abandon he felt—the anticipation—was greater than any he'd known.

Whatever pulled at him pulled again, and this time he turned his attention within to identify it.

The staff. He did not have it any longer, and the moment of panic that struck had him scrambling for the surface. He broke through, gasping and floundering, beneath a sky filled with a scarred brown world that he knew was his home.

Because I'm swimming with the d'jin—light-bearers—in a lunar sea.

Limned in the light of Lasthome, the arches of the Moon Wizard's Ladder rose up in the night like vast white bones. He turned toward them, knowing somehow that if he only swam through those arches, he would find himself in the colder waters of the Ghosting Crests.

Except, he realized, *that I am dreaming now.*

And even with that knowledge, he struggled to find the thread of reality he needed to drag himself back to wakefulness. He felt heavy, weighed down, and the warmth of the water longed to give him rest.

Vlad opened his eyes, disoriented and groggy, and felt the wetness of his own drool upon his face. *When had he fallen asleep?* He'd been sitting in the chair, discussing Neb's visit with Elder Reeve. And now he slouched in the chair, his body sluggish and his mind groggy. The others stirred to life around him, their own movement slow and hesitant as they sat up carefully from where they'd fallen to the floor.

He felt the staff pushed into his hand as Elder Reeve leaned over him. When Vlad spoke, it was a whisper. "What happened?"

The bearded old priest shook his head, his eyes glazed. "I do not know, Lord Tam."

Vlad pulled focus from the staff and sat up, suddenly alert. Children whimpered and adults whispered as he studied the room. Amylé D'Anjite still slept, stretched out upon the sofa. And Jin—

Vlad gasped as his eyes widened. *She's gone.* His eyes scanned the room faster now, taking it all in. There was something different now, a sweet scent lingering on the air, and as he took it in, he used the staff to trace its roots. On the table, near the door, stood a vase of white flowers. How long had they been there?

He looked to Elder Reeve. "Those flowers. Who brought them in?"

The priest looked to the vase. "Sister Tarma, I think." He glanced around the room, his eyes finding the empty couch. "She's gone, as well."

They took my daughter but left me the staff.

These, he suspected, were the very ones who'd taken his grandson along with the Crimson Empress and her mother Chandra. *And my knives,* he thought. And more and more, he suspected these were also the ones who'd helped fund the Lunarists' campaign, adding terror to his work here in Ahm's Glory.

But who are they?

Vlad sighed. He'd been on his way to find out when the kin-dragon fell upon him. And he doubted now that he would get closer to them without somehow forcing his way.

He looked again to the Younger God stretched out and sleeping peacefully. He'd done this somehow with the staff and knew instinctively that he could undo it when the time came. But what to do with her?

And what had Neb told him? She was unwell. The boy had thought he could treat her somehow.

Vlad glanced back to Elder Reeve. "I'd like you to try to arrange another meeting with your mysterious friends," he said.

The priest nodded. "I will, Lord."

"And tell them to keep my kin safe until I come for them or risk my wrath."

The Lunarist paled. "Yes, Lord."

Vlad climbed slowly to his feet and limped to the girl, using the staff to bear his weight. Each step ached, his muscles and joints protesting as he went. When he reached her side, he dropped to his knees and rested a hand upon her forehead, calling upon the staff as he stared into her sleeping face.

He saw them both upon their different moons. One was the perfect summer, the heat dry and the sky blue beneath a blue-green world that he knew was a Lasthome that hadn't existed now for millennia. The girl was young, her hair long and blond and caught by the wind as she stood upon that living tower and gazed out to the Seaway, watching the line of crystalline ships on parade.

The other was a storm at twilight, the sky gray and the wind cold upon the dead bones of the Firsthome Temple. A broken, barren Lasthome hung in the sky, and the old woman watched it and growled beneath her breath.

"Hello," he said to both of them.

They both turned to him, unaware of the other, and when he saw that the old one recognized him, he dismissed the girl. She opened her mouth once before vanishing.

"You are the one to treat with first," he said. "I am Lord Vlad Li Tam of House Li Tam. I would know why you attacked me, unprovoked?"

She spat. "Unprovoked?" She stood to full height and pointed to the dead world above. He saw crisp anger in her fierce blue eyes. "You and your kind have murdered your parents and feasted upon their blood. You've murdered each other again and again, destroying Lasthome and proving out the Founders' Counsel."

Founders' Counsel? It was an unfamiliar term, and he raised his eyebrows to it. He would ask about it later. For now, he had other work to accomplish. "What is it you wish to accomplish by attacking me?"

But he knew the answer when her eyes found the staff. He held it up. "You want this?"

"The tools of the—"

He waved off the remaining words. "Yes," he said. "I've been told." He leaned forward. "I can tell that you're angry. I am angry, too. The people here murdered my family. They are the children of Y'Zir, and when I finish punishing them, I will no longer need this tool." He extended the staff to her. "Nebios Whym lays claim to it, but I have no loyalty to him."

Her eyes raged, but her voice was calm. "Nebios Whym must not restore the Continuity Engine. The Founders' Counsel was clear and the decision made when Lasthome was established. Before I saw what the Downunders did, I took my father's view that the Founders had lost their path."

Vlad tried to piece together the words but found them vague, almost cryptic. Still, she fed him enough that he could set his hook and catch another fish that would help him move the river. His eyes narrowed. "If I gave it to you, what would you do with it?"

She regarded him for a moment, and he watched her eyes soften with thought before they hardened with resolve. "I would let it finally end," she said.

Do not go down this path, my love. He felt her words through the staff, moving into his arm and spreading throughout his body like warmth.

Vlad dreaded his disobedience, but even as the shame tickled at him, he glanced around the room. He'd lost his knives and he'd lost the children. He'd lost his daughter. But his tool belt was growing.

He fixed his eyes upon Amylé D'Anjite and did easily what he needed to do. "I will help you let it end," he said, "if you will help me finish punishing them."

The Younger God smiled. "I will help you."

Vlad returned the smile but saw easily behind hers. *Does she see so easily behind mine?* he wondered. "Good," he said. "Then wait here until I call you forth."

He didn't wait for the look of surprise on her face to finish registering. He squeezed the staff and shuffled her to the side like the turned page of a book.

"Hello, Lady D'Anjite," he said as he bent his smile into the other dream. The girl looked up from crying at the edge of her tower.

"Who are you?" she asked.

"My name," he said, "is Vlad Li Tam."

Her face and voice were panicked. "Where is Neb? I was with him and then—"

"Neb was called away," he said.

She stifled a sob. "I don't know what's happening to me."

Vlad stepped over to her and put an arm around her shaking shoulders. "It's okay, Lady D'Anjite," he said. "I can explain everything."

And then he did, telling the young girl everything she needed to know in order to best serve his purposes. He would shore up this aspect of the divided woman and keep the other one asleep until he needed her. Then Vlad Li Tam would push this one back into the darkness and rouse the wrath of heaven from her slumber.

Marta

Time in Behemoth passed without meaning or marker, and Marta found enough of it marched past that she was no longer bored. She'd explored every corner, every room that she could get to within the gigantic metal beast. She'd watched the fish in the catch tanks below; she'd learned to harvest the sea-water gardens located in the same space and had even spent hours watching the water scrub itself through a series of sponges as the massive machine made it drinkable.

Once she'd run out of places to explore, Marta had turned to her companions. She'd spent as much time with Isaak as possible, despite the fact that he spent most of his time in that state he refused to call sleep, his eyes flashing dimly as he sat propped in a corner. Being with him, just sitting silently nearby, his metal hand in hers, was sufficient. But she'd also taken it upon herself to steer into her fear regarding Ire, the Y'Zirite woman, and had even talked the woman into showing her some of the stances for a beginner with the knife.

Still, with all of this, Marta was ready to see the sky. It's what she was thinking about when Ire's knife clanged against her own unready hand to send her blade skittering across the floor.

"You were somewhere else," the woman said as she bent over the girl. "And you weren't planted." The woman used her feet to guide Marta's, shifting them to a more solid stance. "Like so."

"Sorry," Marta mumbled.

Ire smiled. "Don't even start me on your grip," she said, nodding to the knife.

Marta recovered the knife and offered it, handle first, to the woman. "My mind was elsewhere."

"Yes. I could tell." Ire slid the knife back into her sheath. "Let's take a break."

Marta followed Ire as they left the room and took the corridor down to the galley. There, the Blood Scout scooped two shells of water from the cistern and handed one to the girl. They sat and sipped.

Marta had learned what she could of the woman, despite how very guarded Ire Li Tam was. The life she'd lived—from the early years before her death was faked to her first years in the blood cult where her grandfather had planted her—fascinated the girl. Marta had grown up all her life hearing from her father how everyone must do their part. This woman's part had involved giving up her home and growing up in a strange place, adopting their horrific customs and climbing the ranks to become the elite of the elite. And all for the purpose of one day making a journey across the Churning Wastes to bear word to a sister who thought her dead, bidding her come to Y'Zir.

She studied the woman. Her hair was growing out, red and unruly, stark against the white scars of Y'Zir carved into her flesh. Ire was tall and lithe, her muscles hidden beneath a slenderness that Marta knew better than to mistake for weakness. And at first, she'd smiled little. But in the days they'd spent together, the woman had become more human.

"So do you think we're nearly there?" Marta asked as she sipped the water.

Ire nodded. "I do."

Marta swallowed. Once they arrived, she knew Isaak would try to keep her from following. She wasn't sure exactly how, but she knew he would just as surely as she knew she would do her best not to let him leave her behind. "I wish I knew what was going to happen."

Ire Li Tam sighed. "I think we all do. My father is . . . unpredictable."

"I think fathers can be that way," Marta said. "That's why we have mothers."

The thought of her mother was an ache, and she thought she saw a similar shadow cross Ire's face. "I don't remember my mother," the woman said. "The children of House Li Tam are usually separated early from whomever their mothers happen to be."

Marta tried to imagine it but couldn't. "My mother died at Windwir."

The woman regarded Marta with calculating eyes. "Loss can make us strong and show us our path."

"Yes," Marta said. "And sometimes it just hurts."

Ire nodded. "Aye."

She thought for a moment, taking another drink from the shell. The water was cool and sweet. "But at least with your family, it's to serve a higher purpose."

The shadow passed over Ire's face again. "That is what we're taught," she said. "Oddly enough, the Y'Zirites also believe their cuts and scars are for a higher purpose. And the Androfrancines believed something very similar about serving their light."

Everyone, Marta thought, believing they did their part. And yet each group acted against the others, full of conviction and confidence. House Li Tam was largely gone, according to Ire Li Tam, cut away beneath the Y'Zirite knives. But not before using that very House to bring down Windwir and the Androfrancine Order, paving the way for an invasion of the Named Lands. An invasion that came with schools and evangelists and a new way of life. The Y'Zirites doing *their* part.

She couldn't think of the city without thinking of Isaak. And when it came to mind, that small part of her that hated him for being the weapon that killed her mother came to life and she had to settle it down. Fortunately, the love was bigger.

Love is always bigger. It stirred up a memory, and she glanced to Ire. "What about the Lunarists?"

She blinked. "What about them?"

"Did they also have a way . . . a path?"

Ire nodded. "Certainly. They believed that the secrets of where we came from were hidden upon the moon with the last of the Younger Gods—that the moon was still inhabited." Marta watched the woman draw from memory, her brows furrowed. "They believed in a coming time of restoration. Their doctrine was largely derived from the idea that five gifts had been given to us. The first two were choice and love." She wrinkled her brow. "I think will and intelligence were two of the others, but it's been years since I studied them."

Marta opened her mouth to ask a question but closed it when she felt the slightest change in the vibration and dull hum of Behemoth's engines. Her stomach fluttered, and she met Ire's eyes. "We're slowing down," she said.

"And rising," Ire added.

They were on their feet simultaneously, moving for the door. When they reached the corridor, Isaak was moving toward the hatch at the end.

Marta caught up to him. "Are we there?"

He looked down at her. "No. But we are very close. We're preparing to enter the canal."

The thought of the sky flooded her, and Marta felt an unexpected hope flood her as well. The idea of seeing the sun, the sky, maybe even land, made her mouth suddenly want to smile. "Are we going all the way up?"

Isaak nodded. "I need to check our position." His eyes flashed red as he inclined his head. "And I thought you might like to breathe the fresh air while you can."

They waited there by the hatch for what seemed an hour, saying

nothing. Marta was startled when Isaak suddenly took hold of the
wheel and spun it until the door swung open. She was even more
startled when he quickly scooped her up into his arms to carry her
through waist-deep water out into the opening mouth.

The sunlight blinded her after so long in the dim red light of Behemoth's belly. She blinked at it, shielding her eyes with her upraised
hand. Beyond it, she saw dark cliffs and a blue sky. Isaak carried her
to the edge of the mouth and placed her feet on the high metal ridges
at the base of the beast's metal teeth. Ire came up beside her.

"The Barrens of Espira," the Blood Guard said.

"Yes," Isaak replied.

Marta followed their eyes out across dark waters and drew in a
lungful of air that tasted different from any she'd breathed before. It
tasted bitter and dry, the way she imagined bone powder to taste, and
she suspected it was blown down from the high black cliff-tops.

Behemoth pointed toward a slight impression set into the cliffs
ahead of them, and as they moved slowly closer, Marta saw that it was
an opening. She wasn't sure of how large until a ship emerged from it,
long and low and dark.

Ire Li Tam gasped, and Marta heard a slight whistle from deep
inside Isaak.

The ship was followed by another and another in short succession,
and when they turned in Behemoth's direction, she felt Isaak's hand
tighten in her own. "Who are they?"

But she knew who they had to be even before Ire answered. "Y'Zirite
Imperial Navy."

Isaak leaned out to study them, and Marta wondered if he saw more
with his jeweled eyes than they could. He was quiet, his head moving
over the vessels. "But they fly no flags," he said.

The ships continued, and Behemoth did not adjust its course. It
moved slowly, its metal body clanking through the water, on a course
that would take it within an easy arrow flight of the Y'Zirites. As the
Y'Zirite vessels drew closer, Marta saw the people that lined its railing, pointing to the massive beast she stood within. Still, even seeing
them, the ships made no effort to slow or change course.

"And they are not wearing uniforms," Ire added.

The ships were even closer now, and a man in a robe stood in the
bow of the lead ship. He waved and Isaak returned the gesture. Marta
and Ire did the same.

Then the man began pointing aft and as she followed his finger,

Marta watched as a large patch of black cloth—a makeshift flag—unfurled upon the mast's highest point.

Painted in white upon it stood a tree, and she knew it instantly. She was in the field again, hearing the words and feeling the wind rise up for the sowing. "It's from the dream," she whispered.

When Isaak spoke, she heard awe in his voice for the first time, and it made goose-skin break out over her body. "Yes," he said. "It is."

Ire's voice held wonder in it as well. "These are ships from Ahm's Glory," she said. "They are refugees."

"No," Isaak said as the ships moved past them. He looked first to Ire Li Tam and then to Marta. "They are not refugees." He looked back, his eyes upon the single flag they sailed under. "They are pilgrims of the dream."

And Marta wasn't sure exactly what a pilgrim was, but the tone with which he said it, and the tiny intake of breath from Ire Li Tam, were all she needed to know that it was a wonder of sorts she now beheld.

Marta closed her eyes and marked the moment, savoring the sunlight on her face and dreading the return she knew she must soon make, back into the belly of the beast.

Chapter 10

Winters

The muddy streets of Caldus Bay were drying as sunlight broke through a high layer of clouds and Winteria drew in a deep breath of the cold morning air. Erys walked beside her, moving with the deliberate stride of a soldier though they had no particular destination.

"I do not understand why I am doing this," the officer said as she glanced to Winters.

Winters pushed to keep up. She'd been taking lunch alone in her room when Erys had come for her with boots and coat in hand. "Walk with me," Erys had said, barely giving enough time to boot up and follow her out into the afternoon sun. They'd exited from the back of the house and slipped out a small gate, unaccompanied by any guards that Winters could see.

Now she looked at the woman. "I know why you are doing this," she said. "It's because you remember the dream; you remember how it felt."

Their eyes met briefly, and Erys looked away. "I do remember it." Her voice was hushed and solemn. "It's like nothing I've experienced before."

"I've not, either," Winters said. Of course, it wasn't technically true. She'd had dreams her whole life, and she'd even shared some of them with Neb. But even those were nothing like this one. It was a moment, pregnant with hope and history, shared by a vast multitude. *Felt by all of us.* "But I carry it within me and I long to follow it home."

The officer said nothing for a moment, and Winters felt the change of subject like the opening and closing of doors in a hallway. "So I will send you in the custody of a squad of infantry. I considered sending my scouts with you, but I need them elsewhere. I've told them that unless you take them into harm's way, they're to escort you and your associates wherever you require." They turned and moved up a slight hill, away from the center of town. "And that they are to await orders from me regarding your final disposition. I will also provide whatever supplies you require." She sighed and Winters heard resolve in it. "Including the voice magicks."

"Thank you," Winters said.

Erys looked back at her. "Don't give me reason to regret this choice."

She shook her head. "I will not."

The woman nodded once. "Good. Now where will you start?"

It was a good question, and Winters had given it some thought. The answer had been easier coming than she'd expected it to be. "I'll start here, of course," she said. "In Caldus Bay."

Erys looked surprised. "Here?"

She nodded. "Yes. There are ships here. I need ships. And even with the war, there's still enough traffic to carry word farther down the coast." She scanned the buildings around them, then looked off toward the forest. "I just need a good place to gather everyone."

"We've used the docks. It gets cold, but there's plenty of space."

They continued discussing logistics as they walked, but Winters could tell that Erys had said all she needed to say both by the questions she now asked and the way her pace quickened. They rounded another corner and found themselves back at the manor where they'd started.

Erys stopped Winters at the door even as the guard there opened it. "I cannot come tonight," she said, "for obvious reasons. But I do wish you well, Lady Winteria."

Winters smiled and inclined her head. "Thank you for your help, Lieutenant Erys." She searched the woman's eyes and found the pain there quickly. But beside it, she saw something else—a yearning, an ache for something new and real to hang onto.

Because she's lost everything. And she was going to lose more, Winters wagered, with what was coming. Whatever the Androfrancines released was going to decimate this woman's ranks and likely take her own life as well. Winters had thought about this, tossing and turning in her bed to find a way to warn her. And from the guilt of wanting to save this one but not the whole of them. She'd made a compromise with herself. "Come with us, Erys."

The Y'Zirite officer blinked. "Come with you?"

Winters reached out a hand and put it on the woman's shoulder. "To the moon. Yes. Come home with us." She narrowed her eyebrows. "I will need strong leaders who remember the dream. Leave this behind and join us."

The woman regarded her, her eyes showing surprise on an otherwise placid face. She didn't answer. Instead, she turned to the guard. "See her to Sergeant Kyla. Tell the sergeant to get Lady Winteria whatever she needs."

The soldier saluted, and Erys returned the gesture. Then, with another nod to Winters, the lieutenant was moving into the manor with that deliberate stride, leaving her in the care of her escort.

Winters spent the day making arrangements both for the journey she would undertake in the morning and the meeting she would host tonight. At one point, she checked in with Tertius and Hebda, updating the two Androfrancines on her plans even as she put them to work bearing her message to the mayor and dock steward of Caldus Bay. She considered getting word to the New Espiran, Captain Thrall, but decided he and his people were likely aware of the changes in her situation and monitoring her whereabouts from hiding. By late afternoon, she'd done all she could, including reoutfitting herself with a new pack, bedroll and fresh clothing from the Y'Zirite quartermaster.

As the sun prepared to set, Winters dressed in the simple clothing she'd laid out for the event and went downstairs to meet her escort and her Androfrancine traveling companions.

Hebda and Tertius waited by the door, both dressed in trousers and shirts that made them look more like locals than Androfrancines. She took up her boots and looked up with surprise when Erys joined them.

"I've changed my mind," the lieutenant said. "I've decided to personally monitor tonight's gathering."

When they set out into the fading light, Winters felt the moths fluttering in her stomach again. Certainly she'd made her share of speeches and proclamations, and this would be no different.

Still, it felt different and she knew it was this new dream that made it so.

Bring them to the dream. The words and the voice that whispered them had haunted her now for days. "I will bring them," she whispered.

They made their way down to the docks, and as they approached, she heard a buzz that grew to a rumble. Lanterns scattered the docks and the shoreline around it where pockets of people gathered. And it was a larger crowd than she'd imagined possible for such a small town, the men, women and children standing or sitting on whatever dry patches they could find as the temperature dropped and their breath billowed on the evening air.

She let the Y'Zirites lead her and the others to a section of the high dock that gave her the widest view of the crowd, and as she climbed the stairs to it, her hand moved to the small phial of voice magicks in her pocket. Gauging the size of the audience, she knew she would need very little of the bitter fluid. Even that little bit would carry her voice far beyond the town.

A small group of men waited for her, and one separated from them to walk toward her. He was an older, heavyset man with thinning hair. Erys spoke first.

"Lady Winteria, this is Mayor Harnim."

Winters inclined her head first. "I'm honored to meet you."

He flushed. "The honor is mine, Lady Winteria."

The redness in his face brought heat to her own cheeks. *He has been moved by the dream.* The others with him also, she realized, as they gathered around her and introductions were made. Then, the others settled into the plain wooden chairs that had been brought for them.

As Winters approached the railing of the dock with the mayor by her side, a gasp rippled through the audience as those who'd been seated surged to their feet to catch sight of her. The noise of the crowd was such that the mayor's brief introduction was largely lost and he offered a weak smile to her as he took his seat.

She returned it, then drew out the phial. Unstopping it, she touched the tip of her tongue to it to taste the smallest, bitter drop.

She felt the warmth moving down her throat, and she cleared her voice softly, listening to the rumble of it move out from her like distant thunder. "I am Winteria bat Mardic," she declared in a whisper that roared out into the night. "You know me from the dream we shared."

A cheer rose up from the audience and she remained quiet, waiting for them to finish. As she waited, she scanned the audience. The fishermen and sailors were easy to pick out, many of them listening from the boats and ships that were docked there. But there were also families and Y'Zirite soldiers.

She smiled. "You remember our dream."

She saw the nods, and though she'd thought carefully about what she would say and had even scribbled out a few notes to keep her moving forward, Winters left the papers in her pocket and instead willed the words to work their way directly from her heart.

She started with the dream that had brought her riding forth to Windwir's aid, a hidden and dreaming queen among the Marshers. She recounted meeting Neb, the Homeseeker, and the events that followed. As she spoke, she felt a connection with the people and watched their rapt faces as she whispered to them, her voice booming from the magicks that enhanced it.

And as she spoke, a movement to the left caught her eye: a tall, slender man dressed in clothes that hung too loosely from his frame. His white hair peeked out beneath a fisherman's cap and his eyes were on her, bright as the look of wonderment and love upon his face as he hung upon her words.

It was not a face burning with light and rage and terror—not like the last time she had seen him—and it snared her, causing her to stumble over her words as she felt something powerful stirring within her.

It was all she could do not to stop and go to him in that moment. Her hands shook and she seized the railing, forcing her eyes away from him as she continued.

But even as she looked away, Winteria bat Mardic smiled and knew that Neb saw that smile from where he watched among the crowd. And knowing brought more heat to her face. But Winters poured that passion into her words, eyes chancing along the way to meet the eyes of her Homeseeker as she brought her people once more to the dream.

Petronus

The jungle swept beneath them as the airship sailed east of the Firsthome Temple, and Petronus chuckled his amazement.

The pilothouse offered a wide view forward, starboard and port, with mirrors on hand cranks that could be deployed to view aft. The wheel and acceleration lever were simple affairs, and to the left of the wheel was a series of smaller levers and switches and a row of glass-encased dials. The captain had taken the wheel, dismissing the pilot to make room for their visitors.

Nadja laughed. "You look like a boy just now."

He chuckled again and glanced at the girl in time to see her blush. "I'm flying," he said.

She shrugged. "You flew to the moon."

Petronus looked back to the window, watching the shadow of the airship speed across a carpet of green. "I did. And now I'm flying again. It's—" He paused, trying to find the right word. "Remarkable."

"Yes," she said. "It is."

He looked at the instruments and the captain's hands upon the wheel. "Surely you fly all the time?"

"From time to time. But not on the moon." Her smile widened. "Not with Pope Petronus."

Now he blushed. Just one more way that he found this younger body responding to her. *You are seventy-two years old,* he told himself. *No, seventy-three?* He did the math, then gave up. For now— and for the days he had left—he was thirty. He'd been in his forties when he'd done the things she so openly admired during his papacy. Of course, she'd not been born yet when he'd done those things. "You overestimate my value to history, Ambassador," he said.

She grinned. "Take us south now, Captain."

He nodded and turned the wheel slowly. As the vessel began its turn, Petronus took hold of the railing. Nadja took hold of him, her hands sudden upon his arm as she stumbled against him and steadied herself. She was slow to release him, and Petronus found he didn't mind.

She was like nothing he'd seen before. So young and yet easily a hundredfold more intelligent than any of the Androfrancine scholars he'd known during his time in the Order. The young ambassador was richly versed not only in her own culture and history but that of the Named Lands, the Empire of Y'Zir and the deeper history of the times before: the days of Frederico—the fallen, fugitive czar who had called the New Espirans to their work—and before that, aeons of myth from what they would consider the time of the Elder Gods. The Outward Journey of the People, she called it. And she told the stories from those times with eyes that shone with the same wonder he suspected his own held.

Now I've gone from avoiding meals with her to longing for them. More than that, he'd taken most of them with her. They'd also walked alongside

the Temple Canal and talked about the future. And now, they flew
to the moon.

Ahead, the green of the jungle ended and a sea that matched the
color of the sky stretched out to blur into an indistinct horizon. Petronus scanned it, his heart lurching with nostalgia that took him back
to a childhood spent fishing on the waters of Caldus Bay. When he was
young, he'd longed to escape his father's trade, and by the time he
was in his forties, he'd come back to it. It was more honest, easier on
the heart and soul, than the backward dream he'd served within the
Order.

Three black specks in the distance caught his eye and he squinted
at them. His vision was much stronger now than it had been even in
his youth—yet another gift from Aver-Tal-Ka's sacrifice—and Petronus could just pick out the dark sails as they flew closer. "There are
ships in the sea," he said, glancing to Nadja.

Her face paled and her brow furrowed as she scanned the horizon.
"I don't see—"

"I see them," the captain said. His hands moved quickly over the
instrument panel, and Petronus felt the slightest tickling in his feet as
something deep in the vessel buzzed to life. "Let's hope they didn't
see us. We have the sun in our favor."

The vibration built until Petronus felt it in his ears. He knew the
mechanism he heard was beyond anything he'd seen during his time
within the Order and that it was the device that allowed the New Espiran ships to move about the skies of Lasthome unseen by the people
they observed.

He felt Nadja's hand upon his shoulder. "They are Y'Zirite ships,"
she said.

Petronus nodded. "Aye." He looked at her. "Is it safe to get a better
look?"

She looked to the captain, raising an eyebrow. "Is it?"

"We wouldn't want to get too close, but yes. I think it's safe."

Already, Petronus was calculating what he could of their odds
against the Y'Zirites. He started with his own resources and then
worked from memory through what he knew of their new allies. From
the standpoint of numbers, he needed count no further. They didn't
have the capacity to face down even one ship, let alone three. Not by
sheer numbers. And despite the mechanical wonders Petronus had
seen on their vessel and in the hands of its crew, he'd not seen a single
weapon.

They were over the sea now, and the ships were clearer in his vision—two frigates escorting a troop transport, the decks crawling with uniformed men moving with intent. Petronus measured their speed and checked the distance to the mouth of the Temple Canal they sailed for. He could see it from this altitude but suspected they were still several hours from sighting it themselves. Still, the Firsthome Temple behind them was a landmark that dominated the horizon, making it easy for the Y'Zirites to find it.

"They definitely have us outnumbered," Petronus said. He glanced to Nadja. "Certainly you have the means to defend yourself?"

Her brow furrowed at his words. "Means, yes." She paused, and he read in the line of her jaw how uncomfortable she was. "But we avoid those situations at all costs. Our work in the world depends upon being hidden observers, gathering knowledge for the Time of Sowing. We do not interfere."

For some reason, the firmness in her jaw and the sudden hardness in her eyes started a low-grade anger guttering in him. "So what are you going to do?"

She said nothing and looked away.

Finally, he repeated himself. "Ambassador Thrall," he said, "what are you going to do?"

She met his eyes. "I will return you to the temple and then withdraw the airship."

He blinked and felt the anger growing along with his surprise. "You're withdrawing?"

Now she repeated herself. "We do not interfere."

"Surely," he said, "it is time to consider changing that tactic." He heard coldness in his voice. "You yourself say that the fulfillment of Frederico's Bargain is near. Your noninterference could harm the success of your work here."

She shook her head. "We will avoid interference and continue to observe quietly. We will record whatever transpires here for entry into the library." Her tone was firm, but her eyes were unsteady, glancing away again.

Petronus opened his mouth to ask her to reconsider, then closed it. The New Espirans would have been useful, but he did not need their resources to deal with this new threat. He needed the silver crescent that lay in his room back in the temple. Neb and his steel kin-dragon would be more than enough to handle the three wooden ships. But Nadja's cold resolve on the matter caught him off guard, especially given how familiar they'd become over the past several days. Of course, it made sense that duty would come first for the girl.

I was just as resolved in my loyalty to the Order's work. He'd already started aggressively climbing the hierarchy at her age, and it was that commitment to the letter of their law that carried him.

Petronus found the anger dissipating as quickly as it began, and he sighed. "Okay. Then it's best you get me back now."

He saw something like relief pull at her face, though she tried to mask it. Her mouth was firm, but her eyes betrayed the hope that he wasn't disappointed in her. She glanced away and to the captain. "Take us in."

He wasn't sure why, but Petronus felt the need to somehow reassure her. He lifted his hand and settled it upon her shoulder, though he found no words to accompany the gesture. He kept his hand there as the ship banked and the massive structure of the Firsthome Temple loomed ahead of them, and as they turned, he felt the woman shift on her feet, brushing her body against his as she found her footing. Only this time she did not pull away.

And still Petronus did not lift his hand. He stood with her, his mind busily recounting their weak numbers and wondering how quickly Neb could be back to them, and he left his hand where it rested. Something about her warm skin beneath it soothed and stilled him, and it struck him suddenly that he'd never felt anything quite like that before.

Why does touching her give me peace?

Petronus did not know, and as he asked himself he felt the urge to remove his hand, drop it to his side.

But he resisted that urge, and when Nadja Thrall looked over her shoulder to smile weakly at him, he smiled back and then found himself surprised by that as well.

Neb

The sun hung low in the west when Neb slipped from the forest and onto the coastline two leagues east of town.

He cleared his voice, eyes moving over the rocks to his left and right. "Are you here?"

Neb started when the man appeared. "Yes, Lord Whym. Commander Pardeau bid me watch for you. I am Endrys Thrall, captain of *Amal's Perspective*."

The man wore a New Espiran uniform beneath his black cloak. His hood was thrown back to reveal short red hair and bright blue eyes. Neb saw the resemblance immediately, even as he connected the names. "You are Ambassador Thrall's brother."

The captain nodded. "Yes."

Neb scanned the beach again and the sky above it. There was no evidence of the airship, though he knew it couldn't be far. He looked back to Thrall. "How much assistance can you render?"

"I can provide transportation, but my orders are to not interfere and to gather relevant information for the Sowing."

The Sowing. He had heard the word before and still wasn't certain of what it meant. He'd seen the saplings they'd carried into the Firsthome Temple's library, and he'd watched them scoop the first of that vast chamber's soil to lay trees like white bones into the ground, branches already laden with jewels of purple and blue. They'd planted them near a Watching Tree. Nadja had explained them to him as best she could, but it still staggered Neb that somehow all of the data—all of the history—they had gathered had somehow been grown into saplings that would grow into trees like their neighbors, full of the knowledge of Lasthome gathered by Frederico's disciples. Neb pushed his memory of the library aside and looked over his shoulder to the town behind him. "So you have observers in Caldus Bay?"

"Yes. And we know where Winteria bat Mardic is. We also know where she will be in a few hours."

Neb felt his eyebrow raise. "Where?"

"The Y'Zirites are holding her in one of the larger manors, though she appears to have significant freedom. She's called for a meeting this evening. By way of voice magicks." The captain's face had the same flushed excitement Neb had seen in Nadja when discussing Named Lands history. His eyes were bright. "It's the dream."

Neb felt a moment of loss. It was something he'd been meant to share with her. It had been his calling, as the Homeseeker, to open the Firsthome Temple. Instead, Petronus had played his part when Isaak and Winters dreamed the Final Dream and gave the old pope what he needed to translate the People's story and open the tower's doors. He'd missed it, locked away with Amylé within the temple. But he'd heard it described, each time with an awe and wonder that was palpable. He found himself wishing desperately he could've shared it, not just with Winters but also with the others.

It's one more reminder that I am not one of them.

Neb swallowed the sudden sadness that washed through him and looked at his silver robes. "I will need more suitable clothing. Is that something you can help with?"

"I can."

"And you've offered transportation. Just how far will that offer carry us?"

"Anywhere in the Named Lands for now," Thrall said. "But ultimately to the moon if that becomes necessary."

Neb inclined his head. "Thank you, Captain Thrall."

He returned the gesture. "I am pleased to meet you, Lord Whym, and to do my part in the Bargain's fulfillment."

Neb blushed at the man's sincerity. "It is a mutual pleasure."

"Now," the man said, "if you'll wait a few minutes, I will have more appropriate clothing brought to you." Before he'd finished speaking, Endrys Thrall was gone and Neb stood alone upon the shore. He stood still and listened to waves licking at the rocky coastline and wind murmuring through the pines behind him. The thought that he was just a few hours from seeing her settled into his stomach with an ache, and he wondered how she would look at him this time. The terror on her face there in the Machtvolk Territories had haunted him. But maybe with the clothes, without his skin and eyes and hair burning white, she would not be afraid.

And maybe she had seen worse since then. It was hard to imagine worse, the memory of her naked form covered in the bleeding cuts of Y'Zir still hard upon him. He remembered those same blades upon his own skin and the screams they'd raised from him, staked out in the Churning Wastes as the Blood Guard sought to stop the antiphon.

He heard the softest clearing of a voice behind him and turned. A woman stood before him now, dressed in the rough clothing of a villager. She held a bundle of clothes under her arm and a pair of low boots in her hand. "Lord Whym," she said as she inclined her head.

He took the clothes she offered. She placed a small cloth purse on top of them. "If you're quiet," she said, "you should have no problem. The Y'Zirites have little will to fight or police left now, and they've become complacent. Their behavior with Lady Winteria has us curious, so we will be near you even if you don't see us."

It had Neb curious as well. He was certain some of this change was

Vlad Li Tam's handiwork, though he'd not spent enough time in Ahm's Glory to hear everything that had transpired. Something dark beyond the plague that ravaged the empire, he knew—something that was whispered in tones too soft to hear. And of course, some of it was Winters herself and the dream she'd shared with them.

He forced his mind back to the woman in front of him. "I'll do my best to keep hidden," he said.

She smiled briefly. "I will see you in town."

He returned the smile, and as she turned and moved for the tree line, Neb caught the hem of his robe between his thumb and forefinger, touching the slick fabric and willing it to shrink, pulling itself tight against his skin so that he could slip into clothes that smelled faintly of fish and wood smoke. After pulling on the boots, he turned for the town and made his way back, his white hair tucked beneath a fisherman's cap.

The town was less quiet than Neb imagined it would be. The streets were drying beneath rays of sunlight slowly choked by clouds, and people were out in it, talking at their fences and from their doorways.

"She is speaking tonight down at the dock. About the dream." He heard hope in the voices and light in the eyes, though once they glanced at him as he passed by, they went quiet and looked away.

Neb had never visited Caldus Bay before, though he'd heard Petronus speak of it plenty of times during their grave-digging work at Windwir. It was easy enough to spot the inn where the old man had spent his last thirty years drinking and composing off-color limericks with his friends. And once Neb stood before its door, the smell of fresh roast pork and newly baked bread set his stomach to growling. He touched the purse at his belt and slipped inside.

He took a small table in the corner and watched the room. It was busier than he would've expected, with sailors making up about half of the clientele and a scattering of local loggers and fishermen who created a natural border splitting the room. In another corner, two old men fussed over a game of Queen's War. The innkeeper and his wife worked the bar, sending a young woman Neb suspected was their daughter out into the room with platters of food and tankards of beer.

Neb checked his purse and, satisfied with what he saw, ordered the roast pork. They served it with hot potatoes covered in molten cheese and with a baked apple drizzled in firespice, its hot cinnamon flavor a perfect companion to the tender meat. Neb ate quietly, chasing the food with a crisp, pale ale, while he listened to the room.

At one point, a man with a lute took up another corner and started playing and singing quietly as the patrons kept his tankard full with pours from their own. Neb heard familiar songs of love and loss under the dull mumble of the crowd, and the sense of quiet community that overcame him was as warm as the nearby fire. He ate slowly and savored the island of peace until he saw people gathering up their coats as the air filled with excitement.

Neb paid and followed them out into the evening, suddenly aware of the ache in his stomach.

I'm going to see her. And afterward, he would talk with her though he didn't know what exactly he would say.

The crowd gathered along the docks and shore, and he pushed his way through them to take up a place where he could see the elevated portion of the high dock where a small group stood around wooden chairs. Neb saw several Y'Zirite soldiers posted at points nearby, their watchful eyes scanning the crowd. And he saw Winters, though it still took him by surprise to see the mud and ash of her faith replaced with the scars of her cutting. Beside her, he saw two other men, and one of them sank his heart, bringing a lump to his throat.

Brother Hebda is with her. He'd hit the man he'd thought was his father for so long the last time he'd seen him. Learning that he'd been deceived, even left intentionally behind to watch Windwir fall, had snapped something off in his heart and flooded him with rage and he'd broken Hebda's nose with his fist. Now that anger, over time, had turned to sorrow those few times he let his mind wander back to the man.

Neb swallowed. *I will have to face him, too.*

Another man tried to introduce Winters now, his voice largely lost on the excited mumble of the crowd. When he gave up with a sheepish smile and Winters took the railing, the crowd swelled to their feet with a roar, and when the woman spoke, her voice rumbled out under the power of voice magicks. It raised the hair on Neb's arms.

"We've been told," Winteria bat Mardic said, "that change is the path life takes." She paused. "And the dream we have shared marks this as a time to embrace change and choose a different path than those we've chosen before."

As she spoke, Neb felt her words resonating within him as her voice marched out over them and into the gathering dusk. She spoke of the dream, and as she did, he found himself swept up in the wonder of it and in the wonder of the woman she had become. She was confident, articulate, passionate and . . . beautiful.

She spoke for at least thirty minutes before her wandering eyes found his and recognized him. He watched her take hold of the rail, her face flushed as she stumbled over her words. And when she smiled, Neb felt the heat rising in his own cheeks.

When she found her voice again, it was heavy with emotion. "My people have waited for their new home for thousands of years, huddling in the north while our dream unfolded. Now at the conclusion of those years of dreaming, I know that it was larger than the Marsh-folk who dreamed it. Our call homeward was broader than my people."

She glanced at Neb again, and this time her smile turned playful. "The way to the moon is now open," she said, "and I call upon Nebios Whym, the Homeseeker—no, the *Homefinder*—to come and tell us of it."

There was a buzz of whispering as all eyes turned in the direction that Winters now stared, and Neb blinked, paralyzed by her unexpected invitation. But when she raised her eyebrows to him and her smile widened, and when he heard the excited murmuring around him as the crowd fell back to leave him a path to the dock, Neb took a deep breath and made his way to her, eyes still locked on hers.

He paused before her and glanced to Hebda. The man's face was washed in grief, and the Androfrancine looked away. When Winters put her hands upon his shoulders, he looked back to her. "Tell us about the moon, Nebios. Tell us about the home you have found us."

Then she kissed him, and he tasted the faintest hint of the sour, bitter blood magicks in her mouth as the world tipped and spun from the softness of her tongue. The crowd cheered, and Nebios turned to face them.

"I . . ." Neb paused and took another deep breath. "I am Nebios Whym, son of Whym and Homefinder," he said. Then he told them about the moon and everything he'd found there, easing into his words as he went.

For a moment, everything felt suddenly right again after too long not, and he knew it was the woman who stood beside him, watching him with open admiration upon her face. *She isn't afraid of me anymore.* The joy of that realization threatened to burst his heart.

He kept his remarks brief, distracted by the sense of peace he'd fallen into. But Nebios Whym knew better than to trust it, and midway into his description of the Firsthome Temple, he heard Petronus's tinny voice whispering from the crescent in his pouch. And the urgency of it told Neb that this moment of peace, like so many that had come before it, could not last for long.

Chapter 11

Jin Li Tam

Awareness leaked slowly into Jin Li Tam, at first muffled voices, then bright light when she opened her eyes and a sharp pain that started from the back of her skull and worked its way forward.

"Lady Tam?" It was a man's voice.

Jin tried to turn her head. *Father?* No, not him. Another voice. She closed her eyes again and worked her tongue around a dust-dry mouth. What had happened? She remembered her father facing down the kin-dragon, then turning on her as she threw herself at him. Beyond that, everything was lost in fog.

She felt a hand upon her shoulder, and she willed her own hand to slap it away but it refused. "Lady Tam?"

Jin opened her eyes again and blinked. The light no longer stabbed at her, and her head was a dull ache that kept time with her heart. She lay stretched out on a narrow cot, and she felt the vibration of something not unlike the engines that propelled her father's Iron Armada tickling her through the bedframe. She licked her lips and tried to raise her head. "Who . . . ?" The question was too much effort, and she fell back into the pillow.

"I am Commander Finiz Pardeau of the New Espiran Council Expeditionary Force," the man said. He was blurry before her, older with close-cropped white hair and a leathery face. "We've kept you sedated for the journey for security purposes, but it's time to wake up. We're disembarking soon, and I need you able to walk."

His words were slow to register. *New Espira.* She'd never heard of it, nor any kind of expeditionary force. And as her focus returned, she realized she'd also never seen a uniform quite like the one this man wore. And the room was unfamiliar to her, too. Walls of metal, light from glass orbs that glowed white and flickered in time with the vibration of what she assumed must be engines somewhere aft.

Finally she found more words, slurred through the dryness of her mouth. "Where are you taking me?"

He regarded her, his eyes hard. "I'm not at liberty to disclose that. But someplace safe." He stood up from her bedside. "There is food and water on the table; fresh clothing at the foot of the bed."

Her disorientation turned to anger, but it sounded more like panic in her raised voice. "I have more questions."

Commander Pardeau paused at the door and smiled. "There will be plenty of time for answers after we've disembarked."

Then he let himself out.

Jin lay still and breathed through the disorientation, counting as she felt herself grow more centered. It was finally the promise of water that forced her to sit up. Her mouth was a desert, and her throat ached.

How long was I asleep? She added it to her list of questions, reciting them internally as she sat and gathered her will to stand. When she stood, the room dipped and weaved then stabilized as her eyes found the metal pitcher that sat in the center of the table beside a platter of sliced fruits and cheeses and a loaf of black bread.

The room moved again, and now she realized it wasn't just her perception. It had moved—jumped a bit. The ripples in the water proved it. She pulled out a chair and sat at the table, lifting the pitcher with shaking hands to pour into a matching metal cup. She sipped and let the water settle into her empty stomach.

The room took on more definition. It was much like the cabin of any other ship. A single bed, a small table and chair. There was a porthole, but it was covered from the outside. It made sense that they would limit her visibility. What didn't make sense was how she had come to be their prisoner . . . or why. But she suspected her father had something to do with it. *More for the list,* she thought.

The ship moved again, not like anything she'd experienced at sea. There was also a slight change in the engine speed as the room shifted.

She heard the vibration wind up and settle down, now feeling it through a hand pressed flat against the surface of the table.

She drank more water, then braved the fruit and cheese. She nibbled at them, cataloging her questions and studying the room. The single door was no doubt guarded. The blocked porthole meant they did not want her to know where they were or where they were going.

Her stomach finally protested and she stood from the table. The clothing at the foot of the bed was simple—trousers and a shirt not unlike those the commander wore, though all insignia of rank had been removed. They were accompanied by low-cut leather boots and a matching belt. Jin shucked out of her sleep shift, noting the absence of her Y'Zirite uniform, and pulled on the shirt and trousers.

She reached for the boots and the room lurched violently as the distant, high-pitched sound of tearing metal reached her ears. Jin fell across the room as it tilted, her thigh striking the table. She caught herself, heart racing, as the room shuddered and rolled the other direction.

What manner of vessel is this? Obviously not one that rode upon the sea, and the alternative made her eyes go wide even as the ship bounced again, this time lifting her from the ground and tossing her onto her back. She struck the bed frame as she fell and felt a sharp pain spread out from her shoulder.

The vibration cut out as the walls and floor started shaking. She thought she smelled the faint trace of smoke in the air and felt the room slowly tipping as what she imagined must be the bow of the vessel pointed downward and they started descending.

The door opened, and Commander Pardeau staggered into the cabin, his face sober. "We've been attacked."

Another sound of metal ripping as the ship shuddered and bucked again. He fell into her, his hands catching her arms and turning her so that his body absorbed the impact as they struck the wall.

The vessel pitched and rolled, and she felt his arm encircling her as he rolled with the room. With his free hand, he snatched the corner of the bed's thin mattress and used it to shield them. Jin was dimly aware of a guard trying to enter the room only to strike his head against the doorjamb as he was tossed into the hallway beyond.

The vibration was gone now, replaced by the growing roar of their descent. The lights flickered and then went dark. They bounced around the room, the mattress and the commander who wielded it shielding her from the worst damage. At one point, her head struck the corner of the table, and she winced as lightning laced her vision. The roar continued to build until it reached a crescendo in a deafening crash that threatened to rip the cabin apart as the walls crumpled and tore.

Jin closed her eyes and her mouth, holding her breath, letting the fear wash through her as they landed in a corner and were held there by the momentum of the ship as it plowed into the ground. She held on to the man who held her until finally they were at rest, wrapped in a twisted steel cocoon of wreckage perforated by starlight.

She lay still, releasing her breath and sucking in air that smelled of smoke and dust. Pardeau tried to move, his breath ragged, and when she put her hands on him she felt the slick heat of his blood. Beyond the cabin, she heard the groans and cries of other wounded. She moved beneath the man and heard him gasp in pain. "I'll get help," she said.

His voice gurgled from a mouthful of blood. "Too late for that," he said. Then he clutched at her with the one hand that seemed to work. "You have to keep moving. North by northwest to Endicott Station."

Endicott Station. She'd not heard of it before. "What is Endicott Station? Why were you taking me there?"

The commander coughed, and she felt his body spasm against her. "I'm taking you . . ." His words failed, falling to another fit of coughing. "Classified."

There were voices calling out now in the wreckage around her, weak voices and voices filled with fear and pain. And the sounds of life that she heard beyond the cabin alarmed her in contrast to the weakness in the commander's voice. "What is classified? Where were you taking me?"

"I'm taking you . . . to your . . . son."

Jin Li Tam blinked into the darkness, unsure of the words she'd heard. *My son?* "Jakob is dead," she said. Her voice was flat and hollow. "How can you possibly take me to him?"

But the commander's only reply was the rattle of his failing breath, and when she repeated her question, she resisted the urge to shake him. The impact of his words had already slipped past the guard of her heart, flooding her with a sudden and impossible hope that she knew she could not afford. And when other hands finally pulled at his cooling body, she heard her own voice broken by a sob.

"He's dead," Jin said. But those hands that now pulled at her could not have known she spoke of her son, the light of her life so recently snuffed out, and not the man who'd given his life to save hers. "He's dead."

Still, that hope ran loose within Jin Li Tam, forty-second daughter of Vlad Li Tam, and Great Mother of Jakob the Child of Promise, as she let those hands guide her out of the smoldering wreckage and under a blanket of stars made blurry by smoke and tears.

Rudolfo

Rudolfo crouched in deep shadows cast by pine and ferns, watching the Y'Zirites as they patrolled the hunting manor's perimeter. So far, he'd counted six unmagicked Blood Guard, and a careful sweep of the area with his monoscope assured him there were no blood-magicked guards on the prowl.

But that could change quickly. He closed his eyes for a moment, drawing in a slow breath against the scout magicks that burned through his body, savoring the focus they now gave his wrath.

He'd lost count of the days since the kin-raven and its unbearable news. He had no idea how long he'd lain in his tears, sobbing and raging, once his body had given out and there'd been nothing left to break and no energy left to break with. Nothing left, that is, but his need to know more and his need to put his knives to work. Breaking was not enough. He needed to cut in the way that he had been cut and give the tangle of feelings that boiled over in him some place to go. *And learn more of my son's last days.*

He felt the tears for but a moment and blinked them away, finding a grip once more on the knife handle that anger provided him. The magicks helped, though his legs twitched with the need to run; his arms twitched with the need to thrust and slash his way into the house he now watched.

Rudolfo felt Renard's fingers upon his shoulder. *Just six. But there is a platoon of regulars billeted in the gamekeeper's cabin. And a squad and a half in the house itself.*

He placed his own hand on Renard's arm. *Are you confident of our men and our path?* Renard had initially resisted Rudolfo's mad scheme when Rudolfo had laid it out before him in a low and controlled voice, eyes still red from mourning his son. But Esarov had supported the plan and had offered up a squad of his own hidden Delta scouts to help, and Orius had reluctantly concurred, his concerns whispered from the beak of a moon swallow. They'd even managed to secure aid from a handful of local resistance members. It was a small group, but they had the advantage of striking a stunned opponent.

I am confident, General, Renard replied.

Rudolfo drew in another breath, held and released it, letting the filling and emptying of his lungs center him. He'd not heard it himself, but word was his song traveled fast across the Named Lands, sung loudly in taverns beneath the nervous eyes of an Y'Zirite occupation that had no idea how numbered its days were. He tucked away the monoscope. *Now let's give them something new to sing about.*

Aye, General.

Rudolfo drew his knives and started his count as Renard moved down the line, his eyes moving from guard to guard as they took their turns. The manor was deep enough into the forest that its fence was more decorative, marking the beginning of the grounds proper and the edge of the forest that surrounded it. He'd counted four doors and assumed there were Y'Zirite regulars posted inside each. The top floor was where the Daughters of Ahm, the spiritual wing of the Y'Zirite Empire, were housed. They were kept apart from the military command structure, though the Daughters fed them young acolytes for Blood Guard training and were attached to units to provide leadership, instruction and discipline in matters of faith.

Rudolfo stood, his lips moving as the numbers counted down. When he reached zero, he did not hesitate. He moved out of the deeper shadows and trusted the clouded night sky to hide him. Somewhere to the northeast, captured deer were released and driven toward the manor by magicked scouts, the noise as they crashed through the underbrush covering the soft whisper of boots over ground. Rudolfo moved now, too, clicking his tongue softly in time with his feet to keep the scouts to his left and right aware of his position. He held his knives tightly as he ran, angling between the Blood Guard on patrol even as a whistle of alarm went up among them. They were fast, their hands moving to the small phials they wore at their throats. As the closest Blood Guard unstopped the phial and poured the contents into her mouth, Rudolfo surged forward and fell upon her with his knives.

As she dropped to the ground, her heart and lungs pierced, the Y'Zirite scout twitched and vanished, the magicks taking hold of her body even as she breathed her last. Rudolfo heard the other falling beside him and pressed on for the narrow servants' door that already opened, a curious-faced soldier peering out into the night.

Rudolfo reached him first and brought the man down with thrusts to the lung and heart again. The knives in his hands were not as balanced as his father's, but made of newer, lighter steel and sharp as a straight razor. Stepping over the fallen guard, Rudolfo moved into the hallway and clicked his tongue again to bring Renard and his men around him.

Esarov's maps were accurate so far, and they quickly found the stairs. But now the Y'Zirites—stunned initially—were putting up more fight. The next soldier went down harder, leaving a cut on Rudolfo's forearm that stung. The others pressed in tight alongside him now as they took the stairs, and when they reached the top, they lost their first man when the Blood Guard fell upon them.

The Y'Zirite blood magicks and numbers gave their enemy an advantage after the surprise wore off. It took Rudolfo and two other scouts to bring down one Blood Guard at the ready. And no less than three of the elite Y'Zirite troops awaited them at the door marking the wing of living quarters. Rudolfo came out of that storm of knives with multiple lacerations on his arms and a long cut on his thigh, but the satisfaction of his blade deep in flesh fed his cold rage, and he smiled grimly as they threw open the doors and raced the corridor beyond them.

The sound of full alarm reached his ears now, and his smile widened. The Delta sappers were at their work, keeping the Y'Zirite focus scattered. The stables burned now, horses driven into the woods to hamper pursuit, and if all held to plan, fires were set in the gamekeeper's cabin and in the kitchen below.

Rudolfo counted the doors, his magicked feet whispering over the thick carpet. He'd committed the maps and notes to memory, going over them all carefully with the men before pushing the sheaf of papers into the fire and watching them burn. He'd sent his first message by moon swallow soon after, ordering the Physician Benoit south from the Ninefold Forest to Caldus Bay and arranging the secret hire of an isolated farmhouse.

Rudolfo took the door at the far end of the hall, knowing Renard and the others would take their doors as well. When he kicked down the locked door, he saw the woman, still in her sleep shift, working frantically at the latch of her window.

"Hold," Rudolfo said.

But she did not hold. With her hands still furtively working the lock, she looked over her shoulder, and in the dim light he saw the frightened, pale face of a woman past her sixties, her iron hair cut short.

Rudolfo advanced, hearing the sound of a scuffle in the hallway behind him. "Hold," he said again, and this time she turned her entire body toward him, the small knife up and ready.

Rudolfo leaped forward, knocking the knife away. "You are Sister Tamray, Chief among the Daughters of Ahm for the redemption of the Named Lands." His words were a statement, not a question, and she lunged at him with her fingernails now, her voice rising in a loud cry of anger and fear.

He hit her, hard, and felt momentary shame at how satisfying it was. She fell, and he knelt onto her back, pinning her arms beneath her, as he sheathed a knife and fumbled for the powders in his pouch. Kallacaine for sleep and scout magicks for concealment. It wasn't an optimal combination—the risk of the two working together to stop her heart and lungs was high. But this woman was dead in days otherwise.

Not that what awaits her will be better. It would be decidedly worse. But he'd been beneath their knives, and he'd seen the handiwork of their blades upon his home. And now, though he knew in a fog that there was much more to it, this blood-loving cult of knives had taken his son away from him.

No, some voice deeper in him whispered. *Vlad Li Tam did this.* But Rudolfo pushed that voice aside and focused on the woman beneath him.

"Kill me and be done," she said. Rudolfo took advantage of her open mouth to push the first handful of powders into it. She spat and bit at him.

He leaned close to her ear. "I will," he said. "In time." She bucked against him, and as she moved, he felt his rage rising. It lent him strength, and he held her in place as the kallacaine took hold. He wanted to resist, wanted to wait for Benoit's report after his first redemptive cuts, but asking through his Physician of Penitent Torture and hearing by the bird or by courier left something urgent within him unsatisfied. "Tell me," he whispered, "what you know about the death of Lord Jakob, your Child of Promise?"

Her words were slurred beyond recognition from the drugs and from the side of her face being pressed into the carpet, but at his words, he saw the fight go out of her eyes and her mouth go slack. Now he could the see the hollowed-out shell that she was, and his sudden kinship with her struck him like a boot to his gut. The woman's tears were sudden and her sob was real, and he felt his own stirring to meet her there on the common ground of an inconsolable and shared grief.

In that moment, some part of Rudolfo recognized that this woman had also suffered a loss—one that she had not caused him personally—and that empathy threatened the cold, distant place he needed to be in order to keep moving forward. In order to not collapse beneath the weight of too much loss.

Behind him, the sound of fighting continued, and Renard's low whistle from the doorway told him that it was time to exit. He pushed the scout powders into Sister Tamray's open, drooling mouth and felt her body tremor beneath him as the magicks took hold.

He pulled the woman up onto his back, feeling the weight of her upon him. He could give her over to a younger, stronger man, but he did not want to. He'd chosen this path and would see it through. *For my son,* he thought, but as he thought it, Rudolfo knew he lied.

I do this for myself. Too much cut away over a lifetime, and it was time to do his own cutting in turn. And the man he knew was actually responsible—the man he should've killed two years ago as Vlad Li Tam burned his family's secret history in the Named Lands—was too far away and too out of reach for him to cut. These Y'Zirites would have to do, even if it was under the pretext of gathering intelligence and adding to the myth he was becoming.

But even as he raced that Whymer Maze of justification, the hounds of grief snapping at his heels, Rudolfo knew that regardless of anyone's part, it was he himself who was responsible. He'd failed to protect his child, and that failure was his to pay for ultimately. He took a deep breath and then released it.

He felt the wound ache on his chest and shifted the woman's weight upon his back. *Some knives we bring upon ourselves,* he realized.

Then, growling beneath the burden he bore, Rudolfo found his footing and ran after his men, the sorrow once more safely tucked away within his rage.

Vlad Li Tam

There were signs of recent fighting in the streets, and Vlad Li Tam smiled at his handiwork as he moved quickly through the stillness of predawn. Beside him, silver robe rippling behind her like water, Amylé D'Anjite matched his pace.

He made no effort to hide them now. They were more than a match for whatever remained of the Y'Zirite military, and he wanted to be seen entering the palace. They took the most direct route to the massive courtyard that housed both the Imperial Palace and the Temple of the Daughters of Ahm. The statue of the Wizard King still lay broken across the paving stones, and in the gray, as the first of the stars began to fade overhead, it looked like the corpse of a god stretched out, hands pointing to Vlad as he approached.

As he walked, he considered the woman beside him. Vlad knew their alliance was tentative at best. He'd stayed up for hours answering her questions—inventing answers where he needed to and admitting ignorance where he could. Still, he'd controlled the flow of information, shaping her perceptions like a sculptor shaped clay, building her into a tool that he would only be able to use in a limited way. And once she knew the truth of his manipulations—or if the old crone he'd locked away somehow got free—Amylé would turn on him and likely be his ending. He'd defeated her before, when she had the help of her kin-dragon, but he was under no illusions of doing so a second time, without the element of surprise in his favor. And he was getting more tired as his body burned away. It would take nothing for her to catch him off guard.

So I must never be off guard. And he must keep her anger and curiosity engaged in the direction that best served his purposes: the descendants of Y'Zir and what they had done to her people, to her father.

Time wound down, narrowing like a noose, and he had more to do than when he started now that his forty-second daughter had been taken from him. The metal man, Isaak, would arrive soon, and a confrontation over the staff brewed there, though Vlad was confident of that outcome. But not long after that encounter, Neb would return also demanding the staff of him.

And if I am finished, I will give it to him. He certainly wouldn't give it to Amylé, and he knew he couldn't keep it much longer. He'd dreamed the dream like everyone else, and he knew that the staff belonged in the tower and that whatever blew upon that wind as Winters cried out upon the plain came by way of the parents' tool in the parent's hand.

A pair of Blood Guard changed direction in the courtyard, turning to intercept Vlad and his companion. He slowed and Amylé slowed beside him. "Be ready," he said.

In response, he saw her robes begin to shift, tightening until the silver fabric clung to her body. He felt heat rising from her and smelled the slightest scent of ozone on the air. But beneath it, he also smelled her fear.

The Blood Guard approached, and Vlad called out before they could see who he was. "We require immediate audience with Regent Eliz Xhum. Tell him Vlad Li Tam has come to parley."

They reached for the phials of blood magick at their throats, then paused and looked at one another. Something unspoken passed between them, and one of them ran for the palace gates while the other stood back and watched Vlad and Amylé from a distance. Vlad looked to the massive building beyond the gates and wondered how easy it would be to storm it now, with Amylé by his side, strengthened by the blood of the earth. Part of him craved it. The more direct path of violence committed by his own hands. But there were eyes upon him even when he could not see them. He'd still not met them, but he knew they were out there. They'd taken his grandson and his daughter, along with the knives his father had hidden here for the time of his arrival— children of his household who'd been embedded into Y'Zirite culture, like Ire Li Tam, his thirty-second daughter. Whoever they were, they watched from the shadows. As did the Y'Zirites, their eyes dark with grief and wide with fear.

It is important that they watch. They will be the ones to tell their children what they saw. They will be the ones to write down their parents' cautionary tales and pass them in turn to their children. It made no sense to deal only with the problem of the day when the problem of centuries or even millennia could be dealt with at the same time. Lessons learned in blood to be remembered and recounted.

Vlad smiled.

When Xhum and his escort arrived, the regent was easy to pick out by his uniform and cloak. He was easily twenty years younger than Vlad, but the man's eyes made him look older. Vlad saw the grief in them and beneath that grief, a defiance he could respect. A tall woman in dark robes, her long iron hair braided and over her shoulder, stood beside him. She leaned over and whispered something to the regent at the sight of Amylé but was otherwise silent.

They came without bravado or pomp. A simple squad of Blood

Guard walked in formation around them, unmagicked but alert, their
knives sheathed.

They know they cannot hope to stand against us.

Vlad waited until they stopped and made eye contact with the regent again. "I've come to offer you terms, Regent Eliz Xhum." He used
the staff to project his voice, letting it boom out over the city.

The regent blinked slowly, his mouth working around a reply that
he thought twice about delivering. Finally, he swallowed. His eyes went
to Amylé and then returned to Vlad. The defiance was there still,
but muted by something else. "What terms do you offer, Lord Tam?"

He kept his voice level, certain it could be heard at least ten leagues
away. "An opportunity to survive what is coming," Vlad said. "In three
days' time, Ahm's Glory will be struck down. Those who wish to survive it will leave what they have behind and flee now, while they are
able. Otherwise, those taken by plague and sword will be joined by
those taken in a death worse than either."

The regent's eyes narrowed. "Forgive me, Lord Tam," he said, "but
I do not hear any terms offered thus far. Only threats of violence."

Vlad smiled, though it felt weary and false. "I will permit you and
what remains of your government to organize an evacuation and leave
in an orderly fashion if you cooperate with me."

The regent glanced at the gray-haired woman beside him. "What
does my cooperation entail?"

"First, I require the spellbook. I know you've had it removed from
the city. It is needed elsewhere." Vlad watched the two of them as he
said it and saw another quick exchange of glances that spoke volumes.
She knows where it is.

He tucked that knowledge aside and continued. "Second, whatever
remains of the Wizard King Ahm Y'Zir is to be staked in the courtyard. The rest of you may go where you will. But Ahm Y'Zir remains
behind to pay for his sins and fall with his city."

He'd confronted the beast in Chandra's dreams—an ancient mechanical spider that bore what was left of the old wizard in a crystalline orb. The beast was chained somewhere deep beneath them, driven
insane by time and the magicks that preserved him. His next confrontation would end Y'Zir's life upon this earth and finish what P'Andro
Whym had started on his Night of Purging.

Vlad watched the gears turning behind Regent Xhum's eyes.
"I cannot agree to these terms," the man finally said.

Vlad raised his voice. "Then the blood of this city will be upon your

head, and I will have what I require regardless of your agreement."
Then he slid his thumb over the silver of the staff, dropping to a whisper as he turned on the old woman.

"What is your name?" He heard the power in his words and saw
her eyes widen. He felt his eyebrows furrow as he concentrated. *What
is your name?*

"I am Sister Elsbet, Chief Mother of the Daughters of Ahm."

He tightened his grip on the staff. "Where have you hidden the
spellbook, Sister Elsbet?"

The Blood Guard moved forward now, drawing their knives and
reaching for the phials at their throats. Vlad looked to Amylé and she
nodded, blazing white as she drew strength from the blood of the earth
that wrapped her. As the light built, she shrieked at the sky and the
sky shrieked back at her.

Vlad had hoped that would be enough but knew better than to trust
it. He pounded the staff upon the ground, the force of it sending two
of the Blood Guard to their knees. "Enough," he roared over the beating of the kin-dragon's wings.

The Blood Guard scattered as the beast dropped into the courtyard and pulled Amylé into itself. Relentless, they threw themselves
at the beast, but its tail, claws and teeth cut through them without
effort.

Then Vlad turned his attention back to Elsbet. His voice rose, and
with it, her face paled. "Where is the spellbook?"

Her mouth twisted as he pulled the words from her. "It's been taken
to the convent at El Shapir for safekeeping." With it came the image
of stone buildings at the foot of steep, bare mountains.

From the corner of his eye, he saw Amylé dispatching the last of
the Blood Guard, tearing into them in a blur of movement Vlad could
barely follow.

He released his hold on Elsbet and turned to the regent. "Tell your
master I will dig him out of the smoldering basements of his city once
I've burned it to ash."

Amylé, tucked away within her kin-dragon, returned to his side.
The dragon's nostrils flared as it gulped air.

The regent stared at the dragon but did not allow himself to look
at the bloody piles of cloth and flesh that used to be his squad of Blood
Guard. "I will tell Lord Y'Zir personally," he said. He glanced at Elsbet
and then looked back to Vlad. "There is a matter I wish to inquire
about, Lord Tam."

Vlad inclined his head. "Inquire."

"Your daughter is missing. She was last seen tracking you. Do you have any idea of her whereabouts? Our search parties have come back empty-handed. I'm sure you're as concerned as we are about her well-being."

"No, Regent Xhum," he said. "I am not concerned. My daughter is dead. She tried to interfere with my work and I killed her." He savored the slight widening of the man's eyes, the slight flaring of a nostril. "Don't be surprised. I murdered my grandson and your Crimson Empress without the slightest remorse. I am a Tam. My children are arrows fired into the heart of the world."

He saw sorrow flood Elsbet's face, but the regent maintained his composure. The eyes held less defiance now, though, and he nodded slowly. Then, stiff-backed, he turned away and walked slowly toward the palace gate.

Elsbet lingered. "Your father," she said, "would be ashamed of you, Vlad."

He met her eyes and read in them that she'd known the man somehow. "Perhaps for many other things," Vlad said, "but not for this. He fully understood his sins in this matter, I'll wager."

Or else Vlad's father would not have brought him here for this work, brought his forty-second daughter here as well, hiding knives for them—other Tams tucked away in Y'Zir—to cut this evil from the world.

Vlad waited for the woman to turn away, and when she did, he turned to the kin-dragon. "Can you find the convent at El Shapir?"

The beast nodded, and her voice filled his head. *I can carry us there. Hold still.* The kin-dragon reared up on its haunches, its two forelegs opening to take Vlad into an embrace. He held the staff and closed his eyes as the cool metal met his skin. Then, he was in the beast and was the beast. He heard through its ears, saw through its eyes, smelled through its nose. And at the same time, he was aware of himself folded into some compartment within the creature, held in place, his hands still upon the staff.

They lifted off, and he felt the vertigo of watching the sky spin and right itself as they built altitude. *I am flying,* he thought.

Yes, she answered. *It is exhilarating.* She paused. *But I am disturbed, Lord Tam.*

He tried to pull his senses back away from the rush of the wind and the feel of it upon metal skin he knew was not his own, the over-powering smell of smoke and decay and burned citrus. *What disturbs you, Lady?* He thought it would be the violence. He was confident she'd never killed before today.

But her response surprised him. *You lie easily and effectively about terrible things.*

When it serves my purpose. He forced calm into his mind. *Sometimes a higher purpose calls upon us to do or say terrible things.*

She was quiet for a moment and once more, the flight distracted him. He had no power to move the beast, but he felt everything that it felt, saw what it saw—which now was the rush of wind and the rush of barren landscape below. *I hope,* she said, *you are not lying to me as well.*

And, of course, he was. But not completely. He'd been truthful about his family beneath the Y'Zirite blades even if he'd fabricated kin-clave between their houses and a manufactured message from her father whispered down through his line for the day that she was finally found by House Li Tam and able to avenge herself upon her family's direst foe. And he'd been truthful about the ruse involving the children and his daughter. But he'd told her they were safely hidden away with allies.

The best lies, he knew, were at least two-thirds true.

If he could, Vlad Li Tam would have smiled reassuringly. *I have no reason to lie to you, Lady D'Anjite. You and Nebios were chosen—hidden away for millennia, even—to finally end Y'zir's hold on the People once and for all. And once we have the spellbook, that work can truly begin.*

Like all the other lies, it came easy to him. He was, after all, a Tam.

Chapter

12

Winters

A new moon hung in the sky, bathing the clouds in blue-green light when the crowd finally dispersed at the docks. It had gone well—better than she expected. Neb's surprise appearance with his tales of the moon, combined with her discourse on the dream, had won the night.

Winters had watched the crowd, their faces shining with awe as Neb described the jungles and seas, the ruins and the Firsthome Temple. At first he'd been nervous, but he'd grown into his words, and after a few minutes he had his listeners by the reins, steering them as he went. She'd lost her fear of him instantly. It was hard to even recall what had frightened her so much in the first place. He'd changed, certainly. He was more confident in some ways, less in others. And there was a sadness in him now that she could see, peeking out from someplace deep where he kept it hidden.

He has been broken by all of this. Of course, they all had been. And that realization dragged her back to the loss of Jakob, the loss of Hanric and the others. But Neb's words wouldn't let her linger in those losses. She saw the longing they inspired in the others, and she felt it herself.

A homecoming is upon us. When he'd finished speaking, she spoke a bit more, and the words were there, upon the tip of her tongue. "A homecoming is upon us," she said to the crowd. "Come home with me."

A cheer went up. And even as it echoed into the night, Winters heard a quieter affirmation. *Yes, Daughter of Shadrus. A homecoming is upon you indeed.*

Of course, even after she dismissed them, the crowd was not finished. She and Neb spent easily the next hour being stopped by men, women, even children, with questions about the moon and the dream. And then, most fruitful of all, there were the captains. They approached her after the others had left. They were open-minded, having experienced the dream, but were also businessmen. If the Y'Zirite Navy gave way as Winters believed they would, the captains saw quickly the benefit of offering their vessels up for hire and made that clear to her.

And then suddenly, it was just her and Neb and the small entourage that accompanied them. She'd watch him slip away a few times, a silver crescent pressed to his ear as he scowled and asked questions into it tersely.

When he returned this time, he slipped the artifact into his battered leather pouch. "I have to go," he said, glancing to Lieutenant Erys and her Blood Guard.

Winters felt her heart fall, and it surprised her. "So soon?"

He nodded, and she could see the hesitation in his eyes. *He doesn't want to leave me.* She heard the same in his voice when he spoke. "I won't be gone so long this time."

Still, she'd only just realized how badly she missed him, and the idea of being separated again was an unexpected knife in her ribs. She looked from the young man to her captor, but before she could say anything, the officer offered a smile that caught Winters off guard. "Perhaps you should escort your friend to the edge of town and meet us back at the manor when you've finished. You've a journey to pack for, Lady Winteria."

Winters blushed and inclined her head. "Thank you, Lieutenant."

The lieutenant looked from her to Neb. "Do not test my goodwill and spirit her away, Homefinder."

Neb blushed as well but said nothing.

Winters watched the others leave, and when they'd vanished, she held out her hand. Neb stared at it for a moment before taking it. He let her lead, and she guided them toward darker streets that meandered slowly out of the town. She glanced at him as they walked. "Was that Petronus? On the moon?"

"Yes."

She'd seen him in the dream and had not recognized him at first. He'd looked so different. "Is he really so young now?"

"Yes."

She looked to him again and saw for a moment the slouched shoulders and castaway look of the boy she'd fallen fell in love with what seemed so long ago. She juxtaposed that boy against the man she'd so recently seen speaking to the crowd, his voice full of wonder and passion as he described their new home. And between the two, she tried to find that terrifying being of light and rage she'd seen not so long ago, but she couldn't see that Neb anymore. "And he needs you?"

He hesitated and looked around, making sure no one was near enough to catch his low voice. "There are Y'Zirites en route. I need to . . ." His words trailed off as he considered them. "I need to deal with them."

Winters took him in, dressed in the rough clothing of a fisherman. "How will you do that?"

"Deal with them or return to the moon?"

"Both," she said.

His brow furrowed. They were at the edge of town now. "I don't want to scare you."

I don't think you can anymore, she thought. There was nothing about him now that frightened her. Instead, she had feelings she'd forgotten in their time apart. She glanced at him. "I want to know," she said.

He nodded. "Okay."

They continued walking until the sky was lost to the overshadowing pine forest. They were quiet, moving slowly hand in hand, until he stopped.

"This is it," Neb said.

She met his eyes and felt her mouth go dry. The idea of him leaving felt like a sharp knife on her skin, and it surprised her to feel that way. "But you'll be back soon?"

He nodded. "I will. I also need to go and get the staff from Vlad Li Tam. Unless Isaak is successful."

Winters felt an unexpected rush of anger at the mention of his name. *Does he know?* Behind the anger, the grief threatened to leak out, and the words came even faster. "Tam killed Lord Jakob."

Neb blinked. "He did?"

She watched his face fall as the news set in, and that part of her that had stirred back to life was dashed beneath the cold water of the agony she saw in his eyes. When he spoke, he stammered. "It's because we didn't get the staff in time," he said.

Winters shook her head. "You had no control of that, Nebios."

He sighed, and she could hear the frustration and weariness in his voice. "But I should have. I'm the Homeseeker, right? But none of it went as it should. Petronus opened the temple; I was trapped inside. Aver-Tal-Ka gave his life because of that. We didn't get the staff; Vlad Li Tam has used it to terrorize the Y'Zirites, and he's murdered Lord Rudolfo's son—" Here, Neb's voice broke, and his sob made Winters do the same. "He could've never gotten close to Jakob without the staff." She saw tears forming in his eyes and felt her own rising up. "It's not how the dream meant for things to go."

"No," she said. "But I think the dreams we've followed were never meant to be exact. In thousands of years of dreaming, we never saw the possibility that my own people might forsake the dream in favor of the bloody Y'Zirite knives my sister offered them. And if the Watcher hadn't removed the Final Dream from the Book of Dreaming Kings, I would've dreamed it myself, sharing it only with you. But because that happened—and because I needed a way to get that dream to you and Petronus—the dream meant for two has become a dream shared with all." She heard her voice flooding with passion. "And you saw them tonight. It's giving them hope. Some of them will come with us, and we will start something new in a new place." She took his hands in hers and looked up at him. "We have paid a terrible price, all of us, but at the end of it, home rises before us. A new home for whoever wishes."

As she said it, Winters watched the realization dawn upon him. "Whoever wishes?"

She nodded. "Yes. We all shared this new dream. Anyone who wishes should heed it and come home."

Doubt clouded his face. "I don't see how—"

Winters stretched up onto her tiptoes to silence him with a kiss. It was brief—the merest peck—though a part of her wanted to linger. Still he blushed, and she took advantage of his silence. "We don't need to know how all of it will work right now. You need to get the staff and tend to matters at the temple. But give the Y'Zirites the option to lay down their cutting knives and join us."

"And Tam?"

She needed no time to consider it. Her words marched out quickly and clearly. "No," she said. "Not Tam." She couldn't bring herself to say the rest of it, but Neb's eyes and the line of his jaw told her he already knew. *I want him to die for what he's done.* "But he must give over the staff. The violence has to stop, Neb."

She saw something wash over his face that she couldn't quite read. Was it guilt? "I will do my best," he said, looking away quickly.

She stepped back from him. "Now," she said. "Show me."

He blushed, then took a deep breath. The sound that came from his throat was not like anything she'd heard before. And Winters jumped when she heard a cry that echoed his own, this from deeper in the forest east of the road they stood upon.

Something large moved through the trees. She heard the breaking of branches and the crunch of feet in the underbrush.

When it stepped onto the road she gasped. It was a massive beast, dark and ambiguous with no moonlight to illuminate it. Still, she knew what it was. "A kin-dragon."

He nodded. "Yes."

"You ride it?"

"It's . . . hard to explain," he said.

She smiled. "You can tell me later. Go do what needs doing, Nebios Homefinder. Find me when you're done."

"I will." Now he was awkward, shifting on his feet as his voice hesitated. "I'm sorry I was gone so long," he said. "I'm sorry I—"

This time, when she kissed him, she gave herself to the kiss and felt the moment when he gave himself to it as well. When they finished, she held him close, then pushed him toward the kin-dragon.

As he approached it, the beast reared up, opening its forearms and embracing Neb. There was a slight pop, a flash of light, and a shift in the air. When Winters blinked away the brightness, she saw that Neb was gone now and only the kin-dragon remained. It took a step toward her and inclined its great head toward her.

She returned the gesture, then stepped back as Neb unfurled his wings. He lifted with ease, branches slapping against the massive body as he took off. Winters watched him break through the evergreen ceiling, pine needles and broken twigs raining down as he went. Then she heard a loud buzz as the wings beat faster. The kin-dragon hovered a moment, its head still inclined, then shot south.

And Winteria bat Mardic turned back toward Caldus Bay to finish packing for her journey, the memory of his kiss like magicks on her lips, warming her entire body as she walked.

Ria

Ria shivered from the cold as she tugged on her pants and coat. Her fire had gone out sometime in the night, and her aide was nowhere to be found; but it was the nightmare that had pushed her out of sleep, not the room's dropping temperature.

For the first several days, she had not left her command cabin at the edge of Windwir. She'd heard Sister Elsbet's voice leaking from the kin-raven—the old woman unable to keep the grief from her voice as she recounted all that had transpired—and lost all sense of time and place. Garyt and the ravener's faces had gone pale, and without a word, she'd retreated and locked herself away. On the second day, her grief had swelled into a rage she did not know how to still, and by the third day, she'd understood just how she'd failed.

I did not finish the kin-healing. No, Rudolfo had interrupted their work and she had run out of time. The magisters didn't get what they needed to fully alchemize the Tam blood and distill it into the magicks that would give Lord Jakob life.

The weight of it threatened her faith. And the nightmare, she realized, was merely a symptom of that threat. She'd been falling, and she'd stopped screaming long enough to hear someone else screaming on the hot night wind. She'd twisted and turned, suddenly aware of her wings as she moved in the direction of the scream.

There. In the distance, she saw the tower and lunged for it. These eyes—better than her own—saw the old woman clearly there. And the old woman, it seemed, saw her. She stood in silver robes, a silver staff held loosely in her hand.

"How does a Downunder come to fly a dragon?" the old woman called out.

Ria landed heavily, her six claws digging into the tower's surface, and wasn't prepared at all for the solid crack and the bright flash of light that spilled her naked onto the ground when the woman's staff connected with her.

"The tools of the parents," the old woman said as she lifted Ria up with ease, "are not toys for the children."

Then, as Ria screamed, the old woman tossed her with ease over the edge of the tower and cackled as she plummeted down.

Now she took another deep breath and held it as she shoved one foot and then the other into her waiting boots.

She is some aspect of me, she thought. The Androfrancines were wrong about many things, but their understanding of the hidden world of dreams—aether not withstanding—was significant. She'd used some of that knowledge to help counter the dreams she'd fought to suppress most of her life. Ria suspected that the old woman represented the full fruit of her anger and self-hatred—a product of her guilt regarding Vlad. The tone of the old woman's scolding was that of a disappointed and angry parent.

Ria went out into the night and noticed immediately how dark the camp was. It wasn't uncommon for it to be quiet this late at night. But never dark unless they were at alarm and trying to stay hidden. The moon was veiled behind clouds and gave limited light. And her guards were gone.

Ria glanced behind her to the knife belt hanging near the headboard of her narrow bed. She slipped back inside quietly and grabbed it up, buckling it on beneath her coat. Then she closed the door behind her and gave a low, inquiring whistle as she stepped onto the frozen mud path.

No answer drifted back.

Ria moved along the path toward the mess hall and enlisted quarters. She found her aide lying outside the hall, his platter of food freezing on the ground and his tin cup in his hand. She went to him and crouched, a knife slipping into her hand by habit as she checked his body.

No wounds. Ria looked around. There was no movement and no sound other than the wind. She whistled third alarm and waited to hear its chorus picked up by the rest. Silence.

The galley's door stood ajar, and she moved to it, glancing inside. There were more bodies, and the magnitude of it twisted in her gut.

She whistled third alarm again and finally heard it echoed deeper in the camp. Farther out another whistle answered the second. Following the sound of alarm, Ria made her way across the camp. She paused at the officers' galley and poked her head in. She recognized Sister Gwendolyn by her robes and saw Magister Captain Onell stretched out beside her.

Poison? It seemed the most likely. She counted the other bodies and then closed the door.

"Lady Winteria." She looked up at the familiar voice. Garyt had been with her from early on. His grandfather had been one of her sister's most trusted elders. He'd converted quietly and said little about it. But he spent his meal periods poring over his copy of the gospel and had taken the mark not long after the Mass of the Falling Moon. Ria herself had administered it.

Now he looked frightened and recently dragged from sleep.

"Captain," she said. "What do you know?"

"I suspect poison, but it's too soon to tell. I've not been able to locate any living magisters or Daughters." A handful of soldiers came shuffling along the path, their eyes and mouths open wide with fear. Garyt whistled them over. "The Blood Guard are all dead, too."

Ria regarded the men as they approached. She could smell their terror. "Search every building. Do not disturb the dead. Gather up the living and set them to searching as well. I want to know our numbers. And I want to know what's happened here."

"Yes, Lady Winteria."

She joined in the search, and by dawn she had the numbers. All of the Blood Scouts. All of the magisters and the Daughters of Ahm. All of the officers in the Y'Zirite army, and nearly half of the Machtvolk. And even more surprising, the kin-ravens were dead along with the camp's ravener. Ria was left with a handful of Y'Zirite and Machtvolk infantry and camp servants and an even smaller number of Machtvolk officers like Garyt. And there was evidence that some of those surviving had already deserted, fleeing south. At best, their faith had been shaken to the point of apostasy, and at worst they pursued the new dream and had forsaken the promises carved into their very flesh.

And that is without knowing fully what has happened in Y'Zir. Rumors were certainly doing what rumors did in any army, but she'd made no formal announcement about the news she'd received.

How do you announce the death of hope? A wave of powerlessness washed over her, and she sat down heavily in the snow, dropping her end of the body she was helping Garyt haul from the mess tent to the wagon.

She thought she saw a flash of something upon his face, and she suspected it was worry. He laid down his end of the corpse. "Lady Winteria?"

She waved him away, fighting a sudden rush of tears. "I'm fine, Captain."

He squatted beside her. "Darkness is upon us," he said in a quiet voice. "And there are whisperings of an even greater darkness back in Y'Zir."

She held her breath a moment and tried to regain her focus and composure. "Yes," she said. "And we must do our best to be light in that darkness."

He nodded and waited beside her, his face grim, until she climbed to her feet. "What is your plan?"

They wrestled the stiff Blood Guard into the wagon with the others. "We'll pack our dead in the snow and await word from the couriers. We can't dispose of the bodies until the magisters have had a chance to examine them. We need to resupply with whatever game or fish we can find. Every provision in the camp is suspect at this point."

Garyt nodded. "I'll have it all packed in the snow as well so it can be checked."

They returned to the galley slowly and took hold of the last body there. Other wagons were being loaded throughout the camp, and the bodies were being packed into snowdrifts beyond the small town of wooden buildings that served the work at Windwir. Once the last were buried, Ria knew she'd need to find something to say to the others. Some word of encouragement to carry them through this latest bit of dark. But she had no idea what that word would be. First, Yazmeera and her officers had been assassinated. Then, the Crimson Empress and the Child of Promise. And now, most of her leadership was dead and yet somehow she was spared.

She wanted to offer her people some kind of strength, but faith in the promises of Ahm Y'Zir had been her strength and her life. A faith reinforced by the cuts she'd given and received over the course of her life in service to those beliefs.

And now, Winteria the Elder thought as she loaded one last corpse into the wagon, *my faith has been cut out of me.*

And she had done it to herself. Tam may have been the knife, but she was the wielding hand. She had cut him, and now he had cut them all.

Not him. Me.

Closing her eyes against the wind and tears, Ria leaned into the cold and swallowed the rancid taste of her shame.

Lysias

Winter still held the northern Machtvolk Territories with fang and claw, and General Lysias shivered against it beneath his blankets.

They'd left the Beneath Places just three days earlier after being harried by the kin-wolves and the Blood Guard that followed after them. He'd seen the remains of his forces whittled down to nearly nothing, certainly not enough to be of conventional use in what was coming. Still, they'd brought down the kin-wolves and what he estimated to be half of the Blood Guard. It was time for the rats to resurface. He'd never favored the idea of fighting outside their element. These were men of the great Ninefold Forest, accustomed to snow and woodland, not tunnels and caves.

So he'd brought them up through an access shaft thirty leagues southeast of the Papal Summer Palace, well north of the Desolation of Windwir. Lysias had seen the Gray Guard intelligence on the excavation of that dead city and thought it a likely place to observe firsthand whether or not his mission had succeeded.

And rendezvous with Tybard's forces. He hoped the lieutenant had sustained fewer losses. They could resupply at Windwir if the weapon was successful and reassess their role in what came next.

Tomorrow their forward scouts should reach the Y'Zirite camp and start gathering information for him. He'd already sent two of his fastest scouts south and west, magicked, to establish communication with Orius and with Tybard. Once he'd rejoined whatever remained of his men they could take the camp—if the pathogen had worked as planned, and if that surgical removal of their elite forces and their leadership had the expected impact on Y'Zirite military effectiveness.

Lysias looked out over the moonlit snow in the clearing beyond their dark, cold camp. It was a quiet night, the only noise the sound of his men breathing as they slept. He'd tried to join them but couldn't. His mind kept returning to the dream. It had awakened something in him—a curiosity perhaps, or maybe an urge. As if one of those falling seeds had penetrated his heart and taken root there, started to grow.

But growing what? He did not know, but he found himself suddenly thinking of a day when his life might be simpler. Where he might have a house and a garden and spend afternoons at a pub. Put away the uniform and the sword. Unknot his scarf of rank.

It was not something he'd ever considered before. Until the dream, he'd assumed he would serve Rudolfo as a general until the day he was too old to do so. It was familiar to him; he'd been serving since he graduated from the Entrolusian City-States's famed Academy. But now, for the first time in his life, something unfamiliar whispered to him, kept him from sleep with its insistent tone.

A light buzz reached his ears, and his eyes went to the clearing. He squinted and saw something small flying across the field of snow. It flew low and straight, stopping suddenly to hover. As it turned, he puckered his lips to whistle them to third alarm. The object drew closer, slowing as it approached, and Lysias forced himself to release his held breath.

It's one of Orius's birds. The moon swallow beat its silver wings, hovering now just an arm's length away. Lysias felt the cool breeze of it on his cheek and stretched out his hand.

It hopped lightly into his palm and cocked its head. The beak opened, but the voice he heard leaking out wasn't Orius. It was Rudolfo. "Lysias, I hope this finds you. Renard insists it will. When you've finished your work, rally with Philemus and the Wandering Army at Windwir and bring it into the war." His voice was different, colder and controlled, and it lowered now. "Harry the foe southward as you will; I will communicate rendezvous details soon. We will drive the Y'Zirites into the sea or cut them to the ground. We will take back our home."

When the bird finished, it closed its beak, blinked, then opened it again and waited. It took him a moment to realize that it was expecting a reply. Lysias cleared his voice. "Message received."

A few of the men had stirred awake around him at the sound of Lord Rudolfo's voice. They gasped now as the moon swallow shot up from Lysias's hands to flee across the clearing and vanish into the forest.

He looked after it for a time and then sighed, drawing the blanket up to his chin. He'd forsaken the notion of a tent, propping himself instead against a pine for the few hours he thought he might sleep. Most of the others had done the same, and soon their breathing became deep and steady again as they drifted off.

He himself must've also nodded a bit, because the gentle whistle to second alarm startled him alert. He pushed the blanket aside as he dragged his short blade from beneath it, rising to a crouch as he did.

He heard commotion from the other side of the camp and set out for it at a jog, mindful of the men he dodged as he made his way to the source of the alarm. He wasn't sure how much time had passed—hours, though, by the gray in the sky.

Two scouts stood over a man they'd tied and hooded, and in the dim light, Lysias saw the dark Y'Zirite uniform. "What do we have here?"

The first scout straightened and inclined his head. "A deserter, General."

A deserter. He crouched and lifted the hood to reveal the scarred, white face of a young man. "Is this true? Have you deserted?"

The soldier nodded, his eyes wide. He said something at first in a language that Lysias didn't comprehend, then paused and spoke in halting Landlish. "Dead."

"Who's dead?"

The young man spoke again, the words jumbled together and holding no meaning for Lysias. But he didn't need to understand the boy's language to read his terror. And while it stood to reason that he might be scared of having been caught by the Gypsy Scouts, it was more reasonable that he was afraid of whatever had driven him to abandon his post and flee. And Lysias was confident of what that was. He'd seen firsthand what the Androfrancine pathogen could do.

Lysias slowed his own words and lowered his voice. "I need you to focus. Who is dead?"

But it was no use. The man regarded Lysias and then regarded the scout, his face blank. "Dead," he said again.

"We found him sleeping about ten leagues west. It looks like he came from the north."

Lysias nodded. "Magick a half-squad and have them trace his steps back. I want to know where he came from."

And if it's truly started. Of course, he knew it had. And judging by the terror in the young soldier's voice, the wideness of his eyes, the way his nostrils flared, the Androfrancine pathogen was having the desired effect on Y'Zirite morale. He would know soon enough, between this and Windwir.

Lysias turned his attention back to the prisoner. "Where are you going?" At the man's blank look, he pointed south, pantomimed running with his hands.

The soldier nodded, then looked up, squinting at the sky. His brow furrowed, and finally he pointed to the snow and started drawing in it with his finger.

At first Lysias didn't recognize it, but slowly the image took shape. *It's the tree from the dream.*

The man pointed to it and smiled. Lysias nodded and returned the smile. Then the man laughed, and it was like music in the silent forest. There was joy and hope in that laughter, and it unsettled Lysias.

He has lost something and found something. He could see it on the soldier's face: a balance between the fear that drove him to flee and the beckoning of a new home.

For the first time in his career, Lysias contemplated fleeing himself, taking an almost lascivious pride in the notion of stealing a boat with this young Y'Zirite and sailing for the moon. It was a passing notion that he chuckled away.

It wasn't as surprising as his next thought, which was to strip the boy of his uniform, dress him in the garb of a Forester, and send him along to Caldus Bay where he might have the hope of a ship. Lysias contemplated that possibility for a full minute.

But in the end, he did what he knew must be done, and that did not surprise him at all. General Lysias pushed his blade into the Y'Zirite soldier's heart from behind and, after the body fell and kicked its last, he watched the Y'Zirite blood darken the snow-drawn tree until the image melted into nothing recognizable at all.

Petronus

The night wind was warm upon Petronus, and he stifled a yawn as he watched the ships at anchor far below. He'd not slept, staying up to argue with Nadja instead. The young ambassador was more stubborn than the oldest, staunchest arch-scholar, and his level of frustration was unexpected. Still, she'd not budged.

"We avoid involvement," she said. "A key component of our mission is to be unseen and unknown, to observe and record from a place of anonymity in history."

Despite the firmness of her jaw, he'd seen the truth in her eyes as she said it. *She wants to help us.* Once he'd seen that, he'd stopped arguing as fiercely, and as her hackles lowered, Petronus steered the conversation elsewhere before leaving her in the quarters they'd made for her in the temple. Her decision to stay when the others withdrew had surprised him, and now, in hindsight, he could see her conflicted desire to interfere despite the position required of her office.

And something more.

The girl made him feel odd, but he was growing more comfortable with it. Her conflict went beyond wanting to help, and his own conflict regarding the young ambassador surprised him. And though he doubted very much that they would need her help, Petronus liked that the girl was near.

He looked at the ships in the canal. They were only a few hours out from the temple now, and he expected they'd resume course at dawn. Depending upon Neb, of course. He felt the fabric of his robe, pressing it between his thumb and forefinger as he willed the garment to shrink and cling to his skin. Petronus knew he could do his fair share with his command of the blood of the earth, but it was the dragon that gave them the advantage and assured their success.

Even as he thought about it, he felt the wind pick up around him. He turned to watch the kin-dragon drop to the roof of the temple lightly. It stretched, and when it lifted off, Neb crouched in the shadow of its wings.

He was dressed in the familiar woolens of a fisherman that reminded Petronus of home. "Father," he said with a nod.

"It's good to see you, Neb."

He turned back to the southern view and Neb joined him. "There are three more behind them," the young man said. "They just left the Seaway."

He looked to Neb. The last time he'd encountered Y'Zirite ships, he'd sunk them. "You let them pass?"

"These flew a different flag," Neb said. "A white tree. But they were Y'Zirite ships."

The dream. It had brought out the New Espirans, and now it brought out others, it seemed. "What will you do?"

"I was with Winters," he said, and then stopped as his cheeks flushed red.

Petronus smiled. "Good. You waited long enough."

Neb nodded. "She spoke to a crowd. She talked about the dream and even had me talk about what we've found here on the moon."

Petronus felt his eyebrows rise. "Where was this crowd?"

"Caldus Bay," Neb said. "Even the Y'Zirites were there. Ships' captains, too."

What she was doing struck him, and Petronus wondered why it felt like an ambush. He said aloud without realizing it, "She is calling her people home."

"But not the way I imagined it," Neb said. "The dreams that brought us here don't speak to this."

"Because this is something new being birthed," Petronus said. And for some unexplainable reason, it felt right to him. The notion of the Marsh Queen calling out those who wished to join her for the great Homecoming. A chance to start anew in a new home. "Maybe the best dreams allow for new dreams to emerge. After all, change *is* the path life takes." He'd heard that all his life, and he'd meditated upon it as a most sacred truth for most of his adulthood.

"Yes," Neb said. "Change is the path. I think we need to change, too. I think Winters is right. This is a new home for any who would seek it."

The idea was nearly as confounding as Esarov's nonsense about democracy, and Petronus wanted to argue with Neb, tell him that it was idealistic to believe that such vastly different worldviews—vastly different cultures—could all decide simply to live together in peace. But yet it would be change—and from that change, what new life might spring forth?

Petronus looked at the scarred visage of Lasthome as it filled the sky. After millennia of self-destruction, surely it was time for something different.

Change is the path life takes. He would not be around to see the fruit from whatever tree they planted here upon the moon. *But it has to be better than what we've done before.* "So how do you propose we greet these . . . guests?"

"I think," Neb said, "we'll greet them personally and inquire of their intentions." Then he laughed. "Let's run, old man." He turned away, tugging at the fisherman's clothes as he made for the temple's hatch. He was naked by the time he entered the temple, conjuring silver robes at a whisper as Petronus tried to keep up.

They ran the temple's stairs silently with Neb in the lead. Once they left through its wide gate, they ran side by side on the trail they'd beaten down along the side of the canal. It was a familiar course and Petronus gave his feet to it, rejoicing in the wind upon his face and the air moving in and out of his lungs as his legs pumped to keep up with Neb. The sky was already gray with the light of Lasthome, dimming the stars and casting the jungle in murky twilight a full two hours before dawn.

The birds came to life, a tentative and mixed choir that faded behind them as they raced by. Occasionally a fish jumped in the canal, breaking the calm water's surface with a splash. Petronus had caught some of the fat bass that swam the canal. He'd cooked them for Nadja; they'd been sweet to the taste, and the memory of it made his stomach growl.

I need to fish more and run less. But still, he pressed on. They ran until the ships squatted before them in the water. Then they stopped and crouched in the shadows of the jungle, taking inventory of the situation.

He could see men on the decks—just the handful needed to stand watch—and no evidence that they'd come ashore here as of yet. This near, the temple loomed up ahead of them, filling the sky. They waited until about an hour before sunrise; then Neb stepped onto the shore across from the first ship and Petronus followed after.

"Hail the ship," Neb cried out with a raised hand.

There was a sudden flurry of activity as a bell rang. Men poured onto the decks of each vessel, taking up positions. Many were armed with bows or spears.

"Hail the shore," a voice finally called in reply.

Neb's voice was clear in the predawn air. "I would hold parley with your commanding officer. I will wait here on shore."

Petronus watched as a longboat was lowered and men scrambled down into it to row ashore. Sailors scrambled over the side to pull the boat onto the sand. A man and a woman—both in their late forties—stepped out together, steadied by the arms of their escort. The man wore the uniform of a naval commander, and the woman wore the robes of an Y'Zirite priestess.

"I am Sister Agnes of the Daughters of Ahm," the woman said. "This is Commander Eltara of the Y'Zirite Third Fleet. He commands the military and the vessels; I oversee the mission."

Neb inclined his head. "I am Nebios Whym. This is Father Petronus."

Their eyes widened at the mention of his name, and Petronus smiled. *They know me.* They should. His sacrifice, as the Last Son of P'Andro Whym, was a part of their gospel, enacted by Ria so long ago with one slice of her knife across his throat before she brought him coughing and sputtering back to life with her blood magicks.

"You are the Abomination," Sister Agnes said as she took Neb in. She said nothing when she looked to Petronus, but he could see her working the cipher of what exactly he had become.

"That," Neb said, "is a matter of perspective. But I prefer Neb or Lord Whym to Abomination." He smiled, but Petronus saw it was devoid of humor. "I am the steward of the temple you now approach."

The woman's own smile was cold. "We approach the Moon Wizard's Tower in the name of Lord Ahm Y'Zir. The House of Y'Zir holds claim to these lands, having been the last to vacate them."

"There is an older claim," Neb said. "They were deeded by my people to the House of Shadrus to be held in trust."

Agnes raised her eyebrows. "The House of Shadrus was incorporated into House Y'Zir millennia ago."

"Not by choice," Neb said.

"Perhaps," she said, "our respective experts in lands-right law should meet and examine these claims together?"

Neb looked around. "I think we are the only respective experts to be found in the present moment. If you would like to leave and return when you are more fully prepared, I can grant you escort to the Seaway."

The woman regarded Neb and said nothing, her tightly drawn mouth saying more than her words could have. The commander glanced at her and spoke. "Our mission is primarily one of peace and exploration," he said.

Petronus wanted to chuckle, but Neb did it first. "A false peace, to be sure," the young man said. "I've been beneath your Y'Zirite blades. They were anything but peaceful. And I spent a long winter burying the bodies at Windwir." He paused. "Still, if your mission is one of peace, lay down your arms and I will show you the Firsthome Temple."

The commander pursed his lips, considering the two of them. "Regardless of your claim," he said, "I'm not certain the two of you are sufficient to persuade us."

Neb smiled. "Then by all means, return with your law experts and we will convene a proper parley."

Eltara's face went red, and Agnes leaned over to whisper something to him. He nodded and she spoke. "We have heard of your exploits in the north, Abomination. The blood of the earth makes you strong, but not invincible."

The blood of the earth is the least of your problems, Petronus thought. Then he waited for his friend to prove it to them.

Neb

Neb watched the Y'Zirites as they watched him and pondered his words with care. There were moments—too many of them—where he felt more like the boy he had been rather than the man he was becoming. This was one of those moments, standing on the shore of a lunar canal surrounded by a jungle slowly waking to a new day.

Of course, he'd fallen hard into adulthood, reorphaned by the fall of Windwir and then slowly dragged beneath the great machine of dreams and prophecy as he discovered he was not even in the vicinity of who he'd thought he would be. He'd been young when the fire had taken his home, and he'd started down this very different path. But in those days during the War for Windwir, he'd risen to the challenge, commanding an army of gravediggers in Petronus's absence. Now, to stand beside the old Pope and confront the enemy that had brought down Windwir, he felt young indeed.

And yet the words he'd needed found him. He glanced to Petronus, then back to Commander Eltara and Sister Agnes. "I am asking you once more to reconsider," he said. "Lay down your arms and show us that you've come in peace. Or return to Y'Zir and come back with others more capable of seeing a better path than needless bloodshed."

The two of them said nothing. With a glance to their men, they turned to the longboat and walked back to it. Neb watched them row away and felt the knot in his stomach growing.

They will not leave. He wasn't certain that they would engage the two of them either, and when he saw the deckhands scrambling to raise sails and anchors, he knew their intentions. "They're going to sail on as if we aren't even here," he said.

Petronus nodded. "Yes."

Neb sighed. When he'd sunk the earlier ships there had been no conversation and very little else to make it personal. He'd even closed his eyes at the time, dropping the massive weight of his kin-dragon through the wooden ships like a boulder from the sky, never seeing the cost in human life. "I wish there was another way," he said.

He saw compassion on Petronus's face. "I wish it, too."

The ships were slowly moving now, Sister Agnes and Commander Eltara watching smugly from the bow of the last vessel.

"You should return to the temple," he told Petronus. "Have Rafe ready the ship." At the man's nod, Neb filled his lungs and summoned the kin-dragon.

It called to him from a distance as it burst up from the eastern jungle, red in the light of the rising sun. The kin-dragon's wings beat the sky as it rose and then dropped onto Neb, enfolding him and pulling him into the belly of the beast.

He felt his body become one with the dragon, felt his wings take hold as he hovered, felt his lungs filling with air that stank of salt and the myriad odors of the Y'Zirite vessels and their crew.

Neb roared and watched wide eyes go wider still at the sound of it. It was clear that the Y'Zirites had not expected this development, and he took advantage of it to launch himself upward even as their archers sent a volley of arrows toward him. They clattered off his metal skin as he climbed out of range and hovered. He positioned himself above the last vessel—the one that held the senior leaders—and then dove for it, building speed as he bent his wings and straightened his neck.

He tucked his wings in and curled himself into as tight a ball as he could just before impacting and felt the deck splinter as he broke through it with ease. Once he felt the inside of the hull, he tore into it with his claws, opening the ship up to a flood of warm salt water. Then, he pushed himself up from the wreckage to launch himself back into the air.

Neb built altitude and held, studying his handiwork. The ship sank, though it would be a shallow grave in the canal. There were bodies scattered amid the debris, more of them swimming and flailing about than not, which pleased him.

He'd not tried to speak from the kin-dragon, but now he felt compelled and cleared his voice. It was a deep bass that rumbled like thunder over the jungle.

"I do not wish to harm you further," Neb said. "The moon is closed to the Empire of Y'Zir until peace is treated for. Take your people aboard and return to the Seaway."

Neb waited and watched as the ships slowed and boats were lowered. He saw the commander pulled from the water but no sign of Sister Agnes. Already he felt remorse and hoped they were savvy enough not to press him. Surely they saw their wooden ships and wooden arrows were not going to win them any ground.

He felt the heat of the sun on his silver skin, and a shudder washed over him. Petronus had told him the story of the People, reading it to him as they walked around the temple. That he was one of them, descended from a species that had bent the universe to its whims, still astonished him. As did the magick—or what seemed it—that they took for granted. Below him, his enemies felt an astonishment of their own.

Once the two remaining ships were loaded with survivors and under way, Neb kept pace with them as they retreated. After staying with them for an hour, he swung out over the jungle and built speed for the coastline as he climbed higher into the sky. From this altitude, he could see the pillars of the Seaway in the distance and the three small specks upon the water. He'd flown over them at night, so he was confident that he'd not yet been noticed, though he'd picked them out well enough with the sharp eyes the kin-dragon afforded him. But now, Neb thought, it was time to be seen.

He approached slowly, giving the ships a wide berth as he swung around them, gliding on his wings. At night, the decks of these three had been crowded with sleeping forms, indicating that they were carrying far more people than the vessels he'd just turned away. But now in the daylight, the forms moved about, pointing and shouting to him as he passed by. And these were not predominantly military, though he saw a few uniforms scattered throughout. Of course the most distinguishing difference was the absence of the Y'Zirite flag and the presence instead of a hand-painted flag—a white tree against a dark field. Neb had not shared the dream with the others—as far as he knew, he and Amylé D'Anjite were the only two not to have experienced the dream. But he'd seen this tree on banners in Caldus Bay among those gathered to hear Winters speak.

A thought occurred to him, and he thought it again. *These are People of the Dream.* They were Winters's people and—despite not having the dream in common with them—they were his people as well.

But unlike those he'd spoken to in Caldus Bay, these had come in Y'Zirite ships. *The same dream calls them home.*

Neb matched his speed to that of the ships, flying with them as he gradually descended. Once the wind of his wings whipped at their flags and sails, he backed off to hover. The ships were overloaded and tipping as they crowded the rail to see this latest lunar wonder. All in all, Neb saw a few pikes but no bows, and none of the weapons were at the ready.

He flew ahead and rose above the bow of the first ship, feeling a kinship with them that swelled up within him. He was a child of the dreams, those he shared with Winters and those he shared with the mechoservitors. Both had carried him here, just as a new dream had carried those below him.

"The People of the Dream are welcome here," Neb cried out, his voice the roaring of many waters. "The time of Homecoming is upon us all."

There was a moment of silence, and when their cheer rose up, it deafened the cheers he'd heard in Caldus Bay and in the Ninefold

Forest. These were the heartfelt cries of people beneath the knives too long, tears streaking over the scars of the gospel carved into their flesh.

Neb saw joy upon those faces, heard it within their shouts. And relief. And hope. Unsure of what else to say, he repeated himself. "The People of the Dream are welcome here."

Then Nebios Whym turned his nose toward the Firsthome Temple and beat his wings against the morning sky.

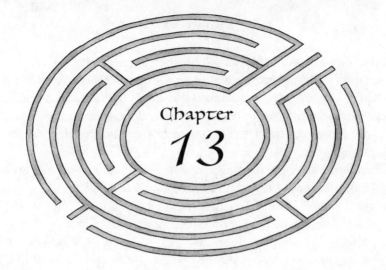

Chapter 13

Jin Li Tam

The Barrens of the Old World were eerily silent as Jin Li Tam matched her step to the line of survivors ahead and behind her. Overhead, the sun was relentless in its heat, her skin red from burns that stung by day and ached through the cool nights.

She moved slowly, head down, eyes darting left and right as she monitored a landscape that stretched flat and dark as far as she could see.

These are the ashes of the Wizard Wars.

She'd learned the stories as a child, taught of course that they were largely apocryphal. The ruins of the Old World after Raj Y'Zir's silver army laid waste to Frederico's empire. Then, according to myth, the Moon Wizard had gathered what survivors remained and led them to a new world and a new start beneath his reign and the reign of his descendants. Of course that new world had long been razed, reduced to a wasteland more habitable than this but not by much.

The person ahead of her—a woman in a torn uniform and short blond hair—stopped, and Jin Li Tam did the same at an order barked somewhere up the line in a language she did not understand.

Jin sat where she was and waited for her ration of water, trying not to lick her chapped and blistered lips.

They'd buried their dead and what of the wreckage they could. Then they had stretched out sheets of what looked and felt like metallic cloth, covering what was too large to bury. She'd watched them run wires to something akin to a sunstone buried nearby, and when those wires were attached to the cloth, it shimmered and vanished, leaving only the appearance of flat, dark ground beneath it. It was a type of scout magick, she knew, but nothing like the ones she was familiar with.

That had been four days ago, and now they moved toward an uncertain rendezvous. During that time, she'd learned what she could about the New Espirans, but that hadn't been much. The survivors, haggard from grief and fear, had been largely tight-lipped, though it was obvious that some of them understood Landlish. She knew that they were very concerned about being seen, doing their utmost to hide any evidence of the crash site while the woman who'd inherited command stood to the side, a dark stone in her fist. Jin had attempted to engage the officer repeatedly then and over the days they'd slowly traversed the wasted landscape. But the woman had offered her nothing in the way of information other than promises that her questions would be answered in due time.

Still, Pardeau's whispered words haunted her with each step and chewed at her each time they stopped. Could Jakob somehow be alive?

She'd resisted the notion for the first day, her memory flooded with that horrible night. She could still smell the smoke, could still see her father there on the rooftop as he hurled the children away and downward into the raging fire.

But by the second day beneath that blistering sun, Jin realized that the commander's last words had taken root. She had seen what her father had wanted her to see. He'd seeded her fears and told her exactly what he intended to do in his earlier encounter with her in the aether.

Of course it wasn't the first time House Li Tam had used misdirection and fear to bend perceptions in favor of their work. And of all the children of House Li Tam, Vlad was the master of such manipulations.

He'd tried to tell her so just before she fell upon him with her knives. *Things are not as they seem.*

By the third day, Jin Li Tam was convinced of the ruse. It had all the sensibilities of a Tam strategy. The only way to eradicate the Y'Zirite threat was to undermine the one thing it needed to maintain its power over people and motivate blind obedience.

Their faith.

Her father had done great damage prior to his attack on the palace. He'd incited terror with his plagues and fires, reducing the population and destabilizing the government. But to destroy a faith, Jin realized, you had to destroy the objects of that faith. Take away that which was believed upon and hoped in and the rest would fall into chaos, anarchy and despair.

Even me.

And it appeared to have worked. But it brought forward another question to perplex her here on the fourth day.

Vlad's plan was dependent upon everyone's belief—including and especially hers—that the Child of Promise and the Crimson Empress were dead. And the easiest way to assure that belief was to actually go through with their murder. Anything else was to risk discovery and unravel whatever other plans Vlad Li Tam had for the Empire of Y'Zir.

And yet he concocted a clever bit of misdirection instead. Why?

Vlad Li Tam had used his children, his nephews and his nieces, his entire family as weapons and tools in whatever work he deemed necessary in the Named Lands. The lives of two small children were nothing to him in the greater scheme of his perceived higher good.

Why had he spared them?

Perhaps, she thought, he was changing. Certainly the events of the last few years had changed the course of her own river. The desolation of Windwir and everything that followed were as transformative as they were traumatic.

She looked up and down the line and drank the last of her water ration, then stood when the others stood behind and before her. Jin felt the ache of too many leagues in her feet and knees, and felt the blistering sun upon her face and neck.

They shuffled off northward, and once again she fell into the rhythm of one foot before the other, her mind once more working the Whymer Maze of her circumstances.

They'd marched two hours when movement on the horizon ahead brought them to a halt. She shielded her eyes from the setting sun and watched a single figure moving toward them at impossible speed.

"Lady Tam." She took her eyes off the movement and met those of the woman who'd taken over command. It was the first time the woman had addressed her in four days.

Her eyes went back to the approaching runner. "Yes?"

"You will be going on ahead of us," she said. "And I am now authorized to tell you that your son—as well as several members of your family and First Captain Aedric—await you beyond Endicott Station."

Even though she'd spent days pondering the possibility, the sudden assurance from this woman that Jakob lived rocked her back on her heels and brought about a sob she could not contain.

The woman placed a hand upon her shoulder. "I'm sorry I could not answer your questions earlier. I was under orders until your safety could be assured."

Jin looked to the single figure rapidly closing the distance between them. "You're sending me ahead with one man, and that assures my safety?"

The commander shook her head. "Not a man."

She squinted at it and now saw the fine dark cloud of dust that rose behind it as it moved. She'd seen a similar loping run before, and when the last of the setting sun reflected off a metal surface, she understood. "A mechoservitor."

"Yes. An automaton. You will be safe in its care."

Jin nodded. As it drew closer, she saw that it was a twin to the Watcher, though it was a dull silver and showed less age and wear than its dark, time-pitted cousin.

The metal man stopped, looming above them, and the commander whispered something into the black stone she held.

"Lady Tam," the mechoservitor said in a low voice as it inclined its head. "I am to bear you to Endicott Station."

She was so used to interacting with Isaak that she instinctively inclined her own head. "Thank you." She looked to the woman now. "What about the rest of you?"

"The rescue party is two days out. The council wants you out of harm's way as soon as possible."

Jin nodded. The mechoservitor turned and stooped, exposing its back to her. She climbed on and felt its hands slip back to grip her legs as she clutched to the cold metal neck. "Be safe," she said over her shoulder.

But any reply was lost as the metal man lurched into an awkward run that steadied as it built speed. Soon, they moved at top speed across the wasteland as the sky went dark periwinkle and the first of the moon spilled its eerie light upon the ashes of the world.

My son is still alive, Jin Li Tam thought.

And that thought banished the aching from her bones, transformed the desolation that surrounded her, weighed upon her, into an unexpected oasis of grace and peace.

Rudolfo

Wet ferns slapped at Rudolfo's buckskinned legs as he ran the forest. To his left and right, the soft clicks of the Delta scouts marked their formation. He ran unmagicked for a change, enjoying a break from the nausea and vertigo that the scout powders still gave him.

As he ran, he thought about Sister Tamray and her screams.

It had taken a few days for Physician Benoit to break the woman, but he had. And Rudolfo, of course, had been there for it. They'd kept her hidden away, stockpiling enough untainted water to keep her alive indefinitely. And though Benoit and the Gypsy King had both questioned her, they'd expected little intelligence. The salted knives would cut nothing useful from her already scarred flesh.

But when Benoit had begun peeling away the words of her gospel, something had snapped within her.

Before Windwir, Rudolfo had—like his father before him—frequently sat in to observe the Physicians of Penitent Torture at their work. After Windwir and after what the Y'Zirite knives had already cut from the world, he'd dismantled Tormentor's Row, using its stones as part of the new library.

But this time, there was nothing redemptive, nothing penitent, about the act. For her, at least. He sat and watched, merely waiting for her to feel the blade the way he had felt every blade since the days of his earliest memory. And for Rudolfo, it had become an act of almost worship.

Finally, she had screamed, and the sound of it was like a hymn in the basement corner where they'd put the Physician's table and knives. Rudolfo smiled at the memory of it.

Ahead, he heard a low whistle and slowed as the magicked escort around him matched his stride. A group of figures separated from the deeper shadows of the forest.

"Hail, Rudolfo," a gruff voice called.

"Hail, Orius," he answered.

The general had aged in the years since Rudolfo had seen him, but he felt the strength in the man's grip as they clasped hands. "It is good to see you, General."

The old Gray Guard inclined his head and winked with his single eye. "And you as well, General."

Rudolfo smiled at the use of his military title. "I take it your venture was successful?"

Orius nodded. "Aye. I'll show you." He turned, and Rudolfo followed him as the Gray Guard fell in around them. He heard the clicking as his scouts took up positions farther out and was surprised when he had to work to keep up with the Androfrancine. "It was simple to take the estate with the leadership neutralized."

They broke into the clearing, and Rudolfo saw the outbuildings and main house of another Entrolusian estate—this one commandeered by the military to billet officers fresh to the front from Y'Zir.

The bodies of fallen Y'Zirites scattered the grounds, and soldiers of the Gray Guard moved among them. Orius and his entourage moved past them and climbed the wide steps to the main doors. They toured the building quickly, and Rudolfo felt astonishment and delight warring for dominance over his mood as he tallied the bodies.

"The pathogen," Orius said as he used his boot to turn the body of an Y'Zirite captain, "took out all of their officers and Blood Guard along with some of their infantry. They were truly a headless snake."

Rudolfo released his held breath, remembering the banquet not so many days past. "Gods," he said. "What a weapon."

Orius nodded. "I wish we had more tricks in our arsenal, but I think it will suffice."

More. Rudolfo's eyes narrowed at this. "I can't imagine needing more."

Orius met his eyes briefly and said nothing. But the moment was enough to bring Isaak's warning about the man to mind. Still, it was difficult for Rudolfo to be overly concerned. He'd come here fresh from the first screams of his captive. He'd had little sympathy for the Y'Zirites before the kin-raven arrived. Since its dark message, he had none at all and relished the blades that would cut Y'Zir from his world. And when he was finished here, if the old man still lived, Rudolfo would find Vlad Li Tam and do what he should've done that day beside the bonfire of his family's secret histories.

"A stronger arsenal is usually more prudent than less," the Androfrancine general said. "But I think this war is nearly won." His eyes took on a softer tone. "Though I am sorry for what it has cost you."

Yes. Rudolfo tasted the bitterness in his reply. "It's cost us all far too much, General."

They moved through the house, finally settling into a parlor off the kitchen that had been cleared of bodies. Hot chai awaited on a small table nestled between the chairs. Renard waited in one of them and stood as they approached.

At a nod from Orius they all sat.

"I've word from Lysias and Philemus," Rudolfo said. "They are rendezvousing near Windwir."

"Have you given thought to strategy?"

Rudolfo took a mug and sipped from it. "If we've truly severed the snake's head, it's only a matter of cleanup."

"Yes," Orius said. "We've contacted resistance leaders in Turam and on the Emerald Coasts. We're also coordinating with Esarov on the Delta. Between those scattered resources, my Gray Guard remnant, and your Wandering Army, we should be able to put down the remaining stray Y'Zirite dogs." He unrolled a map and moved the kettle and mugs around on the table until it fit. Then he pointed. "Pylos is our biggest problem."

Rudolfo nodded. The entire nation had been slaughtered when the Y'Zirites unleashed plague spiders upon them, fulfilling yet more of their dark prophecies. Open land with cities and towns and farms completely depopulated and ready for new occupants. It had become the logical foothold for the invasion and was a wide-open space where Y'Zirites could hide. "I concur. The Divided Isle will also be difficult."

Renard spoke up now. "I've been in contact with Countess Merrique, and she is confident that they'll be successful with minimal assistance from the mainland forces." He tapped the city of Merrique on the map and inclined his head toward Rudolfo. "And she says you gave them quite a leg up before you left."

It felt like forever ago. But Rudolfo, for the third time in his life, was faced with a moment against which he measured the flow of time. It had been the day his parents died. And then the day Windwir fell. And for a brief time, the day his son was born. But now, he marked the time by the day he heard his wife's voice first slipping from the kin-raven's open beak.

Rudolfo, my love.

He closed his eyes and forced his attention back to the men he sat with. Orius had just finished speaking and was looking at him expectantly.

"I'm sorry," Rudolfo said. Then he sipped his chai. "I was preoccupied."

Orius offered a smile that looked too fierce to be reassuring. "Dark times, General. But I was inquiring about your plans for the Wandering Army once they rendezvous with Lysias? Would the Foresters be up for cleaning out Pylos?"

Rudolfo had pondered the same question over the last few nights when he wasn't thinking about his prisoner. Or his son. "I believe we would be up to the task, General."

Orius gave him a hard look. "No prisoners. And no retreat to Y'Zir."

The steel in that single eye resonated with Rudolfo. Isaak was right to keep the spell from his hands. That weapon did not have the precision of a blade held in skilled hands. "No prisoners," he agreed, "and no retreat."

Orius dug into his tunic and pulled out a flask. He opened it and poured a healthy amount into his chai. He held it out to Rudolfo, and for the first time in a while, the Gypsy King had absolutely no interest in it. He did not need it to cut the edge of his pain, knew from that abandoned path that it couldn't ever do more than dull it. And with it, dull the edge that made him sharp.

Instead, Rudolfo rested his hand upon the pommel of his knife and meditated upon the new path and new cutting ahead.

Vlad Li Tam

The small enclave at the base of the Y'Zirite crèche's impenetrable southern mountain range looked deserted from the air as the kin-dragon approached. They'd flown less than an hour, covering the leagues quickly while Vlad Li Tam watched the landscape roll by with wonder and nausea.

The Y'Zirite lands were not nearly as verdant as the Named Lands, and with the dragon's nose, Vlad had taken in the aroma of unfamiliar flora and fauna for league upon league. Y'Zir's larger population put more strain upon the resources available, giving them much larger cities and towns and a highly industrialized agricultural system to keep people fed.

Of course, he'd also taken in the plague fires and the smell of burning flesh on the outskirts of those cities. And inwardly, he'd smiled at each of the smoking pyres they'd passed.

Now, as Amylé held them in place, hovering above the convent, Vlad studied the buildings below.

The convent was nestled against the side of the mountain and walled off with a single approach, much like the Papal Summer Palace, though this place had none of the pomp and splendor of the Andro-francines' colors of kin-clave.

It appears abandoned, Amylé's voice spoke into his head.

Yes, he agreed. There hadn't been enough time for a kin-raven, and to his knowledge, their casting in the aether—even using a chain of casters to cover the range—would take time to go this far. If they had been warned, it was recently. *Can we land?*

She didn't answer. Instead, she blinked, and a silver sheen fell over Vlad's vision as she swept the area again with the kin-dragon's eyes. *She's looking for Blood Guard,* Vlad realized. She sniffed the air again, and Vlad felt the dragon's lungs filling. *I would pick up the scent if they were hiding in the buildings,* she said. Then the dragon's head tipped as she listened. Nothing.

She slowed their wings and let them drop slowly, all the while turning the beast's head and snout this way and that to scan the ground below. They settled onto the ground, and Vlad felt a moment of vertigo as everything went white. Then he found himself standing in the courtyard next to Amylé D'Anjite. He could feel the wind of the kin-dragon's wings behind him as it lifted off to hover overhead.

Vlad tapped the staff once upon the ground to amplify his voice. "You know why I am here. Do not make me come find you," he called out. His words echoed out across the small square and between the scattered buildings. They were simple structures made of stone and undecorated with the courtyard and its single well in common between them. He could pick out the blood shrine and the kitchen and armory and had to assume the other buildings were administrative space, barracks and living quarters. The stable, near the gate, appeared empty.

Vlad looked to Amylé. It was the first time he'd seen her face since she'd killed Xhum's escort. He could see the lines of worry and exhaustion in her face and eyes. He'd sent his children in to kill or be killed many times, but they'd spent a lifetime being shaped and sharpened for their roles. He'd only had days with this girl, and she'd had no training. Her sharpening had been rushed. "How are you? After . . ." He searched for the right word. "After events at the palace?"

Her eyes met his. "I do not like how I feel, Lord Tam. But I'm the daughter of a captain. I grew up with the military, following him from post to post, before he hid me away near the end of the war." Those blue eyes narrowed, and the silver robes she wore started to constrict and shine brighter. "I know how my father felt about Y'Zir and what he did to my people on the moon when he took the Firsthome Temple. . . . What he did to my father. What his children and children's children have wrought here." She stretched out a hand and ran a finger along one of Vlad's thousand scars. "What they've done to you and your family and to themselves with their knives and their faith." She dropped her hand and looked away. "I do not like how I feel, but I do not need to. I need to honor my House and finish this war once and for all."

Good. A river bent. And if that somehow changed, he had the other one tucked away. But he knew bringing her forward would likely be the end of him. *And everyone else.* He offered her a weak smile. "Agreed. We will honor our Houses together then."

"But," she said, "I don't know anything about this spellbook you seek. When I met Nebios he went on about Moon Wizards and ladders and towers. I told him there was no such thing."

"I suspect you'll know it when you see it," Vlad said. He held up the staff. "Just like you knew this was the administrator's rod for the Firsthome Temple and not the staff of a Moon Wizard."

"Yes. But first we must find it."

The kin-dragon hovered above them, its wings gusting the courtyard. Vlad walked to the well and checked its bucket. It was wet. "They've not been gone long."

But where? They'd kept an eye out as they approached and had seen no sign of anyone on foot or mounted for hundreds of leagues. And if they'd been warned, it couldn't have been too long ago. Which meant they were hiding nearby.

Someplace the dragon cannot smell them. Unless the Y'Zirites had some magick for masking scent. Certainly if word had reached them, then it had also warned them about the beast that carried them. Vlad looked to Amylé. "Could they be underground?"

She nodded. "They could be in the Beneath Places," she said. "The hatches are airtight."

"Then we search the buildings for a hatch."

They split up and took a building at a time. Vlad started with what appeared to be an administrative center while Amylé approached the armory. He went through the building office by office, the staff giving him a light that pulsed in time to the headache that grew behind his eyes.

Even the slightest use hurts me now.

Vlad wasted no time, peering into each office and mentally measuring the space to identify any rooms that might be closed off or tucked behind hidden doors. He turned carpets but didn't expect he would find anything there. He couldn't imagine anyone staying behind to cover a hatch back up.

He exited the building through another door and found himself next within a barracks attached to a small armory. He started with the armory, the lock breaking off at a touch from the staff that made him wince.

The weapons and armor racks were empty, as was the smaller case he suspected held their blood magick phials. He gave the rest of the room a cursory glance and then entered the barracks. The beds were scattered with various bits of clothing and gear that had been left behind in a hasty packing process, giving him more of the puzzle. They had prioritized weapons and armor over their clothing and field gear. A low whistle from outside turned him back to the door.

Amylé waited across the courtyard. "The food in the galley is still warm, and there were pipes in the blood shrine that led to a basement. I think our hatch is there."

Yes. It made sense if they were mixing human blood with the blood of the earth. The same way they had concocted the cure for his grandson and Petronus's resurrection from the dead. And brewed their deadly scout magicks, the blood making them far more powerful than the powders taken from the earth. Blood distilleries meant access to a bargaining pool.

Vlad moved across the courtyard to join her. "They've not been gone long. And they're well-armed."

The thin sheath of silver that covered her brightened, and Vlad felt the heat of it. "So are we," Amylé D'Anjite said.

He followed her into the blood shrine and stopped abruptly as a sudden wave of terror and despair struck him.

It is the first time I've seen a cutting table since Ria.

The last time he'd seen one, he'd been on it. And he'd watched his family die one by one, hearing the last words that they cried out to him from beneath their blades, each of them dying while honoring him. He stifled a sob and felt a wave of nausea strike him.

Amylé reached out to steady him. "Are you okay?"

He could not take his eyes off the table. But he also could not answer. His voice would not obey him. Instead, he shook off her hand and pushed his way into the shrine. He forced his eyes away and to the door just past it. Amylé overtook him and went through first. "The stairs are here."

The pipes were there, too, running down along the staircase she approached. He stretched out a tentative hand and touched one, expecting it to be warm.

It was cold.

Vlad sighed. *I will turn my pain into an army.*

The basement contained cells and more cutting tables, along with all of the equipment necessary. The door she'd found was set into a wall that accessed an area beyond the shrine above. It was locked by key, but at a nod from Vlad, Amylé kicked it in with ease.

The dark tunnel stretched back into the mountain, and they followed it lit by the dim shine of Amylé's silver suit. At the end of the corridor, Vlad saw the hatch. The cipher on it was similar to a Rufello lock but older and much larger.

"How do we open it?" Amylé asked.

Vlad closed his eyes and gripped the staff. It hummed in his hand, and as it built in pitch, he touched the tip of it to the lock. *Open.*

He opened his eyes.

Nothing. Vlad drew in a deep breath and held it. "Open," he shouted.

Then he brought the staff down hard upon it. The metal flashed bright enough to blind him, and a roar filled the tunnel as the hatch collapsed upon itself and fell in smoldering, white-hot pieces. Farther below, he heard screams and smiled.

"It seems they were waiting for us," he said.

"Let's not disappoint them," Amylé said.

The smile on her face and the heat rising from her body in waves made Vlad shudder. Either he'd not buried the raging old woman deep enough, or he had brought this out in her. Neither option pleased him. Still, Vlad Li Tam stood back and let her descend the ladder first. And he did not hurry when he heard the sounds of battle below. He needed her strong and confident, and he knew the blood would give her that.

Because she is part of my army now.

Still, as he climbed down after her clutching at his staff, Vlad Li Tam wondered what he was awakening within this girl and whether or not even that tool of the parents would be enough to contain her once she came fully into her own.

Chapter
14

Marta

The field was white with seed beneath a summer sun, and Marta stood with her father and mother and brother, laughing together as if they'd not been together in a long while. Isaak was there, too. And others she did not recognize but knew she should.

She opened her mouth to ask her mother how the market at Windwir was and then closed it when she felt the world shake. She waited and noted something was different.

We've stopped moving.

Marta sat up, the sound of laughter still ringing in her ears. She blinked into the dim red light of her cabin and climbed to her feet. They were unsteady now that Behemoth was no longer moving after so long traveling at top speed. She'd kept her pack ready and slept with her boots on since they'd entered the canal. And her training with Ire paid off now as she moved faster than a rabbit out into the corridor, still buckling on her knife belt and its pouch of bullets for her sling.

It could already be too late. She knew Isaak intended to prevent her from following him, though she had no idea what form that might take. She only knew that she had to be quicker.

The hatch at the end of the hallway stood open, and Ire Li Tam waited there. She raced to her. "Where's Isaak?"

Ire nodded beyond the hatch. "He's out there. He's waiting to talk with you."

Marta slowed at the news as her fear of being abandoned was suddenly replaced by butterflies. She looked through the hatch. "What does he want to talk to me about?"

Ire's green eyes met hers. "I suspect he's going to ask you to stay here. It's what he asked me."

"And you're staying?"

Ire looked away. "I will not be accompanying him. He says he needs to go alone."

"But you swore your blades to—"

Ire Li Tam cut her off quickly. "Regardless." The tone was sharp enough the Marta closed her open mouth. "Now go talk with him."

Marta swallowed and forced her feet to carry her through the hatch and into Behemoth's open mouth. Beyond the jagged teeth, she saw the dim light of morning. Isaak stood in his robe, his red eyes sharp and clear.

"Hello, little hu—" Isaak interrupted himself. "Hello, Marta."

She inclined her head and approached, wading into the water. "Isaak. What are you doing?"

"I'm going to take the staff from Vlad Li Tam and return it to the tower." Something whispered beneath his metal skin, and his eyes dimmed briefly. "I know you wish to come with me, and I told you I would prevent you."

Marta waited. When he didn't continue, she released an exasperated breath. "And will you?"

He shook his head. "I won't. But I will tell you this: I do not want you to come with me. I want you to stay with Ire Li Tam." He took a tentative step toward her. "The second gift given is difficult at times. For you, it creates the need to be near me and to not let me face Lord Tam alone. For me, it creates the need to protect you from the very real danger that I know he is." The metal man sighed. Whenever he did, it touched something in her, and this time it made her want to suddenly cry. Again, Isaak paused.

"It's because we love each other," she finally said.

He looked down at her. "It is." Now he crouched so that he was suddenly eye level with her. "And I am not going to prevent you from coming with me. But I am going to ask you, because we love each other, to please stay with Ire Li Tam. When I am finished with Lord Tam I will return, and we will rendezvous with Nebios Whym."

Marta blinked at the tears. The morning her mother left for Windwir suddenly ambushed her. "But what if you *don't* come back?"

"If I don't come back, then you certainly would not have survived coming with me," Isaak said. "And I will have ceased to function knowing that I kept you safe."

She met his eyes and then looked out into the gloom. In the distance she saw the lights of what she assumed was the city of Ahm's Glory. Then she looked down. "Okay," she said.

Isaak's metal hands settled onto her shoulders. "Thank you," he said.

She looked up and wiped her nose. "But you better come back."

Isaak nodded. "I will." Then he rose to full height and turned for the edge of the mouth and the wooden dock just beyond it.

The weight of the conversation struck Marta, and her fear was different now—grounded in something she could count on now as true. *Because we love each other.* And so she could honor his first gift with her second, and he could do the same.

She watched him climb up onto the dock and set out for the city. He was lost in the darkness when she turned to the hatch. Ire stood in its red light, two packs in her hands. "Is he gone?"

She nodded. "But I thought we—"

"He asked you to stay with me. Correct?"

"Yes, but—"

Ire splashed into the water and crossed to the teeth. "So then stay with me." Then she hopped lightly out and onto the dock. "Quickly."

Marta let Ire help her over the teeth and onto the abandoned dock. Then she strapped on the pack that the Blood Scout handed her. When she finished, she made sure her knife and sling were both within easy reach.

Ire pulled out a small pouch and a steel phial from her pack. "Look at these. Do you know what they are?"

Marta shook her head.

She held up the phial. "These are blood magicks. They will kill you. You would have needed to start building a tolerance to them years ago to use these magicks now." Then she held up the pouch. "These are scout powders. Too many of them will kill you, too, but with small doses now you can begin to build tolerance and practice using them." Then she drew a silk thread with a loop from beneath the sleeve of her shirt. "This is a running line." She slipped it over the girl's hand and pulled it tight. "Do you understand?"

Marta nodded.

Ire Li Tam shook a tiny amount of the powder into the palm of her hand. "Open your mouth and put out your tongue."

She did as she was told, wincing at the bitterness of the powder as Ire placed a pinch of it onto her tongue.

"Swallow that." As Marta did, Ire wet her thumb and used it to dab the powder onto the girl's forehead.

Marta felt her stomach twist as vertigo made her light-headed. She felt a sudden strength surge through her as her nostrils and ears flooded with distant smells and sounds. The darkness brightened a bit, and she realized that she was panting.

"It's okay," Ire said. "Breathe." The Blood Guard took in a deep breath and then released it. "Like this. Breathe."

Marta breathed. Finally she held up her hands. She could not see them. "I'm . . . magicked."

"Just like a Gypsy Scout," Ire said.

"How long will it last?"

Ire was fading now, too, as the powders from her hand did their work. She licked the remainder and was gone. "About an hour. So let's make the most of it." Then she tugged at the lead-line. "Are you ready to run?"

"Aye," Marta said.

She could smell smoke from the city that burned ahead of them, and in that smoke, she smelled death. But Marta was not afraid. Fueled by love and magicks, she stretched out her legs and ran faster than she had ever run before.

Neb

The moon rose slowly over the Desolation of Windwir, and Neb sat on the overlook and watched it. This was the place he'd stood and felt the racking pain of a city's death. It had turned his hair white and tangled his tongue up in the random words of P'Andro Whym for a time. It had brought him to Winters and to the dreaming.

And everyone else.

He wasn't sure why he'd come here. There was so much to do, so many things to check on. Petronus was preparing for the arrival of pilgrims and already busy assigning housing in the vastly spacious Firsthome Temple. The New Espirans, to Neb's knowledge, remained aloof and simply observed. And here, on Lasthome, Winters had been clear about where she felt his focus should be.

Getting the staff from Tam. Agreement or no, he needed it and she was right. It was time to stop the bloodshed both here and in Y'Zir.

And keep an eye on the pilgrims bound for their new home. He'd come in over the horn to check progress and was pleased to see vessels sailing for the rendezvous. Farther north, he flew over the campfires of the Marshers and Tam survivors who moved south through the Churning Wastes, shepherded by mechoservitors, carrying what they owned upon their backs as they set out for their long-promised home.

And as he saw from the abandoned Y'Zirite camp below, there was also a war to finish and a home to rebuild.

Neb sighed and shifted his position against the tree.

He was quiet for a time, listening to the silence and watching his breath upon the air.

He must have slept, because when he opened his eyes, the world had changed. It was a bright second summer day, and the city on the plains below thrived with life. He could hear the buzz of it from here. On the Third River, ships bobbed at the docks. The colors of kinclave flew over the city, and Neb's breath caught at the sight of it.

"I come here to remember how it was," a reedy voice said behind him.

He turned and looked. It was Isaak, but not the newer version Winters had told him about. It was the Isaak he remembered first meeting, with his damaged leg and his Androfrancine robes. A gout of steam hissed from the mechoservitor's exhaust grate. Neb looked back to the city. "How is it . . . ?" He couldn't finish the sentence.

"We are in the aether. My use of the dreamstone seems to have connected me to it, and I am able to project much farther in the aether than anticipated." The mechoservitor paused, its eye-shutters flashing open and closed. "But we cannot stay long. The aether is monitored."

Neb's eyes narrowed. "Where are you, Isaak?"

Isaak stretched out a hand and put it on Neb's shoulder. "It is not necessary for you to know where I am," he said. But his metal fingers, pressed lightly into his skin, said otherwise. *I intend to recover the staff from Lord Tam. Your assistance may be required.*

He had reached Ahm's Glory, then. The sigh Neb released was louder than he expected. "I will reach you by dawn," he said.

Neb sat up, shivering in the dark, and climbed to his feet. The city

was gone now, and its snow-covered grave stretched out below, interrupted only by the Y'Zirite camp and the scaffolding and dirt piles of
their excavation. He turned his back and slipped under the cover of
the evergreens.

The kin-dragon was waiting for him in the clearing where he'd left
it, and Neb clucked his tongue at it. He'd spent nearly all of his time
in the beast these days, and he wondered if he shouldn't name it. He
shrugged the sentimentality aside as it reared up on its hind legs and
exposed its stomach to Neb. He let the creature encircle him with its
forelegs and draw Neb into itself. He felt the heat and closed his eyes
against the flash of light, opening them slowly as he adjusted to the
sudden change in his body. He flexed the wings and then flapped them
against the night air.

It was time to return to Y'Zir and join Isaak. Together, they should
be able to get the staff away from Tam. But first Neb needed to even
up his chances. When he launched himself skyward, it was not to the
southeast in the direction of Y'Zir but to the northeast in the direction of Rudolfo's Seventh Forest Manor and the library he built there.

Neb stayed low and built speed quickly, not caring if he was seen
as he sped across the forested hills and then the open snow-sweep of
the Prairie Sea. He found the manor quickly and had the kin-dragon
drop him in the forest to the west of it. Then he found the trail he'd
walked back in the days before Sethbert's trial.

Have this destroyed, Petronus had told him, handing over the cloth-
wrapped item. But Neb hadn't. Instead, he'd buried it. And now he
looked for the rock he'd used to mark its resting place two springs
behind him.

It wasn't as easy in the dark and snow, but he found the tree he'd
placed it near and from there, heated the silver suit he wore until the
ground around him grew spongy and snow began to melt.

He found the stone and dug up the hand cannon that was wrapped
in oilcloth and buried beneath it.

Then Neb called down his dragon and had it take him the short
hop to Library Hill, aware of third alarm being whistled beneath him
as he flashed past the lights of Rudolfo's manor.

He landed in the library's courtyard and exited the kin-dragon before the dumbstruck guards could magick themselves. Neb raised his
hands. "Stand down," he said. "It's Nebios ben Hebda." He gave his
former name by instinct and then corrected himself. "Nebios Whym."
He paused. The guards were already slowing. "The Homeseeker."

"Homefinder," a metallic voice said from the library's porch.

Neb looked up. The forest guards, knives drawn, looked as well. "Brother Hezekiah?"

The mechoservitor clanked forward. "No. My designation is Malachi, formerly Mechoservitor Four. I have stayed behind with two of my brothers to oversee the library in Hezekiah's absence."

Neb walked toward the stairs. "I need your help. Is Brother Charles's workshop still functional?"

The metal man nodded. An officer of the Gypsy Scouts approached, and Neb turned to him. "Good evening, Captain. I apologize for my sudden appearance."

The man's eyes were wide at the massive beast that crouched behind Neb. Neb was certain that they'd seen nothing like it. "Lieutenant Nebios? Ornys told me you'd paid us a visit a few nights back. The Marshers were singing about it all the way out of town."

Neb offered him a weak smile. "I resigned my commission to pursue the dream," he said. "I'm here on urgent business." He added the next words because there was no reason not to. "From the moon."

The officer looked up, then back to the dragon. "We'll surely not keep you."

The guards fell back, and Neb approached the mechoservitor. He carefully unwrapped the package. "Do you know what this is?"

The mechoservitor lifted the weapon up and turned it over in its metal hands. "I do."

"Can you make it operational and instruct me in its use and loading?"

Malachi clicked something on the weapon, and it came apart in two pieces. "Yes," the metal man said. "I suspect I can. Let's go to Father's workshop and see if everything I need is there." The mechoservitor glanced at the kin-dragon. "I may require blast powder."

"I can get you whatever you need," Neb said. "But I need this by morning."

The mechoservitor inclined its head. "Yes, Lord Whym."

Then it turned and reentered the library, waiting for Neb to follow just inside the open door.

When Neb entered, he felt the soft carpet upon his feet and a warm blast of air that smelled like paper. He closed his eyes against it and gulped it in as the door closed behind him. He opened them and took in the foyer. There were portraits here of Rudolfo and Jin Li Tam, along with glass cases containing artifacts from the age of the Androfrancine

Order. He wanted to linger here, because the last time he'd visited, they were just finishing the basements and still hauling in the timber and stones for the main buildings. It had been a muddy hill.

Still, Malachi's long legs moved quickly, and Neb left the foyer behind for the first massive room. It was lined with shelves, each crammed full of books that were still so new they'd barely been opened.

Again the desire to stay was strong, but he forced himself to keep up with Malachi. When the metal man stopped suddenly, Neb stumbled into his back. He felt the sudden heat of steam as it released from the exhaust grate.

"It occurs to me, Lord Whym, that this is the first time you have seen our work here in the Ninefold Forest."

"It is," Neb said.

"Perhaps you would like to look around while I inventory supplies and determine what is required to restore the hand cannon? I can find you when I know exactly what I need and when it can be ready."

Neb looked at the hand cannon and then to the books. He would be useless in the workshop, and the smell of paper was overpowering. Intoxicating in its sudden comfort.

It reminds me of home. He'd grown up in the Great Library. And nights after a day full of fear and panic, he dreamed of those days. Of the feel of a book in his hands and the smell of its pages in his nose.

He stretched out a finger to touch a spine. It was Arch-Behaviorist Lemuire's *On Y'Zirite Resurgence*, a classic he'd read in school. Neb turned to the mechoservitor and inclined his head. "Thank you, Malachi. I would like that very much."

"Pull down anything you want," Malachi said. "We have aides who will shelve them in the morning."

Neb smiled, remembering that work himself. Then he wandered the rows and lost himself in all of the words. It was much smaller than the library it tried to live up to, but it was still easily the largest repository of knowledge in the Named Lands.

And elsewhere, Neb knew, there were other repositories. The New Espirans had spent millennia in hiding, gathering knowledge and prepping seedlings for a library he had yet to explore—the Library of Elder Days—in the Firsthome Temple.

It's . . . the light. No, Neb thought. It really wasn't. But it reflected the light like a mirror. And after so much dark, Neb was ready for this reminder of why they pressed forward.

Of why I am having a weapon repaired so that I can kill a man and take something away from him.

Neb shuddered and took down another book, much preferring its weight and balance in his palm to that of the Androfrancine hand cannon.

Then, for a time, he lost himself in words there in that place of light. But Nebios Whym knew all the while that darkness awaited him and that soon enough he must return to it.

Winters

It is hard to awaken after so long asleep.

The voice drifted to her in a dark, warm place, and Winters thought at first that the voice referred to her. And she suspected that indeed she *was* sleeping, though when she opened her eyes against the dark there was only more darkness there. Darkness and the voice.

But they tell me that the way to the moon is open, and I can feel the Seaway's engine pulsing in my veins.

Winters opened her mouth to speak, but no words came out. Furrowing her brow, she pushed the words out from her like a prayer. *Who are you?*

I am the Grandmother. Bring them to the dream, Child.

Winters closed her eyes. *Where are we?*

We are in the World-womb.

World-womb? Winters tried to move but found she couldn't. Every muscle was suffused with a liquid warmth that pulsed through her. *I do not understand.*

Winters felt the Grandmother's chuckle like a ripple in the warmth. *No. And I've forgotten most of it. Imagine waking up and discovering you are older than anyone who ever went before you?* Then the voice took on a note of sadness. *And discovering that you can no longer remember those who came before. Or even those who came with.*

Winters floated silently in that place and felt the questions growing even as sleep pulled at her. The voice was distant now, and she was suddenly aware of the cold.

Bring them to the dream, Child of Shadrus.

She opened her eyes with the words still echoing in her mind. Then she rubbed her face and blinked into the predawn gloom. "I'm trying to," she said. The voice had become stronger, and now it was in her dreams more frequently.

Winters crawled out of her bedroll and dug her coat from the bottom of it. Then she pulled on her boots and climbed down from the covered wagon parked by the side of the road. She picked her way around the water-filled ruts, slipping in the mud as she made her way for the fire where the Y'Zirite soldiers gathered. Erys had sent her with some of her lowest-ranking infantry. The lieutenant claimed she needed her others elsewhere, but Winters was convinced it was another evidence of the woman's unwillingness to hold her prisoner.

Hebda and Tertius waited there, too. Hebda was crouched over a kettle pouring chai. She'd thought about sending them around the horn with the ships but was still not confident of what to do with them. Hebda's—and the Order's—manipulation of Neb along with Tertius's secret assignment for the Office for the Preservation of the Light while serving as her tutor represented a way of doing things that was untenable. They'd proven her concerns justifiable yet again when they'd protested her invitation to Erys.

Still, she'd pressed the woman, knowing the Androfrancine weapon would kill her as surely as it had killed her superiors at Rudolfo's Markday Feast. "Bring down the Y'Zirite flag," she'd told her. "Release your soldiers to make their own choices and meet me on the moon."

The lieutenant had smiled. "You are persistent. And you know nothing about me."

"I know enough," Winters said. She wished she could grab her by the shoulders, shake her, and tell her that she would be dead in days if she did not listen. But Winters, as much as she hated the death that was coming, understood that it was necessary for those they left behind. *Because only some will reach for this new dream.* So instead, she met the woman's eyes. "And I know a better life awaits you there than here," she finally said.

"You may be right," the woman said. And then she'd sent them off with a wave into the early morning.

Now Winters picked her way to a place at the fire and took the steaming metal cup Hebda pushed into her hands. "How did you sleep?"

She sipped the hot chai. "I'm dreaming still."

Tertius looked up at this. "That is . . . unusual."

Winters pushed aside the guilt that mumbled at her. "I should be writing them down." After a lifetime of dreaming and carefully recording those dreams, it seemed foreign not to.

The old scholar cleared his voice. "Are they about the moon?"

Winters shook her head. "No. I don't think so. There is a voice. Someone called the Grandmother. But she mentioned the Seaway."

They glanced at the Y'Zirite soldiers. One appeared to be dozing in his armor. The other was either disinterested in their conversation or couldn't understand it. Neither of them spoke much Landlish.

"They could just be dreams," Hebda said. "You've been under a great deal of stress."

She smiled at him and took another sip from the chai. "I don't know what I would do if suddenly I just dreamed normal dreams."

Tertius chuckled. "Aye. That would be something."

She'd spent her lifetime dreaming, culminating in the Final Dream that, like a river, had jumped its bed and taken a new course. Winters was confident that though this new dream was different—along with its new voice—the gist of it remained the same. There was a time when she'd fervently believed it was Heaven—the beyond that her people went to after wandering the Beneath Places when they died—that guided her dreams.

Winters yawned. "Regardless, I'm dreaming more than sleeping."

They drank their chai in silence after that, and when they finished, the sun was up and casting its watery light upon the muddy road. After they'd loaded their gear back into the wagon, she crawled up into the front next to the Y'Zirite tasked with the drive. "The next town is ten leagues up the road," Winters said after consulting the map beneath the driving bench. The soldier nodded.

Then Winters reached into her pocket and curled her fingers around the phial of voice magicks. She'd started up the preaching yesterday morning, drawing from her and Neb's talk on the docks and expounding upon it and, of course, drawing from the dream itself and the white tree full of promise.

She sighed as she examined the phial in her hand. If Erys chose not to take her advice, the woman was likely dead. And if it weren't for Winters's heritage, she'd be dead by now as well. She'd used blood magicks off and on since childhood, especially the voice magicks of late. For the longest time, Hanric had used them for her, bellowing out his War Sermons as her shadow when he took the Marsher army to field. But she'd been using them since his death, most notably when she climbed the spire with her Wicker Throne strapped upon her back to declare herself as Queen of the Marsh.

And now, because that river had changed, she no longer preached the War Sermon that set her and her people apart from the others in this place. Instead, she unstopped the phial and touched a drop of the black, sour liquid to her tongue. There was thunder in her voice when she cleared it, and then, as the wagon bumped along the rutted road, Winters preached.

The moon was still in the sky as she described what Neb and the others had found there and as she recounted the dream she had unintentionally shared with the world. Winters kept her voice even and calm, letting it roll out into the early morning for league upon league. She laid the dream out before them and invited them to meet with her in the town ahead to hear more.

And two hours later, when they rolled into the town of Oxenford at the edge of the Third River, Winters saw that not only had a crowd gathered but some of the townsfolk had erected a makeshift shelter for them to stand beneath along with a platform and a pulpit for her to speak from to keep them from a persistent rain. She took to the platform with no fanfare or introduction and went straight to it. The last of the voice magicks lent her voice power over the wind.

During the talk, she thought she saw Endrys Thrall in the crowd, though this time he was dressed as a lumberman. Still, his eyes had shone bright from his place near the front as he hung upon her every word. She singled him out to talk to afterward, but by the time she finished, he was nowhere to be seen. And the people, eager to give something of themselves back to her in light of what she'd given them, quickly dragged her off to the town's hall to regale her and her companions with the best of the town's cooking. That night, she would sleep in a bed, and then in the morning she would get up and they would head north to do the same thing again.

And if her words had any impact, then others would also rise up early in the morning. Only they would go south to Caldus Bay for the ships that waited there. And as they went, others would join them. Y'Zirites and Named Landers alike.

Yes, that ancient voice whispered. *The Time of Sowing is upon us, Daughter of Shadrus.*

Winters looked up from her half-full plate to see if any of the others had heard it. The others were busy laughing or talking or eating.

I've spent my lifetime seeing and hearing things no one else could and convincing myself it was Heaven.

But perhaps, Winters thought, where these notions came from was unimportant. Perhaps, she thought as she slowly chewed her roast rabbit, the heaven or hell they made from these revelations were more important than their origins.

Winters looked at the room around her. In the midst of war, here was laughter and warmth and a longing for home.

No, she realized. *In this moment, we are home.*

And Winteria bat Mardic smiled at the revelation.

Chapter 15

Lysias

The sun rose over the Y'Zirite camp at Windwir as Lysias watched his scouts slip out into morning fog and vanish beneath fresh magicks.

He and the leftovers of his forces had met up with Tybard and his men the night before, and the most recent moon sparrow from Rudolfo informed them that Philemus and the Wandering Army would arrive the following day. Lysias had considered waiting until Philemus arrived, but movement in the camp in the hours before dawn hinted that the few Y'Zirite survivors remaining were preparing to abandon the site.

Cold water from the melting snow he lay in trickled into his boots and seeped through his uniform. He grimaced and turned to Tybard. "How many were there at last count?"

"Forty-seven," he said. "There have been four desertions."

Lysias's eyebrows furrowed. That meant four more shallow graves. Rudolfo had been clear on the matter of prisoners, and Lysias had operated with the same ruthless pragmatism before he'd even received those orders when he'd dispatched the young Y'Zirite soldier just a few days earlier. There was no kin-clave with Y'Zir governing the treatment of prisoners of war, and he landed on the same side of that cipher as Rudolfo and Orius in sending a strong and final message to the invaders—a message now reinforced by the pathogen's sharp scalpel and the promise that the same awaited any other Y'Zirites who followed.

Which of course raised another curiosity—a concern even—to the surface. "And you're certain the woman the scouts identified among them is Ria?"

The captain nodded. "We believe so. The Firstfall Axe is in her quarters, and the others are deferring to her leadership."

It didn't seem possible. Lysias was fairly confident that Ria had used blood magicks for her visit to the Seventh Forest Manor back in the days just before the bombing that had led to Rudolfo enlisting Lysias to build the Ninefold Forest a standing army. And yet the Androfrancine pathogen hadn't affected her.

Lysias squinted down at the camp. The Gypsy Scouts were impossible to pick out in the morning gloom as they carefully approached and took up their positions. When they struck, it would be fast and hard, but they would leave an opening that funneled any who fled into the blades of Lysias's waiting infantry.

He glanced at Tybard again. The younger man's lips moved as he counted silently, his eyes fixed on the buildings below. Just as he stopped counting, Lysias heard the whistle of alarm rising from the camp mixed with the sounds of combat. The skirmishes were largely out of view, hidden by the clustered buildings, but from time to time, he saw a running form suddenly beset by an invisible attacker and brought down to thrash in the muddy snow. Lysias waited, remembering the long-past days when he was the scout and his general watched from safety. He'd gruffly given up those days, finally convinced by his own superiors that the Academy and a career in leadership were a better use of his skills.

Movement from the corner of the closest building caught his eye. It was a swath of green cloth—the color of peace—extended slowly upon a broken spear. The man holding it was a young Machtvolk— his uniform nearly indistinguishable from the Y'Zirites. Lysias knew his scouts surrounded the man with drawn blades.

The man knew it, too, and raised his voice along with his flag. "I am Garyt ben Urlin," he shouted. "I serve the true Queen of the Marsh, Winteria bat Mardic the Younger and hold kin-clave with the Ninefold Forest Houses."

I know that name. He was the Marsher that Rudolfo had pledged support to. Until the birds had died, he'd fed what intelligence he could to the Foresters.

"Hold," he shouted to the scouts.

Then Lysias stood, and Tybard shot him a questioning look. "I don't think it's safe to approach yet, General."

"It's safe enough," he said. His voice had more growl in it than he'd intended, but this was an unexpected turn. Slowly he picked his way down the hill, and as he did, he saw the first of the Y'Zirites attempt a retreat. As the infantry fell upon them, Lysias continued making his way toward the man and his green flag.

He was halfway there and the fight on his left was gaining in ferocity when a shriek rang out across the gloomy snow. "Traitor!"

Lysias slipped, caught off guard, and regained his footing as he turned his eyes in the direction of the voice. He saw nothing but a flurry of snow and mud erupt as invisible objects collided. He heard the magick-muffled ring of steel on steel and watched as Garyt tumbled into the snow and clawed his way out of the fight.

Lysias drew one of his knives and pressed forward. Tybard caught up to him now, already fading from sight as his magicks took hold. "We can't afford to risk you, General. Let us deal with this."

But it was obvious to him as he watched that the attacker fought under blood magicks. They held their own easily against four of Rudolfo's best scouts. And though he didn't know how it was possible, he suspected it was Ria. The sound of her voice had bolstered the last of her forces, though it was only a matter of time. The Forest Army was new, but now they fought in the snow and mud and not in tunnels beneath the ground, and Lysias was pleased with their effectiveness.

Hopefully it is just Ria and no others. He knew anyone could use the blood magicks . . . once. But without a lifetime of slow exposure, they would ultimately kill the user within three days. And from what he'd heard, it was a painful death. Still, he couldn't afford to waste men.

He moved slower now, eyes on the scouts. Garyt was clear of the fight now, and Lysias knew he needed to make a decision soon. They were wearing her down. Rudolfo might not concur, but if this was the Machtvolk queen, she had ties to the very beginning of the conspiracy to bring down Windwir and the Androfrancines and open the doors for a carefully planned invasion of the Named Lands a generation in the making. She had a great deal of intelligence both on Y'Zir's military forces and plans in the Named Lands and also on the homeland where she'd been raised.

Lysias sighed. "Take her alive," he shouted above the sounds of battle. Then he looked to Garyt ben Urlin. "Him too." He whistled for a medico and when one approached he pointed to the grunting, splashing patch of mud. "Get your kallacaine ready. You're going to need a lot."

"Aye, sir." The medico pulled a satchel from the pouch on his belt. Then he pulled another and made his way carefully down to the edge of the fight.

Now Ria howled, and Lysias thought he heard something in it beyond the rage she expressed with her feet and blades and teeth. It was the cry of something lost and forsaken, something broken and despairing. And for some reason Lysias's mind flashed back to the Y'Zirite boy and his tree drawn in the snow.

Because her cries are the counterpoint of the dream. A lamentation in contrast to that hymn. Because, he realized, she knew was losing.

To his left, the infantry had finished up. They gathered now in the care of their sergeants as the medicos made their rounds. He moved closer and watched as the medico leaped in once Ria was secure. "Hold her mouth open," he said. Then he leaned forward to get the kallacaine into her.

They dosed her twice before she finally succumbed. "Manacle her and keep her down," Lysias told the medico. "She is your responsibility. Tybard, assign this man a security detail and secure a wagon and horses."

Lysias didn't wait for an answer. Instead, he turned to Garyt. "Find this man a better uniform. He's under guard until we've had a chance to communicate with General Rudolfo." He met the Marsher's eyes. "Understood?"

He nodded. "Aye, General. But ultimately, I intend to join my queen on the homeward journey."

The man was fortunate to have been spared the pathogen. Lysias wasn't sure exactly how many Marshfolk had used the blood magicks in the days before and after Ria's rise to power. "Understood," Lysias said. "I am certain that if you're being truthful, Rudolfo will honor your kin-clave."

Garyt inclined his head. "Thank you, General."

Lysias returned the gesture. Then he forced himself away from his new prisoner and in the direction of men who needed praising for a job well done.

He only hoped Rudolfo would feel the same way when he learned that Lysias had spared Ria's life.

Vlad Li Tam

They moved quickly through the Beneath Places, Amylé out ahead, light blazing from her as she ran the corridors. Vlad kept up with her as best he could, already aware of how much strength and stamina he drew from the staff.

Twice they encountered magicked Blood Guard. With the first group, he drew the magicks from their bodies while Amylé laid into them with hands and feet. The second time, though, he held back and watched in awe as she defeated them without his help.

She is getting better with practice. The young woman had steel in her, and a childhood spent with the military had given her access to excellent training. *And now I simply show her how to build her pain into an army.*

An army he could use in his war. Alongside his own.

Another ambush ahead. He saw the flash as her body suit absorbed the impact of an invisible blade.

Vlad tapped his staff and then swung it out ahead, feeling it make contact. Then he grabbed hold of the thin black thread of blood magicks and tugged it into the staff. He felt the metal heating and pulsing in his hand. He shoved it forward again, connecting with another.

And then they were moving again.

The Y'Zirites were easy enough to track. Most of the branching tunnels had been sealed off, leaving only a few viable paths. And the one they ran now ended at a closed hatch ahead.

Vlad swung the staff at the locking mechanism, feeling the impact in his hands even as the staff flashed and the hatch sparked. On the third blow, the door swung open. Three men in black robes waited, each raising hands that bore dark rings.

Magisters.

Vlad raised the staff quickly as the rings popped and electricity leapt from them. He felt the fire of it burning into his hands even as something heavy struck his legs and tumbled him to the floor.

The magisters were not alone. Magicked Blood Guard hemmed them in. The chamber beyond them had no visible exit, and half of it was some kind of liquid. This was not another ambush. This was a last stand.

"Conceal me," he heard Amylé shout to his right before the silver light that surrounded her swelled and then went out. Still, he saw the evidence of her work as she moved through the Blood Guard one at a time.

As he fell, Vlad heard a gentle cough followed by another and another. And with each, he felt the slightest sting. It took a moment for him to realize what was happening.

Darts. Whatever they'd put on them was fast-acting, and he already felt his muscles trying to seize. The staff fell out of his hands as he struggled to roll onto his back. He closed his eyes and stretched out his fingers, feeling the heat of the Firstfall steel as it crackled with whatever energy the magisters' rings employed. Vlad forced his hand around the staff and roared his frustration at the fire that engulfed his arm. He pushed with another shout, and this time their rings exploded, taking fingers with them as they did.

Vlad's vision grayed at the edges now, and his tongue felt swollen in his mouth as he tried to call to Amylé. He took a deep breath and pulled from the staff, drawing its power into himself like kallaberry smoke through a pipe, bidding it flood him and chase down whatever toxin they had laced their darts with.

He crawled to his knees, then pushed himself up only to slump against the wall. From here, he could see the uniformed men in the shadows, the long tubes held ready in their hands as they took aim at him.

He'd seen the Y'Zirite thorn rifles from a distance, but this was his first encounter with them. He raised the staff against them but knew he couldn't use it to deflect their darts and wasn't even confident he could stay conscious long enough to counter the toxins.

He didn't have to. Amylé shrieked, and in her cry there was a sense of abandon to rage and despair rising off the Younger God in waves. At the crescendo of that shriek, she moved through the last of the magisters and fell upon the soldiers and their thorn rifles.

The tubes coughed, and the silver light that shone from her burned the thorns to cinders as they struck her. Behind them, Vlad saw the two women huddled there and smiled.

"You have something that I need," he said to them.

Then the gray finally caught up to him, and Vlad Li Tam collapsed under the weight of it.

～

He swam in light, the song all around him now in shades of undulating blue and green.

She was there, though he couldn't remember her name. She held him, and her dark eyes were full of sorrow and fear. "Oh my love," she said, "the tools of the parents are not the toys of children."

Still, even at her words, he reached out for the staff, but it wasn't there. And the panic from that discovery brought him up from dreaming.

"Where is the staff?"

It hummed to life in Amylé's hands and lit the space he lay in. They were above ground again and tucked away in one of the convent's private rooms. "It is right here, Lord Tam."

His mouth was dry, and talking hurt. He tried to sit up, his eyes never leaving the staff in her hands. "What happened?"

"I carried you back out after I finished with the Y'Zirites." He didn't like the look on her face—it was almost beatific as she stared at the staff, and her voice sounded far away.

He looked around. "And the spellbook?"

She laughed. "Not a book after all." She reached into her pocket and pulled out a small dark object. "And you were right: I recognized it."

She held it up to the light from the staff, and Vlad recognized it too, though this one was made of a smooth, black stone. But otherwise, it was an approximate replica of a ring he had seen—and had even kissed—more times than he cared to count.

The spellbook of Y'Zir is a ring. Plain, large, and cut to the same pattern as the papal signet of the Androfrancine Order, though theirs had been made of Firstfall steel.

He climbed slowly to his feet and held out his hand, suddenly unsure if the girl was really going to give it to him. But she dropped the ring into his waiting palm and then passed the staff over to him.

He studied the ring and then slipped it onto his finger.

The voice was in his head as soon as the ring touched his skin. *Library access authorized.*

His brow furrowed. "It's granting me access to a library."

"Yes," she said. "Back at the Firsthome Temple. The Library of Elder Days."

Vlad closed his eyes and felt something like wind, only from deep within, tugging at him. He let it pull him, and when he opened his eyes, he saw a forest. Trees scattered across a field of grass, branches heavy with gems that sparkled in the white light.

No, he realized. *Not a forest. A room.* He blinked. *A forest within a room.*

Men in blue uniforms were tending a row of saplings and looked up, their eyes wide.

"Where am I?" Vlad Li Tam asked.

He felt a hand on his arm and realized it was Amylé. "You're still here. But the rod and ring will give you access to the Firsthome Temple."

He looked back to the room and saw the men in blue leaving at a brisk pace. He stretched a hand out to one of the closest trees, touching the green gem that sparkled from its branch. It sung beneath his fingertip, and as it did, Vlad's mind opened and information fell into it like boulders into a well.

He sat at the rushing images and closed his eyes against them.

"Oh," he finally said. "Oh my."

"Yes," she said. "It's a lot."

Just that momentary touch had flooded him. The People, ancient and tenacious, had risen up from their first home—had risen and fallen, fallen and risen across millions of years of time and space. He'd felt it. He'd seen it. All within a flash, and it left him slack-jawed.

He looked at the girl, and she made sense now in a way that she hadn't before. He looked at the staff in his hands and saw that it, too, made sense somehow differently.

"Oh," Vlad Li Tam finally said again. Then he stood.

Amylé stood with him. "What next?"

And what came next made sense to him now, too, in a way that it hadn't before. Vlad Li Tam sighed. "Now it is time to bring the age of Y'Zir to a close," he said.

And the smile on Amylé D'Anjite's face as he said it assured Vlad that the river of her life still bent where he willed it. But something in her eyes told him that he may not be able to count on that much longer.

Still, that was to be expected of any Tam allies.

And even with that expectation, Vlad Li Tam knew that yet another unwitting ally awaited him in Ahm's Glory to help him cut Y'Zir from the world.

Rudolfo

The forest was hung in ribbons of mist in the hour before dawn, and Rudolfo walked it, pretending he was alone. Someone followed him—he wasn't sure if it was one his men disobeying his orders or one of Ori-us's Gray Guard following their own general's. Whoever it was hadn't bothered to magick themselves, but they still did a decent-enough job staying hidden and quiet. And that fact led him to believe it was indeed one of his own farther down the ridge that Rudolfo now slowly climbed.

He forced himself not to look back over his shoulder and instead forced his mind back to the Whymer Maze that robbed his sleep. He'd already been preoccupied, his mind full of the map of Pylos he'd been going over in preparation for his rendezvous with Phile-mus and the others. But then the messages—both by moon swallow and by courier—had caught up to him at the end of his day as they settled into yet another reclusive hunting manor on their journey north.

Some of it was good news. The cleanup was going as planned, and there really wasn't much fight left in Entrolusia. There was still fight-ing in Turam and on the Emerald Coasts, but Rudolfo suspected strongly that Pylos would be the last holdout.

And some of the news, he suspected, could also be fortuitous, though it initially didn't feel likely.

Ria lives. Rudolfo had not expected that. Somehow, the woman had survived the pathogen despite her use of blood magicks. Lysias had even confirmed that she continued to drink the water without inci-dent. He'd not expected this, and as if it weren't enough of a surprise, the other bird had brought information from the south.

Winters is preaching a new sermon. For some reason, he'd thought the girl had left the Named Lands. Her people were already in the Churn-ing Wastes, led by the mechoservitors. He'd wanted to send scouts to see her safely out of the Y'Zirites' care, but Esarov and Orius had assured him that she was provided for along with the Androfrancines who accompanied her. At their word, he'd arranged the requisite let-ters of introduction and credit in Caldus Bay.

And these sisters—both users of the various blood magicks forbid-den within the Named Lands—lived still despite the weapon. Ria had been under the blood magicks when they'd taken her. And Winters moved north, according to the report from Orius's scouts, using voice magicks—technically, a blood magick of sorts—as she preached about the dream.

It was having an impact. Orius also reported on Y'Zirites and ref-ugees within the Named Lands all making pilgrimage to the coast in search of vessels they might hire. And after years of economic uncertainty, the ship owners and captains—all having experienced the dream—were curious about what resources and opportunities to extend trade routes might exist with the Seaway now granting access somehow to the lunar seas. At the end of two years of war a real end was in sight. Y'Zir's back was being broken, both here and at home. But what waited at the end of the war? Something new grew on the horizon, and people who had lost everything were gravitating toward it. Orius himself reported Androfrancine deserters, and Rudolfo expected some of his own might join them.

All of it made his head hurt. And it kept his mind from the one place it wanted and dreaded most going.

Rudolfo had been a parent all of two years, and already it had so redefined him that it took vast effort for him to accept the roles and purposes that had once filled his life.

Jakob changed everything.

After being a father, how could any man return to simply being a king and general? *And yet somehow I must.*

Rudolfo exhaled and watched the cloud rising from his breath. He crested the ridge and followed it north, savoring the damp, cold morning. He'd spend his day on horseback. Before learning of Ria's capture, he'd thought he'd start west to meet Philemus and the others in the scattered villages north of Pylos proper. But now he suspected he would ride directly north.

Rudolfo found a tree and leaned against it, looking back over the ground he'd covered and the distant lights of the manor. Whoever it was, they were good at not being seen. He squinted back, eyes scanning from tree to tree. Nothing.

Rudolfo jumped at the low whistle just to his left.

"Hail, General," a voice growled.

Renard.

Rudolfo released the hilt of his knife. "You are good at the woodlands for a Waster," he said.

The man stepped from the shadows. "I spent time—quietly—on this side of the Wall. Times when Hebda wasn't digging."

Rudolfo nodded. He never could fathom Androfrancine chastity and held no judgment for anyone who couldn't live up to that rather impossible expectation. Of course, until Jin Li Tam, he'd not even been able to consider monogamy as any less impossible. "Well, I thought you were a Gypsy Scout. And they are the best of the best."

Renard inclined his head. "Thank you, General." His face darkened. "How are you doing?"

Something in the man's tone reminded him of Gregoric, and Rudolfo felt the ache of loss. He thought about his friend more and more
and wondered how that man would've responded to all of the events
that had unfolded since Windwir's destruction.

*If Gregoric had been here she'd have never left the Named Lands with my
boy.*

He tried hard to keep the edge of his rage away from Jin Li Tam. It
was hard to blame her for a nature he'd known existed in the first
place. She had been shaped and dropped into his life by the same
man who had murdered Rudolfo's family. *Now all of my family,* he realized, because he had to accept the hard truth that the woman he
loved had never truly been his. She had always been her father's
daughter—a child of House Li Tam. Still, there were times when his
anger toward her flared as well, and he was grateful that she was nowhere near.

He looked up at Renard, realizing he had still not answered the
man's question. "I am . . ." He let the words fall into the snow and
glanced away. The sudden tears behind his eyes ambushed him, and
he blinked into the cold air, hoping Renard couldn't see. "I am weary,
Renard."

"I think we all are," Renard said. "We have all lost a great deal and
have had to live in our rage to keep that loss from crippling us." His
eyes narrowed. "It changes us, I think. It's changed Hebda. He carried his secrets about Neb admirably until Neb learned those secrets
and could hate him for it. And the light's gone out of his eyes the few
times I've seen him." He shifted against the tree. "Orius has changed,
too. He's less reasoned and pragmatic now. The man I knew would
have never considered using the spell in light of what happened to
Windwir."

Rudolfo nodded. He didn't need to look far to see the changes in
himself. They'd been building one upon the other, and he'd never
thought any change could be so profound as the birth of his son.

But the death of his son had brought a profundity all its own, and
it crushed and ground him like teeth during his every waking moment.
Because it wasn't just that loss but every loss leading up to it back to
that first loss of his twin brother, Isaak.

He wiped a renegade tear away and forced the shame of it down.
"It has changed me," Rudolfo said, "and I fear not for the better in

many ways. But I cannot take the time to fathom those changes until I know my home is free."

"Aye," Renard agreed. "And that should be sooner rather than later. Orius is moving north to intercept Lysias and take Ria into custody."

Rudolfo's brow furrowed. "What does he intend to do with her?" Orius had said very little on the subject when they met briefly the afternoon before.

The Waste guide shrugged. "He'll interrogate her first. And then I think he means to make an example of her. There on the grave of Windwir."

This surprised Rudolfo. The war had already left the north. The vast majority of Marshers had rejected Winters's plea and stayed behind. And the army—supplemented and led by Y'Zirite officers—had largely been wiped out by the pathogen. "That seems out of the way to send a message." He stroked his beard. "And to whom is he sending it exactly?"

"I think maybe to himself," Renard said in a quiet voice. He paused, considering his words. "Orius is not well, General. He is also working with Blakely and Symeon to mount an expedition to the Y'Zirite crèche once peace is restored in the Named Lands."

Rudolfo felt the ice that suddenly settled in his stomach. First the spell. *And now the Androfrancine general meant to commit genocide of his own.* "Are you certain of this?"

Renard nodded and looked away. "He's asked me to lead it." He paused. "But I have no intention of doing so. I plan to find Hebda and head to the moon when things are settled here. If Neb will have us."

"And what did he say to that?"

Renard shrugged. "I've not told him." Then he met Rudolfo's eyes. "But I am telling you. And I'm also warning you." Then he said the words again. "Orius is not well."

Rudolfo nodded.

Renard nodded in return. Then, without another word, he turned and began making his way back down the tree line. The sky was gray now, and the world was washed in the light of the setting moon.

Rudolfo sighed. Orius would have to be dealt with. The war had changed him, had swallowed the man he had once been.

It's changed me too. Initially, it had changed him for the better. He'd torn down Tormentor's Row and built its stones into the library. He'd become a father and taken a queen. But then somewhere in the north, after the library bombing and after the fog of firespice wore

off, something more fierce and ruthless than he'd known before had
risen up inside of him. And then had gone feral at the news of his
son's death.

But even in that place of rage and hatred, Rudolfo could not bring
himself to the place of endorsing genocide.

And yet I am keeping an Y'Zirite alive so I can hear her scream again. And
though he didn't agree with taking the pathogen abroad, the notion of
Ria being made an example of brought him a satisfaction mingled
with shame.

Renard wasn't moving as quietly as before and made little effort to
conceal himself. Rudolfo picked him easily out among the shadows
farther down the path they'd made. He set out to follow and found his
feet suddenly felt as heavy and cold as his heart.

Still, Lord Rudolfo of the Ninefold Forest, General of the Wandering Army, put one foot in front of the other upon his chosen path and
hoped the coming day would warm him.

Jin Li Tam

Her dreams were full of the smell of the blasted lands they ran
through as Jin Li Tam slept fitfully on the mechoservitor's back. She'd
stayed awake as long as she could, but eventually all of the walking
and the aching in her bones from the crash and from the blood magicks
had caught up with her and she'd let sleep take her. Jakob had flooded
her dreams, too.

He was her last thought before she slept; her first upon waking. *He
is alive.*

A part of her still didn't want to let herself hope. But she hoped
anyway, and as the sun rose, she saw a small enclave of old buildings.
Facing her, she also saw a figure stand up slowly from a chair that sat
by itself. From a distance, she could not pick out any specific details,
but the metal man covered the distance quickly.

The man was maybe a decade or two older than Rudolfo and
younger than her father, his hair receding. He wore plain dark trousers and a matching shirt. He smiled as the automaton slowed.

"Lady Tam," he said, inclining his head to her.

Her voice was sharper than she wanted it to be as she climbed down
from the mechoservitor. "Where is my son? Take me to him."

"I will," he said. "My name is Cyril Thrall. I am one of the watchmen of Endicott Station." He turned to the metal server. "Automaton Re-ish," he said, his tone changing to one of command, "you may return to stasis."

"Yes, Watchman Thrall," the metal man said while bowing deeply. Then it moved toward one of the buildings with a liquid grace Charles's reproductions had lost.

After it vanished through a heavy metal door, she looked around them at the dilapidated buildings. They were old, but not as old as the blasted wastes that surrounded them for league upon desolate league. The rising sun cast them in shades of crimson.

"Follow me," the watchman said after the metal door closed. He set off at a quick walk, abandoning his plain wooden chair where it sat.

Jin matched his pace and listened to the morning air. The small enclave was wrapped in silence, their feet the only sounds until he worked the lever and opened a rusty door. He ushered her inside and then closed the door behind them as he drew a stone from his pocket. He closed his eyes briefly, then nodded to another door.

They entered the room, and he stooped to push back an ancient carpet. Jin had heard of the hatches leading into the Beneath Places, but she'd not seen one until now. The metal was pitted and ancient, but the wheel spun easily as her guide entered the cipher. It swung open without a sound, revealing the ladder downward.

They are keeping him in the Beneath Places.

"If you'll kindly descend first," the watchman said, "I will close the hatch behind us."

She looked down the dimly lit shaft, then glanced back to the man. The look on her face must have betrayed her sudden lack of trust.

"Lady Tam," he said, "I assure you I am not your enemy. I was here the night they brought your son and the others, and I am eager to see you reunited."

Her eyes locked with his. "Where are they?"

"You will see them in just a few minutes." He offered a weak smile. "You have weathered the most difficult of times, Lady, so your suspicion is fully warranted. But we truly are allies and friends."

She had question after question, but she knew this was the wrong time and Cyril Thrall was likely the wrong person. So she turned and found the ladder's rungs with her feet, then climbed down. Cyril closed the hatch and followed, his breathing heavier when they reached the bottom. He led them down a corridor that eventually revealed yet another hatch, this one set into the wall.

She gasped when he spun it open. The room was lit by lichen that reflected eerily off a quicksilver pond that she knew had to be one of the bargaining pools of old. A white tree at the shoreline waited, its limbs heavy with purple fruit. Cyril Thrall approached the tree.

He pulled a fruit down from the tree and handed it to her. "Eat this," he said.

She held it up to the dim light. It had skin like a plum but was as large as an apple. "I don't understand. How will this take me to my son?"

The watchman smiled. "It is difficult to explain," he said. "But eat the fruit and you will see your son. He is waiting." He closed his eyes, and his brow furrowed for a moment. "Aedric is with him."

Aedric? She vaguely remembered the New Espiran officer telling her the same when she'd sent Jin with the metal man. She'd not seen the Gypsy Scout since they'd landed. But she knew better than to be surprised that Rudolfo's first captain would find her son. She bit into the fruit, feeling its juice run down her chin. The meat was sharp and sweet and sour all at once. "I don't—"

"Chew and swallow please."

She did, and his hand was in his pocket again. "Endicott Station translation commencing."

She opened her mouth to say something but didn't have a chance.

"I'm sorry," Cyril Thrall said as he pushed her quickly and effectively into the bargaining pool. And as soon as she touched it, Jin Li Tam felt vertigo within a flash of light, and then suddenly she *was* light, racing veins of silver for seconds that slowed and blurred with speed all at once until she rose gasping and sputtering from the silver pool.

Her anger flashed. "What in the hells are you—"

But Cyril Thrall was gone.

No, she realized, I'm gone.

The pool was larger, the chamber much larger and better lit, and instead of a single tree, a grove of them grew here. Men in uniform waited to pull her to shore, and an older woman in silver robes stood with them.

"Lady Tam," she said, "I am Elyna Gras, chief administrator of the New Espira Council Expeditionary Force. I am pleased to welcome you to New Espira."

But Jin Li Tam barely heard the woman's words, because a curly-haired head appeared at the edge of the grove, joined suddenly by another. "Jakob!"

The toddler laughed. "Mama!"

And in that moment, she heard nothing else. Nor did she see Aedric smiling in the background. She pushed past everyone, ignored the little girl who stood with her son, and scooped the little boy up into her arms. She flooded herself with the feel of him, the smell of him, as she crushed him to herself and sobbed with the force of a reunion Jin Li Tam had both dared and not dared to hope for.

Chapter

16

Petronus

Petronus took the stairs three at a time and still wasn't winded when he reached the library. He'd been down at the canal welcoming new arrivals from Y'Zir when word reached him. He'd excused himself and ran for the temple at top speed.

An old man with a staff suddenly appeared in the library. Then disappeared moments later.

Nadja Thrall was waiting for him there, along with four young men wearing the uniform of the New Espiran Council Expeditionary Force. She smiled and inclined her head. "Father Petronus," she said.

He felt blood rushing to his cheeks but didn't know exactly why. *Or I know but don't want to acknowledge it.* It was something in the way she looked at him. A look he'd not experienced often since his youth on the bay, before he joined the Order. And he was always surprised to see her. Other than their work in the library, tending the newly planted saplings, her people had been scarce. She'd been less scarce, turning up for meals or largely unnecessary meetings. "Ambassador Thrall," he said. "I came as quickly as I could. I heard we had an intruder in the library?"

She nodded to the men. "Tell him what you saw."

Petronus didn't yet completely grasp their rank structure or insignia but assumed the one who spoke was higher ranking because he was slightly older than the others. "An old man wearing robes. Long red hair streaked in white, tangled beard, slight frame. He held a silver staff and wore a black ring."

It's Vlad. He glanced at Nadja and raised his eyebrows.

"It is consistent with recent sightings of Vlad Li Tam by our people in Ahm's Glory. And this means he's found what you call the spellbook along with the Staff of Y'Zir."

Petronus felt his brow furrow. "How in the nine hells did he find his way here?"

"I have experts on the ship who can explain it better," Nadja said. She extended her hand. "But walk with me and I'll tell you what I can."

Petronus flushed again but took her hand even with the others watching. They paid no mind to it at all, but it wasn't the first time the New Espiran culture had surprised him. Her hand was warm and firm in his as she led him deeper into the forested room. "You are familiar with the legends of the Last Weeping Czar Frederico and the Moon Wizard's daughter Amal Y'Zir?"

"Some of them," he said. "Very little from those times survived the Age of Laughing Madness." He thought about it. "Very little likely made it over in that first migration after the Wizard Wars. And we didn't have the opportunity to mount expeditions to that part of the world."

"When they established New Espira, they left behind careful instructions. You've seen some of them in the form of the letter I showed you on the day that we met. Amal Y'Zir spent her childhood in the temple and left behind what information she could for us. Including the care and cultivation of the knowledge trees." She stopped in front of a tree that Petronus recognized. It was the small one in the center with the dark rings, guarded by a Watching Tree. She touched one of the rings and jumped when the Watching Tree stirred to life. Then she laughed. "This is your spellbook," she said. "They provide access to the library remotely by way of the aether. But you need the administrator's rod to grant access."

Petronus stared at the tree in wonder. "So you wear the ring and you have a library at your disposal wherever you are."

She nodded. "Yes. Somehow. I don't begin to understand it." She grinned. "I studied Androfrancine leadership and philosophy. Not ancient technology."

Technology, not magic. He'd largely grown to believe that was true the longer he'd studied the teachings of P'Andro Whym. But now it was being proven true, and his own body, now in touch with his heritage

as one of the People, reminded him daily that the ancients they'd re-
vered as Younger Gods were actually their ancestors. His chuckle was
more like a bark. "Astonishing."

She moved closer to him, and he fought the urge to pull back.
"Which?"

Petronus felt his body respond to the look in her eyes. It wasn't a
look he'd seen often, and he felt shame chewing at him. *She is a child.*
But the way she watched him and laughed when they talked over their
meals, and the topics they'd spanned, had invigorated him. And there
was something charming about it—he the youngest Androfrancine
Pope and she the youngest New Espiran ambassador. He realized that
he hadn't answered her and blushed, looking away. "Both," he finally
said. Then he changed the subject. "So Vlad Li Tam paid us a visit. I
wonder if he will be coming back."

"I imagine he will."

Petronus nodded. "I will post a watch."

Their small party had grown now, with the arrivals of people called
by the dream. Some, he suspected, would eventually return home via
the Seaway. But most came with what little they had and wanted to
join in whatever was happening at the Firsthome Temple. So some had
been tasked with hunting, some with fishing, some with exploring and
others with cooking and cleaning, each to their skills. It wasn't unlike
the beginnings of the gravediggers' army. There was work to be done
and new hands arriving to help every few days. And now they had a
few new jobs—guards in the library to let him know if his old friend
showed up again.

Maybe I can persuade him to put aside his wrath and give Neb the staff. He
doubted it.

Nadja was walking deeper into the orchard now, and Petronus followed. "I wanted to talk with you about something, Petros."

She'd not called him that before, and it caught him off guard. It
was a childhood nickname and the name he'd taken after leaving the
papacy. That name on her lips stopped his feet. "Yes?"

They were far from the entrance now, where the light was softer,
and the gems upon the trees cast Nadja's hair in greens and reds and
gold. She turned. "The day we saw the ships and I told you we would
not involve ourselves. It disappointed you."

He shook his head. "I think it surprised me. Your people have
labored in secrecy and silence for millennia toward this day, and now
it is threatened by war. You have technology that would assure our

victory over forces that have sought to keep the tower away from us since the days of this so-called Downunder War Y'Zir started." He paused and took a breath. "I can understand not interfering in order to capture events as they unfolded. But now, at the end, it seems more prudent to intervene."

She nodded. "I do not disagree with you. It was a difficult decision to abide by, but . . ." She smiled, and her eyes took on a playful note that caught him off guard.

"But what?"

"I am not a pope. I answer to the council, and they give me my orders. But I was tempted. You are a pope, after all."

Petronus laughed. "Technically, I am no longer a pope."

"True," she said. "But you *are* a Younger God."

In that moment he felt a bit like one, and Petronus smiled.

Her eyes went serious. "Still," she said. "I do not always blindly follow even my own backward dream." She paused and met his eyes. The stark blue of them was disorienting. "When Nebios arrives in Ahm's Glory, there are elements within the council that are inclined to aid him." Then she smiled slowly and inclined her head.

Petronus returned the gesture. "Thank you, Ambassador."

"You're welcome, Petros."

He blushed. Then he stepped deeper into the forest and changed the subject as any good Androfrancine would. "This is truly astonishing," he said. "But you should have seen the Great Library."

She followed him. "I did see it. Through the aether projections our people captured over time."

That fascinated him. The stones they carried allowed them to communicate, and other stones allowed them to capture images, sounds and other sensory detail for use in the aether. It was all somehow related to the dreamstones—both the large one they'd used to reach him with the Final Dream and the smaller ones the Y'Zirite Blood Guard carried. He'd seen a facsimile of the Great Library himself—pulled from his own memory—when Aver-Tal-Ka had him cocooned.

The wonder of it all made him blink. "And now all of that is here in the Firsthome Temple?" The saplings had seemed to be thriving when he'd looked in on them earlier.

"Yes," she said. "You—Pope Petronus of the Androfrancine Order—you are in the library. And also as a Younger God brought back from the depths of time."

"And you, Ambassador Thrall?"

She grinned. "I'm young. My story is still being written." Then Nadja looked around. "But yes. Someday my story should be here, too."

Petronus paused as a thought struck him. "Did the New Espirans capture the Final Dream?"

Now her cheeks flushed. "Some of us watch it daily."

And in that moment, when her eyes met his, they shared a moment of awe. Then, as she pulled him close to her and began to kiss his mouth, Petronus felt more shared awe and wonder as he kissed her back and kept on kissing her until his body joined hers in knowing exactly what it was meant to do there in the shadows of such ancient, primal knowledge.

Neb

The morning sun was cast in brown light as Ahm's Glory and its dead smoldered, belching smoke into the sky that Neb knew made the far horizon hazy after weeks of burning. He'd flown in from the south, passing over the canals and tipping his wings to the vessels that sailed there. They'd stripped their Y'Zirite colors and flew instead the flag of the white tree.

There are more and more of them. And there were others, too, trickling out of the city from all directions as they fled. They'd noticed the kin-dragon, but once he'd landed and sent it out to patrol, they'd paid him no mind.

He clutched the satchel tightly and stayed to the shadows as he went. His flyover of the city had revealed that most of the military were focused in the vicinity of the palace, with a small force attached to the Imperial Magisters. No one seemed to notice the white-haired man in silver robes as he hurried toward what had once been the market district.

He slipped a hand into the satchel, finding the crescent and drawing it out. "Okay," he whispered into the silver artifact. "I'm close now."

Petronus's voice was tinny and distant. "I'm assured by the ambassador that you will be met. Proceed to the fish stalls on T'Erick's Way."

Neb looked around. The streets were marked, but not in any language he comprehended. "I'm not sure how to find that, Father."

There was silence on the other end for a moment; then Petronus spoke again. "The street off the main thoroughfare leading to the palace. It's marked with a statue of Ahm's brother."

Neb continued, his eyes moving over the few passersby he encountered. The city was nearly abandoned, and when the meditation bells chimed, no one paused or even gave it any mind.

These people have lost their faith. No, he realized. It had been systematically taken from them by the man he came to face. And by today's end, he planned to have that staff in his hands. The ring, too, that somehow connected Tam to the library.

He tucked the crescent back into the pouch, his hand brushing against the cloth-wrapped hand cannon he'd left the Ninefold Forest with that morning. He'd not fired it, but he'd practiced loading and unloading it several times under Hezekiah's careful tutelage. He had five spare cartridges—a handful of lead balls and blast powder wrapped in waxed paper—but he knew that given how long it took to prepare the weapon, he would likely only get one shot. And he would need to be close.

Neb swallowed the copper taste of violence in his mouth and set out again. Soon, he saw the statue marking T'Erick's Way and turned right, still keeping to the shadows, until he found the first of the abandoned stalls.

Hail, Homefinder.

The voice in his head brought Neb to a stop, and he looked around. A woman separated herself from a group of refugees loading a cart. She was at least a decade older than Neb, her face lined in Y'Zirite scars but the rest of her hidden in dirty robes and a silk head scarf. She briefly met his eyes as she sidled up beside him. *Follow me.*

Neb followed, struggling to keep up with her shorter legs. They slipped into an alley before she spoke in a low voice. "I have better-suited clothing for you if you wish it."

Neb shook his head. "No one's paid me any attention. I think it's fine."

Her smile was tight. "They are paying attention, Lord Whym. But there's no one left to raise the alarm to. The regent has what remains of the Blood Guard and military organizing an evacuation of the government. But they are definitely monitoring the aether with diligence now that Lord Tam has accessed the library, so we must be careful there. So far, the subaether remains out of the Y'Zirites' reach." She inclined her head to him. "I am Captain Vanya." Then she opened a door and held it for him to enter. It was the back room to some long-closed shop, and two men waited there by a table. One held a thorn rifle. Vanya followed Neb inside and closed the door.

Neb looked at the men and then back to the captain. "Where is your ship?"

She shook her head. "No ship. We've lost three ships since the Seaway opened, and the council has grounded the fleet." Vanya exchanged glances with her men. "And our involvement is not exactly sanctioned by the council."

It was the first Neb had heard of the downed ships. "Is it the Y'Zirites?"

The captain looked to one of the men. "No. We believe it's something that crossed through from the moon. Possibly another kin-dragon."

Neb nodded. That made sense. He and Petronus and the others had been brought down by something—the mechoservitors described it as something large and silver and fast. He swallowed, not wanting to ask the next question. "Do you think it's Amylé?"

One of the men, the older of the two, cleared his voice. "It is likely a third kin-dragon." He paused. "Or more. Amal Y'Zir's memoirs tell of them guarding the lunar skies in her childhood. Our military historians suspect they were used to maintain air superiority during the Downunder War before Y'Zir brought them back to the moon and closed the Seaway. It's possible that with restored access to Lasthome, they are continuing that mission."

Neb's brow furrowed. "But Ambassador Thrall's vessel hasn't been attacked."

The man shrugged. "We only have theories."

"Regardless," Captain Vanya interrupted, "we have other business to attend." She looked at Neb. "Do you believe you can get the staff and ring from Tam? Because if it is indeed kin-dragons, that staff is our best hope of redirecting them and getting the council's fleet back in the air."

That staff seems to be the best hope for a lot of things. And yet Neb still had no idea how to use it. His best hope was that if Vlad Li Tam could figure it out, then he should also be able to do the same, especially given his heritage. But first, he had to find the man. He looked at the captain. "The ambassador thought you might be able to help."

She nodded. "We know where he is. He was seen returning late last night. Unfortunately, we've already pulled our embedded agents among the Lunarists that he is staying with."

And for what was coming, Neb would not want Tam hiding among the Lunarists. He fully expected unless the hand cannon worked, it was going to take everything he had to bring the man down, and he wanted to minimize the risk to anyone caught in the path of this coming storm.

Now she reached under her robes and pulled out a gem like the others Neb had seen them whispering into around the Temple. "This will let you reach us if we become separated."

He took it and felt the dry warmth of her hands as she pressed his own fingers closed around it. "You can use it audibly," she said. Then she blinked. *And with practice you can use it by direct cortical transmission.* Her face was sober as her voice lowered. "Giving you this will likely cost me my commission with the council," she said. "And your physiology will give this much greater range than ours, so use it carefully and understand that though the Y'Zirites and mechoservitors won't hear you in the subaether, *my* people—both the ones in favor of this intervention and those who are not—will hear." She winked at it. "So whisper, Nebios Whym."

He nodded and tucked the gem into his satchel. Captain Vanya moved closer to the lamp and held up her head for the two men who waited there. "How do I look?"

The one who had spoken pulled a small canister and brush from his pouch and opened it. Then he dabbed at her face. "You'll pass."

Their scars are painted on. Neb watched as they checked each other's clothing and paint. It still baffled him that this group, hidden from them all, had watched them quietly from the shadows, bidden to do so by the Last Weeping Czar and his companion, Amal Y'Zir, once they knew that the Wizard Wars were lost to Raj Y'Zir and his silver army. That bargain wrought by Frederico somehow included Neb and the line of Whym along with both the metal dream and the dream that Winters's people followed—the Dream That Shadrus Drank.

They'd hidden the staff and ring for him to find. And Amal Y'Zir had sealed the temple upon her last visit when she'd set the mechoservitor to its harp and poisoned the bargaining pool behind her. All building to today.

Neb felt the weight of millennia in his stomach and swallowed. And he felt the weight of the hand cannon in the satchel at his side—the very weapon that had taken Pope Resolute's life in a faked suicide that, ironically, Vlad Li Tam himself had arranged.

And now, if I need to, I kill him with it. But Neb had no doubt he would need to. He did not think the old man would surrender the staff.

A light tap at the door made Neb start as Vanya and her men drew knives. He rubbed the fabric of his sleeve and drew the silver garment up tight, feeling his body flood with strength as the blood of the earth empowered him.

The door opened slowly. "Lord Nebios Whym," a metallic voice whispered into the room. "Do not be alarmed."

A tall robed figure ducked into the room and swept off its hood, revealing a silver face set with red jeweled eyes that burned like the Watcher's. At first sight, Neb thought it was the Watcher—only newer. But as it limped across the room, he knew just who approached him with inclined head. "Isaak," he said. Before he realized what he was doing, Neb had crossed the room to embrace the metal man. He looked nothing like the mechoservitor he'd seen in the aether. Or the one he'd seen give his last to save him from the Watcher and send him to the moon. But he was here, and between the two of them, Neb thought they might have a chance against Tam.

"I'm glad you're well, Isaak," Neb said, stepping back.

Then Captain Vanya stepped forward, eyes narrow. "And how exactly did you find us?"

Isaak's eyes flickered bright and then dim. "I am able to monitor both the aether and the subaether in my current configuration."

Neb saw the frustration on her face and heard it in her voice. "And were you followed?"

"I do not believe so, Captain Vanya."

The use of her name transformed her anger into a moment of bewilderment. She opened her mouth to speak, but Isaak continued before she could.

"I assure you, I am here to help Lord Whym acquire what is necessary for his work. Your operations in Ahm's Glory are not compromised in any way." He looked at the older man. "And I concur with your theory regarding the kin-dragons. My cousins' experience upon the moon corroborate it."

The man inclined his head, staring at Isaak as he did. "You were in the dream," he said. "You stood with Winteria bat Mardic."

Now Isaak inclined his head. "I was the conduit for the Final Dream."

The man's voice was matter-of-fact, devoid of any judgment. "And the conduit for the Fall of Windwir."

Isaak looked away. "Yes."

There was silence until Neb cleared his voice. "I think it's time to go," he said.

They left one at a time, pausing in the shadows of the doorway to space themselves out along the street. Vanya led, and Neb and Isaak walked side by side beside her. The others followed.

They went quietly, taking streets and alleys largely abandoned, and those few they encountered averted their eyes as if they did not want to see. Neb counted the minutes, and after nine of them had passed, Vanya whistled low at the entrance of a dark alley. Neb heard a crackle and the slightest pop, and a man in plain black clothing appeared. Vanya drew close to him and Neb joined her. "What do we know?"

"Tam is there with the Lunarists," the man said. "They've been gathering supplies. I think they're preparing for a move." He passed her a gem and she held it, closing her eyes.

Vanya opened her eyes and gave the gem back to him. "Looks like they're leaving the city. How many times has the kin-dragon been out?"

"Three times. It's out now, Captain."

Neb felt his eyebrows furrow. *What is she up to?* "How long have its trips taken?"

"A few hours."

Neb calculated. She could go nearly anywhere in that amount of time. Even to the moon with the Seaway open. "I think it's to our advantage that she's gone." He frowned. "But it would be better to lure him out and spare as many of the Lunarists as we can."

Isaak's eyes flickered beneath his hood. "I concur, Lord Whym. I do not believe Lord Tam is going to freely relinquish the staff and ring." The metal man sighed, and Neb heard the weariness in it alongside the resolution. "Statistical analysis favors a ninety-four percent likelihood that he will resort to violence."

Yes. Neb was certain of it, and he swallowed against the fear that stirred beneath the surface of his own resolve. He offered a sigh of his own. "Yes," Neb said. "I am prepared to kill him for it." The satchel grew heavier as he said the words, and Nebios Whym took a deep breath. Then he nodded to Captain Vanya. "We're ready," he said.

And Neb hoped as he said it that they truly were.

Winters

Wind rattled the windows of the borrowed room where Winters tossed in yet another borrowed bed. She'd found it harder and harder to sleep, and she suspected it was more than just the voice magicks she used.

It is the work I'm doing. The sermon was increasingly the easier part. But afterward, the hours of talking—of answering questions there really were no answers for yet—mixed in with the feasting and dancing late into the night and left her mind running through it all again and again hours after she'd crawled into bed.

Winters couldn't blame them for being curious. She was, herself, and she'd had no opportunity to really think much about the questions they now asked her.

How will we govern? Will I be their queen? What of the Homefinder? What is his role, and where is he now? She'd spent her lifetime dreaming of a home, and now that it was found, she was uncertain what to do with it. The questions daunted her, and before the unintended sharing of the Final Dream, she'd just assumed she and her people would continue as they always had—a council of twelve elders that shared the burden of government with her so that she was free to . . .

To do what? The council had given her the freedom to dream and explore those dreams. And when he'd lived, Hanric had also helped keep her focus there. But those dreams had fulfilled their purpose. And now a new dream—an accidental dream—had her gathering people she'd never imagined calling her own to a home she never imagined sharing in this way. And from that dream, others took root that seemed less intentional. The dreams of Grandmother and of the angry old woman.

Though they do not feel like dreams.

Still, sleep meant they likely waited for her, and that was less appealing now than the racing thoughts of what her purpose would be beyond this role of dream catcher once she settled into her new home.

Winters sighed and sat up, looking around the room. It was in a larger house, its family already en route to Caldus Bay and the waiting ships. The Y'Zirites had been pleased to accept it when the mayor offered it up, and now they occupied the larger of the bedrooms while Tertius and Hebda made use of the smallest. They'd given her this one because of its proximity to a bathing room, though she'd not taken advantage of it. It was not a night to be nostalgic for her caves and the hot springs she'd bathed in when her life was simpler.

Winters dressed quickly in the dark, knowing what she did would likely make her guards unhappy—her friends as well—if they found out. But she suspected it would be simple enough to keep them from finding out. She strapped on her knives and slipped into her rain cloak, gripping her boots in her hands and letting herself into the hallway silently. She padded to the back door in her socks, then slipped her boots on and cracked the door quietly open into the windy night.

She stepped onto the stone porch and pushed the door carefully closed behind her, scanning the open yard before her. The house was southwest of town in a less densely wooded region near a creek that branched off of the Second River. Of course, she'd had no real plan other than getting out of that room. And now that she stood in the cold, the wind tugging at her cloak, Winters realized she had no idea what to do now.

Still, waiting on the porch to decide wasn't prudent. So she set out at a slow walk toward the tree line, drawn by the sound of water over rocks. The wind was cold upon her until she left the clearing and entered the wood. The creek was larger than she remembered it earlier, or maybe it just seemed louder in the dead of night. The snow here was melting, and the ground beneath was spongy and soft beneath her boots.

"Hail, Lady Winteria," a quiet voice whispered to her left. She jumped, her knives out and ready before she had time to think.

A tall form stood two spans away from her, hands upraised. The voice was familiar, but she couldn't place it. "I mean no harm," the man said.

Captain Endrys Thrall. Winters released her held breath and sheathed her knives. "Captain Thrall," she said. "You have a way of turning up near bodies of water when young women are walking alone."

He smiled and lowered his hands. "I'm sorry it's taken me so long to reach you. Our fleet was grounded and it's made transportation . . . challenging."

Winters felt her eyes narrowing. "Why are you following me?"

"The council has assigned my crew and me to monitor your mission and offer what limited support we can. The ambassador awaits you on the moon to negotiate the full terms and conditions of the treaty between the House of Shadrus and the New Espiran Council."

"So you're keeping watch over me?"

He nodded. "Until you're safely to the moon, Lady Winteria. I will bear you there myself once my ship is cleared to launch."

She'd really given no thought to how she might get to the moon. No, she realized, that wasn't true. And she blushed, remembering the one time she'd allowed herself to think about arriving on the moon with Neb, carried to her new home by kin-dragon. She felt the heat in her cheeks and ears and was grateful for the darkness. "I assume," she said, "that you are not just monitoring me but the greater situation here in the Named Lands?"

"Primarily you," he said. "But I also have observers keeping an eye on nearby military movements."

She'd heard little. Everyone had been so focused on the dream and the moon. "How near?"

He looked away. "I was coming for you when you stepped outside the house."

Coming for me? She glanced back in the direction of the house. She made the connection and turned on him. "What's happening?"

"Gray Guard forces augmented with Delta Scouts," he said. "Members of the resistance reported your escort. Orius knew you were being held captive—loosely—by the Y'Zirites. He's been receiving intelligence on your movements since your first sermon at Caldus Bay." The captain's face was obscured by the night, but his chuckle said enough. "The general apparently has no love of you or your people."

Winters smiled. "We took his eye before I was born." Then her smile faded as she remembered her last encounter with the man. The hatred and rage she'd seen in him when he'd demanded the Seven Cacophonic Deaths from Isaak. "Orius is a dangerous man," she said.

"Yes," he said. "And so I'm here."

She looked back to the house again. "Do we have time to get Hebda and Tertius?"

Endrys Thrall shook his head. "No. But they're Androfrancines. But once they captured your sister, I—"

Winters felt the wind go out of her. "They captured Ria?"

It made sense. They shared the same parents, so of course her older sister would survive the Androfrancine pathogen.

There was an awkward silence. "They have. I thought you knew."

She shook her head. "No one is talking to me about anything but the dream."

The captain nodded. "She was taken near Windwir. They're planning to execute her there."

Winters blinked into the darkness. "Who is?"

"General Orius. Rudolfo's man, Lysias, captured her and handed her over to the Androfrancines."

Her eyes narrowed. "Is Rudolfo aware of this plan?"

But of course, she knew he was. She remembered him standing over the Y'Zirites they had rooted out of the Ninefold Forest, the coldness in his voice as he banished them—banished the very man that had raised him after his parents had been murdered. And Ria's surgical work upon House Li Tam and its master had sent Vlad Li Tam to Y'Zir. *Where he murdered Rudolfo's son.*

"I believe so. He is sending the Wandering Army ahead to Pylos under Philemus's command."

"What are they doing with the other prisoners?"

He glanced to the house again, and his tone was somber. "Lady Winteria, there *are* no other prisoners. Some have fled for your ships, but with their scars they'll be easily culled from the others. Between the Entrolusian resistance and the Androfrancine forces, I doubt many Y'Zirites will leave the Named Lands unless Orius is dissuaded from this course of action."

She felt the weight of it in her stomach. "We have to get to them first," she said as she turned to the house. "I have no love of the Y'Zirites, but our escorts do not deserve to be slaughtered in their sleep like—"

His hand upon her shoulder, suddenly firm, interrupted her. "It's too late," he said in a low voice. "It is not our place typically to interfere, but they had orders to take you as well, and my sister and I concurred that minimal intervention was in the best interest of the Shared Dream. Your new home is on the moon."

The way he said it made the words sound almost sacred, and in that moment, Winters knew something about Endrys Thrall that she hadn't known before.

He is a follower of the dream. The Shared Dream. And his allegiance to it was already trumping his allegiance to the council and the uniform he wore on its behalf. She stared through the trees to the house and watched one by one as the few lights within went out. She heard the shrieks first and then the shouting.

Winters took another step forward, and Endrys kept pace with her, his hand again settling on her shoulder. "There is nothing you can do there," he said. "I think it's time to get you home, Lady Winteria."

But my people are not gathered. The thought was a knife in her soul.

Now they will gather themselves. The words you've sown will spread. She recognized the ancient voice and shook it out of her head.

"I'm not ready to go home," Winters said.

"We should discuss it on the move," Endrys said. "We have a safe-house in a neighboring village where some of my crew are waiting." He set off at a brisk walk downriver, and Winters walked beside him.

She waited until they were half a league out before she spoke again. "How would you get me to the moon if your vessels are grounded?"

He glanced at her. "Getting you to the moon would likely be worth risking an airship. But I could also always escort you to the coast and hire a ship."

Winters thought of the Y'Zirites and then of their lieutenant. And then, she thought about her sister. Ria had certainly earned an execution. *But even Sethbert had a trial, sham though it was.* And Ria herself had interrupted Petronus's trial only to execute the old Pope herself. Killing Ria was a message—likely for those of the Marshers who'd survived the pathogen. And it was a vengeful, vicarious act for those who'd survived the Y'Zirite invasion overall. Certainly her own people had committed their share of symbolic violence. Blood was a powerful message.

The problem with blood was that it continued to call for more. Blood for blood, eye for eye, ear for ear.

And Winteria bat Mardic sighed, because she knew Orius's message was meant for her as well. And because she knew that she must find some other refrain to answer with that would not be more of the same.

(D)arta

The alley stank of smoke and rotten fish, and Marta fought the urge to gag as she waited for Ire Li Tam. Her stomach still clenched and roiled from her brief time under the magicks, and her head still throbbed. The stench and the heat of this place didn't help either.

She had better return for me. It had occurred to her that the Blood Guard might abandon her now that they were deeper into the city, but how was that safer than leaving her behind in the first place? No, Marta was confident that Ire would return.

She closed her eyes. When she did, she could feel the tug of the running line and the twist and turn as they ran from alley to alley. Ire had tucked her into this forgotten corner as her magicks sputtered out.

"You're done for now," Ire said. "I will find you proper attire and check on Isaak."

And now, it had been more than an hour since the woman had left her here. She looked down the length of the alley from the shadowy dead end where she crouched. The wall behind her was still cool from her sweat, but her clothes were dry now as the temperature climbed.

She felt the slightest breeze against her cheek. "Hail, Martyna."

Marta inclined her head in the direction of the Blood Guard's voice. "I was getting worried," she said.

A bundle of cloth appeared on the ground before her. "Put these on," Ire said. "Quickly."

There was a sense of urgency in her voice, and Marta stooped to pick up the robes of a Daughter of Ahm acolyte. "Where did you find these?"

Ire avoided the question. "We need to hurry. Isaak and Neb are approaching my father."

Marta started pulling her other clothing off and felt Ire's hands firmly upon her shoulders. "There is no time for that. Put them on over what you're wearing."

She is scared. Marta pulled the robes and cowl on. They were light-weight, but combined with what she already wore, the heat would be stifling and her mobility would be hampered.

She felt the hands upon her shoulders again, and this time Ire's voice was nearby and at head level with Marta as she crouched before the girl. "Now we walk. We need to find someplace safe to put you until whatever storm is coming has passed. And then I need to see how I might assist them in their work."

Marta wasn't going to ask, and when the words came out, it was more a statement than a question. "Against your father."

"Yes. Now let's go."

She felt the string slip over her wrist, then felt it go taut as Ire pulled her along. Marta matched her pace to that of the Blood Guard and tried to memorize her surroundings as they emerged from the alley into weak sunlight. This was her first visit to a large city, and she found it overwhelming despite the quietness of the streets. She couldn't imagine how much more overwhelming it would be if it bustled with the activity and noise of life.

They moved down the street at a brisk pace before slipping into another alley. Ire pulled her up short just inside. "If we get separated for more than an hour, return to Behemoth and I will meet you there if I can." Marta could tell by the woman's voice that she crouched before her again. "But you need to understand that Isaak and I may not come back."

Marta nodded. "I know." But acknowledging it made her stomach hurt, and she had to believe that Isaak would return for her no matter what. She could not afford to think otherwise without her world losing its meaning.

"Behemoth is your only way home unless we come back," Ire said, her tone severe.

Marta resisted answering again and focused instead on trying to memorize her surroundings. She wasn't sure she could find her way back to the docks. And she also resisted telling the woman that Behemoth could not carry her home because Isaak was her home now and if he did not return, she became homeless.

They continued moving until they reached an alley that opened on a squat two-story building. The line went tight long before Marta left the shadows, and Ire Li Tam's mouth was near her ear when she whispered, "That is where my father is hiding with the Lunarists." Marta felt a hand firm upon her neck, swiveling her head to the right. "That alley there is where Isaak and the others are waiting." Ire turned her head yet again, this time to the left. "That alley will take you to the main thoroughfare that we took from the docks. You should be able to find your way back to Behemoth from there. Do you understand?"

Marta nodded.

"Good. Now we wait."

They'd not waited long when a robed figure stepped into the wide street to approach the building. She recognized the robes and the limp instantly and suddenly felt a wrongness in the moment that chilled her stomach and caught her breath in her throat. *No, Isaak. Don't go.*

As if hearing her, the metal man stopped and cast his red eyes toward the alley where she crouched in shadow. When he did, she started and pulled at the running line to sure that Ire was near. Instead of a tug in reply, the thread hung loose.

Isaak continued toward the building's main door, and Marta held her breath as he brought up his metal fist and then knocked—three times—upon the door. "Lord Tam," his voice intoned, "I've come to parley with you."

Without waiting for an answer, Isaak opened the door and slipped inside. When it closed behind him, Marta saw movement near the mouth of the alley where the others hid. A tall, slender man stepped from the shadows. He had long, white hair and wore a suit of silver that clung to his thin frame and reminded her of Isaak's smooth, mirror-like metal skin. She suspected it was the Homeseeker, Neb, and he watched the door Isaak had gone through with a worried brow.

Marta wasn't sure how long she sat and watched, but when it happened, it was sudden and it made her jump. First, there was a scream from above as something large dropped from the sky in a tornado of wings and claws. And as it landed with another blood-chilling shriek, the door bust outward and Isaak leapt from the building with an old man upon his back and raced toward her. The old man had one arm around Isaak's throat, a long silver rod tucked beneath his other.

Marta pressed herself back against the wall, trying to close her eyes but unable to as they moved past her, gaining speed. There were shouts now as others poured out of the building and scattered. All the while, the kin-dragon pressed Neb and the others, keeping them from pursuit.

She felt a hand grab her arm. "Open wide."

Marta opened her mouth and tasted the bitterness of the powder Ire dabbed upon her tongue. Then she felt the Blood Guard's thumb as it smeared her forehead. It hit her stomach first, and she fought the urge to throw up even as her head began to pound.

Then the running line was reattached and she was once again doing her best to stay on her feet and keep up with Ire Li Tam.

And try to understand what just happened.

But Marta knew—and hated knowing with each slap of her feet against the cobblestones—that whether or not she understood it, whatever it was could not possibly be good.

Chapter 17

Jin Li Tam

Sunlight streamed through large crystalline windows when the sound of children playing brought Jin Li Tam awake. Her first sensation was the sharp blade of cutting sorrow that her own child—Jakob, the Child of Promise—was gone. But then a new awareness seized her and she sat upright quickly, the sheets falling away.

"Jakob?"

She heard a familiar laugh. Then, a girl's giggle—one she also recognized—joined in. Small hands slapped at the door, followed by a brief knock.

"Great Mother?" There was hesitation at the use of the title, and it was not a voice Jin recognized. "Lady Tam?" She covered herself as the door swung open a crack. "I'm sorry to disturb you, but Jakob is very excited to see you. Amara, too." The face was young and scarred; she knew she'd seen it before. With the others when she'd arrived, she was certain.

Yes. She remembered now. All of them had met her there at the edge of the quicksilver pond, and then the New Espiran medicos and a stern female physician had looked her over, checking her for injuries from the crash, she assumed. They'd spoken quickly in a language she could not follow, softer and more fluid than the Y'Zirite tongue she'd become competent in. But that memory—and all other thought—fell away at the sight of Jakob leaping for the bed and scrambling to find a purchase. She reached for him and pulled him to her, burying her face in his hair to inhale the scent of him.

The woman came in. Behind her, Aedric stood and managed to look somber in the light-colored cotton trousers and silk shirt he wore. "You probably won't remember me," she said. It took Jin Li Tam this long to realize the woman was speaking V'Ral. "We were all pretty disoriented when we arrived, as well." Amara hugged at the woman's leg, smiling at Jin Li Tam from behind her. "I'm Chandra. I was the Vessel of Grace before Lord Tam saved me."

She was vaguely aware of the woman's role, and her eyebrows went up as she swallowed the rage and the retort that the mention of her father raised up in her. Instead, she took the woman's offered hand. "You are Amara's mother."

Chandra nodded. "Though she was taken from me early and given to the Daughters while I was prepared for my ministry."

Jin heard bitterness in the woman's voice and identified with it. For the briefest moment, she thought of answering and held the words in her mouth. *My father convinced me he murdered my child.* Then she swallowed them and blinked at the sudden tears as Jakob poked at her face with his fingers. "Mama sad?"

He said it in V'Ral, then said it again in Landlish. "Sad?"

She pulled him closer and closed her eyes. "No," she said. "Not anymore."

"I think we'll leave the two of you alone for a bit," Chandra said as she lifted Amara up into her arms.

Jin Li Tam nodded. "Thank you."

"The council chief will want to meet you soon. There are clothes laid out for you." Then Chandra pulled the door closed.

She wasn't sure how long she lay there playing with Jakob. It felt like hours, and it wasn't time enough. But she marked the shift in him as he grew hungry and finally climbed up from the bed to see what awaited her.

She dressed quickly in the cottons and silks that reminded her of the loose-fitting wear she'd grown up with in the near-tropical heat of the Emerald Coasts. Near the clothes, she found that someone had laid out bread and cheese and fruits of a variety that were unfamiliar to her on a small table in the sitting area. She fixed a plate and took it back to the bed, handing Jakob a piece of cheese.

"Mara?" She looked at him for a moment, trying to figure out which language he was asking in, before she recognized the question. *He's asking for his friend.* Of course, it made sense. He was accustomed to having meals with the others now.

"We'll go find them soon," she said.

After eating something that was too tart to be a pear, a slice of heavy whole-grain bread, and a handful of berries that tasted like plums, Jin Li Tam slipped on the low-cut walking shoes that waited by her door. Then, holding hands with Jakob, she let herself out into a common room. It had two doors on each wall leading, she assumed, into guest chambers similar to her own. Aedric waited there on a sofa of unfamiliar material. He stood at the sight of her and inclined his head. "Lady Tam," he said. Then he winked at the boy. "Lord Jakob."

"First Captain Aedric," she said, returning his gesture of respect. "How do you come to be here with my son?" Jin felt anger beneath her words despite the relief.

Aedric's gaze was level, and his words and face held no regret. "I helped your father take the children, Lady."

"And then we," another voice said from the opposite corner of the room, "took the children and the people with them away from your father and brought them here." A woman in silver robes stepped through an open door, and Jin Li Tam's eyes narrowed as she tried to place her familiarity. It was the woman who had met her when she'd first arrived. She'd introduced herself as an administrator with the New Espiran Council.

She smiled as she approached and extended a hand. "Welcome again to New Espira, Lady Tam." Then, as if reading her mind. "Elyna Gras. I'm the elected chief administrator for the council that governs our mission."

"And the one responsible for taking my son away from me?"

The woman met her eyes, and the humor in them surprised her. But there was compassion in the woman's voice. "Oh no. That was all your father's doing. But I did give the order to bring your son and the others here so that we could keep them safe in the midst of the Y'Zirite collapse." She paused. "Please keep in mind that I also gave the order to bring *you* here, Great Mother. That order cost me a ship and a dear friend in Commander Pardeau."

The commander's face flashed before her for a moment and slowed Jin's search for a reply. Her anger sputtered and sparked but couldn't hold. Finally, she found the only words that felt right in the moment. "Thank you," she said. She heard the slightest break in her voice as she said it.

Administrator Gras inclined her head. "You are most welcome. Though there is another who interceded on your behalf that you may find more worthy of your gratitude. Usually the council does not intervene in such direct ways, and I must admit that I was initially opposed to the"—she paused here to search for the best word—"to the suggested course of action."

Another who interceded on my behalf. Jin furrowed her brow. "I will hope to have the pleasure of thanking them."

When the woman in robes suddenly clapped, Jin started and Jakob burst out in laughter. "Yes," she said. "It's why I've come. I thought you'd be awake. She is awake, too, so it is a good time."

The way the woman spoke piqued Jin's curiosity. "I would be pleased to meet her."

Administrator Gras smiled. "Good. Let's go then." She looked to Chandra. "We should bring the children to her. She's been waiting."

Aedric started to stand, and the woman's hand settled onto his shoulder. "I think just the mothers and their children this time, Captain. They'll be in good care."

Jin noticed the flash of anger in his eyes but pretended not to as she moved to the door with Jakob in tow.

She wasn't certain what she'd expected, but stepping out into the New Espiran late morning challenged every other day she had stepped out into. Absolutely nothing felt right about it.

The bright light she'd seen penetrating the crystalline windows came from a sun that was too small and hung suspended above them. And the villa they occupied sat on patch of close-cropped grass at the edge of a river that sloped gently upward to a horizon lost in haze. It was so disorienting that she found herself clutching Jakob's hand more tightly. Still, she forced herself to look around. She saw stands of trees and other villas and a landscape that rolled out and slowly up. Farther out, she saw light reflecting from the silver of an airship as it made its way across the sky.

But what kind of sky? It wasn't like any she'd seen before. It was haze and light without blue and without clouds.

She looked back at the administrator, and the compassion on her face told Jin Li Tam that she understood. The woman's voice was gentle when she spoke. "It is difficult to adjust to," she said. "Some of our people have found the outside world overwhelming in its differences from our home here. We've even had to bring home field-workers and reassign them."

"What is this place?"

"The People—the ones you refer to as the Younger Gods—established places called crèches. Your Named Lands occupies one. The Empire of Y'Zir occupies another two." A guarded look passed over her face, and her smile pulled slightly at the corner of her mouth. "There are others. The Last Weeping Czar, Frederico, and his Lady Amal Y'Zir guided our people to this one millennia ago when he established our charter and launched our great work."

Jin looked around. She saw few people, but those she did see wore loose-fitting garments made of a type of silk she was unfamiliar with. The cut of the clothing was odd, but so were the colors. And the designs of the scattered buildings, even the way the trees grew and the style of paving stone, were different. But the sun and the horizon were the most baffling to her. They threatened her with vertigo and a tinge of nausea.

She glanced at Jakob, but he didn't seem to notice it at all. Of course, he'd been here longer. Then she looked to the administrator and saw the compassion on her face. "It is hard to get used to at first," the woman said. "Just like it's hard for our people to adjust to the above spaces." She paused. "Your stars, for instance. Most New Espirans never see the stars. Or the sun."

Jin's mouth went dry as the words settled in. *The above spaces.* "We're . . ." The words were so inconceivable to her that she lost her way and had to start again. "We're underground?"

Administrator Gras nodded. "We are." Then she looked to the light that pretended to be a sun. "The People established this crèche at the center of Lasthome. They called it the World-womb. It would be difficult to explain—there is good reason their descendants grew to see them as gods. But long before Lasthome was formed for them, the People had harnessed the power of suns and gravity, had solved the mysteries of mass and light that would let them expand beyond the confines of their Firsthome. We've lived here, in the Hidden Crèche, since Frederico and Amal Y'Zir led us to this place in the great Under-Exodus. Here, he established the bargain that has now come to term."

Jin released her held breath and looked around again. Four uniformed men waited near a large, ornate wagon with six steel wheels and no horses. One of them lowered steps and helped the administrator aboard. Then they helped Jin up, and Chandra passed the children up to her one at a time. The interior was paneled in mahogany, with cushioned benches running along the walls.

Once everyone was aboard, two of the uniformed men climbed onto the back, and the other two climbed into the driving bench at the front. Jin couldn't see what they did exactly, but she heard a hiss and a low rumble as the wagon started moving. It rode easy, and the children played in the aisle between the benches as they made their way down a white road beside the river.

When the voice filled her head, Jin was caught off guard.

Yes. It was old and dry and far away. *At long last, the Time of Sowing is upon us and the People are restored to their heritage. I look forward to meeting you, Great Mother.*

Jin blinked the voice away and looked around at the others. The administrator was watching her. "Did you hear that?"

The woman smiled. "Of course I did." She looked out the window. "We'll be there soon."

Not knowing what else to do, Jin Li Tam divided her attention between watching the children play and watching the strange landscape roll past the window of the horseless wagon that carried them. Some part of her—the part that belonged to her father—thought maybe she should be more frightened than she was and more focused upon the Tam cunning that kept her family alive and in control. But that part was distant to her now, lost in the sound and sight of her son and the wonders of this new place. So instead, Jin Li Tam found herself flooded with curiosity and gave herself the luxury of a wandering mind for the first time in too many years.

Ria

She climbed in hot fog that clung to her, blinded her, burned her lungs as she raced, and when Ria burst through the door at the end of her climb, she spilled out into a night scattered with stars the likes of which she'd never seen.

And there, on the horizon, a blue-green world rose to add its light to the stars.

Ria gasped and turned, taking in the view.

It is the tower from my dreams. And she didn't want to believe it, but she knew it must surely be the Moon Wizard's Tower, the one that had been unsealed by Winters.

"You again." The voice was no longer enraged but curious, and Ria turned toward it. The old woman cocked her head and sniffed.

"You reek of the Downunders," she said as her eyes narrowed. Then she stepped forward. "But you are more than that. What is your name?"

Ria stammered, trying to make her tongue work. "Winteria bat Mardic the Elder. I am called Ria." She paused and took a step back as the woman advanced another step. "Are you going to throw me from the tower again?"

"I might," the old woman said, "if you don't tell me how you came to be here."

Ria shook her head. "I don't know. Is this the Moon Wizard's Tower?"

The woman laughed, and it was a cackle on the air. "Oh no. No, it isn't that. This is a hidden part of the aether that my captor created specifically for me." She took another step, her eyes narrowing even further. "So you can imagine, I'm sure, my curiosity as to how you seem to come and go."

Ria took another step back and glanced over her shoulder. The edge of the tower was still some distance behind her. "I do not know," she said again. "I thought I was dreaming."

The woman stopped, sniffed again. "It is a type of dreaming," she said. Then she smiled and nodded. "Have you ever seen it before?"

Ria looked and saw the world rising over the lunar horizon, its blue-green light reflected upon the waters of sea like polished glass. "No," she said. "It's beautiful."

"It was," the woman said. "Until the Y'Zir and his Downunders burned it past recognition." The woman sighed. "And after all these years of watching it. Seeing what it was. Seeing what it is now." Ria saw something in her eyes that was both soft and hard. "I've come around to understanding they were right. It must all end."

And Ria understood the love in the woman's voice when she said it, along with the despair and grief. She opened her mouth to say so and the tower shook, throwing her to the ground.

"What's happening?" Ria climbed to her knees.

The old woman hadn't moved. She watched with a bemused look upon her face. Once more the tower lurched, and Ria toppled again as a rush of cold water from an impossibly distant sea struck her in the face.

"Wake up," the old woman said. The tower shook again. "Wake up."

Ria forced her eyes open and blinked as another rush of water struck her. She choked on it and tried to raise her hands but couldn't.

She felt the icy chill of it in her hair and running down her neck and shoulders.

The medico leaned over her, a metal cup in one hand as the other gripped her shoulder and shook. "You need to wake up now."

She tried to make her mouth work, but it was cotton and her tongue stuck to the roof of it. The young Gray Guard put down the cup and used both hands to sit her upright against the wall. He used his fingers to pry open first one eye and then the other before finally standing. "She will be lethargic and unfocused for an hour or so, General."

"That's fine, Sergeant."

She looked in the direction of the voice and matched the familiarity of the voice with the man who stood in the doorway of her cell.

And it was her cell, truly, she realized as she looked around at the plain log walls and the straw mat and blankets beneath her.

I am in Windwir. In the stockade they built there. It felt contrary to her vague recollections of awakening on horseback before more powders were washed down her throat to spin her back into oblivion.

Ria tried to look around and found she couldn't hold her head up. Her eyes didn't want to stay open either.

"You can leave us," Orius said.

The medico stood and moved out of view. But Orius replaced him, crouching before her. He smiled, and it was sinister against the backdrop of his eyepatch and scar. "Welcome back," he said. "I thought Windwir would be a good place for our conversation."

She blinked more of the fog away. She tried to reply, but her voice was the faintest croak.

Orius hand was warm and firm along the side of her face. "It will largely be a one-sided conversation," he said, "because you have nothing to say that I have any interest in hearing. And initially, it will be a conversation of few words." He caressed her face lightly, and she felt the rough calluses of his fingertips. It was a confusing sensation made all the more so when his other fist came up to smash into her nose. Her throat flooded with the taste of her blood, and the back of her head cracked against the wooden wall despite the hand that held it firmly up.

Orius leaned in, his mouth near her ear. "First," he said in a low voice, "I want to speak with you about the Desolation of Windwir and the genocide of my people." The fist came up again, connecting with her eye and temple, sending bright light flashing against the back of her eyes. "I thought about using knives, but your kind like that too much. So I decided to write my message in bruises rather than scars."

She opened her mouth without any idea what reply she could give, and as she did, his fist again connected, this time splitting her lip open. Then Orius stood and let his feet do the work as she tried to curl herself into a ball and find the corner. He was grunting with exertion, the small room choked with the smell of sweat and blood, when he finally stopped and called for a chair.

Ria lay still against the wall, panting and wheezing while he sat and sipped water, regarding her with a single eye that held no emotion in it. The pain had begun sharply but already dulled as she gave herself to it.

"I think I was clear," General Orius finally said, "but I'll be back tomorrow to continue that conversation." He leaned forward. "Before I go and let Sergeant Bayrn clean you up, I thought I'd update you on the relevant issues of our present conflict, as is fitting a woman of your office." He smiled when he said it. "Your leadership in the Named Lands has been surgically removed. Your remaining forces are being routed. Your faith has lost its saviors, and the empire is in collapse. And now that we have an effective means of removing the Y'Zirite threat completely, we intend to do so at our earliest convenience." His smile widened. "Everything you've worked for has come to nothing. And once I feel I've communicated that message clearly enough to you, you will be executed here on the grave of the Androfrancine Order."

Then he stood, kicked her once more, hard in the kidney, and left.

When the medico returned, she kept her eyes closed and tried to remain quiet as he located and treated what wounds he could, and when he poured the kallacaine into her mouth again, she welcomed it and the warm darkness it offered her. And as she slipped into that place, she knew Orius would continue their conversation until he eventually took her head, and it no longer mattered to her. She'd lost Mal what seemed forever ago. And now she'd lost her faith and all of her reasons for believing. And she'd lost the war.

Losing her life would be a gift that Ria could wait for, though she hoped it wouldn't be long.

Rudolfo

Firelight danced shadows across the Wandering Army's campsite, and Rudolfo watched from those shadows, smiling, as Philemus and Lysias rallied the men.

He'd pushed the magicked horse hard as his Gypsy Scouts panted to keep up, and he'd made their rendezvous on the southern banks of the First River just twenty leagues south of Windwir. Here, Philemus would split off the bulk of the Wandering Army along with what survived of Lysias's regular army and press on for Pylos, sweeping up the leftover Y'Zirite forces as they went. Lysias would remain behind with a small elite corps of scouts and veterans to liaison with the Gray Guard. Rudolfo had planned to ride with Philemus, but now, with Winters moving north and Lysias preparing to execute Ria, he knew his place was Windwir.

To avert what injustice I can in our pursuit of justice. He sighed and closed his eyes. Philemus had already spoken, and Lysias was winding down. Overhead, the sky was clear and the moon was up.

"And if our king, our general, were with us," Lysias cried out to the soldiers, "he would tell us to stand firm and take back our home for the forest and for the light!"

Voices picked up the call. "For the forest and for the light!"

Rudolfo smiled and stood from behind the barrels where he crouched. This was his cue, and he sprang lightly to the back of the wagon, whipping off his hood. "General Lysias," he shouted out, "I must disagree with you. For if I were here, I would say to my men, 'Eat hearty, drink long, for you've Y'Zirites to hunt upon the morrow and your king and general would not have you do so on empty stomachs and heads full of words.'"

A whisper rushed out from the men closest, and it became a roar as Rudolfo raised his hands and laughed. He hopped down from the wagon and moved through the soldiers as they parted for him until he stood with Philemus and Lysias. "Under-sheriff and first captain of my Gypsy Scouts," he said, "have you what I entrusted to you?"

Philemus nodded and drew the turban from beneath his uniform. "I do, my king."

The men roared even louder as Rudolfo took it and put it on. "I am Rudolfo," he shouted, "Lord of the Ninefold Forest Houses and General of the Wandering Army." He paused as they cheered him. "'That damned Rudolfo' to those I've bested in battle or in bed."

He turned and regarded Philemus and Lysias. "And you," he said. "General Lysias and Captain Philemus, you have each distinguished yourselves in your service to my men. And your service to my men is service to me. You bear my grace beyond my wiliest words. And when this war is finally laid to rest, you'll both see clearly the extent of that grace."

Rudolfo turned and took in the camp. "As you all shall. So eat, drink, hunt well, and come home to me safely."

As the men shouted and raised their hands in salute, Rudolfo inclined his head and kept it low until they were quiet again. "Hunt well," he said again. "For Jakob, for the forest and for the light."

They repeated his words until they became a pulse and when that massive pounding heart reached its crescendo, he nodded and shot Philemus and Lysias a glance.

"Fill up now," Philemus bellowed out over the crowd. "We strike camp at dawn for Pylos."

Then they slipped away to a tent they'd set aside for their surprise guest.

"I think that rallied them well," Lysias said as they pushed through the canvas door into warmth created by a small field stove. A pot bubbled upon it and he pointed to it. "Chai?"

Rudolfo nodded. "Please."

The tent was laid out in familiar fashion. A small desk, a few chairs and a narrow cot. Lysias dug out three metal cups and passed them around. He poured a generous helping of firespice into both his and Philemus's mugs but passed Rudolfo's without either a word or glance. *Polished grace.* He was the one who'd told him in the far north that his men needed a leader, not a drunk. But even then, he'd carried that message to him with strength tempered by grace.

Now Rudolfo regarded the old man and saw something beneath the surface of him he'd not seen before. "How are you, Lysias? And has there been any word of Lynnae?"

The general shook his head. "None. There is no way to know what to expect. From what we know, the imperial capital is in collapse along with the Y'Zirite faith and government. But she's resourceful and she's with Lady Tam and First Captain Aedric—two equally formidable forces of nature. So I try to trust in that and focus on providing them a home to come back to."

Rudolfo nodded. "Aye."

Lysias's eyes softened. "And you, Rudolfo?" He left off the title, and Rudolfo was glad for it in the moment.

"I am . . ." He paused and felt the hardness in his throat, the water at the edges of his eyes. "I am lost, Lysias, and yet I'm clear of eye and mind and I know the path."

Lysias glanced away. "I find myself questioning paths again." His voice was low and far away. "I served Sethbert until my first war of questions forced a change—and then I helped bring Sethbert to justice and Erlund into power. But now . . ." He sat, glanced at Philemus and then Rudolfo again. "Now, I find myself wishing I'd asked more questions twenty, even forty years ago. I find myself wondering what would've happened if I'd settled into some other way of life. Learned to tend a home and a garden rather than a barracks and a soldier's kit."

Rudolfo nodded. "Alas, we cannot change the past. But there is the future. And what we learn from the past can help shape it. What we do not learn from it can help destroy it."

Lysias sipped his chai and glanced away before echoing Rudolfo's own thoughts. "Then by the gods, I hope we learn something from all of this."

Yes. But so far, he'd seen no evidence. Cascading violence in response to violence. Genocide for genocide. And from what little he'd learned of Y'Zir's history, blood feuds between houses going back millennia.

Rudolfo lifted his cup and savored the heat against his cold hands. "I hope so, too." He took a drink, held the strong chai in his mouth before swallowing it. Then he sat back in his chair. "So what do we know?"

"Eyes in the camp tell us Orius is beating her. He's calling it an 'ongoing conversation,' " Lysias said. "We've not heard when he plans to execute her."

If Orius wanted to make a strong statement to the Named Lands, he'd have brought her down to the Delta for execution. But Rudolfo suspected the canny old Gray Guard was making a statement for history—and to Ria personally—about the Y'Zirite invasion, and he was ending it for her on the very ground where it had begun. And her death on the Plains of Windwir would be remembered the same way Rudolfo's assassination of Yazmeera would be: a part of the legends that would reinforce the memory of these times.

Lysias continued. "We've also received word that he has Hebda and Tertius confined to quarters pending disciplinary action. There was talk of having Winters arrested as well. All for their role in Isaak's and the other mechoservitors' escapes."

Rudolfo sighed. "I fear Orius may not be learning from the past. I will speak to him about it tomorrow." Then he looked to Philemus. "And your men are ready for the work ahead?"

"Aye, General. We'll drive them to the sea and take no prisoners."

Rudolfo smiled. "Good." There was a low whistle at the tent flap. "Enter," he said.

A Gypsy Scout stepped in, his hand extended. There, nestled in his palm, was a moon sparrow. It fluttered. "A bird for you, General Rudolfo, from the Androfrancine camp."

Rudolfo stretched out his hand. "Here, bird. I am Rudolfo."

It chirped, recognizing his voice, then hopped from the scout to Rudolfo's hand. The scout let himself out and the bird cocked its head, dark eyes regarding Rudolfo as the beak opened and a faraway voice leaked out.

"Hail, Rudolfo," Orius said. "Forward scouts report that you are bound for Windwir. Your talents and leadership are best used in Pylos with your men, as previously discussed. Good hunting, General. We will debrief in a fortnight when the Y'Zirite threat has been removed from the Named Lands."

The bird closed its beak. Rudolfo waited and watched it for a moment, stroking his beard as he considered the man's bold dismissal of his closest ally. Then he looked to Lysias. "I don't think a response is necessary." He stood and went to the door, slipping the bird outside with a whisper that sent it north.

In that moment, he suddenly remembered releasing another bird what seemed so long ago somewhere near this very spot. It was a raven with the red thread of war tied upon it. Rudolfo wondered what thread he would tie to the message-less bird he sent now.

He shook the thought away, suddenly aware of how tired he was. "What other business do we have, gentlemen?"

"We have the Marsher," Lysias said, and Rudolfo closed his eyes.

"Remind me?"

"He has been sending us intelligence on the Machtvolk since Winters and Lady Tam were in the north. I did not want to turn him over to Orius with Ria, so he's been in one of our uniforms and kept out of sight. Garyt ben Urlin. He's a grandchild of one of the council members."

"I'm assuming," Rudolfo asked, "that he is bound for the moon with his people, then?"

There was a brief look that washed across Lysias's face, and Rudolfo suddenly saw the conflicting emotion in the man's eyes. *He wants to go, too.* It was that dream. Even Rudolfo felt its pull.

"That is his expressed desire, Lord. If you release him to do so."

"Certainly I do," he said. "Send him to the quartermaster for anything he might need and arrange for his passage, Lysias."

Rudolfo met the man's eyes again, but the conflict was gone now. Still, it set Rudolfo thinking, and even after the two officers excused themselves and after he had crawled into the narrow cot, he found himself contemplating that look.

Lysias longed for some kind of home.

And Orius had his longing for revenge.

What do I long for? He'd longed for home, and that was lost to him now with the loss of his son and his queen. He'd longed for revenge, and already he saw that path was closing to him, too.

It was just as he drifted into sleep that it struck him.

All I want, Rudolfo thought, *is to live in peace among my people and give the world more light than it had before my time in it.*

And warmer than any down quilt, that thought carried the Gypsy King into a solid sleep filled with the smell of books and the lamplit rows of the pine shelves they rested upon in the library he raised at home.

Vlad Li Tam

Wind whipped at Vlad's face as he clung to the metal man's neck. Twice he'd nearly lost the staff as it banged into the corners of buildings or the poles of empty market stalls, and once they'd rounded a corner to stumble into a small group of refugees that he drove the metal man over to the sound of bones breaking beneath the metal feet.

It was far easier than he'd realized. Isaak had entered the room, and with a flick of the staff, Vlad had paralyzed him. Then, laying his hand—and the ring he wore—upon Isaak's chest, he'd commanded him with a basic sentence and they'd fled.

He counted the turns and time and looked up as they passed into their last alley. They were near the Magisters College now. When Isaak slowed, Vlad climbed down and waited while the metal man removed the metal hatch that would give them access to the city's sewer system. Vlad climbed down first, eyes watering from the stench, and waited for the metal man to put the lid in place and then join him.

There was no need for Isaak to carry him here, and Vlad set out at a brisk walk. "Follow me, mechoservitor."

He heard the soft whistle and hum as Isaak complied. Vlad reached into the aether with a tentative probing thought. *Amylé?*

She had been waiting for him. *I am here, Lord Tam.*

It will not be long now. He took them left and then right as he maneuvered them beneath the college and found two of the Lunarists waiting at the hole they'd made in the wall, each dressed for fast travel.

"Is everyone here?" Vlad asked as he approached.

They nodded with sober eyes. He moved past them, and Isaak followed. He'd run the route himself with the others, and when he slipped into the college's sub-basement, he knew which route to take for the hatch.

More Lunarists waited there, and the others from the sewers joined them as well. Then, Vlad descended into the Beneath Places with the army his pain had fashioned him.

The others gathered in the room. Most were men—older—but a few were young, and there were a few women as well. Their priest was gone along with their families, bound now for the moon in an Y'Zirite vessel they'd liberated. These that remained had chosen to, and now they watched Vlad in the dim light of the lichen that grew overhead.

Vlad took a deep breath. "Sit down, Isaak. This will be brief."

The metal man's eyes fluttered, and he sat heavily upon the floor. He stepped forward and pressed the ring against the silver head. *I require access.*

Access granted. Vlad's eyes narrowed against the swell of noise and light, and then he found himself in the library. He could smell the paper and the burning oil of lamps turned low. *This is the place he retreats to.* Vlad knew it was merely a construct within the fabric of the aether but marveled at the detail Isaak had put into it. A robed figure seated at a long table looked up from a book. "Lord Tam," the metal voice wheezed. "What are you doing? I've come to implore you to—"

"Isaak," he said, raising his hand, "I know why you think you've come, but I can assure you that it isn't as you believe. You are here because I called you here with this staff. And when I have finished with this staff, I will keep my word and give it to young Nebios to carry back to his new home where it belongs." The feelings were there again, and he ignored all of them except for the ones that served his army best. He took a breath. "There is something you've carried for far too long, and I must take it from you."

The metal man started to shake, and here, in this place, Vlad could see that this wasn't the mechoservitor he'd run with so recently but the original version—the one Rudolfo had found in the crater of the old library. Steam released from Isaak's exhaust grate, and his eyes flooded with rusty tears. "I am the only one that can carry it, Lord Tam."

Vlad shook his head. "No. I can bear it." And then he stretched out the staff and closed his eyes and waited. It was there beneath the surface, the two songs that defined the existence of this metal man Charles had brought back from the grave of the old world. He heard the Song of Sowing that was Frederico's Canticle for the Fallen Moon first—and saw within it the motes of light that were the code woven into it. The information had given Charles's re-creations what they needed—when they discovered the silver crescent that played it over and over again—to find Neb and to prepare the antiphon to carry them to the moon. And behind that melody, the Seven Cacophonic Deaths of Xhum Y'Zir stirred—a storm of notes that also bore a code though Vlad saw immediately that it had been corrupted and twisted beyond its original purpose. He closed his eyes and separated out the songs, drawing the one to him through the staff, internalizing it so that he could study it. He saw each bend and twist in the words and melody that Xhum Y'Zir had composed during all those years hidden away, plotting his vengeance upon the people who had murdered his sons. As he drew it into the staff, he touched the ring with his thumb. *Open.*

Another stream of information flowed into him, and he felt the deep roots of the Library of Elder Days lay hold of his mind, tucked away in the grove within the Firsthome Temple. It wasn't a complete river—there were parts of the grove that had gone dead, and he suspected that the first Y'Zir, or perhaps the last of the Younger Gods, had something to do with that. Most of the pre-Lasthome history and nearly all of the early history of the people who settled here was gone. But as he dug about, he found the threads that matched what he drew from Isaak.

Then Vlad brought both streams of information together and felt himself moved by the power as they intersected and expanded with a thump that he could feel in his brain. Together, he saw the sum total of it as it danced and warbled, beams of light bending and shifting.

Isaak opened his mouth and closed it as his eyes flashed amber. A low whistle built deep inside his chest cavity, and Vlad closed his eyes and tapped the staff upon Isaak's metal chest once again. There was a spark and a flash. And then Isaak went limp.

"Upon awakening," Vlad told him, "you will flee this place at top speed and you will find the girl you came with. You will flee Ahm's Glory, and you will not stop until you are both safe. Then you will find my grandson Jakob and my daughter Jin Li Tam in Endicott. You will see them safely back into the care of his father in the Named Lands. Only my daughter or Lord Rudolfo may release you from this command. Do you understand?" He swallowed and winced against the sharp ache in his left temple as the metal man nodded once. "You will not remember this conversation." Then he paused and looked again at the bundle of notes and words and light.

There. He made the change—dulling the one note that would blunt this terrible weapon. And then Vlad made another—sharpening the note where Isaak and the others would need to look to finish their work in this world. "But you *will* remember *this*," he said. "Y'Zir bent the People's Song of Shaping into his Cacophonic Deaths, and *here* is where you begin to bend it back into its original shape." He stepped back. "Okay. Now. Wake up, Isaak. And flee."

Isaak leaped to his feet and raced for the door. Vlad did not wait and he did not watch. Time, he knew, was of the essence. He turned to his people. "Lie down with me, children," he said to them in a low voice heavy with emotion he wanted to discount and pretend was not present in this moment. Then Vlad Li Tam joined them on the floor.

He lowered them into sleep and joined them in the aether. He shaped the space for them, drawing from the library where he needed to. They all sat about him in a field, and in the distance, a massive white tree blossomed.

"It's time," Vlad said, and they nodded. He held up a sack that materialized in his hand when he wished it to. "The fruit that Amylé has gathered will get you where you need to go and keep you alive long enough for the sequence to initiate. When you arrive, you will likely feel disoriented. Stay in the Beneath Places until you've got your wits back. Then make your way to your assigned target by whatever means necessary. You only have three days, but most of you won't need more than a day." He paused. "After that, find a central location and sing it out, loud and long." He looked at them and tried to make eye contact with each, but there were too many before the pause became unwieldy. "This hymn," he said in a somber tone, "will end millennia of darkness and bring back the time of the Younger Gods so long unremembered and uncelebrated by all but you."

Then, he taught them the last song that they would ever sing. And when he finished, he woke them and they passed the fruit among them, starting with Vlad himself. He held each piece up in supplication before taking a bite and passing it around. Then, after, he blessed them and sent them out to be his own choir, and they received his blessing, eager to be the mouthpiece of his violent worship. They left quickly, racing down the shafts and corridors he'd pressed into their minds, slipping into the quicksilver with hands and faces still sticky from the fruit they'd eaten.

When he was alone, Vlad sat in silence. For a single moment he allowed the weight of his choices up to and including this one to settle fully upon his back. It bowed him, but it did not break him, and finally Vlad Li Tam stood.

It is because I have already been broken.

Then he slowly shuffled out of the room and made his way to the stairs.

The hallways of the Magisters College were empty, and Vlad let himself out into the courtyard. A few men in dark robes moved about, noting him with looks of concern. He ignored them and went to a bench near a large fountain carved from obsidian.

He inhaled the scent of the city and took in the smudged horizon. *Now.*

Amylé did not answer, but he knew she heard. He saw a flash of silver two leagues to his west as she rose above the city. And as her wings beat furiously, the kin-dragon fled north.

Closing his eyes, Vlad squeezed the staff tightly and willed it to sustain him as he offered up a hymn to those who had been taken from him, cut away by the blades of Y'Zir.

And as the ground shook and the fire fell, Vlad Li Tam laughed and wept in delight and in despair at the glory of his handiwork.

Chapter
18

Marta

Marta ran, her nose filled with the reek of vomit and smoke and her wrist numb from Ire Li Tam's running line. Behind them, the shrieking of the kin-dragon pierced the air, mingled with the shouts of the New Espirans and the crashing sound of walls collapsing as the beast thrashed about in close quarters.

"Look straight ahead," Ire whispered harshly after Marta had thrown up. "Don't look at the ground."

But looking ahead didn't seem to help much. And looking down was worse. *Because I cannot see my own feet.*

They'd followed Isaak and Vlad Li Tam as best they could, dodging down alleys and avenues until finally losing them.

Ire pulled them into an alley where they found a dark corner. Marta blessed the pause in running that it granted her and tried to catch her breath. The kin-dragon's cries were farther apart now.

"I don't understand what he's doing," Marta finally said. "Where are they going?"

"I don't either," Ire replied, "but my father is at the center of it, and it does not bode well. The Imperial Magisters College is near, but I do not know what he would seek there."

Marta rubbed life back into her wrist and tried to keep worry at bay. Something had gone wrong. She was certain of it. And Ire's tone was a confirmation. "Then we should go to the college," she said.

This time, Ire slipped the line around her wrist. "How is your stomach?"

It roiled again, and she felt a buzzing that built behind her eyes and made the world seem to vibrate just slightly around her. "Better," Marta said.

"Then let's run."

They left by the back of the alley and down a street lined with nicer houses. Marta tried to keep her focus straight ahead, but the newness of everything drew her eye—the colors, the stone buildings and palm trees, the few people that were out, their skin covered in silk and scars.

Ire pulled her around a corner, and suddenly they were on a thoroughfare leading to a large, dark series of buildings tucked behind a wall. "They probably entered through the sewers," Ire said.

Marta opened her mouth to answer and then fell to her knees as her head exploded in light and noise.

MARTA!

She cried out at the weight of his voice as it fell upon her and flooded her mind. "Isaak?"

She looked up to see a flash of silver as something hurtled over the wall and crashed into the cobblestones just outside the gate, sending up a shower of broken stone and dust. Isaak's eyes glowed like blood in the haze, and they turned toward her.

He was a wordless blur as he closed the distance between them. And it was as if he saw right through the magicks. His metal hand shot out and grabbed her wrist.

Marta resisted as he pulled her toward him. "Isaak? What are you doing?" He said nothing as he scooped her up, and she felt panic rising. Marta kicked and punched at him. "Put me down."

But instead, he put her over his shoulder and started to run. The silk line that tied her to Ire snapped, and Marta screamed.

Do not be afraid, little human.

And at the same time, another voice nearby panted in her ear. "I'm here, Marta."

But Marta suspected that even with her blood magicks, Ire Li Tam would not be able to keep up with Isaak. And even as she thought it, she felt the metal man lurch forward and build speed.

He is not limping anymore. Instead, he took longer and longer strides, as they raced toward the larger, wider thoroughfares leading out of the city.

They were within sight of a massive gate when everything went quiet around them in a way that defied Marta's sensibilities, and over the rise of that silence, somewhere far behind them, she heard a single note ring out. It was the last clear thing she heard before cacophony swallowed them.

Close your eyes, little human.

She did, but even closed, they could not prevent the light piercing her even as the noise did the same. The ground began to shake, and it took Marta a moment to realize that the high-pitched whine that built on top of the other sounds was Isaak as he surged ahead.

And it was in that moment that Marta understood what was happening. "Ire," she said. "We can't leave Ire." Isaak said nothing, and she wrestled against his grip. Marta gritted her teeth and furrowed her brow with concentration. *Isaak.*

He faltered at his name and lurched to the left as he lifted Ire Li Tam and swung her heavily over his right shoulder. Then he slowed, and steadied beneath the weight of both of them.

They were two leagues out of the city when a wave of hot wind lifted them and tossed them to the side of the highway not far from the edge of a canal. She looked up from the sand and dirt to see a pillar of fire behind them—far too close—before Isaak had her up by the ankle and over his shoulder again.

Roiling clouds of dust and debris spread out around them as the heat and noise grew unbearable, and she heard the hiss of the water boiling away. She could smell hair and cloth burning and could not tell if it was hers or Ire li Tam's.

This, Marta realized with an uncontrollable sob, *is how my mother died.*

Isaak slowed finally, and a shift in the temperature brought her eyes open. They were beneath a bridge now, the canal waters burned away to the dry stone floor. He set them down carefully, turned to take in the pillar of smoke and fire that filled the sky behind them, and knelt.

Then Isaak hung his head in his hands and wept. His shoulders chugged as the whine deep within him became a squeal. Marta watched, the impulse to go to him and take him in her arms at war with the horror she felt.

The thought came again and would not let go. *This is how my mother died.*

"Oh Isaak," she finally said with a sob of her own. "What did he do to you?"

Isaak said nothing, and perhaps it was his silence along with the steaming tears overflowing his jeweled eyes that eroded her fear. She was head-to-head with him there on his knees, and she encircled him with her arms, pulling his metal body toward her. His metal surface was hot against the patches where her own clothing had been burned away, and Marta closed her eyes against the pain. Not knowing what else to say, she held him and repeated her question. "What did he do to you?"

She felt hands upon her, gentle but firm. "Are you injured?"

Marta paused. She was certain that she was. But beyond the heat, she could not determine how or where. "I'm fine," she said.

Isaak's sobbing ceased, and he climbed to his feet. "I must go," he said, lifting Marta as he did.

"No," she said. "Not yet, Isaak." She wriggled in his grip, and this time he loosened it and she climbed down. "We're safe here."

"I concur," Isaak said, "and now that you are safe, I am compelled to find Lady Tam and Lord Jakob and return them safely to the Named Lands."

Compelled? She blinked. "I do not know what that means, Isaak."

"I'll warrant," Ire said, "that it means my father is about his business."

Vlad Li Tam took the spell from him and then used it on the city himself. "Did Lord Tam tell you to find them?"

Isaak shook his head. "I do not remember. I remember running him to the Lunarists beneath the Magisters College. I remember waking up compelled to carry you to safety. And then I remember . . ." He paused, and something low whistled deep in his torso. His eyes flashed red, then went dark for a moment. "Oh," he finally said. And then his voice changed, and Marta assumed that it was Vlad Li Tam that she heard speaking now. "Y'Zir bent the People's Song of Shaping into his Cacophonic Deaths, and *here* is where you begin to bend it back into its original shape."

Isaak's eyes flashed again.

"I don't understand," Marta said.

Isaak's voice was far away as he watched the pillar of ash and fire fill the sky. "He has altered it in some way that I have yet to fully comprehend. But this is the last time it will be used as a weapon." There was a touch of wonder in the metal man's voice. "I will need to do extensive calculations, but his alterations point toward the possibility of further alterations that would restore it to its original purpose."

The Song of Shaping. Marta wondered about it and would've asked, but Isaak turned away suddenly. "Now that you are safe, I must assure the safety of Lord Jakob and Lady Tam," Isaak said.

Marta felt the anger and let it out in the icy tone she adopted. "How are you going to do that? And how do you know we'll be safe once you abandon us here?"

His eyes dulled and sparked. "I'm not abandoning you. Ire Li Tam will keep you safe. She is—"

The Blood Guard interrupted him, and Marta turned in the direction of her voice and saw the slightest warble of light where she crouched. "She isn't able to guarantee her *own* safety, let alone the girl's. So if Marta's safety is part of my father's directive to you, her safest place is by your side, metal man."

Isaak sighed. "Your reasoning is sound."

"And I am not leaving Ire," Marta said. "So if we go, we all go together."

When he spoke next, he sounded more like his old self, and Marta felt a stir of gratitude. "I am compelled to go, but I am not compelled to go alone or at a pace that would be considered harmful to my companions."

"Good," Marta said. "Then let's go."

They put the pyre of Ahm's Glory to their backs and walked as ash snowed down upon them. Isaak limped again as they went, and Marta thought perhaps now it was even more pronounced.

This is how my mother died, she thought again.

Then Marta turned her back upon the desolation and fixed her eyes upon her home, following him in faith she couldn't fathom.

Through fire and under sea, Marta thought, *beneath the ground and in dreams upon the moon, I am with you, my love.*

Petronus

The library was dark but for the dim, rainbow glow of gems that hung low upon the branches, and Petronus sat in that space and pondered.

I am too old for this. But even as he thought it, he chuckled. Certainly as a younger man he'd violated his vow of chastity a time or two. And he'd found in those moments that everything worked as it should. In the days following those dalliances, he'd found himself hungering for more. But it was a dragon that went easily back to sleep.

Until now.

He'd chosen this tree for its sentimental value, and he felt the stirring in his body as he remembered the moment that Nadja Thrall slid onto his lap, the warm skin of the tree pressing against his back even as her warmth enfolded him. He sighed.

"Too old," he mumbled. But he wasn't. He was closer to seventy-five now, but with a body in better shape than his own at thirty. And having a tryst, it seemed, with an ambassador in her twenties.

Something tickled at Petronus's ears, and a split second later, the room shook slightly as a vibration passed slowly through the tower. He climbed carefully to his feet, cocking his ear.

The tickle was gone.

An earthquake, maybe? He couldn't recall the tower moving before. But whatever it was, it had been mild. Still, it bore investigating. Petronus savored the feeling of the bark upon his back and the memory of Nadja Thrall and their first time together, here in a library of trees in a tower on the moon, for another moment. Then he climbed to his feet.

He heard the cough near the center of the library and stopped. "Hello?"

Something croaked, and Petronus moved toward the sound. There, at the foot of the tree bearing the dark rings, lay a pile of burnt skin and bone propped up upon a silver staff and shimmering with silver light.

Petronus took a cautious step forward. "Who are you?"

A burnt and scarred face looked up at him. "Oh my friend," Vlad Li Tam said, "you've grown young again."

Petronus crouched and studied the man that lay before him. The hair and clothing had been mostly burned away, but even before whatever calamity had overtaken his old friend, he'd wasted away to nearly nothing. Vlad had never been a large man, but he'd been powerfully built and now was skin and bone. "What's happened to you?"

Vlad coughed. "The tools of the parents."

Petronus remembered the quote. *Are not toys for children.* He nodded, thinking of the blood of Aver-Tal-Ka that fused with his own to grant him access to the temple but at the cost—at some point soon, he knew—of his life.

"Where is Neb? We need that staff, Vlad. It is time to lay it down."

"Neb is close," Vlad croaked. "And I'm finished with it now." The tattered old man tried to stand and couldn't. He raised a finger to the dark rings that hung low before them. Petronus saw a matching ring upon it. "You are authorized," Vlad whispered.

The tree shook slightly, and the Watching Tree beside it turned its dark eyes toward Petronus for a moment. But he forced his attention back to Vlad Li Tam.

"Have Neb bring you back to the tower," Petronus said. "We can treat your wounds. The war is nearly over, and we've new waters to fish."

Vlad shook his head. "Sorry, old friend. Only one fish left for me to hook." He coughed again. "Tell them I am sorry."

Petronus leaned forward. "Tell who?"

"All of them. My daughter. Rudolfo." He paused for another fit of coughing. "And Isaak."

Petronus's stomach sank. "What have you done, Vlad?"

Their eyes met for a moment before Vlad looked away. "You are authorized," he whispered again, and then vanished.

Petronus stood and took a hesitant step toward the tree. He stretched out a finger to touch one of the rings and felt that it was warm to his touch. Holding his breath, he slid his finger into it and then pulled it from the branch. It came away easily, and the flood of light and sound that swept him away as it did so dropped Petronus to his knees.

"Oh," he said as the Library of Elder Days introduced herself to him in a cascade of data.

Petronus wasn't sure how long he knelt there as it all unfolded itself before him. It felt like hours but was likely minutes. He saw vast archways leading into deeper and deeper forests of information. And he saw the burn marks where forests had been cut out. He saw the controls for the temple and for the Seaway. Finally, he forced the ring from his finger and tucked it into the pocket of his robe next to the stone Nadja had given him.

As he brushed against it, her voice filled his head. *Petronus?*

He closed his eyes. *Yes?*

Come to the roof, please.

The memory of their second time washed over him as he remembered the grass at the top of the temple and the light of Lasthome washing her pale, supple body. He shook it away and took to the stairs. The urgency in her tone wasn't the same urgency of the last call that had brought him up to her.

He raced the stairs and found her standing with a small collection of New Espirans and settlers. They were watching Lasthome and talking in sober voices.

Petronus squinted up. "What is it?"

Nadja's culture had no shame regarding couplings, and she kissed him quickly when he approached. "Look," she said.

He saw a large dark smudge over the southern continent. "What is it?"

"It was Ahm's Glory," she said. "It's been destroyed."

Petronus felt it like a boot to his stomach. "Neb's there."

She nodded, her eyes rimmed with tears. "Yes. Isaak, too. And others."

Tell them I am sorry. Petronus could not contain the sob that shook him.

Oh Vlad, what have you done?

Y'Zir had cut a city from the world and then cut Vlad's family from him. And now, those cut upon did their own cutting. But at what cost?

He looked away, his mind flooded with the memory of the pillar of smoke and ash upon the sky that drew him back into a papacy he'd laid down years before. "Have we heard from Neb or any of the others?"

Nadja shook her head and opened her mouth to speak. But she was silenced when a collective gasp went up from the small group that gathered.

Petronus looked up and saw the flash of white as it bloomed, went orange, then went dark maybe eight hundred leagues west of Ahm's Glory.

Nadja held a hand up and used it to measure distance. "T'Erick's Fall, I think." And as she said it, once more the tower vibrated.

"We have to reach Neb," Petronus said. A cold terror gripped him, and once more he thought it, *Oh Vlad, what have you done?*

Somehow, he'd taken the spell from Isaak and had used it twice now.

Petronus turned to Nadja. "Keep trying him by the stone. I'll go fetch the crescent."

She nodded, and Petronus saw the fear upon her face. He paused long enough to kiss her again, quickly, before moving for the door and stairs.

He took them three at a time and was halfway to his room when the tower shook again.

And for the third time, Petronus wondered what dark and terrible thing his childhood friend had done with all of his pain and just how far he would go to cut Y'Zir out of the world.

Neb

Neb spat blood and dirt from his mouth as he climbed up from the wreckage of a collapsed wall and looked around for some sign of Isaak and Vlad Li Tam.

One of Vanya's men had died upon impact, and the other had vanished. Vanya lay with her legs pinned beneath more rubble at the other end of the alley, and the kin-dragon shrieked and tore up gouts of cobblestone with its claws.

Neb contorted his mouth and screamed for his own kin-dragon, hearing its reply from a league away. *Guard me.*

Then he tightened the silver suit he wore, feeling strength and calm flood him. Neb took a step toward the kin-dragon. "Amylé," he said. He blinked and tried again. *Amylé.*

The kin-dragon snarled. *I can't believe you would betray your own people, Nebios Whym, in service to these bloodletting children of Y'Zir.*

The accusation caught him off guard. "I don't know what—"

The kin-dragon surged forward, interrupting him, and Neb leaped toward Vanya, feeling the wind of the massive beast's wings as it lunged past.

He lifted the section of wall that held her, his eyes never leaving the dragon as it turned on him again.

His own kin-dragon dropped silently like a massive silver stone to land upon Amylé. A whirlwind of dust and debris spun out from them as they twisted and writhed, tails and legs tangled, then lashing out. Another wall collapsed, and Neb pulled Vanya up and away from the fighting. "We need to find them," he said.

Something, he realized, had gone horribly awry. And not for the first time. All of the carefully laid plans brewing for thousands of years, dreams buried in songs and so many working parts to bring together a whole. Neb supposed the acolytes who had taught him and the other orphans Androfrancine logic and statistics would've have postulated that flaws in execution would be logical and likely for a strategy of such magnitude.

What is Isaak doing? And why? When the door had burst open and they'd come racing out, it was the last thing Neb had expected to see. And before he could pursue, Amylé had engaged them from above.

"Did you see where they went?"

Vanya pointed. "That way." Then she paused. "Sergeant Quinley says they were running toward the Magisters' Quarter."

Neb nodded. "It will be faster if I carry you," he said.

She blanched, then looked to her fallen man and the kin-dragons as they tore at each other. She inclined her head and he lifted her, surprised at how little she weighed.

Then Neb started out at an awkward jog. Behind him, Amylé's kin-dragon shrieked and tried to disengage. They'd gone a few leagues when her voice filled his head. *He's lost them.*

A tickle of fear at the base of Neb's neck spread out into an ocean of cold in his belly. It was a realization that he could not bear to comprehend, and he heard the panic in his voice. "He's controlling Isaak with the staff and ring."

He said it aloud and felt Vanya stiffen in his arms. *If he's controlling Isaak, then we must assume he has access to the Cacophonic Deaths.*

Neb forced the word through the gate of his terrified mind. *Yes.* Then he forced more words through his suddenly dry mouth. "Which means we need to leave now. I can't stop him if I can't find him. And if we stay . . ." He remembered that day as if it were yesterday. There on the hillside, waiting for the man he thought was his father—Brother Hebda, actually a behaviorist from the Office for the Preservation of the Light tasked with monitoring Neb—to return. He'd not returned, and Neb had stood and watched Windwir fall, his brown hair turned white and his speech reduced to glossolalia and bits of Androfrancine scripture as a result of that Desolation. "If we stay," he said, "we die."

He wanted to vomit, and even as the fear overtook him, so did the grief at what was coming. Vanya twisted in his arm as he forced his feet forward. *To me,* he called to the kin-dragon.

"Bring your man back to us quickly," Neb said, cocking his head. Then he tucked her into the alcove of a building. "I may have to fight our way out of here, so wait until I call you."

"What are you going to do?"

He looked to the sky. "I'm going to get us out of here."

MARTA.

The word dropped into his head like a rock, and he felt the pulsing in his temple. He knew the voice, and he shuddered at the urgency he heard. *Isaak? Where are you?*

There was no answer, and he heard a crash half a league to his west. His kin-dragon landed in the open road ahead of him, and the other fell upon it with claws and teeth. Neb held his breath and felt the silver skin tighten against him as he leaped into the fray and pressed for his dragon's offered belly. He felt the solid crush of the other beast as it shifted its weight, and then Neb and his own beast were one as he twisted away from Amylé and her teeth upon his neck. He whipped his tail and kicked his legs against her, surprised when she suddenly released him. Without a word, she beat her wings against the sky, climbing and then speeding north.

Neb scanned the alcove and saw Vanya and Quinley watching him with slack jaws. *Step out and stand closely together,* he sent. They did, and he gently wrapped them into his paws, pulling them against his stomach until the silver skin shifted and they were suddenly tucked inside the kin-dragon in small pockets near where Neb's own body lay. He wasted no time, surging up from the cobblestones and beating his wings furiously as he climbed and built speed.

He felt his skin go cold as the air around him went completely still and a solitary note rose up from somewhere far below. Neb glanced toward it, marking the place as best he could in his memory. Then he beat his wings furiously against what he knew followed soon.

The mechoservitors, even those reconstructed by Brother Charles, had contained some original element that made them immune to the effects of the spell. It had been mechoservitors—of the more ancient variety like the Watcher and Isaak's current form—that had delivered Xhum Y'Zir's death song in the first place, creating the Churning Wastes. Neb could only hope that the same immunity held true for the kin-dragon he flew.

He felt the wind and fire rush over him, and the force of it tumbled Neb through the sky as his wings tried to compensate. Drawing his legs in, he forced himself upward and away. Everything was white heat and then utter darkness as the city started into its second sigh. And as he raced against the expanding pillar of fire and smoke, he could not help but think of that day seemingly so long ago. He'd seen a metal bird—golden—flitting out of the firestorm. And now, he wondered what those below him might see. *Dragons upon the wind of death.*

The darkness released them, and Neb cast about, finally setting them down upon a hill that overlooked the boiling canals and pillar of fire. *Wait for me here,* he sent. *I need to find Tam.*

He pushed them gently out and stood them on the ground, then waited for the two of them to step back. When they were clear of his wings, Neb lifted off again and turned himself back to the desolation. He hovered there, as close as he could fly, and took in the wrath of Vlad Li Tam.

After everything that had transpired, he was once more here in this place overlooking more devastation and loss than any heart could contain. It did not matter that these were the people who had engineered the fall of Windwir or that their knives had carved the words of their faith into his skin while whispering to him. *They called me Abomination.* But truly, the Abomination was whoever had shaped such a vast and terrible weapon and unleashed it upon the world.

He tested the heat as he flew closer, pausing to adjust his course. If he strained his ears to filter out the roaring of cacophony, he could hear the notes of the song at the heart of the fire. Neb pushed and then waited, pushed and then waited, and scanned the ruins and craters with eyes that could see through magicks or smoke with ease.

He had no sense of how long it took before he was able to reach the center and find the withered remains of the man stretched out there in a large smoldering crater. He saw the silver staff clutched in the man's hands and the wide, empty eyes staring into nothing. Neb settled the kin-dragon down and adjusted as its paws settled into the ash. He heard the crunch beneath his feet and felt a stab of memory that drew him back to that forest of bones that he and Petronus had buried during that dark and violent winter.

The season brought Winters to mind. He'd fallen in love with her there amid those graves and had shared that first kiss and those early dreams.

This dream is of our home.

He shook it all away and forced himself to leave the kin-dragon. He wasn't prepared for his body's response. His senses had been bolstered, filtered by the kin-dragon when they were synchronized. But now that it was his lungs, his eyes, his skin, he felt the burn and the heat and the taste, and it was Windwir all over.

He approached Vlad's body. Somewhere not too far north, he heard a shriek. *Guard me,* he told the dragon again.

Vlad's clothing and hair had been burned away, but the staff shone brightly in his skeletal fists. He heard the collision of massive bodies behind him and moved quickly, pulling the sheath of light that protected him close as he reached for the staff.

The grip was firm, and Neb jumped when the wide and wild eyes turned upon him.

He is still alive.

The old man croaked something and jerked the staff away from Neb, knocking him off balance. He fell heavily on his satchel and winced as metal bit into his hip.

Groaning, he rolled and reached in to find the handle of the hand cannon. Vlad was trying to climb to his feet, using the staff as a prop. Neb fumbled with the weapon, pulling it free of the leather bag and the cloth it was wrapped in. "Your work is done now, Vlad," he shouted.

Vlad cackled. "Only one more fish to hook," he said.

The dragons were closer now, and Neb raised the canon. "No," he said, and with the pyre and grave of Windwir fixed steadily behind his eyes along with every bloody river of loss that had flowed into and out of that desolation, Nebios Whym squeezed the trigger and felt the cannon buck and roar in his hand.

Winters

The field stretched out all around her, white and expansive, and Winters sighed as she adjusted her back against the tree. Even in its massive shadow, the air was warm and the scent of the grass and the tree and the fallen seeds was intoxicating. She'd been lulled to sleep, even, until a distant sound jerked her head back.

What was that?

Wind, maybe?

No. She heard it again and climbed slowly to her feet.

Crying.

Winters moved around the base of the tree—easily the size of Rudolfo's giant library—in the direction of the noise. It was a child; that much she could tell.

Winters stopped when a woman's voice rose above the sobbing. "Don't look at it," she said, "or the false promise of it will seduce you. Just wait for me there and I will come to you soon."

"I can't bear it anymore." It was a little girl's voice.

Winters started walking again, this time working harder to stay quiet. She ran one hand along the smooth white skin of the great tree as she went.

The woman's voice dripped with sympathy. "I know, dear. We will make it stop."

Make what stop?

When the voice filled her mind, Winters's feet once more refused to move at the finality in the tone. *All of it.*

Then, somewhere around the bend of the tree, the old woman laughed and the little girl sniffled. "All of it," she said again, and Winters woke up.

She was disoriented at first, wondering why she felt damp and cold, why the bed had become so hard, and then remembered that she slept in the back of a wagon covered with a tarp. She felt about for her pouch and her boots, then crawled from the bedroll and dropped to the ground.

Captain Thrall and the others were already up and making breakfast. To anyone who passed them on the road, they were just another caravan of refugees bound for the Ninefold Forest, and they played the part well, right down to the food they cooked and the exclusive use of Landlish.

She rubbed sleep from her eyes.

Endrys Thrall smiled. "Good morning, Lady Winteria. I trust you slept well?"

She shrugged. "Well enough," she said. "I continue to dream."

She'd found that she had little appetite of late, so while the others ate, she sipped chai and jotted down what she could remember of her dream.

She suspected the woman was the same she'd encountered before but had no idea who the little girl might be. And the old woman had known she was there.

All of it. There was something chilling in the tone, and Winters shuddered at the memory of it. Then she closed her dream log and tucked it back into her pouch.

When they set out, she decided to walk for the first stretch. It was cold and dry for a change as spring approached in the Named Lands. There were birds singing in the forest to either side of the road they followed.

They'd not gone long before the ground shuddered—a long, slow ripple that was enough to throw off her balance but not drop her. The wagon lurched to a halt as the mules protested the shaking ground.

"What was that?" She looked up at Captain Thrall on the wagon.

"I'm not sure," he said. They waited a few minutes, and when nothing followed, he whistled the mules forward and they moved on.

But then, it shook again. Another slight ripple. Followed not long after by another.

Earthquakes were rare in the Named Lands, though they were more common in the far north near the Dragon's Spine where Winters and her people made their home. But this was an unprecedented number—too slight to do any harm. And of late, no earthquake had boded well. She remembered the quake that preceded Windwir and the times she felt the ground shake during Neb's fight with the Watcher. "Something is awry," she said.

Endrys Thrall nodded. "I agree."

They'd not gone much farther when he stopped them and climbed down from the wagon. His face had gone dark, the line of his jaw set with an emotion Winters couldn't place. The young officer pulled a man and a woman from the group off to the side and started a hushed but emotional conversation. The man gasped, and when the woman met Winters's eyes, she saw something terrible there. Like the look on the Y'Zirite lieutenant's face when she told Winters that Jakob had been killed. It chilled her blood, and her fears went to the first place she could think of.

Neb.

Captain Thrall glanced at her, her eyebrows furrowing at the look he must've seen on her face. His mouth became a grim line, and he nodded once before stepping away from the others and approaching her.

"There has been a development," he said in a somber tone. "Word has been relayed that Vlad Li Tam has accessed the Cacophonic Deaths. We have verification of six cities destroyed so far."

Six cities? And one of them, she knew, had to be Ahm's Glory where Neb had gone to face Tam down and take back the staff. She tried to contain the panic that rose up within her. "Neb?"

Endrys put his hand upon her shoulder. "Lord Whym survived the destruction of Ahm's Glory, but I know nothing beyond that."

"What about Marta? And Isaak?" She was reeling, her heart

already being drawn back along the path of loss to the death of Jakob and Hanric and all of the other losses before.

He met her eyes. "Isaak is believed to have escaped. We do not know about the others." The captain looked away. "The council had pulled back its operations in that region due to the instability but—"

Captain Thrall was interrupted as the ground shook again.

Seven cities.

He waited, his face pale, and opened his mouth only to close it again.

Eight cities.

No, she thought. Eight Windwirs. Not nameless Y'Zirite cities, but places with mothers and fathers, sons and daughters all now snuffed out. More light gone from the world for the sake of blood.

Blood for blood.

She felt the tears, but they were more than sorrow. They were anger. There were people in those cities who longed for a new home. She could only hope that they were able to make their way somehow. But Winters knew that for all who made the trek, there were others who for their own reasons could not. And Vlad Li Tam, who had taken so much from the world already, took yet a little more.

The captain's face was kind, and he remained quiet until she spoke. "It wasn't enough," she finally said in a quiet voice, "that he killed the children."

No, he'd taken it even further. Because, she realized, he was dismantling Y'Zir completely. With a bigger knife than the one they'd used to dismantle his family.

Now Endrys had conflicting emotions on his face, and finally he swallowed. "I have more to tell you. I hope you understand why it was necessary to keep this from you before. It was vital that as few people knew as possible, but I think you yourself have said that the time for secrets has passed."

Winters tried to puzzle out what came next by his eyes but had no luck. "Knew what?" Her eyes narrowed and some of that anger leaked into her voice. *"Knew what?"*

He took a deep breath. "The children are alive, Lady Winteria. Lord Tam faked their murder and we intercepted them. They are safe, and Lady Tam is with them now."

It was surreal to feel such unexpected relief flood her alongside of that anger; she had no time to ponder it as the ground shook again.

Nine cities.

But Neb was alive. And Jakob was alive. And these bits of light in such great darkness shone all the brighter for her as Winteria bat Mardic accommodated the shifting of the earth and set herself north to finish her work. Then, at long last, she could go home with her Homefinder and her people and hope to build something better than blood calling endlessly for blood.

Chapter 19

Jin Li Tam

Jin Li Tam lost all sense of time as they moved faster than any horse could have drawn them past sights that overwhelmed her with a sense of wonder she had never known before.

Platforms where people gathered as airships loaded and unloaded passengers moving between buildings of white stone and crystal. At one point, she looked over to Administrator Gras. "If you're able to travel in the way that brought me here," she asked, "why would you bother with these other forms of transportation?"

The woman smiled. "The People—the Younger Gods—could fly to the moon or they could travel instantly through the lightrails, but they chose to sail there instead because it was more enjoyable and could be shared with others. And it paid tribute to their early years when leaving home meant an ocean of saltwater instead of an ocean of stars." She reached into a basket beside her and drew out two pieces of fruit that looked like apples but were deep purple in color. She handed one to each of the children. "Don't you find this more enjoyable than the other experience?"

Jin nodded. And she saw wisdom beneath it all and pondered it as she went back to watching this new world slip past the carriage's open windows.

Soon, the landscape around them began to change. Now they rode a highway surrounded by flat fields freshly harvested, and Jin first noticed the pale white stretches of what she thought must be long ridges of stone beneath the soil, poking up above the ground for sometimes a half league at a time before disappearing again. She could see them out of either side of the carriage's windows, and finally she pointed. "What are those?"

"Those are the roots of Lasthome," Administrator Gras said. "They are more exposed the closer we get to the Firsthome Forest."

The Firsthome Forest. Jin opened her mouth to ask about it and stopped when the carriage suddenly bucked and tipped as the earth trembled around them. The children squealed and tumbled over, Amara's laughter suddenly a cry of pain as her head struck the ornate wooden edge of the bench. Jin lurched forward, falling into Chandra as they swerved off the road and came to a sudden stop.

She glanced at the administrator's face and saw a look upon it that she had not expected. *She is afraid.*

And Jin felt the same fear when suddenly, the light around them guttered, dimming nearly down to nothing for a moment. Now Jakob added his crying to Amara's, and Jin found she'd already scooped him up into her arms. When the light returned, she saw that the white stone ridges were now mottled nearly gray. And she saw the fear deepening on their hostess's face.

"What's happening?"

Elyna Gras tried to compose herself. "I will find out," she said, drawing a small round stone from her pocket and closing her eyes. Then she opened them. "Your father has destroyed Ahm's Glory."

Jin sat with the words for a moment. "He found the spellbook and used it?" It was the first thing that came to mind.

The administrator shook her head. "What you call the Seven Cacophonic Deaths was actually a complex core function of the Continuity Engine. The Y'Zirites spent years studying its notes and finally, Xhum found a way to bend the melody away from shaping and toward destruction. But it isn't magical. And Xhum Y'Zir's twisted version of it did not come from the Library of Elder Days." The guards opened the door to let them out while one of them walked around the carriage, inspecting it for damage, and the other looked down the road with a spyglass.

Jin stepped down, lifting Jakob up into her arms as she scanned the horizon. Already, the mottled color was fading as the roots whitened. And the light above felt brighter, too. The woman's words registered with her, and she glanced back up at the administrator. "If it didn't come from the spellbook, then where did it come from?"

But even as she asked, she answered her own question, and it broke her heart.

Isaak.

Somehow, Vlad Li Tam had bent Isaak in the same way he'd bent every other river around him. Doing the work of House Li Tam no matter what the cost. It was telling that she was more surprised that he had spared the children than she was at the idea of him murdering them, and she'd been flummoxed by his choice there. She'd even begun to afford her father grace, but to use Isaak—who had already been used in such a way—to visit his wrath upon Ahm's Glory moved that grace again out of reach. She made no attempt to hide the tears in her eyes. "He used Isaak."

"It appears so," the administrator said. "We have very few resources in that region, so reports are coming in sporadically."

The driver finished his inspection, and just as they started to climb back into the carriage, the ground shook again, and once more the light faltered.

Gras's face went more pale than it had already been, and she shot a worried look to the driver. "Perhaps we should do this another—"

No. Bring them along. It is time.

The voice was heavy and old and familiar but far away, and Jin had nothing to measure it against. It was warm inside her skull, and it flowed over her.

Gras inclined her head. There was something in the gesture that Jin thought might be resignation. She smiled weakly, but there was grief and fear behind it. "Yes, of course," the woman said.

Jin met Chandra's wide eyes, glad she'd heard it too. Jin wanted to ask, but knew she was going to learn soon enough who it was they went to visit. It waited in line behind all of her other questions about this place and what was happening. They'd not gone long before the wagon shook again. This time, they pressed on but at a slower pace.

The farmlands ended abruptly at the edge of a silver lake that the road they traveled extended beyond, held up by a white bridge made from the same material as the roots. The massive roots disappeared here into the blood of the earth and then reemerged in the distance, climbing up hills into forests of deep green lost in mist leagues ahead. They stopped at the edge of the bridge, and the driver called back through the open window.

"Administrator?"

"Take us ahead quickly, Langston."

He nodded. "Aye, ma'am."

Jin Li Tam clutched Jakob close with one arm while looping her forearm through the leather handle that hung near her head. Her eyes searched the road ahead, looking for some evidence of cracking or other instability, but despite the quakes—seven or eight of them now—the surface continued to remain unblemished. They rolled out onto the bridge and picked up speed.

They had cleared the bridge and were climbing gently into hills covered in trees that looked familiar to Jin Li Tam, though there were slight differences in size and color. "They look like the trees in the Ninefold Forest," she said quietly to Jakob. "The trees at home."

Jakob laughed and pointed out the window. "Papa home?"

Jin swallowed. "Yes."

"They are very much like the trees of the Ninefold Forest. Every crèche was seeded with Firsthome trees."

There was the word again. Sister Elsbet and the Regent Eliz Xhum had also spoken of crèches. The Named Lands was nestled within one. Y'Zir supposedly had eventually grown to occupy two. And there were others.

The light dimmed now as they crested the hill, and the road turned down and deeper into the forest. Jin watched the trees slip past, trying to soak in every type of tree and brush that she could identify. She'd been lulled by the road and the quiet dance of distant shafts of light within the forest when the ground shook again.

It shook one more time before they emerged from the forest to overlook an expanse of grass punctuated here and there by ponds and brooks of silver. And there, in the distance, at the center stood a massive, gray tree, its roots spilling out all around it before running beneath the grassy plain it stood upon. The front window of the carriage gave her only a sense of how large it was.

"This is our Grandmother," Administrator Gras said in a voice filled with reverence. "She's waited a long time to meet Jakob and Amara and the two of you."

Jin blinked. "Grandmother?"

The warm voice flowed through her like honey on a summer day. And yet now, there was another aspect to the voice that Jin could hear. *She is in pain,* she realized.

Come closer, Great Mother.

It wasn't the same tree that she'd seen in the Final Dream. But it was like it. "I need to see," Jin said.

Administrator Gras motioned for them to stop, and the driver let them out.

She couldn't take her eyes off of it. As Jin Li Tam climbed down from the horseless wagon, she looked up and saw a sky full of limbs stretching endlessly away, up and out, until it was lost in the haze above them.

The tree in the dream was the closest she'd come to seeing anything like it, but this tree was ancient and more gray than white, though she had no idea what color it had been before her father destroyed Ahm's Glory.

Or before Windwir. Or before the Age of Laughing Madness.

And how much further back? Even as she thought it, the ground shook again, and Jin Li Tam fell to her knees as the tree went darker and the light around them faded.

This time, the Grandmother Tree groaned, and Jin Li Tam felt the ache of it deep in her heart and bones.

Because it is all connected.

Yes, the Grandmother Tree whispered.

And Jin Li Tam wept at the power of that revelation and at the violence her father's wrath had unleashed upon the world.

Vlad Li Tam

Everything was heat and light and wind and the sound of his broken voice rising above it all, the staff blazing hot within his fist. And then everything was silence and nothing, and Vlad Li Tam moved in and out of awareness.

He opened his eyes and saw only vague shimmering light before them. But when he drew in a great lungful of breath, he tasted ozone and desolation upon it, and all around him he heard the dull roar as the fire that remained devoured what it could.

He'd seen no plague spiders or death golems or any of the remaining Cacophonic Deaths, though he'd forced himself to watch from beginning to end.

The library. He thought he'd remembered the change of temperature and Petronus's voice. Or had he hallucinated it? He coughed, and the pain of it racked his body. Had he said everything that needed saying? He thought he had. And he'd authorized Petronus access to the tower and its library. Petronus would be able to pass that access along. Now Vlad would honor his word and give over the staff. He had but one more fish to hook, and the bait dangled even now—he would not need the staff to land this one into his boat.

The temperature shifted again, and he squeezed the staff to draw some kind of assurance from it. The staff was dead and cold now in his hands. "I will have that from you, you old liar," the old woman said.

He could see her, and though he was still disoriented from the spell, Vlad recognized where they were. He lay in a field of dead grass upon the top of a massive tower, Lasthome filling the sky above them ringed by the stars strong enough to be seen despite the light of that world. "How did you get loose?"

Vlad squeezed the staff again, and once more it was dead in his hands.

The old woman laughed. "I've been loose for a while and biding my time."

He closed his eyes against a stab of pain in his left temple. "Then where is the girl?"

She chuckled. "She is out in the front; I have been whispering in the shadows."

Vlad tried to cast his mind back along the trail to see where along the way he'd left an opening for this aspect of Amylé D'Anjite to get free. It took longer to access his memory with the aching in his bones and the icepick of light behind his temples.

The day we took the ring. When he'd awakened she'd been holding both the staff and the spellbook. He sighed. "What now, then?"

She lunged for him, her hands gripping the staff. "Now I take the staff and shut down the Continuity Engine once and for all." Amylé snarled as she tugged at it. "Your work is done now, Vlad." But when she said it, the voice was suddenly wrong. It was the voice of a man, and the tower was gone. As his brain went to sorting whose voice he heard, the pain in his skull intensified. His eyes burned and his vision blurred now that he was no longer in the aether.

He saw the hazy shape he assumed was Amylé and pulled the staff hard toward himself as she tried to wrench it from his hands. The heat was back, along with the fire in his throat and the taste of ozone in his mouth. He saw the hazy shape of her as she fell, and Vlad tried to stand, using the staff as a prop. "Only one more fish to hook," he said to her, and the voice that roared "No" was followed immediately by an even louder roar as something large caught his shoulder and flipped him around and over to fall in the hot ash and stone and bones of Ahm's Glory.

He lay there a moment and willed the staff to give him strength. But he couldn't feel the staff in his fist or make his arm move. He turned his head to look at his arm, and he saw the staff nearby, still clenched in his fist, the dark ring glistening. But something about the distance or angle was entirely wrong.

How have I broken my arm? More than broken; he could not feel it at all.

He tried to replay the last few seconds to somehow understand what was happening. A form loomed over him, and he blinked. It wasn't Amylé. It was the boy, Nebios, only now he was a man wrapped in silver light, his face and hands and long white hair gray with ash. And he recognized the Androfrancine weapon in his hand.

"Your work is done, Vlad," Neb said as he scooped up the staff.

Vlad watched in rapt wonder as his severed arm went with it, fingers firmly wrapped about the Firstfall steel. He saw the tattered bits of flesh and jagged bone and smelled blast powder on the air.

Neb opened his mouth, and a blur of movement knocked him out of Vlad's field of vision. Vlad watched the staff fall away along with the boy even as that field of vision grayed.

One more fish to hook, he thought as he tried to roll over. Vlad could hear the sounds of combat somewhere to his left, and farther behind that, the kin-dragons fought. He saw his arm where Neb had dropped it, and he stretched his hand toward it. Something surreal in that moment of reaching for his own hand brought a dry cackle to his throat. He pushed himself forward with his feet, feeling the hot ash and stone burn his stomach as he did. He touched his finger, then touched the dark ring.

The library slipped around him as he did, and he closed his eyes against the feeling akin to vertigo that came from having a foot in both places. "Petronus?"

His friend was gone now, and Vlad closed his eyes, pushing again with his feet as his strength faded. He had his wrist now, and he pulled the arm toward himself until he could work the ring from his finger.

He rolled over and could see the staff, but Vlad knew he wouldn't last long enough to reach it. And the two Younger Gods who fought nearby would likely trample him even if he had the strength to make it.

But I still have the ring. Grimacing, he put it into his mouth and waited for enough saliva to coat it before swallowing it. Vlad felt it bruising the inside of his throat as it went down, and when he finished, he lay there gasping.

He jumped when he felt hands suddenly upon him. He looked but saw nothing as fingers pressed words into his forearm. *Lie still and let me treat you.*

He did as he was told as invisible hands tied off a tourniquet and poured powders into his wound. He craned his neck and saw Amylé and Neb thrashing about at the edge of a crater. He tried to stretch and see the staff but couldn't, and then he was being tucked into some kind of fabric and lifted from the ground to move silently and quickly away.

At some point the powders took him, and Vlad slept heavy and dreamless. And when he awoke it was to laughter and the swaying of a ship.

"Welcome aboard the *Kinshark*," Regent Eliz Xhum said as he pulled the sack from Vlad's head.

The mechanical contraption loomed over him, ancient and mottled steel and glass. The orb was clouded with thick green vapor, and something moved within it. A large pink wet eye pressed up to the inside of the glass. "Good to see you, not to be you," a rasping, singsong voice muttered through a mechanical voice box. "Naughty, naughty Vlad Li Tam."

Vlad Li Tam smiled at Ahm Y'Zir, grateful that his bait had been taken and that his work could now be finished.

Lysias

Rudolfo rode into the Gray Guard camp with his back straight, his green turban of office once more upon his head where it belonged, and Lysias was pleased with the strength and resolve he saw in his king.

They'd arisen predawn as the army's camp was struck and not long after had felt the first shakings in the ground. Earthquakes were rare in the Named Lands, and Lysias couldn't remember a time where so many had happened back to back. Strong enough to feel, but slight nonetheless. They'd ridden out on magicked horses, their scouts also magicked and running in formation around them. The ground had continued its shaking, but they'd barely felt it as they raced north.

And now, Orius waited for them with a handful of his officers and a look of smoldering anger on his face. They stood in the same muddy yard amid a scattering of wooden buildings between the edge of the forest and the Desolation of Windwir, where Lysias and his men had captured Ria.

"Hail, Lord Rudolfo," the man said without inclining his head. He turned to Lysias next. "General Lysias."

Rudolfo answered first. "Hail, General Orius, and well-met."

"Well-met." Lysias merely offered the slightest inclination of his head. Then he whistled their magicked scouts to the perimeter of camp in accordance with the Articles of Kin-Clave.

The old Androfrancine grunted. "I'll have your horses seen to. Let's sit down to whatever matter was so urgent that it couldn't wait until Pylos was secure." His single eye glared, and Rudolfo met the stare with aloof disinterest. "I'm sure you'd like to catch up to your army quickly."

Rudolfo seemed to ignore the tone, a feat that Sethbert could never have done, and Lysias smiled. The Gypsy King waved a gloved hand in the air. "My Wandering Army is in capable hands, General. You needn't concern yourself with Pylos."

Lysias waited until Rudolfo dismounted and then followed. He handed his reins over to the young Gray Guard that stepped forward. Then he fell in beside Rudolfo and followed Orius and his aide to a small cabin belching smoke into the dull gray sky from the tin chimney.

The interior was sparsely furnished. Lysias saw that Ria's old command table sat preserved in the corner with open crates nearby and papers partially filed. Near it was a narrow cot piled with army blankets. Orius himself had a small table, largely clear of papers, with three chairs ready. He sat and nodded to his aide, who stepped out and closed the door behind him. Then the Gray Guard general dropped all pretense and what little formality he'd pretended. "What in hells are you doing here, Rudolfo? We've a war to win."

Rudolfo sat. Lysias watched light spark in his dark eyes and saw the quick pull of his mouth. "The war is won, General Orius. What remains is a matter of simple cleanup."

The anger was clear in Orius's voice. "What remains, *Rudolfo*, is assuring that this is the last Y'Zirite Resurgence to rear its backwards, bloody head in this world."

Using the king's name a second time, now emphasized to clearly indicate disregard, brought Lysias's brow together. But Rudolfo didn't let it faze him. His tone remained level and calm, even aloof. "The head is off this snake, *General Orius*." Rudolfo's emphasis conveyed its own message. "I have no concerns about the safety of the Named Lands as far as Y'Zir is concerned." He leaned forward and stroked his beard, eyes narrowing. "However, I do have concerns about our present alliance and our mutuality of purpose," he said. "It has come to my attention that you are holding two Androfrancines—companions of Charles and Queen Winteria bat Mardic the Younger—and intend to try them under Androfrancine law?"

"I do. And my forward scouts have also located Winteria."

Now Lysias heard an edge creep into Rudolfo's voice. "And you intend to try her as well?"

Orius said nothing at first. *He heard the sharp blade in Rudolfo's question.* When he answered, his own eyes narrowed. "I have not yet determined how the Order's best interests are served regarding the deposed dreamer. But she was complicit in Isaak's escape." He paused as if thinking better of it, then did not surprise Lysias in the least by continuing forward. "I would be trying Charles as well had he survived."

"Then I will be brief, Orius," the Gypsy King said. *Now he drops the title.* And there was menace buried in the lightness of his tone as Rudolfo leaned back in the chair. "I have three points of disagreement. First, papacy and its succession is the bedrock of Androfrancine law. Petronus dismantled the papacy and turned over all of the Order's holdings to me. I am the ward of this orphaned order, and I require the release of those men into my custody and that you cease your pursuit of Winteria." Now there was ice in the voice. "Because her Shadow, Hanric, died before my eyes, the young queen in exile has also been one of my collected orphans. I have never had a truer ward than Winteria bat Mardic, and I will take her continued harassment as a personal affront." He waited, and Lysias saw the whiteness of Orius's knuckles as they clutched the edge of the table. "Second, as the truest line of authority based on the actions of the Order's last Pope, Petronus, I abjure you under unction to not release the pathogen beyond our borders. It goes too far, Orius, in a war that is already won." Now Rudolfo smiled. "And third, I support your execution of Winteria the Elder, Usurper of the Marsh Throne. I've come to bear witness to it but ask that I be allowed to speak with her beforehand." He paused. "She is indirectly responsible for the death of my son, and I would have words with her about that."

Orius waited a moment. "May I respond, General?"

Now, Lysias noted, he called him by his military title but not by the title afforded by his turban.

Rudolfo inclined his head. "Please."

"First," Orius said, "my orders came from Introspect the morning that Windwir fell. No countermanding orders have been given, and my mission continues. Succession law allows for the Gray Guard general to function as Pope de facto during times of war when a proper succession plan cannot be followed. It allows for times such as these, when the light is threatened." Now he leaned forward. "I do not recognize Petronus as Pope. His papacy ended long before my orders were issued. I recognize you not as an authority over the Order but as an ally by kin-clave against a common foe." Now there was edge to *his* voice. "And I have continued that position despite the disturbing discovery of your father's complicity in the invasion of the Named Lands and the problematic way in which all House Li Tam and Androfrancine holdings found their way into your coffers as a result of Windwir's fall."

Rudolfo said nothing.

"Second," Orius continued, "I will not release my people into your care, but I will grant clemency to your young ward on the condition that you escort her from the Named Lands immediately. Pylos has ships. I suggest you find her one."

Rudolfo nodded briefly at this.

"And third. I believe we can arrange the execution for this evening and have you on your way back to your army by morning. Does that sound agreeable to you?"

Rudolfo waved his hand again. "I do not find it agreeable, General. But I have heard your position and will ponder an adequate response. Until then, may I call upon your hospitality for myself and my men while we await the arrival of Winters and the departure of her sister?"

Orius nodded. "Certainly." He pursed his lips. "I will have my aide arrange for your men to eat in whatever shifts you require. We are at war; they may certainly avail themselves of our mess tent while magicked. Our kin-clave allows it."

Rudolfo inclined his head. "Thank you."

"And," Orius said, "I will have you shown to the prisoner." He stood, and Lysias heard the man's joints popping and crackling. "Please tell her I will be around to conclude our ongoing conversation later this afternoon."

The aide was waiting outside the door when Orius showed them out and issued a rush of clipped orders. Lysias found himself struggling to keep up with Rudolfo as they made their way across camp to the low, squat building that served as stockade.

The door opened on a small yard and a wall lined with four sturdy doors. Three were open. One was barred and locked from the outside. "Lord Rudolfo and General Lysias are here to see the prisoner," the aide said. "General Orius has approved it."

The guard nodded and went to the closed door, working the key and bar. "She is sedated," he said.

The smell hit Lysias first as soon as the door opened. Feces and vomit and sweat all vying for preeminence on the air. Lysias saw Rudolfo blanch. "She is also soiled," Rudolfo said. "And ill, apparently." He took a step back. "Perhaps you'd like to have her tended to before she meets with more polite company, Sergeant?"

The man's face went red, and he started to salute before inclining his head in a gesture befitting a visiting dignitary. "Yes, Lord Rudolfo."

They stepped outside, and Rudolfo put a hand upon Lysias's shoulder. He translated the words easily. *Have the scouts survey the camp and locate Hebda and Tertius. And get the men fed.*

Lysias made eye contact and nodded his head slightly to show he'd received the message. Then he slipped away. He went to the edge of the camp and whistled low and short. There was the slightest reply, and then a hand found his forearm. *Aye, General.*

He pressed his own words into the offered flesh. *Orius has arranged mess time in shifts. Use it to map the camp. We want to know where they're keeping the other prisoners.*

The scout acknowledged the message, then slipped away to pass the word. Lysias waited, his back to the camp, as he took in the massive grave of Windwir. There were still tall derricks in place and mounds of dirt where the Y'Zirites had desecrated the Androfrancine bones, but otherwise it looked the same as it had when he'd attended Petronus's trial. The night he'd killed Erlund's spymaster, Ignatio, and joined Rudolfo's Ninefold Forest as yet another refugee.

So much had passed since then, and he finally sensed an end coming. He closed his eyes and took in a deep breath, trying to conjure up the image of his daughter's face.

We could leave for the moon together, he thought.

But even as he thought it, Lysias suspected strongly he would find the home he deserved and not the home he longed for when that ending came. And so he turned his back upon the desolation and went in search of his king.

Rudolfo

The room still stank when the guard finally called for Rudolfo. As he entered, he saw Ria had a cot now and she sat at the edge of it wearing the baggy shirt and trousers of an Y'Zirite infantryman.

Her head hung down, her long hair dripping wet from the impromptu bathing. Sitting there, she looked even more like her younger sister. *The resemblance is uncanny.* And Rudolfo saw in the slope of her shoulders the same defeat he'd seen in Winters on the night she'd learned of Hanric's death and the seed of violent rebellion within her people.

He forced the similarities out of mind knowing it did not serve his purpose to associate this dangerous woman with her sister. But as he stood in the doorway of her rough wooden cell, he saw little threat. He looked over to her guard. "When was she fed last?"

The man blinked. "I have food coming, Lord."

Rudolfo nodded. "Knock when it is here," he said. Then he closed the door. They'd put a single chair in the room for him, and he sat in it now, still saying nothing.

He waited and watched her. She made no attempt to raise her head or to speak. He honored her silence with his own, and when the guard knocked at the door, he opened it, took the mess tray from him, and placed it on the cot next to her.

"You should eat, Ria." He did not use her title; it had never been hers as far as Rudolfo was concerned. She'd stolen her sister's throne by careful manipulation and insurrection.

And stole my son from me. He could still remember the hollow, empty look on Vlad Li Tam's face when he'd rescued Vlad from the blood temple where Ria had performed his kin-healing. He remembered the mass grave where the Tams were buried after giving up their last words to their father as he watched from the observation deck beneath Ria's knife. Tam had said something at some point on the journey back. What had he said?

I will build my pain into an army. And that army had murdered Rudolfo's son.

He looked at Ria. She still hadn't moved. "Orius will be by later," he finally said, "to finish your conversation."

She said nothing.

"After that," Rudolfo continued, "you will be executed. I think they're even using your own people's Firstfall Axe."

Ria broke her silence now and surprised Rudolfo. She laughed and it was bitter and dark. When she looked up, he saw the bruises on her face, and when she spoke through split lips, he heard the slur in her speech.

"They are not my people," she said. "My people will come for me. She promised."

Rudolfo's eyebrows furrowed. "The Y'Zirites are routed here. Even now my Wandering Army marches to Pylos to cut the last of them from our lands."

She laughed again, and he heard more than dark and bitter within it now. "They are not my people, either. My people will come for me. She promised."

She must mean her sister. And Rudolfo had no doubt that Winters, despite having her people wrenched from her by this woman, would intervene in the execution if she could. Despite the light that had been lost in these few years, she'd not lost the idealism of her youth. "I do not think anyone is coming for you, Ria."

She went back to silence.

Rudolfo stood. "I will leave you now. I have no parting words for you. The world will be better when you are no longer in it. But your death will not bring back any of the thousands upon thousands your blades and your faith have cut from this world. You live beyond the grace of us all."

She looked up and met his eyes. For just a moment, Rudolfo saw some of the imperious woman he remembered from her days in power. "Orius hunts more than Y'Zirites. He is hunting down the last of the

Machtvolk as well. He's shown me the bodies. They've been left unburied in the forest."

Her sudden shift into clarity caught Rudolfo off guard.

"I will look into it," he said. But even as he said it, he knew he
wouldn't need to look far. It was yet more evidence that Orius had been
tipped into darkness by his pursuit of avenging the light.

Her moment of focus continued, and she kept her eyes fixed on his.
"Do you understand why your family was chosen?"

He shook his head. He'd accepted long ago that there were no answers and that Tam had made his choices for his own reasons—and
later on, when his network was co-opted, made choices based on the
machinations of others in an ironic twist.

"You have been taught all your life that the seven sons of Xhum
Y'Zir were murdered by P'Andro Whym and his scientist scholars. But
Ahm Y'Zir was not murdered. His boyhood friend, P'Andro Whym,
showed mercy on him. He maimed the Wizard King beyond recognition, and the first Rudolfo, the desert thief who led your gypsies into
the forests beyond the Keeper's Wall, hid him away to build a faith and
an empire." She smiled. "That," Ria said, "is how your people were
deeded the Keeper's Crèche."

"Your people were as well," Rudolfo said.

Ria smiled. "No," she said. "All of this—every stone and every blade
of grass upon Lasthome—was deeded to my people. My people made
it out of desolation." Then she went back to staring at the floor.

The sudden shift in her along with the words discomfited Rudolfo.
He stared at her for a moment, then let himself out.

He found Lysias waiting, and he pulled the general aside.

"How is she?" Lysias asked.

Rudolfo wasn't sure how to answer. "Perplexing," he finally said.
And as he did so, his fingers sought Lysias's shoulders. *She says Orius
is hunting Marshers as well as Y'Zirites. There are unburied bodies in the
forest.*

Lysias nodded. "She is that," he answered. *I'll have the scouts investi-
gate. We've located Hebda and Tertius.*

Rudolfo nodded. He had no doubt that they would find the bodies.
And he had no doubt that Orius wouldn't deny it and would instead
defend it vigorously. And it was a line of reasoning that Rudolfo could
understand. When he'd first discovered the hidden Y'Zirites within
his forest, he'd instantly seen the need to purge them from his lands

and to restore a sense of safety to the world. But his father's Y'Zirites had used paint instead of blood and scars in their worship and had done so quietly, without requiring others to participate or embrace their faith. He stood by his decision to banish them but could not fathom solving that problem with a blade himself. Not anymore.

And the Androfrancine general was operating under the belief that he represented the Order under papal authority that superseded Petronus's or his own as the inheritor of the Order.

It cemented Rudolfo's decision to remain behind. The more he saw, the more he realized that even as the threat of Y'Zir diminished a new threat arose.

The threat of what we become as a result of this and what comes after if it isn't resolved.

A cycle was perpetuating itself, and if unchecked, Orius would raise a new Order from the ashes of Windwir not bent upon preserving the light but upon eradicating all darkness. And there was a difference between the two that Rudolfo grew more and more aware of with each passing day.

I will be removing Orius from power. He knew the right path and took it—that is what his men said. But what they didn't realize was that when he arrived to some paths, they weighed him down and made his heart heavy within him. That was a side of the turban he did not show anyone, though for a brief time he'd shown it to Jin Li Tam.

The thought of her sent a ripple of longing and despair through him. Fierce and formidable and her father's daughter. He tried not to think about her now, especially in the days since he'd learned of Jakob. His rage at her decision to leave the Named Lands with their son had never abated. And larger than his rage over her choice and its final, disastrous result was Rudolfo's rage over loving her still.

Because I do not know how to not love her. How much of that was Tam conditioning through their influences over his life? And how much of it was just how love works, drawing opposites together for one reason and keeping them together for another? Rudolfo didn't pretend to know much about love. Love-making was another matter. But for a brief while, he'd loved and had experienced a continent of love to explore both in the eyes of his bride and his son.

Rudolfo sighed. Lysias had already gone to set the scouts to their task. And he now had strategies to implement and a renegade general to confront.

The turban upon his head felt heavy suddenly, and he glanced behind him at the stockade. She'd seemed lucid and clear-headed there at the end. But earlier, he'd heard madness in her voice.

My people will come for me. She promised.

It had to be Winters. Or just the raving of a woman on the edge of sanity. He shook the voice out of his head and checked his knives within their sheaths, checked the pouch of scout powders beneath his shirt.

Then Rudolfo, Lord of the Ninefold Forest, turned himself in the direction of Orius's cabin for one more unpleasant turn upon the trail.

Chapter 20

Winters

Weak afternoon light leaked through gathering clouds when Winters and the others stopped.

Endrys Thrall scanned the road ahead along with the thinning forest that ran along the eastern side, sweeping his slender spyglass to the left and right. "There are magicked scouts in the intersection," he said. "They are moving in our direction." He squinted. "They are wearing Gray Guard colors."

Winters had joined him on the driver's bench after lunch and took the spyglass he offered. "What do we do?"

He closed his eyes for a moment, sending orders out by way of the stone in his hand. She'd seen his crew hide long wooden tubes beneath the household items and foodstuffs one would expect in a wagon of refugees, and now, two of them moved to the back of the wagon, within easy reach. There were five total here with her not counting their captain. She had no idea how many others might be following or keeping pace with them in hiding. "Tell them who you are and that you require audience with Orius. Invoke your kin-clave with the Ninefold Forest for protection. They will likely want to take you with them. Go. We'll join you shortly." He paused again. "My advance party reports that Lord Rudolfo and his General Lysias are in the camp with a full squad of Gypsy Scouts."

Winters swallowed. The last time she'd seen him, he'd been angry over her choice not to tell him about Jin Li Tam's decision to flee the Named Lands with Jakob. He'd been a friend to her and her people, and in that moment she felt her friendship with Jin Li Tam had compromised the man's trust in her.

And what does he know? Surely he'd been told of the events in Y'Zir? But if Endrys Thrall was correct, he couldn't possibly know that his son was still alive. That information had been kept from everyone not directly involved. The death of the Child of Promise and the Crimson Empress were necessary for the dismantling of the Y'Zirite faith and empire. But now that Vlad Li Tam had taken that dismantling even further by unleashing the Seven Cacophonic Deaths, the need for that secret was past.

And maybe, she thought, in bearing that news to him she would redeem that broken trust.

"They're close," Endrys whispered. "Get ready."

"Hail the wagon," a voice ahead in the road called out. "And hail Winteria bat Mardic, the Younger."

Winters answered. "Hail, scout. Which house are you?"

"We serve no house but the light. We are Gray Guard under command of General Orius, sent to escort you to him."

"That is most welcome news," she said, "for I seek audience with the general." She paused. "As well as Lord Rudolfo." Winters didn't wait for them to answer. She stood and reached into her pouch, fishing out a few coins and offering them to Endrys. "Thank you for your hospitality, sir. I wish you success in your new ventures."

Endrys inclined his head and took the coins. "Thank you, Lady. It was my pleasure."

She climbed down and drew a bit of dried black root from her pouch, slipping it into her mouth.

Winters saw the slightest shimmer now of forms in the road ahead of her and approached. "We will make better time if we carry you, Lady."

She shrugged off the hands that reached for her. "No, you will not." Then, feeling the strength of the root settle into her legs, Winters stretched out into a run. It was the first time she'd run under the root since she'd last been with the Gray Guard scouts, running with Renard and Isaak and Marta. Now there was more mud and less snow, but the road itself was solid beneath her lightweight boots.

Winters felt the wind of the scouts as they swept up around her, and then she increased her speed. She poured herself into the run, feeling the cool air upon her face, pulling at her hair. She'd made do now for weeks with the small scout pack she'd picked up along the way, and she cinched it up now tighter.

She wasn't sure how long they ran before she saw the smoke of the Androfrancine camp, and it felt like mere minutes had passed before she was in the camp surrounded by gray uniforms.

Rudolfo, in his green turban and rainbow-colored cloak, stood out from all of them, and when their eyes met, they were not eyes she'd seen before. They were haunted now, and dark circles stood out beneath the Gypsy King's eyes. But the line of his jaw was firm, and he stood straight.

I must tell him.

"Hail, Lady Winteria," Rudolfo said, inclining his head.

"Hail, Lord Rudolfo," she replied as she returned the gesture.

Others were gathering now, and the door of the nearest cabin opened. Orius didn't appear to have missed any sleep or any meals since she'd last seen him, and he barely worked to mask his disdain. "Hail, Winteria," he said. Then he looked in the direction of the magicked scouts. "Leave her with me." He looked at Rudolfo. "I have some questions for her before releasing her into your care, General Rudolfo."

She looked from one man to the other and watched Rudolfo's eyes narrow. He did not speak, and she recognized that he was waiting for her to speak for herself. "I've come seeking audience with you both," she said, "and I will gladly answer questions for you both as well."

Rudolfo smiled; Orius did not. "Come in, then," he said, turning to his open door.

"First," Winters said, "I would see that my sister is well and being cared for as befitting a prisoner of her standing."

"Your sister has no standing," Orius said in a clipped tone, "and is being executed tonight, Winteria. She is being afforded only the care necessary to carry us to that moment."

The general's back was to her when she felt Rudolfo's fingers upon her shoulder. *I've seen to her.*

Winters felt the tension in her neck and forced it away. Then she raised her voice. "No, General Orius. We can talk here."

His voice was short. "Lady Winteria—"

She gave him no room to speak. "My words are for all to bear witness to. Unless you are afraid of the voice of an unarmed girl?"

She watched his back stiffen at her words. When he turned, he had a bemused look upon his face. He glanced to Rudolfo. "Your ward is troublesome, General. Do you wish to indulge her, or do you wish a more civil setting for our discourse?"

Rudolfo met her eyes. "She does not require my indulgence, General. She is the true Queen of the Marsh. I would hear her on whatever terms she proposes."

Orius sighed. "Very well."

Winters looked at the small group that gathered. Most were Gray Guard officers, but a few of the soldiers on guard duty stood about. "I am Winteria bat Mardic," she said, "and as Lord Rudolfo expressed, I am the true Queen of the Marsh. I come under kin-clave as among the first to ride to Windwir's aid upon the day that city fell. I watched the gravediggers bury your people here, General Orius, while my people fought alongside Rudolfo and while Hanric bellowed my War Sermons out upon the wind." She felt the words in her stomach and heard the emotion crack in her voice at the memory of her Shadow, the man who had been a father to her and had been the man the Named Lands thought of as the Marsh King. "The fall of Windwir ended the enmity between the Marshfolk and the Order."

"The fall of Windwir was part of a Marshfolk plot led by your older sister," Orius growled, interrupting her. "With or without your knowledge, it is the truth of it."

"My throne," Winters said, letting anger drip into her voice, "was taken from me as part of an elaborate plot that involved elements from within my house, within House Li Tam. . . ." She nodded. "Lord Rudolfo's House by way of his father, Lord Jakob, along with the Entrolusian Delta and even the Order were all involved. One of Charles's most trusted assistants rescripted Isaak to deliver the spell." She paused at the lump she felt suddenly at the memory of those earthquakes. "All of our houses were infiltrated at some level," she said. "And all of us have lost. Some more than others. But the war is won. The Androfrancine weapon has eliminated the Y'Zirite threat in the Named Lands. And surely you remember the dream? We all shared it. There is more than just an end to war upon our horizon, but a new world to explore and a new home to settle. Those who wish it may come with us, and perhaps together we can start something new. Perhaps we can learn a new path with less blood. Death is a certainty of life, but we have become too good at hastening its arrival." She paused and took a breath, measuring the eyes and faces around her. She had them with her words—all but Orius, who glared at her. "It is time for peace, General. And I have come in that peace to ask you for my sister's life. Exile her into my care, and I will take her from the Named Lands."

The general grunted. "He wants Tertius and Hebda. You want your sister." He looked at Rudolfo. "I'm growing weary, Rudolfo, and we have a war to win. I suggest that you—"

Rudolfo stepped forward and placed himself toe-to-toe. "I suggest that you stand down, General." Then he said something in too low of a voice for Winters to hear, but the general's face went purple as he stepped back and reached for his sword. He opened his mouth, his lips contorted to say something, and then suddenly his eyes went wide.

The others around him went slack-jawed, and Winters heard a hum behind her. Even Rudolfo, hands at his knife hilts, stared in wide-eyed wonder, and she finally turned.

Low and shining in the late afternoon light, a silver airship moved over the plains, a green light of peace alternating with the blue light of inquiry upon its bow.

She'd never seen anything like it before, and that was after seeing more wonders of late than she'd imagined possible—metal men and kin-dragons and now this. The camp went to third alarm, and then a voice called out from the forest.

"Hail the camp," Renard said as he stepped out from the evergreen cover. "I have guests in my company with an interesting story to tell."

And Winteria bat Mardic smiled when Captain Endrys Thrall stepped out, splendid in his New Espiran Council Expeditionary Force uniform, accompanied by two of his other officers, each holding slender wooden tubes, as their ship began its descent on the other side of camp.

Petronus

Voices at the door brought Petronus slowly awake, and he instantly blushed at the location of Ambassador Thrall's hand. "We have company," he whispered into her ginger hair and then summoned his robe silently.

Clothe me.

He felt the light moving over his bare feet as he put them upon the floor. It wove its way over his skin as he stood. His ears were hot. Everyone knew; he was certain of it. Rafe Merrique harangued him about it when it was appropriate to do so, but the old pirate seemed genuinely happy and had invented an entire new line of papal limericks. Nadja's people paid it no mind whatsoever, but he found their culture's sexual values foreign, lacking not just in shame but what he considered a certain propriety.

For the pleasures and privations of the body are a distraction from the light, he thought, quoting the Fourth Precept of P'Andro Whym. *Be ye therefore husbands and fathers to the light and let others bear the baser burdens of our animal instincts.*

He blushed again and opened the door. It was Captain Mikayl, Nadja's aide. Like the ambassador she served, she was young and climbing the Expeditionary Force's ladder quickly.

"Good morning, Father Petronus." She inclined her head. He felt even less comfortable with the title now but had nothing better to offer.

"Good morning, Captain."

"I'm sorry to come early, but there is a development that you and the ambassador should be aware of."

There was a small group behind her. He glanced over his shoulder. Nadja had already put her own robe on and was slipping into the bathing chamber that adjoined their rooms. "We'll be right with you," he said.

Five minutes later, they met the others in the large, brightly lit room that served as the command center. Here, he and Nadja both had tables and aides hard at work. As more and more people showed up to claim their new home, the work had grown too. Hunting parties, mapping parties—though that had become moot once Petronus accessed the library. But rooms were being assigned within the tower, and timber was being logged from the jungle as those who didn't wish to live within that massive structure built homes around it.

He took the mug of chai his aide pushed into his hand. "Thank you. What is this development?"

One of the library tenders stepped forward. His face was flushed with excitement. "I have no idea how it happened. I've checked our initial maps of the tower over and over again."

Petronus sipped the chai and glanced at Nadja. She raised her eyebrows over her own mug. "How what happened?"

"A door," he said. "But it wasn't there before. It's not on any of the maps." He moved to the door. "I'll show you."

Petronus pressed his thumb against the ring on his finger and accessed the library. There, he found the temple schematics and saw the red flashing light. "I think I see it," he said. He squinted into the aether, but it was a section of the library that had been burned out.

"Let's go see it," Nadja said as she placed her mug on the table.

Petronus worked to keep up with her as she set out for the floor that the library took up so much of. When they reached that floor, the librarian took the lead, and Petronus confirmed his suspicions when the door they reached matched the flashing area on the library's schematic.

Nadja touched it. Most doors required the slightest touch to open, and some even anticipated the approach and opened automatically. But this door didn't move. Petronus put his hand next to hers and pulled it back at what he felt. "It's . . . pulsing."

She arched an eyebrow at him. "I don't feel anything."

He put his hand down again and felt the undulating skin beneath it. The door was warm and had a pulse. Of course the entire tower did, but it wasn't as pronounced as here. And he agreed with the librarian: It may be on the schematic, but he and Neb and Rafe had started maps and they'd been validated by the New Espirans. And even on the library's map of the temple, it showed up red and flashing and without any kind of description. He moved his hand over it. *Open.*

Nothing. Petronus put an ear to it and could hear the distant, slow movement. "I think we should post a watch on it," he said.

"I concur," Nadja said. "Do we have any idea when it appeared?"

Petronus slipped back into the library and studied the schematic closely. There was a notation upon it that he suspected was a date, and when he drew that batch of characters to himself, it expanded to show another number—one that appeared to be reducing itself.

Captain Mikayl spoke up. "It was brought to my attention shortly before I woke you."

"I reported it at the end of my shift," the librarian said. "I don't know how many times I passed it before I realized it hadn't been there before."

Petronus straightened. "Well, keep us posted on anything that happens with it." Then he glanced to Mikayl. "I imagine there's more information on Y'Zir?"

The captain nodded, and her face was grim. "There is, Father."

Petronus blushed again at the title. He felt a stab of shame. Vlad Li

Tam had burned down most of the Empire of Y'Zir, and Petronus had been rutting like a first-year acolyte the night before his vows. Of course it hadn't started that way. They'd been talking about what was happening, and it had brought back such stark memories of that day he'd seen Windwir's pyre—and seeing Vlad had brought back such stark memories of the clever, redheaded boy he'd been. And Petronus had found himself suddenly tearing up.

Nadja had reached out to hold him. And then . . .

He'd been embarrassed later. She'd called it a sixth turn on the Five-fold Path of Grief.

But now, as they returned to their shared office and returned to work, the news settled as Captain Mikayl took them through the day's briefing.

Forty-one cities across two crèches. And they'd had people near several of them who had been able to send information back. Not all had made it out. But the devastation was not as widespread as it could have been. It was a limited release—the bearers of the spell had not lived long enough to bring the same level of desolation that Isaak or Xhum Y'Zir's Death Choir had managed. But they had cut forty-one cities out of Y'Zir—and at least half had been unaffected by Vlad's plague when the New Espirans had withdrawn their assets, which meant much higher casualties. It made Windwir look small. But there was more that he wasn't hearing. Knowing glances between Nadja and her aide told him he would need to ask later.

"And Captain Merrique reports Y'Zirite ships in the lunar sea. They appear to be scouting."

Merrique had compelled some of the captains arriving with their pilgrims to help him form a small fleet with which to patrol. Now that Petronus had access to charts and maps, that was making the old pirate's job far easier. "Do we have any idea how many?"

The captain shook her head. "No. And they are not approaching. They flee once sighted."

"And there's been no word from Neb?" He'd tried the crescent shortly after Ahm's Glory fell but had not been able to reach him. He'd also not responded to the stone he now supposedly carried thanks to the New Espiran he was working with.

"We've had little communication with anyone. Our devices utilize the aether and subaether for communication—both of which are less reliable now in those regions." The young captain paused, glancing to

Nadja before continuing. "These kinds of catastrophic events place a great deal of strain on the blood of the earth."

Petronus nodded, though he barely understood. Vlad had obviously used the subaether to speak to him in the library, though he'd had the staff to aid him. Still, the gap between the Androfrancines' best technology (still often believed to be magick) and the New Espirans' was vast. And the gap between theirs and the Younger Gods'—the People's—was even larger.

He hoped once the dust settled more that he'd be able to spend some time with the library. He'd scratched the surface of the People—his people—and their capacity but knew there was so much more.

He looked at the day ahead of him. There were a few Androfrancines who had heeded Winters's dream and had requested time. He also had lunch with Rafe to discuss his plans for the small navy he grew. Petronus had thought the old pirate would head back to Lasthome to try once more to find his lost ship. But so far the smuggler had been content to sail new waters in the sleek crystalline vessel they'd found upon their arrival on the moon.

And we have to find Neb.

Mikayl had finished and stepped out, leaving Petronus alone with Nadja. She looked to him, and her brow furrowed. "Petronus?"

"Yes?"

She stood and slipped a kerchief from her pocket. "Your nose is bleeding."

He sniffed, smelled iron and touched a finger to it. It came away red, and he tried to remember the last time he'd had a nosebleed. It was when Hebda had been speaking to him through the dreamstone, he thought. He'd certainly not had one since.

She touched the cloth to his nose and dabbed the blood away. Her blue eyes narrowed. "Do you feel okay? Maybe you are overdoing it?"

But he felt fine. In fact, Petronus felt better than he'd felt in years. The only shadows were what happened now on Lasthome, and if he thought about it too much, the end he knew was coming.

And this could be the beginning of that end.

Petronus felt fear rise like a lump in his throat, and he looked to the girl who had suddenly become such a different anchor for his tired old heart than the backward dream he'd served for much of his life. *She helps me dream forward,* he realized. And in that moment, he wanted to reach out and hold her again.

But instead, Petronus kissed her forehead and excused himself quickly. Then he went to the roof of the temple with the crescent and sat alone with his thoughts.

Neb

Light erupted between Neb's ears as another fist landed upon his jaw, sending him spinning into a pile of ash and bones. As he fell, he could feel the silver suit straining to protect him.

Amylé's foot lashed out to catch his shoulder, but this time he swung up and caught her behind the knee, sending her sprawling onto him. She twisted and writhed as he worked to get his arm around her throat, and just as he did, he felt the wind go out of him as her knee found his groin.

"Stay down, Nebios," she said. "I've no wish to kill you."

And she could. She wore the suit far better than he did, just as she wore the kin-dragon, understanding how both operated and knowing how to push their limits in ways he couldn't fathom. But as the daughter of an officer during the Downunder War, she'd likely received training on how to use these tools. Neb had fallen into it with the briefest of coaching from the ghost of his long-dead father, and his baptism had been the fight with the Watcher.

Which went about as well as this one. But he doubted Isaak would come back this time and save him. He twisted his head to check on Vlad Li Tam and the staff again but saw nothing but the gray haze of ash they'd kicked up. The nauseating pain was a dull ache, and it joined the thousand other aches in his body. Gritting his teeth, he forced himself up and pulled the suit tighter around him.

I can't beat her. Neb swallowed. "Amylé, we don't need to fight."

Her eyes narrowed. "Are you going to help me?"

He nodded slowly. "I want to. You're ill. And I think Tam took advantage of that illness." He raised his hands and took a tentative step toward her. "Come back to the Firsthome Temple with me. We have the staff and ring. The library will help us."

She laughed. "What you are offering is not the help I require, Nebios. But I know where to find that help."

Amylé took another step closer, and the smell of her, now that he could afford to notice it, intoxicated him.

But he had no time for it. There was a blackened skull in her hand

when it came up suddenly against the side of his head, and Neb felt
his knees go under him as the light and heat around him spun away
into night.

♄

It was dark when he came to and climbed to his feet. He reached for
the crescent in his pouch by instinct. "Petronus?"

Neb tried to orient himself by the glow of distant embers and found
where Vlad had been. But the old man was missing, along with the
staff and the severed arm. "I'm here, Neb," he heard the tinny voice
whisper from far away. "Are you okay? Do you have the staff and ring?"

"I think Amylé has them," he said. He felt the weight in his chest.
"I think she took Tam as well." He suddenly remembered the stone
Captain Vanya had given him and reached for it. It was gone as well.
"She also has my talking stone."

"Do you have any idea where she is going?"

The light of the moon was hazy through the ash that clung to the
air around him. He scanned the scattered pockets of Ahm's Glory that
still glowed and summoned the blood of the earth. "I don't know, but
I would keep an eye out," Neb said. "I'm going to try to find her."

"Be safe, Neb."

"Yes," he said. He stubbed his toe against something and uncov-
ered the hand cannon. He scooped it up and tucked it back into his
pouch. Then he called his kin-dragon.

There was no answer, and he felt a panic rise. The beast had never
failed to answer his call. He shrieked again, this time pouring himself
into the cry.

In the distance, Neb heard a whimper. *Clothe me.*

He pulled the fresh sheath of silver close to his skin and ran in the
direction of the whimper. The noise grew as his feet flew over the
uneven ground. He crested a crater and spotted the kin-dragon.

It lay in a twisted heap in a pool of silver fluid, twitching and kicking the one leg that worked. Two of its four wings had been torn loose,
and one of its eyes had been gouged away and dangled from a wire
that dripped fluid.

Neb approached and it whimpered again, and when he touched its
massive snout, he felt the connection between them. The pain was
intense, and he lifted his hand as if touching a hot stove.

"I'm sorry," he told the fallen beast. He stared at his hand and then
at the large unblinking eye. Then he braced himself and put his hand

back where it had been, taking the pain onto himself and letting it burn away the fog from his mind.

It's dying. He didn't know why he'd lent the kin-dragon immortality in his mind. He'd flown the beast as high in the air as it could go and down into the depths of the sea. Neb had never even considered that it could it be harmed, much less killed.

He closed his eyes and breathed with the beast, ignoring the tinny voice that called for him. When it was finally dead, he opened his eyes.

It gave its life to save me, and I've never given it a name. He'd seen it as a machine—more so than Isaak, who'd proven himself more in so many ways.

Finally, he answered Petronus. "I have another problem," he said. "My kin-dragon is dead. I'm going to try to find Captain Vanya. Please pass word to her if you can through Ambassador Thrall."

The expletives from the crescent were worthy of a fisherman. "I will tell her."

Neb tucked the crescent away and set out for a run back in the direction of the high ground where he had set the New Espirans down. He gave himself to an easy pace until Petronus's voice drifted up to him from the pouch.

"She's lit a fire in the east," Petronus said. "The council has decided to put its fleet back in the air and is sending a ship for you. They've also sent one for Winters."

It won't be fast enough to catch up to Amylé. And he had no idea where she might go. But he was certain that her plans for the staff couldn't be any better than Vlad Li Tam's. "And there have been no sightings of Amylé?"

"No, but we are preparing for her here." The old Pope paused a moment. "And I don't want to worry you, but there are Y'Zirites sneaking about the lunar sea. Merrique is organizing a hunting party."

Neb felt a darkness wash over him. He'd lost the dragon and the staff and ring. The dragon had proven to be their best defense against the Y'Zirites and the staff—in Tam's hands, he'd destroyed a city and somehow reached even beyond it. Petronus had continued speaking, and Neb had missed some of the words. He pushed down the rising despair and tried to listen.

"And remember, Nebios, how far we've come on this dream." Petronus chuckled. "What kind of prophecy thousands of years in the making has any chance of being enacted without error or misstep? We have enough to work with." He also heard something else in the voice besides the exhaustion that rode them all. "And Vlad did something—authorized me somehow—so we have access to the library and the other rings. I've assigned several of the New Espiran librarians. We may not have that particular ring and we may not have the staff, but we have a home. Don't lose sight of that, Son."

He was right, and Neb found himself wondering when it was that he'd gone from a child of P'Andro Whym—an irony that awed him now that he knew his true parentage—to someone who believed in the infallibility of dreams and visions. All along the way, it had been proven again and again that what seemed supernatural or magical was rooted in the advanced sciences of the People. Winters and the Dreaming Kings were experiencing something called the Dream Shadrus Drank— ingested thousands of years ago and activated once they settled into the Lands Beyond the Keeper's Wall. And the other dream—the Canticle for the Fallen Moon that the mechoservitors of Sanctorum Lux had discovered buried deep in the Churning Wastes, whispering harp strings that played the song over and over again. There had been no magick in it—it was a code that only a mechoservitor could break, tucked away to set this so-called Time of Sowing in place after the New Espirans' Time of Tending and Gathering, all part of Frederico's Last Bargain.

And all along this path, I've failed again and again. But had he? The things that had gone wrong were beyond his control. He had no way of knowing about Amylé—she'd lured him into the temple in an attempt to stop whatever it was he'd been sent to do. The mechoservitors had tried to recover the staff, and they had learned ultimately that only Tam could— that hadn't been coded into their dream. Still, Tam found the staff and Petronus unsealed the temple. And the Y'Zirites were no longer much of a threat once the dregs of the empire were dealt with on the moon and elsewhere.

"We had a saying you might remember," Petronus continued. "'Good enough for the Order's work.'"

"You're right," Neb said. He could see the logic, and he reached for it. But he suspected that even if he laid aside his need for the staff, Amylé was going to have to be faced at some point, and she would likely force the issue herself. Something had happened to her—something he feared perhaps Vlad had done to her—and she seemed more dangerous with both aspects of her psyche loose at the same time. He scanned the hills ahead of him. "Tell Winters I will meet her on the moon."

He tucked the crescent away. He could see a fire now on the ridgeline not far from where he'd dropped the others. Neb turned himself toward it and increased his pace. They had worked hard to open this path to a new home. Many had laid down their lives—even among the mechoservitors—in faith spent on these dreams.

Their ability to be wrong proved those dreams were shaped by men and not by gods. *And fulfilled by them as well.*

And as he ran toward the light ahead, Nebios Whym recognized that the lack of magick and presence of fallibility in the dreams made it all more rather than less miraculous in his eyes. Because despite it all, they'd already come so far.

(D)arta

They ran through the day, the heat of Ahm's Glory and the smell of her singed hair turning Marta's stomach as they went. Isaak had run silently, loping at a pace they could sustain until their magicks burned out. Then he'd slowed further.

The few times she'd tried to engage him in conversation, he'd been elusive. And when they finally stopped to rest, he pulled away. That was when she first noticed the other pillars of smoke around them on the distant horizon, barely visible in the fading light and ashy haze.

Oh, Isaak. She tried to count them but kept starting over, and beside her, she heard Ire Li Tam stifle a gasp.

"What in the Nine Hells have you done, Father?" Marta heard anger resigned to heartache in the woman's voice. She scanned the horizon with a hand shielding the light of the lowering sun.

Her father did this. Vlad Li Tam had somehow taken it from Isaak before sending him away, and then he'd used it. She'd never considered that a possibility; she'd assumed that the spell was only accessible by Isaak. That Androfrancine general had wanted it and Isaak had refused to give it to him, and she remembered that day. Isaak would've done violence if necessary to prevent Orius and his men from taking the spell. But Vlad had somehow forced it—with the staff they were looking for, no doubt. The one he'd used to bring the diseases that were already killing the city before this final act burned what was left to ash and bone.

And not just here but other cities as well.

Each of them a Windwir, she thought, with mothers not coming home from markets.

She looked toward Isaak. He stood motionless a stone's throw away, staring at the grave of Ahm's Glory, his eyes dimming and brightening

as he processed. Marta remembered hating him at first once she realized he'd been the cause of Windwir's fall. But then she came to recognize Isaak was as much a victim as every man, woman and child
that died in Windwir. More so, because whatever dark magick had destroyed that city also made Isaak somehow much more than the other
mechoservitors she'd met. It was as if the weight of such sorrow made
the metal man more human.

But now what she saw made her afraid for this metal man she loved.
"Where are we going?"

Ire sat stretched out upon a stone watching the skyline, and Marta
sat down beside her. "I do not know," the Blood Guard said. "We're
running north. And the city was buzzing with news that Lord Jakob
and the Crimson Empress had been killed." The woman swallowed,
and Marta heard an emotion she couldn't exactly place in her voice:
grief mixed with anger, perhaps. "Also murdered by my father."

She looked out at the smoke that choked the horizon, marking the
pyres of distant cities. "Why would he do this?"

Ire's eyes narrowed. "To end Y'Zir once and for all. To assure that
it never happens again. They killed most of House Li Tam in their
kin-healing of him—a redemptive process that involves cleansing by
blood to restore another in that house. In this case, Lord Jakob. The
blood magicks that made his birth possible required a later sacrifice
in order to give him long enough life to reproduce. The Y'Zirite faith
comes to fruition in the children brought about by the union of the
Crimson Empress and the Child of Promise. The death of the children
ends that faith and thousands of years of work. But if the death were
faked, there would always be the possibility of the faithful finding out
and another Resurgence coming to pass." She looked at Marta, her
green eyes softening. "It is a lot to understand, Marta, but all of this—
this cycle of violence—has gone on for a long while. This version of the
faith was born when Ahm Y'Zir was maimed and marooned in the
Wastelands, spared by P'Andro Whym at the last moment and spirited away by Xhum Y'Zir's desert thief, the first Rudolfo."

*So her father thinks to end it once and for all with the Seven Cacophonic
deaths?* Looking at the desolation that stretched out below them, she
could see how it might. Or how it might create pockets of survivors
even more filled with hatred and darkness, biding their time for an
opportunity to keep that bloody wheel of vendetta turning.

"It has to stop at some point," she said to herself. She didn't realize
she'd spoken aloud until Ire answered.

"I've spent my life on these machinations," Ire said, "and I have to concur with you."

Isaak had returned while they were talking and stood waiting for them. Marta climbed to her feet, and Ire did the same. "I have been in touch with the New Espiran Council Expeditionary Force, and our transportation is nearly here," he said in a matter-of-fact tone.

"The what?" Marta glanced to Ire, whose scarred face was washed with the same curiosity.

"The answer is more complicated than we have time for," Isaak said. "But they are friends, and Nebios Whym is with them." He pointed to a place low in the sky just east of them. "There is their ship."

Marta strained her eyes and thought she saw the slightest ripple on the air, though it could've easily been heat. "I don't see anything."

"Their vessels use a technology similar to scout magicks to avoid detection," the metal man said as he took a step toward where he'd pointed.

"But who are they?" She'd lost sight of the distortion and tried to find it again.

"They are friends," a man's voice said. "They are going to take us to Lady Tam and Lord Jakob." Marta looked and saw that two men and a woman had materialized nearby. The man who spoke wore silver robes and was tall. His face was young, but his eyes were old and his hair was milk-white. He had a battered leather satchel that hung from his shoulder. He left the other two behind and moved to Isaak quickly. "Isaak . . . are you okay?"

"I am grieving and full of despair, Lord Whym." The voice was colder and more formal than Marta was accustomed to.

She saw a look of understanding pass over the young man's face, and she knew in that moment based on the compassion in his voice that he was truly a friend to Isaak. "I understand, Isaak," Neb said.

So this, Marta thought, was the Marshers' Homeseeker. She'd heard a bit about him from Isaak and Winters, but he was taller and older than she had imagined him. And his robes seemed to move about him as if they were made of liquid silver.

"I had the staff away from him, but I think Amylé has him now." He grimaced. "Now they're all gone."

Isaak continued staring out over the ruins of Ahm's Glory. "Nothing has gone as we intended it to," he said. "We have failed the dream."

Neb's voice was surprisingly confident, and it went well with the compassion. "The dream itself is fallible," he said. "Because it was fashioned by the same frail creatures who are trying to implement it now." A note of anger rose. "And Tam has been an unexpected element."

Ire spoke up. "But a planned one. My grandfather tucked several of us away to be his knives."

It was as if Neb had noticed her for the first time. "I know that voice," he said. Marta watched several emotions cloud his face. "I didn't think I'd be hearing it again."

Ire's voice was quiet and held regret. "I'm sorry you were hurt by my sisters."

Marta looked from Neb to the woman. "You two know each other?"

Ire nodded. "I had been attacked by kin-wolves. Neb saved me." She glanced away. "My sisters captured him."

"They had help," Neb added.

The Blood Guard ignored the bitter tone and met his eyes. "I am now sworn to Rudolfo and his son, Jakob," Ire said. "These can bear witness to it." She stepped closer to him, squinting. When she spoke there was wonder in her voice. "Your scars have healed."

Scars? Marta also looked and saw nothing that could pass as a scar.

"They have," he said. Then he turned away from Ire Li Tam and faced Isaak. "If she bears your grace then she shall bear mine. But what is it we are to do now, Isaak?"

Isaak shook his head. "I am compelled to see Lord Jakob and Lady Tam safely to the Named Lands."

"With Amylé loose and Tam alive and them in possession of the staff," Neb said, "it isn't safe in the Named Lands." He looked to Ire. "And wasn't Lord Jakob given blood magicks in his infancy?"

She nodded slowly. "He was."

"Then the Named Lands aren't ever going to be safe for Lord Jakob," Neb said, his tone and face sober.

Marta found it all hard to keep up with. Before Isaak's new programming had compelled him to seek out Endicott, Ire had heard talk on the street of Tam murdering Lord Jakob along with the Crimson Empress.

"The Androfrancine pathogen is a lesser concern at this moment," Isaak said, though Marta had no idea what he was talking about. "The staff and ring must be secured."

"I agree," Neb said.

But as they said it, Marta wondered how they hoped to get either. They'd tried once and failed. She wanted to ask but knew better.

"And until then," one of the others spoke up, "it isn't safe anywhere in Y'Zir or the Named Lands . . . for any of us. But it is safe in New Espira, and we should leave while we can."

Marta looked at her; the woman was maybe her mother's age and dressed in torn clothing that looked in keeping with any Y'Zirite commoner. But her scars were smudged—painted on, even—and her face was covered in soot. She spoke Landlish with a heavy accent that was gentler than Ire Li Tam's and the other Y'Zirites'.

"This," Neb said, "is Captain Vanya of the New Espiran Council Expeditionary Force. And her ship is here to carry us to Endicott."

Marta saw a gangplank now materialize and uniformed men and women waiting with hands to pull them up inside. Marta and Ire were hustled off through a cargo bay and into narrow corridors. The New Espirans moved them along quickly, and she looked over her shoulder to make sure Isaak was with them. Once she saw he was aboard, she relaxed and let herself be led. After turning several corners, they arrived in a small room with two cots and a small table and chairs. Marta went to the porthole in the wall but was disappointed to see that it was closed and that there was no access to the shutter that would open it.

She'd swum beneath the sea and seen nothing underwater. Now she would fly and see nothing from the air. So instead she sat and waited for Isaak and thought about what Neb had said. *The dream was fallible because the hands that fashioned it were fallible.*

Marta still thought every day about the Final Dream and could see little that was fallible in it, but she knew it was just the slightest sliver of the larger dreams that had brought them here and had brought them together.

Still, when the others spoke about the Final Dream, it was the tree and Winters's voice booming out that they all remembered. And when Marta thought about the dream she could barely remember the tree and couldn't tell you at all what Winters had said.

No, she thought, because that's not my dream. Her dream was Isaak, standing beside Winters on that plain, hands outstretched to heaven, light shining from his silver body. *He is the only dream I know,* she thought.

And now, wherever Isaak was, his head was bowed and his hands no doubt hung limp at his side as his thoughts dwelt in darkness.

And that, too, Marta realized, *with its craters and winds full of ash and heat, is my dream, perfect and fallible all at once.*

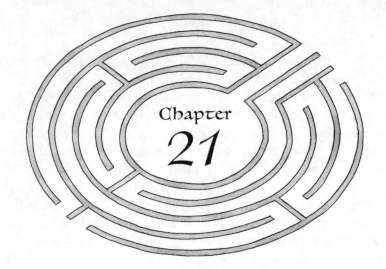

Chapter
21

Jin Li Tam

They parked the wagon in a large flat space at the end of the road, and Jin Li Tam marveled at the vast gray-and-white tree that stretched up to lose itself in hazy light. The massive roots rose up from the field around it, snaking their way to the trunk. Ponds and brooks of silver punctuated the landscape, and the top of the closest root had been planed flat and railings had been installed.

As she lifted Jakob down she felt fingers tickling the inside of her skull. *Yes.*

It was a sleepy voice, an old voice, and Jin felt the weight of longing in that single word.

Bring the children to me.

Jin felt a hand on her shoulder and looked over to see Administrator Gras's warm smile. "It is a lot to take in," she said. "And she's been asleep most of the four thousand years we've tended her. But I can assure you it's perfectly safe."

As if to demonstrate, the woman stepped onto the path and set out for the tree. Jin Li Tam lifted Jakob into her arms, and he resisted but she didn't give in. Instead, she hurried her steps until she was on the root and just behind the administrator. Chandra and Amara followed after, and Jin noted that the soldiers remained behind with the wagon.

As they drew closer, Jin saw that the bark was like nothing she'd seen before. Once it had been white, and now it was more ash-colored, with brighter and darker patches.

"Our scholars' best guess," the administrator said, "is that she's already exceeded her lifespan. And that is despite humanity's best efforts to destroy her." She stretched out a hand and placed it upon the surface, her raised eyebrows encouraging them to do the same.

Jin touched the warm skin and drew back her hand when she felt the pulse. "What is she?"

"She is the Grandmother Tree. Part of the Firstfall of Lasthome."

Jin blinked. "I don't understand." Jakob reached out his own hand, touched the tree, and giggled.

It means I am the oldest surviving member of the People who came here long, long ago to settle this world. Now come closer, Great Mother.

Jin continued skirting the massive tree trunk until she reached an irregularity in the bark.

It was, she realized with a twist in her stomach, an ear. Misshapen and the color of old human flesh. Nearby, a single nostril flared and a blue bloodshot eye blinked open. Below the nostril and beside the eye, a mouth worked its way open. "That is much better. Come where I can see you."

Now Jakob was clapping in his delight and Amara joined in. Jin shifted him in her arms so that he could see better.

"Face," he said, pointing.

The Grandmother Tree's chuckle filled her mind even as she heard it with her ears. *Yes.* "Yes."

Gras brought her face close to the eye. "How are you feeling, Grandmother?"

"Oh," she said. "I ache." *Lean on me, Children.*

Even as she said it, the ground shook again, and Jin leaned in, one hand against the tree and the other holding Jakob close. She felt the skin grow cold as the color darkened even as the light above dimmed. And she heard the old tree groan.

The shaking passed and the tree shuddered. Then the light returned to normal. But the bark was darker and more mottled than it had been before.

Father, what have you done? She glanced to the administrator. "What is it doing to her?"

It is killing me. The lips twisted into a grimace that might've been a smile, and Jin realized there were no teeth in the mouth. "But I was already dying," the Grandmother Tree said. "This is just hastening that day." The eye moved, glancing from Jakob to Amara. *But I am grateful to meet you two especially.* Her voice was gentle. "I can see my People returning in your eyes."

The children were still and quiet, discombobulated by the voice both in their heads and in their ears. Jakob looked at Jin with a look of wonder on his face. "Tree talk," he said.

Amara's face was sad. "Tree sick," she said, adding to Jakob's assessment.

Yes and yes.

Administrator Gras's voice was low as she spoke to Jin. "We didn't think she would survive Xhum Y'Zir's Death Choirs when they created your Churning Wastes. It was weeks of shaking and twilight. But somehow, she held on. She sleeps a lot—for hundreds of years at a time. She was old and dying when Frederico and Amal Y'Zir brought our forebears here in the great Under-Exodus at the end of the Wizard Wars. But she is producing very little new sap these days, and when the reserves are used, it will be gone. That part of Lasthome will disappear forever."

Jin's mind boggled at all of it. "The sap?"

She pointed to a silver pool. "The blood of the earth. It comes from here. From the Grandmother Tree planted at the heart of the world." The woman waved her hand, taking in the forest around them and the soft gentle upward slope of their distant horizons. "And this crèche—it exists for her, and once she is dead, its light will finally fade."

It is coming sooner now, Children.

Something in the tree's tone made Administrator Gras's eyebrows furrow. "We should probably let you rest, Grandmother."

"No," the tired voice whispered. "I rest plenty. Tomorrow's people are here, and I must bless them." *Bring them here.* As the word *here* settled into Jin's mind she saw a section of the tree not far from where they stood now. She moved in that direction, Chandra behind her, as two slender bone-like branches unfolded from the bark.

The branches unfolded further until slender fingers reached from the end of slender arms. Jin also noticed a scar roughly her own length.

Now Administrator Gras stood back and watched, a blue stone in her hand. They were too far away to hear exactly what the mouth murmured, but it sounded like a litany.

May I bless the children, Mothers? Jin nodded, her attention completely taken by the wooden fingers that stroked the top of her son's head.

The branch encircled his waist, the hand holding up the back of his head, and she felt him being lifted. Her first impulse was to hold on, but from the corner of her eye, she saw Amara lifted up as well.

Do not be afraid, the Grandmother Tree whispered in her mind. Jin watched as a seam of light opened in the side of the tree. The bark peeled back like lips, exposing a cavity in the tree that was too pink for wood.

Gently, the branches carried the children into that opening, and when it sealed behind them, Jin's breath went out in a gasp. "What is she doing to them?"

Administrator Gras stared slack-jawed at the scar in the side of the tree. "Something we've never seen before," she said.

From inside the tree, Jin heard muffled laughter, and it soothed her suddenly twisted stomach.

Mama tree good. Where Papa?

The voice filled her mind, and she felt her eyes go wide. *Jakob?*

Now the laughter was inside her, and she found herself stifling a laugh of her own even as her eyes filled with tears she couldn't attach a feeling to.

The seam of light was back now, and slowly, the branches drew the children out. Deep inside the open tree, hazy and lost in red shadows, Jin thought she saw a massive, beating thing. And then, before she could see much more, Jakob was laughing and wrestling in her arms.

The Terms and Conditions of Frederico's Bargain, the ancient voice intoned, *are nearly fulfilled. Their children will need neither blessing nor baptism to remind them of their birthright.*

And as the Grandmother Tree spoke, the earth shook again and the light grew dim once more as a cool wind moved over them. And Jin Li Tam held her son in wonder, tears flowing down her cheeks as he wailed at the groan of pain that filled their minds to overflowing.

Rudolfo

Throughout the unexpected parley Rudolfo found his eyes returning to the ship or at least where it should've been. Once it was tied off, there had been a hum and then a pop before the vessel vanished. Still, he saw men and women emerge as if from nowhere.

The historic nature of it all had trumped protocol, and Orius had brought Hebda and Tertius out for the parley, releasing them into Rudolfo's custody. They sat and listened to the airship captain's introductory remarks, their eyes also going to where the magicked vessel was tethered.

He'd found it all quite implausible but could offer no other explanation. For two millennia, the Androfrancines had believed and taught that the Named Lands was the last pocket of survivors. The Empire of Y'Zir had surprised them all, and now another hidden pocket of survivors stood before them with a hard tale to swallow.

Orius was not budging, keeping the camp at second alarm and the visitors under guard, though they walked about unarmed and with no clear hostile intent. "I find it all quite difficult to believe, Captain," he said. "And if your council were truly our ally, why would they wait and come forward only now, after we've won our own war?"

"For precisely that reason, General Orius," the young man said. Rudolfo studied his face. He had red hair, though of a more copper variety than the Tams. "The council's work of tending and gathering is built upon anonymity and noninterference. Frederico tasked us to watch, wait, and leave an accurate record of the Last Days of Lasthome."

"So if the Y'Zirites had won you would be in parley with them?"

He shook his head. "We'd likely continue on as we have for thousands of years, General. Unless they'd managed to open the Seaway and recover the staff. Then we would have been forced to make contact."

If the young man spoke the truth, his sister was working with Petronus on the moon. Millennia of gathered history and art and other bits of light were being moved into a library there the size and scope of which made Windwir's Great Library look like a grain of sand upon a seashore. And they had Neb and Marta and Isaak.

And the shaking of the earth was the work of Vlad Li Tam.

Orius looked to Rudolfo and Lysias. "You two have been quiet. Do you have any thoughts on this matter?"

Rudolfo stroked his beard. "I think they approached us under the colors of our kin-clave. And if they've come to take Winters to her new home, it solves one of your problems, General. The question is: Shall you also let it solve your others?"

Orius's single eye burned hot with anger for a moment. He nodded to Tertius and Hebda. "These two are yours to do with as you please.

Winters as well." Then he looked to Endrys Thrall. "You and your people are somehow transcribing this occasion?"

He nodded and held up a blue stone. "This captures my full experience."

The general stood. "Then you can bear witness to the execution at sundown. I'm sure you'll want that in your lunar library."

Winters stood, and Rudolfo admired the fire in her eyes. "But General—"

"You are leaving with more than I would normally grant you, Lady Winteria. You may certainly wait aboard the ship if you don't wish to bear witness with the rest of us." He inclined his head to Captain Thrall. "Your people are welcome to our mess hall. Sunset is about an hour away." He smiled. "With the cloud cover lifting, it's going to be quite fetching."

After the general walked away, Rudolfo looked to Winters. "She has earned the axe," he said, "though Orius has made it about far more than justice." He looked to the captain. "Will you or your people intervene in the matter?"

"Only if we're not allowed to leave with Lady Winteria and whichever companions travel with her," Captain Thrall said. "With Lord Tam's activities in the southern hemisphere, time is especially of the essence. It is a two-day flight to the Seaway; our vessels are designed for stealth, not speed."

Rudolfo was confident that Orius wouldn't interfere with their departure if they didn't interfere with his execution. And he was also confident that he would need to implement his plan to remove Orius from power sooner rather than later. The arrival of the New Espirans had merely delayed what was coming.

Rudolfo sighed and then found Winters's eyes upon him. "There is other news for you, Lord Rudolfo, though you may wish it in private," she said.

Rudolfo glanced to Lysias. "I think here is fine."

Then the Gypsy King looked from Winters to the young captain and could tell that this news was not a burden upon them. Still there were already tears forming in the young Marsh Queen's eyes.

"Your son, Lord Jakob, is alive and well, Lord Rudolfo," Captain Thrall said. "As is Lady Tam, the Great Mother. It was a ruse staged by her father to undermine the Y'Zirite faith."

Rudolfo felt the wind go out of him as his knees weakened. He was glad in that moment that he was sitting. Otherwise, he'd have surely collapsed. As it was, he felt his heart burst even as his eyes filled with tears. "My son is alive?"

The young officer nodded. "They are in New Espira. Arrangements will be made for their swift return once it is safe to do so."

It was as if he couldn't hear it. Or maybe that he couldn't hear it enough. "My son is alive?"

Winters's face was already wet, and she nodded. He felt Lysias's hand clap his shoulder, and for a moment Rudolfo lost himself in the transformation that overtook him. Then he paused and his eyebrows furrowed. "What proof do you have of this?"

Captain Thrall held up the blue stone. "Here. Hold it with me and I'll show you."

Rudolfo stretched out a tentative hand and felt the weight of the stone as it settled into his palm. Then Endrys Thrall put his own hand over the top of it. "Close your eyes."

There was mumbling and the smell of the forest and a vast tree, and Jin Li Tam stood with another woman, and each of them held a child up to branches that reached for them, and Jakob laughed and—

He opened his eyes. "Where was this? When?"

"An hour or so ago."

Rudolfo remembered clearly the moment his life changed profoundly when Jakob had come sick and gray into the world on the heels of the Firstborn Feast massacre. And he remembered also the profound moment of change when the kin-raven arrived bearing its dark tidings of loss. And now, this change as hope once more washed out the despair and his lamentation became a hymn. He felt his knees weaken.

My son is alive. Rudolfo met Winters's eyes and then the New Espiran's. "And you intend to bring him home?"

The captain nodded. "Yes. Once it is safe."

Safe. Rudolfo's stomach sank, and he glanced to Lysias and Orius quickly before looking back to Captain Thrall. "What about the pathogen?"

The New Espiran opened his mouth to reply but was cut short when an explosion shook the ground and a patch of sky where the vessel had stood magicked burst into flame and light. The blast knocked Rudolfo over along with the others, tumbling the chairs and table to the tarp-covered ground.

Rudolfo climbed to his feet, his ears still ringing. He scanned the wreckage and saw flaming figures running about in the midst of it, but he couldn't hear the screams. He could see Lysias's lips moving and it took him a moment to register the hands pressing into his shoulder.

Are you injured?

He shook his head. "No," he shouted. Then he turned back to the burning ship. Endrys Thrall was running to the fire now, Winters and Hebda close behind him. Renard was running toward them from the mess hall along with a handful of other soldiers.

He took a step to follow the captain and then stopped when something large crawled out of the wreckage and roared. The sound of it cut through the cotton that filled his ears and chilled his blood. Rudolfo drew his knives and whistled for his scouts, though he doubted there was much they could do.

It was larger than a wagon, with four sets of wings folded back and away as it moved quickly on its six legs, tail thrashing and scattering burning debris. There was another flash, and suddenly a girl stood before the beast.

She was young—not much older than Winters—and her hair was long and golden as straw. Her bright blue eyes shone, and as she stretched out her hands, the silver robe she wore shimmered and then closed in upon her to form a skintight sheath that glowed. "I have come for Winteria bat Mardic," she said. Her eyes fell on Winters. "The Elder. Also known as Ria. Do not interfere with me, Downunders."

She sniffed the air and then looked at Winters again. "You do not belong here either. But you stink of them nonetheless."

Rudolfo saw a look of comprehension register upon Winters's face. "They are my people," she said.

The woman stared at her with a look of bemused disgust. Behind her, the massive creature stretched out its wings and roared again. Captain Thrall and the others had stopped. "Guard me," she told the beast, and it growled.

Then she moved into the camp faster than an unmagicked person should be able to move. "I know she is here."

Rudolfo saw Orius now. He had made it to the door of his cabin and now watched the woman move through his camp with a look of rage upon his face. Whistling the men to third alarm, he advanced on her.

Laughing, she tossed him into the air. He landed heavily with a grunt. She moved on. "Where are you, Child? Where are you, Ria?"

My people will come for me. Rudolfo did not know who this woman was, but Ria had been truthful. And whoever this was had come with fire and a silver beast the likes of which he'd never seen.

He watched as she strode to the building that served as the stockade. She ripped the door off and threw the guard that waited inside out into the mud.

When she came out she held Ria in her arms, cradling her like a child. "Now tell me which one of you is Orius?"

The Gray Guard general groaned from where he lay, and she followed the eyes of his soldiers as they settled upon him. The woman smiled. "Can you stand for me right here?" she asked Ria. Ria nodded.

Then the woman wrapped in silver light approached Orius and scooped him up by the collar of his uniform. "Our conversation will be brief and effective," she told him. "Where is the Firstfall Axe you intended to murder my cousin with?" She followed his glance back to his cabin. "Thank you," she said.

She held up a hand, and Rudolfo watched as the silver of her suit spread out to wrap it in light. Orius screamed when she plunged the hand into his chest. After pulling it out, she dropped him and dropped his beating heart into the mud of Windwir's grave.

Rudolfo's eyebrows furrowed as she took the axe from the cabin. Then the woman spit on Orius's twitching body, gathered Ria back into her arms, and vanished into light as the beast swallowed them, launched itself into the air, and pounded sky for the south.

The look of dread upon Endrys Thrall's face as the captain watched them fly away was enough to raise the hairs on Rudolfo's neck. Still, despite that and despite the screams and the flames, Rudolfo only saw his son held aloft by branches and only heard his laughter on the evening air.

Ria

It was like no other experience she'd had—the sense of flight—and Ria found herself suddenly drunk on the freedom she felt.

More than freedom, she felt the wind upon skin that she knew wasn't hers. And she smelled the forests, wet with the winter's runoff as the snow gave way to spring. She had no control, but she felt the wings as they beat against the sky to move them at an extraordinary speed—so fast that she could already see the farmlands and cities of the Entrolusian Delta stretching out ahead before the beast cut to the east and climbed even higher. The Keeper's Wall, an impenetrable range of mountains running north to south, filled her eyes, and the air grew colder.

I found you, Cousin. The voice was warm, and she tried to answer but found her mouth wouldn't reply. *Now we can set things right that have been wrong for far too long. But rest now.*

She forced her mind into the words. *What will we do first?*

The warmth was back, only now it flooded her, fogging the edges of her vision. The pain she'd grown so used to living in was gone now. And the emptiness was filling up with something else. And now the woman's voice sounded far away as the light faded around Ria. *First we will make you whole. Then we will do what others have lacked the will or means to do and make things right.*

Ria didn't know what any of that meant. She only knew that she wanted to sleep, and when she drifted off, she dreamed of being held in the arms of a warm and loving beast who understood what it meant to have everything that she believed in slowly fall away and become false.

⌀

When she opened her eyes, Ria blinked and wondered if she'd dreamed about flying. She stood in a field, though it was different from the one she'd seen in the other dreams. The tree here was massive but misshapen, twisted, its bark mottled gray with time and disease. It stretched up into hazy mist, its top lost to sight. Around it, ponds and brooks of silver burbled. And before it, she saw the Great Mother and the Vessel of Grace both offering up their children—the Child of Promise and the Crimson Empress—and the tree took them and opened its pink maw to swallow them whole.

Ria screamed and fell into the arms of the woman who suddenly stood there with her. The slender arms enfolded her, and she felt belonging in them as she sobbed.

I don't understand what is happening.

I will show you. She held Ria a moment longer and then released her and stretched out a hand. A blue, round stone sat in it. "I took this from one of the men at the Androfrancine camp. It shows that you've been lied to by the same man who lied to me," she said. "Vlad Li Tam."

The name was a knife in Ria's heart, the source of her shame and her failure. She looked back to the tree. Everything had frozen. The two mothers were staring fearfully at the branches now disappearing into the trunk of the tree.

Now she found her voice. "I don't understand."

"He did not kill them. He hid them away with others of his ilk. He deceived all of you. But he was not the first to deceive you."

The tree was younger now but still mottled. The disease was less pronounced. And now, a stump of a man lay against the tree. He had no legs, no right arm, no left eye. And as he lay, his lips moved as if he talked in his sleep. "This one also deceived you. He took his stories from the same well of lies that the others did and fashioned them into a gospel of vendetta and blood." The voice grew soft. "What would your life have been without Ahm Y'Zir's lie?"

The tree was even younger now. A willowy man dressed in black stood beside a large mechanical spider made of glass and steel. A large bearded man stood beside the tree now, holding the Firstfall Axe and a large silver goblet. He raised it to the tree and then drained down its silver contents. "Or this lie," the voice continued. "The one that Shadrus drank there at the execution of Frederico's Bargain? The one that has haunted your father's line for so long now?"

The question had weight, and she felt it. *What would my life have been?* But another question took preeminence. This woman who had been in her dreams and had promised to come for her had come. And had killed Orius and taken her flying and—

She touched her face where it should've ached. It was no longer puffy and tender. *And healed me in the belly of a monster.*

The tree was gone now, and so was the clearing. All that remained was a large, round hatch in the bottom of a cave dimly lit by the glow of the woman's silver robes.

"Who are you?" Ria finally asked.

"I am Amylé D'Anjite," she said. "I am what your people call a Younger God." Her smile broadened. "And you, Daughter of Salome, are my cousin. My father would have been your uncle."

The rest of the details spun away as the reality settled in. *I am Abomination.*

Yes. The woman's voice was in her head. They were someplace else now. The top of the tower where Ria thought maybe they had met in deeper dreams. Above in the sky, a world hung, whole and beautiful, blue and green. *There are truths that find us sometimes and undo all of the truth we thought we had before.* The world shifted, blurred, and when it came back into focus it was scarred and barren.

And then the scarred world became a ball of light that expanded and expanded until it shattered, sending streaks of light out and away from it.

And then even those truths are ultimately swallowed until nothing remains.

"What is the truth?" Ria asked.

She saw the children again, still held by the branches of the tree, looks of fear upon the mothers' faces. *The truth is that they are also Abomination. The objects of your faith—the very purpose of your faith—were born in service to the same Continuity Engine that the first Y'Zir sought to stop when he stole the Firsthome Temple from my People—from your People. Millennia of careful breeding by the Y'Zirites has brought about a Restoration in these children, giving them back a heritage cast aside long ago. How can they be both Abomination and the heart of Ahm Y'Zir's truth?*

She saw the inconsistencies and asked the same question a second time. "What is truth?"

"You are who you are in spite of what you believe," Amylé said. "Accept the truth and come take the mantle of your birthright." Her eyes grew hard and cold, and she held up the axe. "Then use that birthright to end all of the lying, and silence the Continuity Engine once and for all."

They were back in the cave with the hatch now, and Ria nodded slowly. It was so much to absorb. But at the core, she knew this woman who loved her, who had come for her, was right. The lying needed to stop.

"What do I do?" she asked.

"Follow me," Amylé said. And then she opened the hatch and climbed down. Ria followed her. She'd been into the Beneath Places before briefly, both at Windwir's excavation and up in the north. But she'd never spent much time in them. She'd heard tales and had read some of the magisters' reports.

They descended for what seemed far longer than it probably was. And then set out down a long corridor sloping gently down. They took several twists and turns along the way before they came to a larger room. A silver pond shimmered in the center, and Amylé stepped toward it. "Come with me, Cousin," she whispered. A smile pulled at her lips, and something wide and open in her eyes pulled Ria closer.

She'd never seen it, but she knew that contact with the blood of the earth—without taking proper precautions—was deadly. They lost countless men and women in the distilleries where they blended the blood shed during Y'Zirite cutting rituals with the blood of the earth. She opened her mouth to warn Amylé as her bare foot came down toward the surface of the pond. But when she kept walking, straight out to the center of the pond, standing tall upon the surface, Ria closed her mouth.

Come with me. I will show you how to swim the light.

Ria took a step and then another. She felt the heat of the pond upon the sole of her foot as it supported her weight. Then she fixed her eyes upon Amylé and took another step. And then two more. "I'm—"

She looked down, and as she did, the surface of the pond did more than just collapse beneath her: It sucked her in and pulled her under. She stretched out a hand toward Amylé and opened her mouth to scream only to have it filled with the hot, bittersweet fluid. It flooded her mouth, forcing its way down her throat as the blood of the earth bore her to the bottom of the pond and held her there.

You are of the People, and this world is made for you. The voice was ancient, and it was as if the fluid itself carried the words even farther into her. And with the words, she felt power and she felt understanding, though it was all too much and too fast.

Lift me. It responded, carrying her to the surface.

Amylé smiled when Ria stood up on the pond beside her. "Swim the light with me, Cousin," she said. "I will show you how."

And when Amylé stretched out her hand, Ria took it and laughed at how everything she'd lost had not been anything worth keeping. Then she swam the light in the veins of the world and felt a wholeness she'd never known before.

Chapter
22

Winters

The sun had dropped below the skyline, leaving the sky a bruised and ominous purple when they finished laying Orius to rest. Winters watched from the side with Endrys Thrall and the others as the Androfrancines buried their general and Rudolfo presided over the services. She smiled as he used the opportunity to secure his position as the inheritor of the Order.

"The closest thing you have to a father within your Order has died in service to the light," he said from the edge of Orius's grave, "and now, if you will honor the wisdom of your last Pope, it falls to me to be a father to you."

Because he collects orphans. She watched as he continued.

"And if your fealty to the light will extend to me and to the Ninefold Forest that Pope Petronus chose as Protector of the Light—and to the library that we build—then my grace will be upon you. You may serve as the Gray Guard of the Forest Library. Or you may, at the conclusion of this present conflict, choose to retire and find suitable lives for yourselves within my forests."

He vanished quickly after turning the service over to the new commanding officer—an older captain who had worked closely with Orius. Winters saw the top of his turban vanish into the gray crowd.

Endrys Thrall touched her shoulder. "Neb and Isaak and the others have arrived in New Espira," he said, "and a ship has been dispatched to reach us. My orders are to see you directly to the moon as soon as possible, Lady Winteria."

There was danger in the tone of his voice, and even Hebda picked up on it, shooting her a quick glance. "Has something happened that I should know about, Captain?"

"Amylé D'Anjite is a grave threat to the fulfillment of Frederico's Bargain," he said. "Combined with Vlad Li Tam's course of action in Y'Zir, she not only threatens my people's work, but threatens our very existence. The council has voted for full intervention at whatever cost to assure that the Time of Sowing moves forward."

The tree, white with seed, was behind her eyes now, and she nodded. So much had been spent to reach this time—so many lives lost along the way—and they still really knew so little about what it meant. She'd heard Petronus had accessed the library somehow, and she hoped there would be something there that would eventually tell them what they were to do.

And how and why. She pushed her thoughts away to focus on the captain's words. "The ship had been grounded in the Churning Wastes. It's not far away. We will fly top speed for the Seaway as soon as it arrives," he said. "You should identify who you intend to bring with us."

When he said it, he glanced at Tertius and Hebda. *Renard must've said something to him about my issues with these two.* She followed his gaze and met Hebda's eyes for a moment before the man looked away. But not before she saw shame behind them.

Winters sighed. She'd just urged clemency for her sister, a woman complicit in the fall of Windwir. In a way, these men were complicit as well. Tertius had pretended to hide among her people in order to get close to her and the Book of Dreaming Kings that he studied. Hebda had deceived Neb—even had him convinced he was a ghost back from the dead—and had known the boy would think he'd been buried at Windwir. These men certainly had earned her ire.

But they had also fled Orius with her, and Charles had trusted them. Renard, too. Even now, the Waste guide stood near Hebda, the backs of their hands touching.

She took them in. "There is a place on the moon for you all if you wish it," she said. She'd not asked Neb, and part of her wondered if she should. After all, it was a courtesy to the man she loved.

But she could not move beyond her newest dream—one people

upon the plain, vast and standing within the shadow of that even vaster tree white with the promise of life. And if Neb disagreed with her decision, it did not make her decision any less the right path.

The thought of right paths brought Rudolfo to mind again, and she looked around for him. She didn't see him, but she saw Lysias walking in from the forest.

"Hebda, will you work with Captain Thrall identifying any others among the Androfrancine remnant who should accompany us?"

He nodded. She saw something like relief on his face. "I will. Thank you, Lady Winteria."

She inclined her head but didn't wait for him to return the gesture. Instead, she moved toward Lysias.

"Is he out there?"

He nodded. "He is. But I suspect he wants to be left alone now."

That was his way. And only a few had earned the right to interrupt that solitude he sought at times. *I am likely not one of them.*

Still, she swallowed that fear and moved past Lysias onto the trail.

She made no attempt to move quietly, announcing her approach clearly.

His voice to her left surprised her, and she jumped. "I would expect better of the True Queen of the Marsh. You sound like a herd of elk."

"I didn't want to surprise you."

He chuckled. But when he stepped from the shadows into the fading light of day, his face and beard were wet with tears. "I'm not certain you could."

But she *had* surprised him that day they'd met on the plains not so long ago. And she remembered the anger on his face when he'd learned that she had let his wife and child leave and had kept that information from him at Jin Li Tam's request until it was too late for him to stop that. And until recently, he'd thought his son had died in his mother's care because of it.

"I needed to see you before I go," she said. "A ship is coming for us."

Rudolfo smiled. "You have your new home," he said. "And young Nebios, too."

"I do," she said. "And you have your family." But as Winters said it, she wondered what of Jin Li Tam he truly had and what shape their marriage would take in time of peace. She had high hope for her friends. But the dark look on his face gave her pause.

"Aye," he said. "I have them. But for how long?" Their eyes met. "And where do we go? Jakob cannot stay in the Named Lands with the pathogen here."

"But he's alive, and those problems can be addressed," she said. "Perhaps the pathogen can be neutralized somehow despite what the Androfrancines say. Or perhaps water can be brought in somehow." Winters paused. "And it didn't kill everyone who'd been exposed to blood magicks. It spared my sister and me." She stretched out a tentative hand and touched the Gypsy King's arm. "Despite it all, we've come this far, and I think we'll go farther yet. I have to believe that based on what I've seen."

He nodded. "I concur." Then he chuckled. "I suppose it was too much to hope that we might have less complex problems to solve other than how to port water into the Ninefold Forest from beyond the Named Lands. . . ."

She chuckled with him. "I think we'll have plenty of problems ahead. Two of them just flew off together." But, she realized, they would also have help. They had the New Espirans and what they knew along with the Firsthome Temple and everything contained with the Library of Elder Days.

Once we're finished. She felt the weight of the work behind and the work ahead. Soon she'd be boarding an airship, and in a matter of days she'd be on the moon. Winters looked at the forest around her and wondered when she'd see it again. "I should head back," she said. "But I wanted to say goodbye. I will be taking much that I learned from you with me. I want to thank you for that."

His eyebrows furrowed. "Other than better taste in fine wine and perhaps military strategy, whatever could you have learned from me, Marsh Queen?"

"How to take the right path," she said, "and how to care for the orphaned." She felt a lump in her own throat now. "How to build rather than destroy. They are all things I'm going to need to know how to do."

Rudolfo inclined his head. "I'm honored to have been an aid in our kin-clave. You are a formidable woman, Winteria bat Mardic, and you will rule your people very well indeed."

She smiled. "I thank you, Lord Rudolfo, but I will not rule them. Change is the path life takes. I will be implementing some of Esarov the Democrat's notions, I suspect, as we find the next right path."

Rudolfo snorted. "You will find your way, whatever way it is. I can't imagine *my* people ever wanting that when they can have *me*."

Now she laughed. "We will find our way." There was a moment of silence. "Thank you for your kin-clave and your friendship, Rudolfo."

He inclined his head, and she inclined hers. "And thank you for yours, Winteria." His eyes became sober for a moment. "And I would ask a favor of you."

She felt her eyebrow rise. "Yes?"

Winters sensed his discomfort, and when he spoke, he broke eye contact momentarily. "My scouts tell me that Kember and Ilyna and the others boarded a vessel out of Caldus Bay for the Seaway. They should have arrived by now." He dug a note from his pouch. It was fresh white paper and sealed with his signet. "Would you bear this to them for me?"

She blinked in surprise, remembering that day when he'd banished them. There had been so much ice in his voice, so much steel in his eyes. And now, his eyes were full of tears.

"I fear I do not like the man these times have made of me," he said in a low voice. "They did not make me in the same fashion as they made Vlad Li Tam or Orius, but still I've chosen the wrong paths in the midst of this, and it has cost my soul something I didn't know could be excised from me."

Winters's hand moved to his arm again before she could stop herself. "But these times have also made you a collector of orphans and builder of libraries, Rudolfo. And they have made you a father and a husband and a hero who is sung about in taverns."

He laughed and wiped his tears away. "Aye, they have. And they have made some of my orphans into collectors of orphans themselves." He sighed. "And they have made you wise. Or maybe your dreams did. You will do well, Winteria." He smiled. "And this sounds too much like a goodbye. With the Seaway open, I expect I'll have to sail for the moon myself one day just to say I've done so at least once in my life."

Winters laughed with him, and when they embraced, it was not like the other times. They were on equal footing and shared something between them that they hadn't before.

"Yes," she said. "You must all come visit us upon the moon." Having said it, suddenly all of the darkness was less dark as the silliness of it settled in.

And so Winteria bat Mardic found herself laughing and snorting with a Gypsy King in the forest at the edge of Windwir's grave where all of this had started what seemed so long ago.

16171819202122232425

Vlad Li Tam

The waters of Caldus Bay were calm in the early-morning hours as Vlad Li Tam watched Petros and his father prep the nets. He'd been with them just a few weeks now, and already he'd taken a liking to the serious-minded boy and his somewhat simple family. He could see the wisdom of his father's choice to send him here.

But how much choice was it, my love? And whose choice? The voice was in his head, but it was also behind him and he twisted in the boat to look for her.

Where are you? He strained, leaning out and peering down into the dark and cold water.

There. A spark of blue and green that slowly built as she moved closer.

I am always here for you, my love.

But when he plunged overboard into those icy waters and kicked his way down toward the tendrils of light, swimming into the sound of her song within the water, Vlad Li Tam found nothing and woke up with a sob in his throat.

"False god, stealer of grown-up toys, ruiner of dreams," the gasping and wet voice muttered through its mechanical box. "Murderer of children and desecrater of the holy."

The hold was lit dimly, and he still remained in the chair he'd been tied to. His arm—the one that wasn't there anymore—ached along with the rest of him. And Ahm Y'Zir crouched there over him, the deformed remains of his flesh sealed away in a crystal orb filled with a greenish mist and resting atop a mechanical eight-legged chassis. It clicked two of its metal legs against the hull of the ship near Vlad's feet.

With two others, it lifted the staff. "What have you done to the staff?"

Vlad smiled. "I believe I might have broken it." He was certain of that. Once he'd been given access to the library it had been easy enough to know exactly how to do that if it became necessary.

"And the ring?"

"The girl took it," he lied.

A third leg joined the tapping. "Naughty, naughty Vlad Li Tam."

The doors opened and two Blood Guard admitted Eliz Xhum. "Lord Y'Zir," he said, "we've a raven from Sister Elsbet and the lunar colony."

Lunar colony? He'd expected the regent and Y'Zir to secure the staff and make for the Seaway, but he hadn't anticipated a Y'Zirite colony. But Vlad's life was a long game of changing the course of rivers over time. Erosion and pressure in such a way to feel natural. Because as P'Andro Whym indicated, change was the path life took. But it was P'Andro's brother, T'Erys, who'd showed up far later in the Order's apocryphal origins to note that those changes could be forced and controlled with time and pressure. It was no coincidence that it was under T'Erys's papacy that the secret kin-clave with House Li Tam, the banking and shipbuilding concern of the Named Lands, began to flourish.

So it was expected that things would go wrong. And that there would be plans within plans to deal with the unexpected, unantici- pated and uncontrollable.

Like me. But even now, Vlad knew he'd gone beyond his father's plans. And Vlad could stop with what he'd already done and it would be enough to protect the new dream. Petronus and the others on the moon would have to stand or fall on their own soon enough. But pro- tecting the new dream was not enough. Since their cutting tables and Ria's careful ministrations over him with her knives, he'd needed to do a kin-healing of his own, and Vlad knew that though he could stop, he would not until he was dead or until there were no more Y'Zirites.

Ahm was babbling incoherently now, but he'd stopped the tapping and leaned in so that his filthy glass was inches from Vlad's face. Vlad smelled something foul and rotting and medicinal leaking from the orb. "We will continue later."

Ahm left, and Vlad sagged against the ropes that held him. He felt hands upon him and looked over to see a young woman with dark curly hair bending over his shoulder, unwrapping the bandage to change his dressing.

"I wish," she whispered to him in Landlish, "they would just kill you and be done with it."

The stark honesty and firmness in her tone struck him as odd. As did the Delta accent. From what he saw of her arm and face, she bore no scars. "You're Entrolusian," he said.

She looked at him now, and he saw the hatred smoldering in her brown eyes. "I may kill you myself if they don't do it soon." She jos- tled his stump, and he felt the pain of it shoot like fire through his body. "I keep hoping they'll hurt you for a while first."

She was familiar, and he quickly accessed his inventory of details.

When it registered, his heart sank. "You're Lysias's girl. Jakob's nurse-maid."

She jostled the wound again, and he cried out. "I was until you killed him."

He glanced around, his voice low. "You have to get off this ship. It isn't safe here."

Her dark eyes met his before returning to the wound. "I didn't choose to come here, but I have nowhere else to be."

But you do. And yet to tell her so put Jakob at risk. Jin and Chandra and Amara, too. Because until he finished his work the Y'Zirites could not know the children were still alive.

"This is the *Kinshark*," he said. "There is a lifeboat aft of here. Rafe Merrique kept them well stocked. Get off this ship, Lynnae."

That he'd remembered the name finally and used it had some impact upon her. Still, her laugh was bitter. "And how long would I last on the open sea?" She finished up with the new dressing. "At least on the moon there is the new dream," she said.

Vlad Li Tam had trusted few people in his life beyond his own kin, and even few of them gained his full trust. It was not a part of his economy or the Tam way. He'd trusted his grandson Mal implicitly, and that had been the blind spot that cut away his family from him. And he'd trusted—or more importantly had the blind faith required of a Tam—in his father. And his father—along with Rudolfo's father and Mardic it seemed—had somehow been involved in this plot to destroy Windwir and bring the Y'Zirite Empire to the Named Lands.

"You have no reason to believe me or trust me, Lynnae, but there is a better dream waiting for you. Everything is not what it seems to be. Leave this ship. Right now. Take a lifeboat and go."

"We are in the middle of the ocean," she said.

"Yes," he told her. "You have no reason to trust me. But you should."

She stared at him, and her eyes narrowed for a moment as she looked for something in his. Then they went wide when she found it, and she nodded slowly just once.

After she left, he sagged in the chair and willed himself back to the library.

There was a guard posted and Vlad couldn't risk being overheard, so he passed his message quickly and quietly. "Tell Petronus to have Neb or your people search the Ghosting Crests south of the Moon Wizard's Ladder. There will be a lifeboat there. Its contents are vital to the work of the Ninefold Forest Houses." The man stared at him slack-jawed and Vlad was going to repeat himself when the regent entered the cargo hold. He was smiling in a way that made Vlad uncomfortable.

"I have very good news for you, Vlad," he said. "Lord Y'Zir has determined that I may complete the kin-healing that Ria began with you. Isn't that splendid?"

Vlad met the smile with a laugh of his own. But through his cracked lips and dry throat, it sounded like a bark. "Your faith is dead, Xhum. I've killed it. Your kin-healing serves no purpose."

Eliz Xhum's eyes went violently dark for just a moment, and then it passed. "Yes," he said. "You have killed our faith. And that will make cutting you feel . . . fine indeed. Which is purpose enough for me." He looked around the cargo hold. "I'll have them set up the tables. We should be able to finish most of the cuttings that remain before we take back the tower." He moved to the door, and his smile broadened. "After that, Lord Y'Zir thinks casting you down from the top of it would be fitting, and I have to say that I concur."

Vlad said nothing. Knives meant more pain. And pain was his army. He had his fish upon the line, and he would land it before all was done.

He felt the ache everywhere in him still, deep in his bones, even in the missing arm, and when Vlad Li Tam closed his eyes, he still saw blue-green light always just out of reach and still tasted the cold and briny waters of a sea that pulled him ever down and down.

Petronus

They woke him when Vlad Li Tam's armless ghost appeared, and Petronus rubbed too little sleep from his eyes as he made his way up to the library. Nadja met him on the stairs, and he wasn't sure she'd even slept since she'd slipped out of his room just a few hours earlier.

She caught his hand and squeezed it, then released it and took the lead, forcing him to stretch his legs and keep up.

The library technologist was waiting for them. Petronus yawned. "So what is this about a lifeboat?"

The man glanced at the officer of the watch who stood with him. "Lord Tam said that its contents were vital to the work of the Ninefold Forest Houses."

What could Rudolfo need from a lifeboat in the Ghosting Crests? He glanced at Nadja. "Do you have a ship within reach?"

She nodded. "Surely. Mine." Nadja must've seen the look on his face, because her mouth twisted into half of a bemused smile. "We can be out and back within the day. Though I suspect even a fleet of ships might make it something of a challenge—trying to find a pebble in a prairie."

"Your brother just lost a ship at Windwir," Petronus said. "The skies aren't safe at the moment."

Her blue eyes softened. "We're too close to fulfilling the terms and conditions of the Bargain to count on any safety. Someone once said 'A ship is not made to stay in port, and the light requires we sail out into that unknown with courage.'"

Petronus sighed. It had been his first papal writ, and he felt his ears growing hot.

She continued. "I'd be gone a few days at most. Depending on how the search goes. I could also rendezvous with Endrys, Winters and the others and bring them back with me. We'd likely need more than one ship to search effectively."

He nodded. *What are you up to, Tam?*

Her eyebrows furrowed, and she leaned in and put a finger beneath his nose. It came away red. "You're bleeding again."

It was the third nosebleed. And this time he felt a tickling beneath his scalp—warm with flashes and pops of electricity at the edges of his vision.

Petronus wobbled on his feet as the feeling intensified, and her eyes now had worry in them. "Are you okay?"

"I feel . . ." He had no words, and he reached out a hand to steady himself. That's when he realized the black ring upon his finger was whistling in his skull. He pressed his thumb into it and felt the symptoms instantly lessen.

The command pool has reached maturation, Administrator.

Petronus had not heard this voice before, and he looked up to see if the others registered the same surprise as he did. He waited. "Did you hear that?"

"I think you should sit down." She looked to the technician. "Find us some water."

Petronus shook his head. "No. I'm fine now." He wiped the blood away with his silver sleeve, then watched as the fabric absorbed it into light.

Command pool. He looked up. "The door," he said.

And then, before the others could ask, he moved off toward the

edge of the grove, then followed the room's wall until he reached the
far side with its single door that hadn't been there before Vlad's conversation with him. He looked at the guard. "Has there been any
change?"

She shook her head. "No, Father."

But when he reached out a hand and touched it, he felt it sigh
beneath his touch. *Open.*

The door opened. *You are authorized.*

Vlad had said that as well, and Petronus hadn't understood; but
now, comprehension was dawning like a second summer morn, and
he slipped through the door. It sighed closed behind him, and he heard
Nadja call out—and heard that call cut short utterly when the door
sealed shut.

It was small room, glowing white, and in its center lay a hollowed-
out pool of silver fed by roots the color of bone. And beside the pool
was a large white stone. Standing up from that stone was a staff the
color of piercing white heat.

Petronus reached out for it, curled his fingers around it, and felt
the power shudder through his body. He started to withdraw it, then
stopped.

No. This is not for me. It is for Neb.

He looked at the pool and dipped a hand into it. The fluid was
room-temperature and thick, and as he touched it, the temple became
alive to him. He could see its rooms, its pulse, its temperature, the
health of its roots deep down into Beneath Places they had yet to re-
discover below them. And he saw the sickness in the bargaining pool
beneath them, too—the one that had been poisoned supposedly by
Amal Y'Zir on her last visit to her childhood home.

Holding his breath, Petronus lifted up his robe and climbed into the
pool, settling down. As he did, his clothing evaporated into the pool,
and he felt roots slithering against his bare skin as the temple enfolded
him, drew him down into its heart.

Petronus saw light spinning and careening and heard cacophony
all about him. *It is too much.*

And then he felt the dragons. Not just felt them but saw through
their eyes, smelled through their noses, felt through their skin. There
were three of them left and one that had fallen, its remains in a crater
in the desolation of Ahm's Glory. And he saw the tie that bound one
dragon to its rider but also saw that the dragon was riderless and on
patrol, hunting the skies of Lasthome.

Petronus shifted in the pool and felt the roots hold him tighter. Closing his eyes, he let the roots pull him to the bottom. At first he resisted as the liquid pushed at his mouth and nose; then he gave himself to it and let it fill him, feeling his body contort as it resisted drowning.

He flicked a finger over the ring and brought the library to life within his reach there in the pool, and five minutes later Petronus had the dragons returning to the Seaway and had figured out how to move among them—and how to adjust their telescopic vision—from where he lay. Still, it was not enough. He stood up from the pool and felt the roots release him.

He looked to the staff again and reached out a hand. Then dropped it back to his side. "Clothe me," he whispered.

As the robes spun back around him, he moved to the door and opened it just as Nadja's hand was coming down. Her eyes were wide with fear now, and he could hear panic in her voice. "Where did you go?"

"I don't know how to explain it," Petronus said. "But we have a new staff for Neb. And I'm going to find whatever it is Vlad left for us in the Ghosting Crests."

"*You're* going to find the lifeboat?"

He offered a grim smile. "I think so. Yes." He took her hand. "Let's see."

They left the library and took the stairs to the top of the temple, and Petronus went to the edge and scanned the distant line of sea to the south. He thought perhaps he saw a speck of silver there in the sky, but couldn't be sure at that distance. So instead he raised his head and summoned up the closest approximation to the shriek he'd heard Neb make. And it was as if his throat knew the sound and helped him form it from some lost memory inside his body.

He felt the answer as a tickle in his eardrums, and he called again, looking over to Nadja and the others as he did.

This time he heard the cry upon the wind and smiled at her. "I will be back soon," he said.

Then Petronus leaped, spreading out his hands as if he were diving from the high docks into the waters of Caldus Bay. Only now, where icy cold should have reached out to grab him and drag him down, warm wind pulled at his robes and hair as he fell. He forced his mouth open again to make the cry and then felt the paws of the kin-dragon as they encircled him and drew him in. There was a moment of light and confusion before he felt the wings, smelled the air, saw the jungle and the sky through different eyes.

The next time he roared, Petronus *was* the kin-dragon, and he pounded his wings against the air to carry himself back up the line of the temple. He overshot it and looked down at the faces watching with wonder.

Then he roared again and turned south for the ocean and the Seaway.

Petronus found that even from within the dragon, some part of him stayed connected to the library and he was able to pull up maps that he could see—a ghost image superimposed over the terrain that sped by below. And the map in no way diminished the crisp color of the jungle canopy and the crystalline blue of the lunar sea.

I came to the moon in a vessel, and now I return in the belly of a dragon. Possibly, he thought, the very one that had brought their ship down when they entered the lunar atmosphere.

He'd envied Neb his kin-dragon, and now he saw that it was every experience he'd suspected he was missing out on. And he knew that whatever it was that was happening—however it was that he now controlled the beast—it stemmed from something deep and instinctive that the pool had opened within him.

And he suspected it was because Vlad had commanded it to by authorizing him. *Administrator.*

Petronus watched the sea unfold beneath him and noted the blue-green lights that swam those waters. He'd not seen them before but had heard from Rafe that there were more now than he'd ever seen in all his years aboard the *Kinshark*. The d'jin of old—ghosts of gods stranded in the sea.

He flew low to the water and felt the salt spray of his passage upon his silver skin, smelled the brine of it in his massive nostrils.

The Seaway was ahead now, its massive riblike pillars extending up from the sea to stretch far into the sky. Above it, a silver globe etched with the continents of Lasthome turned slowly and the waters within those arching pillars bubbled a slightly different color.

As he went, he watched for ships and noted two bound for the temple under the flag of the white tree and another heading east. Petronus brought his vision in to note the Y'Zirite markings. *There were more Y'Zirites getting through.* But he suspected that these were the twitches of a warm corpse and easily dealt with once Neb was home.

Home. He was pondering that notion when he flew between the

pillars and everything shifted. Suddenly, the sky was gray and the water
gray, too. And the temperature dropped rapidly as he passed through
the pillars on the other side and found himself in the cold twilight
skies of Lasthome, the moon distant and low in the sky.

Petronus turned south and sent a tentative call to the other two kin-
dragons. They answered, and a few minutes later he joined them
where they circled. He saw the lifeboat and the woman standing within
it, but he didn't recognize her. She stood alone, an oar raised as if it
were a weapon, as she shouted at the massive beasts that swooped and
buzzed about her.

Petronus rolled himself and twisted, taking in the sea and sweeping it with his eyes. Somewhere relatively nearby was a ship, and once
he returned to the command pool, he would task the dragons to find
it. He was afraid he knew where that ship was bound, and he suspected
that his childhood friend was upon it.

And whatever Vlad planned, he'd not wanted this person there
for it.

Petronus focused his eyes again, holding himself steady against the
wind as he studied the woman and the lifeboat. She had the look of a
Delta Entrolusian—curly hair and large dark eyes. And the name on
the lifeboat was unmistakable and familiar.

The Kinshark. The vessel had been lost at sea—suspected captured
by the Y'Zirites after Vlad found one of its metal crew stranded in another of its lifeboats near the Seaway. Now here was another.

Petronus tried out his voice, clearing it and hearing the thunder roll
out as he did. "Who are you? How do you come to be here?"

The woman's fear was noticeable in the pallor of her face, and her
eyes went even wider. But Petronus wasn't prepared for her to drop
the oar and collapse into the bottom of the boat.

With an inward sigh, Petronus brought himself closer to the boat.
Then, he dug around in the corner of his mind where he knew the
knowledge was buried and released his binding to the beast, letting it
drop him into the cold waters of the Ghosting Crests.

Striking out in a breast stroke, he reached the boat easily as the kin-
dragons circled above. Then he pulled himself in. The girl was sitting
up, reaching for the oar again.

"They're here to help," Petronus said. Then, as an afterthought:
"I am here to help, too."

There was recognition in her eyes. "I know you," she said. "You
were in the dream."

Petronus nodded. "I was. Vlad Li Tam told us where to find you. What is he planning? Do you know?"

She shook her head. "I don't think there is much that he can do. The regent and Ahm Y'Zir are taking him to the moon to execute him. They have the staff, but it isn't working."

No, he realized. It wouldn't be. Vlad had seen to that. And the tower had grown a new one for its new administrator. But that, and the matter of exactly where Y'Zir and Xhum were and what to do about them and their prisoner, were all matters that could wait.

"He asked that you be delivered to the Ninefold Forest Houses. Lord Rudolfo is at Windwir, and I intend to bear you to him if you'll allow it."

"Bear me?"

He looked up at the kin-dragons and then back to her. "Yes. I've not done it before, but we'll learn together."

She nodded slowly. Then Petronus went to the bow of the lifeboat and stood, stretching his hands to the sky. The woman jumped when he called for the kin-dragon, but she didn't flinch when it descended suddenly to absorb Petronus. And she didn't make a sound as Petronus then took her into himself and tucked her away.

Then Petronus set out to the north and built speed, his nose and eyes and ears and skin all absorbing the vast sensory cornucopia of his homeworld for what he suspected was both the first and last time.

Chapter
23

Marta

Muffled voices rose in heated discussion as Marta sat with Isaak in the dim room. The metal man had said nothing during their flight, spending those hours largely in his version of sleep. And when they'd disembarked, an old man had met them with a dark look upon his face. He was flanked by other men—these armed with long rods made of wood or something like it. And more surprising, there were metal men with them. Three of them, dark and old and yet like Isaak.

Only nothing like him at all. These didn't speak. They didn't limp. They stared through empty jewellike eyes and did not move until told to.

There was also a woman with them in dressed in robes that indicated some kind of high office. She and Neb had spoken first and then had left together with Ire Li Tam and most of the soldiers.

Then the old man who'd been waiting for them near a plain wooden chair escorted them—followed by the other metal men—into the same low building and ultimately to this back room, where he pointed to a stool. "You can wait here with it if you prefer that to waiting with the others."

They'd waited for an hour when the voices went suddenly quiet. The door opened and the woman stood in it with Neb and Ire behind her. "I'm so sorry for the wait," she said to Marta. Then she looked to Isaak. "You pose us quite a quandary, Mechoservitor Three."

"His name," Marta said, "is Isaak."

"Yes," she said. "But our faith and our system of government doesn't allow for our machines to have names or to function at all in the way that Isaak functions." Her voice was warm, but her eyes were cold. "And we certainly do not use them as weapons."

"It is unfortunately what we were made for, Administrator Gras."

Her eyebrow arched now at his words. "So you know who I am."

Isaak nodded. "My aether and subaether connections were augmented in some way by my contact through the dreamstone. I have full access to New Espiran communication and archives. I am also able to communicate broadly with far more range than my system should permit."

She sighed and looked over her shoulder. "I feared that."

"If you are concerned about my presence in New Espira, I can assure you I only wish to see Lady Tam and Lord Jakob home."

"It is more than that, Isaak." Marta noted the woman's discomfort using the name. "You've been asked for. What do you do when the object of your faith asks something of you that violates the rules of that faith?" She sighed again and looked at him. "Let's go, then."

The other metal men stayed in their alcoves, and Marta followed as Isaak limped out. They went to another room, where they found an open hatch just like the others Marta had seen in the Beneath Places she'd left behind in the Named Lands and more men in uniform waiting along with the old man who had first met them.

They sent Isaak down the metal rungs first and she followed after. When Administrator Gras and the old man reached the bottom, they led them down a corridor until they reached a room with a silver pool and a tree. The old man looked at Isaak with curiosity as he plucked a piece of fruit and passed it to Marta. "Get a good bite," he said, "and swallow it down."

Marta looked around. "What are we doing here?"

But he had already turned to Isaak. "Have you utilized lightway travel before?"

Isaak shook his head. "I have not attempted to. My companions have not been able to do so."

"Translation commencing," the old man said into a stone he held. Then he looked at Marta. "I'm sorry," he said. "Someone will explain later."

The juice was running down her chin, the meat of the fruit still

sweet in her mouth, when he pushed her into the pool and everything
spun away in blue-green light.

She came up gasping and choking and using words her father
would've chastised her over. The room had spun away, and she was in
a grove now standing up to her waist in the same silver fluid that she
had seen disintegrate Gray Guard during their escape from Orius and
his men.

Neb was beside her, and then Isaak was on her other side—and as
they lifted her, she found she could stand upon the surface by a combined act of faith and will and a little help. She walked across the pond,
and once she was on solid ground, she turned in time to see Ire and
Administrator Gras both appear. The administrator lifted Ire up by
the hand, and the two of them approached.

Marta became aware of the others waiting—two women and two
children. One of the women had long hair the color of a sunset, and
she was certain it had to be Lady Tam, Queen of the Ninefold Forest.
Which made the little boy Lord Jakob, the Child of Promise. She had
no idea who the other woman was, but the little girl, she suspected,
must be the Crimson Empress.

Neb and Isaak were standing with Lady Tam. Isaak was quiet, but
Neb was talking excitedly.

Welcome to the Firsthome Forest. Come closer, for time is of the essence.

The voice was deep and rich and warm and familiar and old. Marta
had heard it before, she was certain, somewhere in unremembered
dreams. It filled her head and her heart both, and then she noticed the
tree.

It was nearly as vast as the one in her dream, but it rose up above a
forest like nothing she'd ever seen, and the meadow around it was
pocked with ponds and brooks like the one she now stood beside. And
there were roots like massive bones exposed here and there around it,
leading up to it. The tree might've been white and shining once, full
of seed that awaited some wind to carry it like the one in the dream.
But now it was old and sick and mottled with gray.

And speaking.

The chuckle was warm as well. *Yes.*

Marta took a step forward and felt Neb's hand upon her shoulder.
"This is Marta," he said. "This is Lady Jin Li Tam of the Ninefold Forest Houses and Lord Jakob, Rudolfo's heir. Marta is . . ." Neb looked
at her and tried to find the right word. "Marta is a friend of Isaak's.

She was the first to find him after his regeneration. She traveled with Winters and Charles for a time."

Lady Tam inclined her head and extended her hand from where she towered over her. "Well-met, Marta. Winters is a dear friend of mine. I'm glad Isaak has had you keeping an eye on him."

Marta's tone was matter-of-fact. "He needs it."

The grim look in her eye told Marta that the woman understood that. "This is Lady Chandra, mother of Amara Y'Zir, formerly the Crimson Empress."

"We really do not have much time," Administrator Gras said. She was already walking toward the tree. Marta looked around and realized that they were less alone than she'd thought. Men in uniforms that reflected back the colors of the forest moved about between trees, and in the distance she saw what looked like large horseless wagons. There were also tents of the same material.

"What is happening here?" she asked as the others followed the administrator.

"We are under attack. We have some time—we were able to shunt the lightway to this section of the crèche—but we do not have much." She paused to the side of the root they now walked upon and motioned them ahead of her. "She wishes to speak with Isaak and Neb."

And you, Child. You are Isaak's heart, though he doesn't know it, and you will need my blessing in the days to come.

The administrator frowned, and Marta noted it. *So she hears it, too.* And she didn't approve. She tried to force her focus into that voice and tipped her thoughts in that direction. *Who are you?*

Come and see, Child.

They reached the tree and walked around it until they reached a patch that Marta first though was discoloration. But when it twisted open into a toothless smile, she saw the mouth and stifled a gasp. "Hello, Marta. Use your voice. Let me use my ears."

Farther up the tree, an eye opened and rolled its pupil in her direction.

Marta watched as Isaak leaned toward a flap she recognized now as an ear. His voice was low, though Marta heard it. "I've come to bargain with you, Grandmother," he said.

"Then come and bargain with me. But bring your heart with you, for you will need it."

Farther away still, a pair of branches unfolded and unfolded until she saw rudimentary arms and fingers. They motioned for them to come closer, and Isaak limped toward it. Marta went behind him, her eyes on the beckoning hands.

The tree was opening now, a red light spilling out of it, and Isaak paused. "You cannot come with me," he said.

"She invited me," Marta said. "Did you not know that I am your heart?"

Isaak cocked his head for a moment, and his eyes dimmed and brightened. Then, without a word, he slipped into the tree and Marta followed after.

The walls within were red flesh that smelled sweet in the hot air. Thick purple veins pulsed through the Grandmother's flesh, and a bloody light from a chamber ahead filled the narrow corridor, beating in time with the fluid in the veins. Marta recognized it as the rhythm of a massive, pumping heart.

Now the voice was stronger but only filled her ears, not her head. "Bring your heart to my heart, Isaak."

Isaak hesitated. "I . . . do not wish to," he finally said. "I believe it is unsafe for the human to be here with me, Grandmother."

The laugher was music. "She is not safe anywhere, Isaak, especially here. But I do not think that is your true motive. I think you mean that you do not wish her to bear witness to your bargain." Now she paused. "Ah," she said. "Unsafe because of the harm it will do her."

Isaak said nothing and Marta turned to him. "What does she mean?"

"Enough," Grandmother said. "I'll not have you bickering in the foyer. Bring your heart to my heart, Isaak."

He started moving again, and it seemed to Marta that his limp was more pronounced than ever, his shoulders slouching with the weight of this moment.

The corridor spilled into a small round chamber open around a thick red nodule that beat in time to the light it shed. It was supported below and above by a thick purple vein.

This is the tree's heart. Marta could barely comprehend the idea of a tree having a heart. Or talking. Or inviting them inside for a chat.

"This is where bargains are made," the Grandmother said. "What is yours?"

"Your Codex requires that I be reset and repurposed according to the Terms and Conditions of Frederico's Bargain."

"Not my Codex," Grandmother said. "But the New Espirans', yes."

"I wish you to allow that to happen."

"I am not in any position to prevent it from happening," Grandmother said. "And soon, I'll be in no position to do anything if the Daughter of D'Anjite and Daughter of Salome have their way."

Marta felt her eyebrows go up. "What Codex? What does she mean?"

Grandmother chuckled. "He means that Frederico's children are required by his instructions to erase the human components of Isaak's system, delete or archive all data, and restrict his movement on the lightways and his access to the aether and subaether. Of course, the Codex also requires nonintervention and working in secret—yet you are both here with me now." Her voice lowered. "But what are you asking for, Isaak? You want me to ask the administrator to do that which she wanted to do in the first place—that which I prevented by inviting you here?"

He nodded, and Marta's mouth fell open as she continued. "Where is the mutuality and consideration required by contract, Isaak? Are you going to join the New Espirans and fight the invaders? Or are you going to give me the Cacophonic Deaths that I might use it to prevent my death?"

He said nothing and hung his head.

"I am already dying, Isaak. I will be dead within the century, and with my passing, this crèche will have served its purpose and its resources will be repurposed along with whatever is left of my sap."

The reality of her was dawning on Marta along with what he was asking of her, and she turned on Isaak. "What are you doing, Isaak?"

But she knew what he was doing. He would never be used as a weapon again because he would no longer be Isaak. He would be like the mechoservitors in New Espira, used as tools and machines without names or robes.

"You come with a one-sided bargain, Isaak, and I will instead offer you a blessing."

More branches unfolded at the top of the chamber, but these were moist and fleshy and they draped down to rest upon their foreheads. "I will not give you what you ask for, but I will give you what you need. . . . Does this sound familiar to you, Isaak?"

He nodded. "It is what Pope Petronus told Lord Rudolfo when he asked for a new Pope to be named at the conference where Sethbert was tried."

"Yes. The same holds true of your bargain with me. And so I offer this blessing. Both to you and to your heart."

It was a whisper of discord in a dark cold place and a nearly extinguished light, and then it became melodic. And then harmonic. A song, or at least the first few notes of one.

He showed you this, yes? Rushing light and numbers and symbols and more light.

"Yes," Isaak said. "He deactivated it."

Look closer, Grandmother said. *Listen.*

One note. And then one more to harmonize with it. *There is a song that was lost,* Grandmother whispered. *And then it was found only to be twisted away from its purpose. Your blessing and your bargain is to see the song back to its proper form and find your choir to sing it.*

Now it was colder and darker, and the discordant note was back. Only this time it was the hum of many voices—metal voices—whispering beneath the ice far, far to the north beyond the Dragon's Spine, though Marta didn't understand how she knew this. *I hear them in my sleep but cannot find them. Find them, Isaak, and heal the world with your new song, and it will heal you as well.*

The hands lifted away. "Bear witness to this, Child."

"I do," she said.

"I am not sufficient for this work," Isaak said.

"That is not the truth," Grandmother said with another chuckle. Then she clucked a tongue that Marta couldn't see. "Ask your heart to tell you the truth."

"I am powered by a—"

Marta grabbed his hand and interrupted him. "She means me, Isaak." She didn't wait for him to answer. "And you are sufficient if it is a work you choose. You do not need to be repurposed. I don't know how I feel about traveling the world in search of a song and some mysterious choir, but I do know that I won't go anywhere *without* you and *will* go anywhere with you. You are my home. And I am your heart." She stared over at the tree's beating heart. "Now swear to me by your own heart, Grandmother, that he is free to make his own choices in accordance with the first and second gifts given?"

Her laughter was warm and full now and it made her flesh quiver. "Oh, Child, you are a brave heart, you are. Certainly love and choice prevail."

Marta smiled at the compliment and then lost her footing as the tree suddenly shook.

"And I'm afraid," Grandmother said, "that our time is up and our uninvited guests have arrived."

Marta's smile faded quickly as she glanced at Isaak. It meant he would be leaving soon. He would go out and he would fight, bargain or not, even if the Grandmother was already dying. He would be doing it to save the children. And the others.

And me, she realized.

The realization sparked a sudden panic within, and by instinct she started after him barely comprehending just what his current path might cost.

Because, Marta thought, *he is my heart as well as my home.*

And as Isaak moved down the corridor and Grandmother's branches curled around her, holding her back as she screamed, Marta was reminded that homes could be lost and hearts could be broken.

Neb

It started with the distant warble of an alarm and the waving of trees on the far side of the forest. Neb watched soldiers vanish as they activated the devices that functioned as their equivalent of scout magicks. The reflective nature of their uniforms made them difficult to spot once they were within the shade of the forest, but now they were practically invisible.

Of course, even with their thorn rifles and advanced equipment, Neb knew they couldn't stand against Amylé. And if Ria had joined her . . .

He suspected strongly that alone, he would not last long. He withdrew the crescent. "Petronus?"

Of course, he'd heard nothing from the old man. The administrator had put him in touch with Ambassador Thrall briefly before they arrived to the tree, and she'd told him about the kin-dragons. Hopefully it meant Petronus was on his way. The two of them together—with Isaak—made their odds far better. *But she has the axe.*

And she means to use it on me, Son of Whym.

Her voice in his mind felt like the best of his memories as a child in the Great Library of the Androfrancine Order. Dim-lit aisles of books, the whispering of steam releasing from the library's mechoservitor, the smell of ancient paper—all flooded him as she spoke. She was the distant memory of home.

I will stop her, Grandmother. But as he said it, he knew it was a fervent hope and not a sense of confidence that drove his words. He'd yet to best her when they were one-on-one, and now she brought help. And early reports since their arrival in the translation site were that Ria was every bit as unstoppable as Amylé in their advance upon the Firsthome Forest.

Neb looked at Jin Li Tam. She held Jakob with one arm while her other hand rested near a knife hilt that wasn't there. "You should all wait inside Grandmother with Marta," he said.

The waving of trees stopped as two figures emerged from the forest, moving fast and tossing invisible soldiers aside as they advanced into the meadow.

Amylé held up the Firstfall Axe, and light glinted off its silver surface.

And even at that distance, he felt her, he smelled her, and it washed over him with an ache of longing that he could never be quite prepared for.

No, Neb realized. *It's more.*

Ria stood beside her, and even at that distance he saw Winters in the woman's posture and face. Both of them wore the same suit of light he wore, and Ria held a pair of long knives still dark and wet from cutting her way through the forest.

And Neb wanted them. *It is the Calling.* The People had built into themselves a mating drive that increased or decreased based on their population.

And there appear to be only four of us left.

Neb looked over his shoulder. "You really should wait inside Grandmother," he said again. "There's nothing you're going to be able to do out here, Lady Tam." He didn't add what he wanted to: *I'm not certain of what even I can do.*

Jin Li Tam nodded and glanced to Chandra. Then they turned with their children, and when Isaak emerged from the tree they slipped in with Administrator Gras.

Then Neb tucked the crescent away and checked the hand cannon in his pouch as Isaak stepped up to join him. "I have one shot, and it's not very accurate," he told the metal man. He'd cleaned it and reloaded it but knew now that only close range would be effective. And he did not know if it could penetrate the blood of the earth that she wore.

"Our statistical likelihood of success is twenty-three percent based on my limited analysis."

The New Espirans had limited security forces—they lived in hiding with the world only recently becoming aware of their presence. They had no need of an army, and their Codex required secrecy and noninterference as they gathered for the Time of Sowing. Still, they had access to at least some of the weapons of the olden times.

And a dozen mechoservitors like Isaak. No, nothing like Isaak really. They shared the design, though they were much older. But these mechoservitors had no sense of personhood about them, and they were only used as tools to accomplish tasks, then deactivated until needed again.

When Isaak had first vanished into the tree, he'd breached the subject of sending them in as support with the administrator, and she'd grown pale with the notion.

"The council would never permit such a thing," she had said. He'd tried to press it, but the line of her jaw told him she would not change on this until she saw reason to.

The look on her face as she slipped into the tree told Neb she was closer to seeing reason.

But if she didn't call them soon, it was going to be too late. And if Amylé and Ria prevailed, he doubted the tree would be only thing brought down by the axe.

"I have Amylé," Neb said. He tracked her as she ran the meadow, measuring her steps as she leaped ponds and brooks. Then he surged forward, leaped into the closest brook, and willed himself toward her, letting their bodies pull at each other as he evaporated into light and then reemerged from a pond behind her.

He did not wait and he did not call out. Neb threw himself at her back and brought her down. But as they fell, she kept her grip on the axe and twisted. The smell of her so close, the heat of her body against him, disoriented Neb and he clung to her, dodging her knees and feeling her breath upon the bare skin of his neck.

"Our time is done, Nebios. Don't you see? The People have had millions of years to grow beyond their baser origins on Firsthome. Stand or fall at Lasthome is what they promised, and we fell long ago."

"We are standing still," Neb said. "Stand with us."

Some of her fierceness was losing its edge now that her hands were upon him, and he saw now that her own eyes were wide and her nostrils flared. Then a wave of disgust washed over her face. "See? It's disgusting. They've built survival into our very bodies, but who decided that we deserve to survive?"

Then she jabbed him hard with the handle of the axe even as her knee found a soft place. Amylé tossed him off of her and stood. But when she tried to enter one of the ponds, the blood of the earth refused her.

Amylé roared. "I see you've met our Grandmother and she's favored you." She turned on the tree. "The time of the People has passed."

The Grandmother Tree's voice was in his head. *My sap will not serve those who wish me harm.* Neb had pushed the blood of the earth to the point of refusing him when it was such that it might harm him, and he could only hope this meant that once Amylé's suit burned out, she'd lose the strength, speed and protection it afforded. But Neb couldn't afford to wait, and he had no idea how long her suit was last.

He saw Isaak closing with Ria and watched her knives spark off his metal skin as she danced backward. Then Neb was on his feet and letting the blood of the earth carry him to Amylé. His fist connected with her jaw to send her sprawling, and as he leaped on her again, her feet came up to catch him and toss him aside.

He landed on the pouch and felt the impact of it against his ribs, then rolled off of it quickly to scramble to his feet. As he staggered to the side, he saw Isaak and Ria thrashing about in one of the ponds. And he was vaguely aware of invisible soldiers dodging in and out with their own blades, but they were more the annoyance of summer insects than any kind of real threat or help.

If you can call for help, Neb willed the Grandmother Tree, *this would be a time for it.*

Amylé swung the axe, and he leaped back but felt the wind of it. She shouted as she swung again, and he dodged as the axe bit deeply into the tree; then as she tugged at it, he drew the hand cannon and pulled back the lever.

Neb stepped up to her, pointed it, and pulled its trigger back hard. It popped and smoked but did not fire as it had earlier.

Then Neb saw Amylé's smile and heard her laughter as her free hand came up and took hold of him, lifting him into the air.

"It all ends, Nebios. First here and then I bring the Firstfall Axe to the moon."

Then she tossed him aside and brought the axe down again. And Neb closed his eyes as the Grandmother Tree's howl of pain filled his skull, and the shaking ground beneath him would not let him gain his feet again.

Jin Li Tam

It was already cacophony in the crowded space within when the Grandmother Tree's howl of pain was added to the din. Jin Li Tam closed her eyes against it and held Jakob close to her chest as he wailed.

The girl—Marta—had put up quite a fight, screaming and thrashing about. Chandra was busy soothing Amara; Jin with Jakob. That left Administrator Gras to try to calm Isaak's companion down, and it wasn't a task her years in bureaucracy had prepared her for. Still, eventually the girl calmed down. Until the tree started screaming.

And through it all, the Grandmother's voice continued. "I'm sorry, Children. I don't mean to frighten you."

"I need to see what's happening," Jin said.

Marta's head shot up. "Me too."

I'm not certain it will help you.

But Jin simply repeated herself. "I need to see."

And suddenly, she was far above the clearing looking down, watching the fight unfold as New Espiran soldiers attempted to engage. She saw light glinting off of Isaak's surface as he closed on Ria and then caught Neb knocking Amylé off her feet out of the corner of her eye, closer to the tree. The axe was buried in the tree.

"They aren't going to be enough," she said.

Grandmother's voice was sober, and Jin suspected it was for her alone. *No, Great Mother, they are not.*

"What about the New Espiran mechoservitors?"

"We've deployed them," Gras said, "but without translation capacity they are a full day's run from here. We have airships arriving within an hour, but our vessels have never needed arming. Our technologists have been working on that since the crèche was first breached."

Jin Li Tam winced as she watched Amylé knock Neb into the side of the tree. She heard the thud of his head.

Gras continued. "Last word is that Petronus was en route to the Named Lands, but I don't think he can be back in time to help us."

Jin had seen him in the dream, young and strong—closer to her age than his own seventy-odd years. But even with a kin-dragon and the lightways, it would take Petronus longer than they probably had. Jin turned her attention back to the battlefield. Ria and Isaak fought at the edge of the tree line now; she brandished a long branch at him as he advanced upon her. "I think we will have to find a way to help ourselves."

I am the forty-second daughter of Vlad Li Tam. I can find this path. Her eyes settled on Ria. The woman didn't fight with the same grace she'd seen in her younger sister, but she had a brutality fed by wrath. Still, Jin could not imagine this woman harming Jakob or Amara. Certainly she would harm the others, and Jin was fairly confident that her own role as Great Mother no longer held any merit. *But could she truly harm the children?*

And did that matter? She couldn't fully grasp what it meant to lose the Grandmother Tree, but she sensed that it could not bode well. And it wouldn't stop here. The look on Amylé's face—the look on Ria's, too—was too close to Sethbert's on the day that Windwir fell. There was a reason her grandfather had assured his ascendance to the overseer position for the United City-States. There was madness in him, and she started to see it in his eyes and in his voice after secret meetings. When they'd stopped and sat and drank wine to watch Windwir's pyre on the horizon, he'd laughed.

He had wanted to burn it down. She recognized that same look in Amylé.

"Grandmother," she said, "is there anything we can do?" She thought about it. "What bargains can be made?"

Some part of the tree screamed as the axe bit into her again. But the voice in Jin Li Tam's head was calm. *There are no optimal bargains to be made.*

Isaak went down, and Jin watched the massive branch crash down upon his chest. She saw something spark and heard Marta gasp. *She is watching, too.*

"The time for optimal is past," Jin said.

I can restore one of you. Like Petronus was restored.

Jin knew nothing really about what had happened to Petronus. She'd seen him in the dream, and she'd heard through the administrator that he was working closely with their ambassador upon the moon. Most recently, she'd heard that he had found a way to access the kin-dragons. Whatever had happened to him, it had allowed him to unseal the temple and had shaved forty years off his life.

She closed her eyes and focused her words. *I would have access to the blood of the earth? I would be as strong as Neb or the others?*

For a few hours, yes.

She looked to Amylé and Neb now. He fought about as well as a boy who'd grown up in a library would fight. He'd picked up some skill along the way, but it was not enough against his opponent. Amylé, on the other hand, was practiced precision that smelled more of military training and little practical experience. And Ria fought with the skill of a Blood Guard thrown off balance by her anger.

Jin was already tracing the steps of her knife-dance across the meadow and measuring the distances.

"A few hours would be enough," she said out loud. The mechoservitors would arrive by then. The airships. Petronus, even, could be here by then.

The Grandmother Tree's voice was low now, and Jin sensed only for her. *No, Great Mother, you do not understand.*

What am I not understanding?

If I do this to you, it cannot be undone. You will have only a few hours before your body burns out.

She'd heard about her sister Rae Li Tam's last days, thrashing about as the blood magicks burned out and slowly killed her on her trip back to the Named Lands. *But Petronus survived?*

He was restored slowly, and it burns out slowly. But no, he will not survive his restoration either. But Aver-Tal-Ka was hatched as a safeguard in Frederico's Bargain, and Petronus's sacrifice will bring about the Sowing.

Jin Li Tam swallowed. "I don't need to see any more," she said in a quiet voice. When the fight spun away and she once more stood in the red light of the Grandmother Tree's heart, she looked at the women there with her. "One of us needs to go out and help them. The Grandmother Tree can make us strong like them."

"I'll go," Marta said.

"No," Jin Li Tam said. "I'm the only one here with any combat experience." For the briefest moment the scattered parts of her aligned, and the queen brought her shoulders up even as the mother clung to her son and the Tam within her schemed and spun strategies. She looked at Gras. "Have Petronus bring Rudolfo if he can." Then she looked at Marta. "See Jakob to Ire and Aedric's care until Rudolfo arrives if I am not able to."

She wasn't sure exactly where the New Espirans had spirited her sister to, but she'd been assured of her safety. Still, their rigid protocols were proving to have put them into a corner with only one escape.

But maybe I can reason with them. She doubted it, but she did not doubt that she could beat them. Amylé lacked experience, and her hand-to-hand skills were mechanical and easily predicted. Even Neb was learning, but taking a beating as he did. And Ria could be manipulated with Jakob and her faith.

Jin Li Tam looked at Jakob. "Mama has to go help." She kissed his hair, inhaling the scent of him. He clung, still crying, and she handed him over to Marta.

"I want to go with you," the girl said. "I need to help Isaak."

Jin Li Tam crouched so that she was level with Marta's eyes. "I need you to take care of my son, Marta. He is the Prince of the Ninefold Forest and the delight of my heart." The tears in her eyes ambushed her, along with the lump in her throat. "I will be done quickly, and you will have Isaak back."

Are you certain, Great Mother?

"I wish everyone would stop calling me that," she said as the tears finally slipped down her cheeks. "But yes. I'm certain."

She felt the fleshy branches coil around her and lift her until she was pressed tightly, facefirst, against the tree's great beating heart.

Taste the root of heritage and give yourself to it.

Jin opened her mouth and felt her body seize and her eyes roll back as the Grandmother's sap flowed into her. The more she thrashed, the tighter the branches held her, and sudden bursts of light set the world careening away from her again and again until she realized that it was in synchronicity with the beating heart of the Grandmother Tree.

"Clothe me," Jin Li Tam whispered, and the blood of the earth obeyed her. "Hide me," she said, and she vanished from view. Then, as the vines released her, she flexed her muscles and felt the strength building within her even as calm and a sense of euphoria flooded her.

Then Jin Li Tam, the forty-second daughter of Vlad Li Tam and Queen of the Ninefold Forest, kissed her son upon his forehead and slipped out of the Grandmother Tree to find knives and give herself fully to one last dance.

Chapter 24

Ria

The massive branch struck Isaak, and Ria smiled at the sound of metal groaning beneath the force of its impact. The metal man toppled, and she hit him again from behind.

It was strange, fighting with a mechoservitor so much like the Watcher. That ancient mechanical had at one point in the distant past been Ahm Y'Zir's personal servant and later became the force that helped codify and promote his gospel.

She'd studied on that mechanical's knee from time to time as a child when the Watcher visited the empire. And his stories about the Wizard King's early years in exile had always fascinated her, though some he couldn't share.

But even stranger than fighting the mechoservitor, it amazed her that she held her own. She remembered watching Neb and Isaak fighting the Watcher up in the Machtvolk Territories on the Mass of the Fallen Moon. She'd marveled then, and now she herself was doing damage against him, with strength and speed and focus the likes of which not even the best blood magicks could provide.

You do not need to do this, Child.

The voice surprised her. And she'd heard it before but couldn't place it. Still, it wasn't welcome.

"Get out of my head," she shouted as she shrugged off a magicked soldier, tossing him into a silver pond. They should've evaporated upon contact, but she suspected these New Espiran rats, buried in their war-ren below the ground, had tricks upon tricks in their hidey-holes.

Which they kept to themselves and used to spy upon us all. Amylé had let her listen to the subaether. And she'd seen the wreckage of the ship at Windwir, the men and women in strange uniforms.

The voice of the Grandmother Tree persisted. *You're scaring the children, Winteria.* That stopped her, and Ria looked up at the tree.

"Where are they?"

A voice to her left made her jump. "They are here, Ria. I'm sure she told you."

She knew the voice, and her eyes scanned for some sign of her. "Great Mother, were you part of Vlad's grand deception? Or do you finally now see how deeply the kin-wound in House Li Tam runs?" She thrust the branch in the direction of the voice as she spoke. "Of course you see," Ria said. "Look how easily you took matters into your own hands and spirited Lord Rudolfo's heir away from him in pursuit of your family's constant need to move the world."

Isaak lunged in, and as she turned to fend him off with the branch, she felt a fist from behind into her kidney, driving her to the ground with a howl of pain. "You can't possibly wish to harm your Crimson Empress and your Child of Promise, Ria. Help us stop Amylé before she kills them and maybe kills us all."

She doesn't understand, Ria realized as she pushed herself up from the ground. The pain made her angry, and she let it pour into her words. "They are Abominations. Everything he told us in his gospels were twists and turns on truth and myth to bring back that which Y'Zir had sworn to remove from Lasthome forever when he took the moon from the last of the Younger Gods. He grew old and wise upon their blood, and now his kin wish to bring them back and restore them to power . . . or worse, start the entire cycle over again."

Amylé had explained everything. Ria now saw where her faith had strayed. It had been based upon enough truth to make the falsehoods seem plausible. And at the end of that long labyrinth it was about power and vendetta and not about healing the world.

Because the world cannot be healed. The people who had come here, weary of too long a life and too many rises and falls as a species, had learned that lesson and had declared this to be their last home.

"You yourself are one of these Abominations," Jin Li Tam said. "Your sister, too."

Ria swung in the direction of the voice. "We are the last of the People," she said. "And we decided long ago that we stood or fell at Lasthome." She smiled as she felt the branch connect with something. "We finally, finally fall today."

"I don't believe you will kill my son or Amara," Jin Li Tam said, her voice low and controlled.

"Then bring them to me so we can see together just what I will do." She threw the branch aside and lunged for the body of a soldier. Ria dug a blade out from beneath it and tested it in her hands. It wasn't like anything she'd seen—made of a thin white coral or bone—a long haft and then a blade about the length of a sword, razor sharp and serrated. It did not look like a forged weapon but instead like something grown. Like the thorn rifles that the Y'Zirites grew in their hidden gun fields.

She spun the blade and turned. The slightest whisper to her left betrayed someone—she hoped it was Jin Li Tam—and she thrust.

Finish her and help me. Now it was Amylé's voice in her head, and Ria found herself wanting to scream. When it wasn't voices, it was dreams; and she couldn't remember a time when she hadn't had images or words in her head that had originated elsewhere.

She glanced toward Amylé. The woman was pressed now, her back to the tree as she fended off the other two. But even as she watched, Ria saw the woman's axe lash out and knock Isaak to the side with a cascade of sparks.

Another fist brought her back to the moment, and a realization struck her. *She is toying with me.* These fists were more solid, with the hilt of a knife in them, and so far Jin Li Tam had been careful not to use the blades.

"You think your smooth Tam tongue can sway me," she said as she feinted with the blade and then twisted the handle up to strike something solid and invisible. "But these words only waste your breath." She whipped the blade around again and felt the sharp edge connect lightly and heard Jin Li Tam gasp in pain. Ria smiled.

But the smile didn't live long upon her face. She'd trained with the Blood Guard in her early years and had been a competent fighter, but it had not prepared her for the storm that unleashed now that she'd drawn blood.

She parried the blades away and realized that she could feel the ache in her muscles and her bruised body. Amylé had told her that the blood of the earth would eventually wear off and that there could be a period of time where it required her body to rest before reinfusing her with its strength and protection. *Not yet,* she willed it.

Jin Li Tam's precision and pace increased now, and Ria felt a long hot line of pain along her side as one of the woman's knives connected. "Stand down, Ria, or I will kill you."

She saw another burst of sparks from the corner of her eye and watched Isaak fall as the axe took off one of his legs. Ria laughed and spun away, twisting and swinging her blade in the direction she thought Ji Li Tam had gone. She found air and felt another line of fire, this time along her left shoulder and down her arm. The pain was just registering when she felt something solid strike the back of her knee and she fell facefirst into a pond.

Hide me, she willed the suit, and she felt it move against her skin, but it wasn't working. *Help me.* She wasn't sure if she meant the words for the pool or for the woman who had baptized her into it. She looked up, sputtering, to see Amylé fending Neb off with Isaak at her feet, grappling at her legs.

A hand made a fist in Ria's hair and yanked her back with enough strength that bright light flashed across her vision. Jin flipped Ria onto her back and held her down with a foot planted squarely on her chest as she lifted the long sharp blade.

"Reveal me," the forty-second daughter of Vlad Li Tam said in a low voice.

Ria saw the eyes first and nothing after them. They were cold and blue and devoid of compassion. There was a practicality to their level gaze that made Ria suddenly as cold as those eyes and unable to move.

And there was no smile upon those lips, no slight twitch of victory. They were pursed with resolve. "All of this," Jin Li Tam said, "you brought upon yourself."

As the blade came up, Ria closed her eyes to it. Vlad had told her upon her cutting table that he would build his pain into an army. And in that moment, in the shadow of the Grandmother Tree, Ria realized for the first time that she had pain but that she had fashioned it into nothing at the end of it all and instead had let it shape her in its awkward, bloody hands.

She opened her eyes, as if opening them to truth for the first time, and experienced a moment of confusion as she saw the tree and meadow and sky spin and dance about, saw Amylé fall beneath Neb's fists as Isaak pulled her down, and then came to rest at last to see Jin Li Tam standing over a headless body with a bloody blade gripped in white-knuckled fists. Then light slowly swallowed everything and carried Winteria bat Mardic the Elder, Daughter of Salome, into the waiting dark.

Lysias

The night wind was warmer than usual, moaning through the evergreens, as Lysias walked the perimeter. The camp behind him was bustling with activity as they stacked supplies and queued passengers for the airship just an hour out.

All of it boggled his mind. Invisible ships in the sky. Dragons that hunted them and carried people to and fro. All controlled from the moon. He shook his head and longed for simpler days.

Still, the tree was ever before him now, and he found himself spinning fanciful yarns of what he'd do, retired and free to settle some small tropical farm far from the complexities of kin-clave and the exigencies of war in the shadow of the Moon Wizard's Tower.

"General Lysias? Your sergeant of the watch told me I could find you here." Captain Thrall caught up to him as he turned.

"Yes, Captain?" The young man's face was grave.

"Petronus will be here soon. I've word that we're to send Rudolfo and Winters with him."

He felt his brow furrow. The last message, borne by the man's aide, was that Petronus had retasked the kin-dragons so that the New Espiran fleet was no longer at risk. And that the old Pope himself was en route within one of the very beasts with some urgent matter for Rudolfo's attention. "The general is not expecting to travel. And I do not think he'll willingly leave the Named Lands with so much here to do."

But even before the captain answered, Lysias saw the cloud behind his eyes and felt his stomach sink. "He is needed in New Espira with his son and Lady Tam," the captain said, "and I suspect that he will agree."

There is trouble of some kind. Lysias sighed. Already, his mind spun the list of things that needed doing. He would stay on here and see the Gray Guard remnant back to the Ninefold Forest. Rudolfo had sent the moon sparrows out earlier calling for the capture of any Y'Zirite soldiers found in uniform and not bearing the mark of the white tree; those bound for the moon would not be interfered with. The Wandering Army would join the last of Turam's resistance and clean up

Pylos. He sighed again and looked to the captain. "Let's wake him, then. Have you told Winters already?"

Thrall nodded. "Yes. She is ready."

Lysias turned and made his way back to the camp. Thrall fell in behind him, and they went quietly. When they reached Rudolfo's cabin, he nodded to the guard, tapped at the door, and then opened it. "Lord Rudolfo? Captain Thrall needs a word. It is urgent." Then he stepped back and let the New Espiran in.

He closed the door quietly and found himself filling with dread on the man's behalf. Someone was dead or dying, and as much as he hated it to be anyone, he hoped against hope it was not the boy. Because Rudolfo, as strong as he was, could not weather facing that loss a second time.

And Jin Li Tam is at heart first and foremost a soldier. Certainly a shadowy ghost of a soldier in the Whymer Maze of her father's house, but soldiers were made for war and graveyards were made for soldiers. Not children.

The thought of children brought his own child to mind. He'd not seen her since she'd left for the north with Lady Tam and Lord Jakob. And she'd been in Ahm's Glory. Though the others had been too, and they seemed to be alive. Still, there'd been no word of her among the New Espirans.

Some part of him told Lysias that she could be dead—that she likely *was* dead—but he couldn't accept that. He wanted to believe that it was the power of some fatherly connection to his daughter whispering to him that she still lived, but he knew that he'd done nothing to foster that kind of bond. He'd been away working for an army more bureaucratic than military at least until the War for Windwir. And he'd rejected her and her child there at the end—the one she'd had with the secessionist, the one whose name he could never remember because he'd refused to sit down with them when they showed up at his home unannounced. He'd repaired what damage he could of that when he joined her in the Ninefold Forest to serve Rudolfo and build his standing army. But any bond they had was tenuous, and he knew that the denial he lived in was likely fueled by his own guilt.

I can't afford to believe she is dead, because I failed her as a father and it robs me of the chance to make things right.

He swallowed the shame he felt and looked up to the moon. Maybe he wanted to go there—maybe all of them wanted to go there—because it was a chance to start again and do it differently.

"And I would, too," he told the moon.

But in the end, he was a soldier. An officer in service to a king with an out-of-the-way kingdom rapidly becoming the center of the Named Lands that Windwir once had been. And a war newly won. And new allies from seemingly thin air. And a colony of Marshers, Y'Zirites and other followers of the dream growing upon the moon.

And a dragon bearing a dead Pope, he thought.

Even as he thought it, the camp went to third alarm and he heard a commotion on the other side of camp. He saw something dark moving against the dark sky to hover above the field that marked the edge of Windwir's grave. Lysias moved quickly toward it, noting that both the New Espirans and Gray Guard did the same. He had no doubt that Rudolfo's Gypsy Scouts, magicked and on alert, were nearby and ready.

The kin-dragon settled into the field, and there was a slow build of light that suddenly burst, blinding him momentarily.

When Lysias opened his eyes, a man and woman stood before the beast. The man wore silver robes that shone, and the woman had curly hair and—

Lynnae? He squinted and blinked, taking another step forward. "Lynnae?"

"Father?" Her voice shook, but he knew it and homed in on it like a moon sparrow.

She was in his arms within that instant, sobbing. He held her, his own tears flowing, too. "How?" He tried to find more for his question and could not so he simply asked again. "How?"

"Vlad Li Tam," the man beside her said. And of course, it was Petronus. They'd told him Petronus was coming. But he'd not expected his daughter, and he wouldn't have recognized Petronus if he hadn't known it was him. His balding head had a thick mane of chestnut hair, and he'd lost at least forty years. His compact body was squat and muscular. "He is up to something. I have a dragon looking for the *Kinshark,* but we're not entirely sure if they're still here or if they've crossed the Seaway into the lunar sea."

Lysias released his daughter and wiped his eyes. "Father Petronus," he said, inclining his head. "I do not have adequate words for my gratitude."

Rudolfo was beside him now, and Lysias stood straighter. "Lady Lynnae," he said, "I am glad to see you reunited with your father." His eyes went dark for a moment. "I'll have you reunited with Lord Jakob soon, as well, if you intend to continue in your care of him?" Rudolfo paused and glanced at Lysias. "I have no idea where or how that care will unfold. But he is alive, and I will do whatever is necessary to keep him as such."

Lynnae nodded. "I love him as if he were my own, Lord Rudolfo. When I thought he'd been—"

Rudolfo raised a hand at her choked sob. His own voice cracked. "Then your home is with us. Your place in his life is even more vital now, Lady."

It's Jin Li Tam, then. Lysias felt no shame in his relief. But he did feel shame that the sight of his daughter overjoyed him despite the dark circumstances they faced. And he felt a small stab of guilt that he'd even considered for a moment leaving his duties in the Ninefold Forest in favor of a simpler, quieter life upon the moon. There would be much work to do. And the elation of Jakob's survival still lived in the shadow of threat—the boy's life had been saved by blood magicks, and that bore dark tidings for his return.

Still, Lysias knew, they'd come this far. And now they had new allies. He glanced at the wreckage of the airship now carefully sorted and stacked for removal. Between the New Espirans, the resources of the library mechoservitors and the so-called Library of Elder Days, some solution would be found. It was only a matter of time.

Winters joined them, and Lysias could see that she'd been crying. It was no new thing; his own face was still wet with tears, and he wasn't certain there wouldn't be more. The times they'd lived had been washed in tears of deep sorrow and it seemed imprudent to believe those days were behind them.

But change was indeed the path life took, Lysias knew, and that truth applied to dark circumstances as readily as to comfortable ones.

"You and Philemus know your work," Rudolfo said. "I will be back soon." He glanced to Captain Thrall. "And I'll have an ambassador in tow to begin negotiations with the New Espirans. So have the manor readied for dignitaries and send word to the others." He paused. "And set the mechoservitors remaining to the task of solving our water issue. Have them work with Blakely and Symeon."

Lysias met the man's eyes and saw hard truth accepted there. "We will take care of the home front, Lord Rudolfo. Journey safely."

Rudolfo glanced over his shoulder at the kin-dragon and then back to Lysias. "I should hope so, General." He looked to Lynnae and smiled. "I am pleased that you are safe and sound, Lady Lynnae.

Jakob will be pleased as well." Then he glanced at Petronus. "You're looking well, Father. Take me to my family."

Petronus glanced around and nodded. "I'm new to this, so bear with me." He closed his eyes and stepped back into the beast as it rose up and wrapped his arms around him. There was a flash, and Petronus was gone.

Lysias stepped back and guided his daughter back with him. The kin-dragon opened its arms, and this time Rudolfo stepped forward. He vanished with a flash, and then Winters followed after.

Now all that remained was the kin-dragon, massive and dark as it reflected back the night sky. It stood on two legs and waved four in the air as its two pairs of wings began to beat rapidly. The tail twitched, and Lysias and Lynnae took another three steps back.

Then the dragon launched itself at the sky and climbed quickly to hover above Windwir in the light of the blue-green moon. And it seemed to Lysias that the dragon tipped its head, inclining in respect to a holy place made even holier by the blood that sanctified its ground. The Androfrancines had built their city as an island of light—some hidden and some shining brightly into the world—and Petronus had shepherded that city and its people for a season of his life. And then, while Lysias worked to win the war against Rudolfo and the Marshers, the old Pope had stayed with the boy, Neb, to bury all of those bones.

When the dragon turned south and built speed to crack the sky, Lysias realized Petronus was likely saying his goodbyes. He and Winters, after this, would no doubt be bound for the moon.

But not Lysias. He would never forget the dream and the white tree, and maybe someday, before he died in his sleep peacefully as an old man, he would sail to the moon and see what kind of home the others had made there.

That dream was powerful, but it had reminded him of a more precious dream he had not yet dreamed fully.

Because I love my daughter more than I love the moon, Lysias thought. And he would make a home with her and with Rudolfo and put aside war in favor of something better. Hunting, perhaps, with the little heir and his father if they could find a way to bring the boy home. For now, the fact that Jakob lived was enough.

Lysias smiled and looked to his daughter again. For that brief moment she was six and missing a tooth in a face full of tangled curls.

"There's sweetbread and chai in the galley," he said, reaching a hand out to her.

She took it and smiled. Then in silence, they turned their back upon Windwir's grave and followed the smell of baking bread and frying bacon toward a table waiting for them in a place of warmth and light.

Rudolfo

Not even the wonder of flight, with its smells and sights and wind upon skin, could shake Rudolfo from the anchor that held him to his heavy heart.

My wife is dying. Jin Li Tam had done exactly what he would've expected—had given herself completely to her work, this time the work of saving their child. And now, his wife had hours to live.

It was hard to think of her in that role—she'd only spent a brief amount of time with him, and most of it was during a difficult pregnancy. And they'd been separated as soon as Jakob was born, with those separations continuing until she left the Named Lands with the boy.

Rudolfo had been angry. Not just because of her actions, but because those actions reinforced further what he didn't want to believe—that as hard as he tried, as clever as he was, he could not protect his family, or himself, any better than he had before. He'd lost his brother first. Then his parents. And for a span of days had believed he'd also lost his son. Next he would lose Jin Li Tam, though he doubted he'd ever completely had her. She'd been her father's daughter first and foremost. Death and loss were the counterbalance to life, and in Rudolfo's life, those deaths and losses were initiated by the work of Jin's father, Vlad Li Tam, and his father before him.

And my father, too. He'd been angry about that, as well. He had been angry, it seemed, over many things.

But now the anger leaked out of him and left him with a mix of other emotions that kept him from wondering at the sun upon his wings and the smell of the Ghosting Crests in his wide, flared nostrils. Sorrow and weariness vied for first place in his heart.

I was already weary when it started. He remembered those nights after Windwir fell, unable to sleep, longing for a rest that would not come until the war was finished. Back then, he'd had no idea how long that war would last, how many turns it would take through the Whymer Maze of Tam intrigues and Y'Zirite infiltration to the place where he now rode within a kin-dragon to sit at the side of his dying queen and bring his son back home.

If it could be done. The Androfrancine pathogen was thorough. But now, more than ever before, he found Isaak's words coming back to him. Words he couldn't conjure in the depths of his grief before: to trust him and to trust the dream. But more than that, Rudolfo would trust that between all of the resources they now had, a solution would be found.

Or I will build an aqueduct and bring new water in. . . .

Or, if need be, rule his people from afar.

Whatever came, Rudolfo would find life in it for himself and his son. Very different, he suspected, than the one he'd lived before. He'd spent most of his reigning years learning to balance his sorrow against the pleasures he had once vigorously pursued. He couldn't imagine going back to those days now, awakening in a tangle of limbs to break-fast with the prostitutes he'd kept on his rotation. Now the idea of simply waking up to the sound of a household still sleeping to check on his son before slipping out into a predawn forest to walk the morning dark seemed far more appealing. The notion of spending his evenings with a stack of books was far more appealing than a night of sweating and frolicking. And he knew it was war that had changed him.

The war and the truths it brought to the surface of our hearts.

He didn't notice the landscape changing, or the transition from night to day, until they began to slow and lose altitude. Once they hovered over a small collection of buildings, the sun was high in the sky, though it had only been a handful of hours since they'd left Windwir.

Rudolfo felt the ground beneath his paws, and then as the kin-dragon reared up, he felt a pop in his skull and experienced a strange vertigo as he was suddenly in his own body again and wobbling on the ground.

Petronus and Winters stood beside him, and the now-young Pope guided them both toward the man and the mechoservitors who waited for them.

"I am Cyril Thrall," the man said. "I will see you to New Espira."

Rudolfo hadn't asked for more detail and did not know exactly what he would find. He knew she had made some kind of bargain and that it had allowed her to save the children and this so-called Grandmother

Tree, but he also knew that the ambassador wished to begin talks immediately to establish sanctuary for part of a population that would lose its home in the decades ahead, though most of the New Espirans would gradually relocate to the moon. So however things had gone, there had been losses. But he had more questions than answers, and for now, seeing his son and seeing off his queen were the weights that held him solid.

He followed the man into one of the buildings and down the hatch. The Beneath Places were no wonder to him any more. But this tree and the pool were different. He ate the fruit and followed the man's instructions.

Rudolfo's feet didn't want to obey him, but he forced them out into the pond and was not prepared for the sudden rush of light that swept him away, twisting and spinning, before bringing him back to fall into waiting arms in a pool that was no longer underground but in the shadow of a vast and dying tree beneath a sun that seemed wrong to him somehow.

Neb steadied him and drew him to his feet, guiding him to the shore as they walked upon the surface of the silver liquid. An older woman was doing the same for Petronus and Winters.

The boy had grown into a man in short order. He towered over Rudolfo, his white hair tied back to reveal a face devoid of injury despite the evidence of battle about the clearing. Even now, men in uniform carried bodies away as others stood about the tree assessing damage.

Aedric awaited him on the shore, and Rudolfo saw a look upon his face that told him the man knew he'd earned his general's ire. But it was his best friend's son, and he'd learned to find the right path and choose it from a king who had been more of an uncle to him.

Aedric had known he couldn't stop her effectively, and so he'd done the next best thing and joined her. He was here now and had managed to stay alive through it all. Rudolfo embraced the first captain of his Gypsy Scouts. "It is good to see you, Aedric."

The younger man looked away, his eyes darker than normal. "I'm sorry I wasn't able to see them safely home to you, General."

Rudolfo released him and squeezed his shoulder. "We'll see them home together." *Or find a new one.* He looked around for his family again. Neb was embracing Winters now, lifting her from the ground in his embrace as he kissed her. The sight of that new love reunited was yet another counterbalance to his own moment.

Petronus extended his hand. "Rudolfo, I wish we met under better circumstances. I hope the flight was comfortable; I'm still learning how to do this."

Rudolfo took the hand and flashed a smile he hoped would not show as false. "The flight was magnificent, Father," he said, "and our circumstances have rarely been good." The man's grip was strong now, and suddenly Rudolfo remembered riding down the old man as he tried to sneak out of the Ninefold Forest, on his way to Caldus Bay after Sethbert's trial to establish a network and dig deeper into the mystery of Windwir's fall. They'd had a conversation there upon the road, and Rudolfo had been angry then. He'd asked the man for a new Pope and instead had found himself inheriting an orphaned Order. But brief words about backward dreams and honoring lies had drained Rudolfo's anger then, and he was glad for it because it was the beginning of a new truth for him and life was not finished taking him down its ever-changing Whymer Maze of paths.

"This is Administrator Gras. She is the elected leader of the New Espiran Expeditionary Council."

Rudolfo's eyebrows raised as he took her offered hand. "Administrator. I look forward to talking with you and the ambassador in the very near future."

She inclined her head. "Yes, Lord Rudolfo. But for now, Lady Tam and Lord Jakob are waiting for you." She looked over to Winters. "She'll want to see you as well, Lady Winteria. I'll come for you when it's time."

The girl—no, Rudolfo corrected himself, the young woman—blushed, and Neb did, too. He smiled but hoped they didn't see that it was to hide a wound and not to share their joy. "Take me to my family," he said.

They picked their way across the clearing to the edge of the forest, away from the tree and from the scars of battle. Many of the signs of violence had been removed already but for the two heads that sat upon the shore of a silver pond, a pike of some variety shaped of coral or seashell thrust into the ground between them. He recognized Ria and looked away. The other was the woman who had rescued Ria and killed Orius.

"Gods," he muttered.

"They thought they were," the administrator said. "Lady Tam wanted these left as they are, but I am hoping you will dissuade her of that. It isn't our way."

She took off their heads. Rudolfo released his breath slowly, uncertain why this bothered him. He, who'd only recently enjoyed listening to the screams of his enemy. And not just then but all of the evenings he'd spent in the observation deck of Tormentor's Row, listening to the Physicians of Penitent Torture doing their redemptive work. Back then, he'd no idea it was part of a bond to Y'Zir that held meaning within a framework of faith. But still, it was violence.

And this was violence—brutal, surely—but it was at least in service to something tangible.

He took his eyes from the heads and once more followed the administrator. "I will speak to her about it. I'm certain it was a request based in a moment of emotion that has now passed."

And Winters would want to bury her sister. Probably here, where she had fallen, if they would allow it. And if Jin Li Tam truly could not be saved, he would see her home to the Ninefold Forest. He felt tears again and distracted himself with another look around the clearing. "Where is Isaak?"

The administrator pointed to a pond where several men in a different type of uniform gathered. "He is in the pond being repaired. Lord Whym was able to initiate the cycle." Her eyes flashed to life for a moment. "It has radical implications for our own mechoservitors and other ancient artifacts we've found that we've been unable to repair."

Rudolfo blinked through her words. "And he will be fully functional?"

"Yes, we suspect so. It was Lord Whym's access that allowed his reconstitution in the first place. Our use of the blood of the earth and what you call the bargaining pools is advanced but still limited. Amal Y'Zir granted our people access, but it was access already largely curtailed by the events of the Downunder War."

Ahead, at the edge of the forest, Rudolfo saw a blanket and two figures waiting upon it. He could not help himself. He broke into a run, moving past the administrator. Somewhere in all of those few seconds, Jin Li Tam stood with Jakob in her arms and Rudolfo fell upon them both, laughing and weeping as he crushed them to himself and let his body and his heart quake with the power of that reunion.

Rudolfo was not certain how long they stood there in that embrace. But when they finally sat upon the blanket, he saw that Administrator Gras had quietly excused herself. As they sat, Jakob crawled over into his lap and started playing with his beard. "Papa."

Rudolfo chuckled and inhaled the smell of him, then took him in.

He'd grown in the months since he'd seen him, but he looked exactly as he had in the dreams. "It is good to see you, my little prince." He looked over to Jin Li Tam through a haze of tears. "And you as well, my queen."

She inclined her head, and her hair like a sunrise rushed over her shoulders. She wore a silver robe now like ones Neb and Petronus wore; and like Neb, her body showed no signs of battle whatsoever. But her eyes held vast sadness in them, along with her tears, and she took a breath. "I have many words, Rudolfo, but the most important are that I'm sorry."

Rudolfo shook his head. "Those are not words that need saying now." He looked at Jakob's smile. *He has no idea that he is losing her.* Then again, he was young and his memory of her would be hazy if he remembered her at all. Jakob would not have the same, sharp memory of a twelve-year-old boy watching his mother die. Or his father. That fateful night was a memory that had haunted Rudolfo most of his life.

"No, my love," she said. "They do need saying. I should have trusted you. I should not have left with our son." She paused. "I was a terrible wife."

Rudolfo inclined his head and let that be his gesture of acceptance now. Because in this moment, he could not fathom being angry with her. "You are a formidable queen and a fierce mother," he said. "And the administrator wishes me to discuss your recent victory."

He watched the color rise to her cheeks. "Yes. I'm hoping they can take care of that before it's time to bring Jakob back." Her eyes met his. "They meant to harm him, and I'd only just learned that my father hadn't killed him. I could not bear to lose him a second time." She held his gaze a moment too long, and he saw the tears start before she looked away. "For either of us," she said.

Rudolfo stared at his son. On the surface, he bore Rudolfo's dark skin and hair and eyes. But he had the willowy grace and long limbs of his mother, and Rudolfo knew he would be tall like her. "You did what needed doing. As queens and mothers will."

And as the forty-second daughter of Vlad Li Tam must, he thought but did not say.

Her brow furrowed and she looked up. "I do not have long, but there is more to discuss. Walk with me?"

She stood, and he stood with her, holding Jakob. She took his hand and led him back across the meadow to where the administrator waited with others. Rudolfo shielded Jakob's eyes as they passed Jin's handiwork there upon the shore and noticed that Isaak—shining and new—stood now with Neb, Winters and Petronus at the base of the tree. He also saw another woman holding a child who could have easily been Jakob's sibling.

Jin Li Tam stopped in front of the woman. "This is Chandra and her daughter." He watched her take a breath before saying the name, but he knew the name instantly. "Amara Y'Zir."

"Yes," Rudolfo said. "The Crimson Empress." The two children reached for one another.

"They need refuge, and I am hoping you will offer them a home in the Ninefold Forest," Jin said.

Chandra's scars brought home a realization that he hadn't even considered. "I'm not sure where our home will be," he said. "The Androfrancine weapon has poisoned the water of the Named Lands for anyone exposed to blood magicks. I have the mechoservitors tasked with a solution." He glanced to the tree and the New Espirans and Isaak. "I'm certain we will find a path."

The voice in Rudolfo's head was a surprise, and he jumped. *The children will be fine,* it said. *They have my blessing, and immunity is in their birthright.*

Rudolfo followed the voice, but before he could find it, it filled his head. *Now bring him to me for my last bargain.*

He looked around. "Who is—"

Jin Li Tam squeezed his hand. "It's the Grandmother Tree. And she's right. Jakob and Amara are more like Winters and Neb than they are you and me." She pulled at him. "Come and meet her. She saved us."

He let her lead him to the side of the tree. The others followed. The bark split open, and waving hands ushered them inside. *Come in and bear witness, Children.*

And now finally, as Rudolfo clutched his laughing son close to him and let Jin Li Tam lead him into the pink and meaty orifice of a massive talking tree, he felt the first stirrings of wonder. There in the red light of her beating heart, he saw the Firstfall Axe bound up in pale roots and held above a giant pulsing thing that he thought must surely be a heart.

The heart of the world, Rudolfo thought. But even that wonder was nothing compared to the warm life he clutched close to him in the red light of that place.

He looked at Jin Li Tam, and when their eyes met something wordless passed between them. Rudolfo knew in that moment that he was unlikely to ever sit in the quiet with her and his son again, but the sorrow of that realization was swallowed by the words that filled his head. *Time is of the essence, Children of Lasthome, and the Time of the Sowing is at hand. The People are restored to their heritage, and light is once more sown in darkness. Bear witness now to my final bargain.*

And so Rudolfo stood with the others to bear witness and wondered at how finding a metal man in the ruins of Windwir could bring him so far from home in a life so far beyond his wildest imaginings. And first among those wild imaginings: How much home could change from a place into a person that Rudolfo could hold as tightly within his trembling arms as he did within his breaking heart.

Winters

They stood upon the plain now, the white tree massive and towering above them. It had begun to sing, and Winters wasn't certain when she shifted from the warm, crowded space near the heart of the Grandmother Tree to this wide-open and familiar setting.

Here, she held the Firstfall Axe, and it was heavy in her hands. And she stood with the others—Neb to her left, Jin Li Tam to her right. Petronus stood on the other side of Neb, and Rudolfo stood with Jakob beside his queen. Isaak and Marta were also there, along with Chandra and her daughter, Amara Y'Zir. Administrator Gras stood to the side.

But the old woman hadn't been there. At least not at first, because Winters would've noticed her. She looked to be at least a hundred years old, her hair long and the color of watery milk. Her eyes were green, and her smile was genuine. And she was completely naked.

"Hello, Children," she said. "I would bargain with you here upon the plains of hope and home. Winteria bat Mardic, Child of Shadrus, Daughter of Salome, Last of the Dreaming Tribe, do you stand here of your own free will for the light and for its continuity to bargain in good faith?"

Winters felt something ancient in the words and in the response that welled up inside of her. "I do, Grandmother."

The old woman reached out her hands, and Winters felt them, cold and smooth as paper in the early morning. "Then I require the return of the Firstfall Axe and offer you the healing of the world you leave behind as recompense." Then she slowly inclined her head.

Winters returned the gesture. Then the woman squeezed her hands. The wind rose somewhere distant and whispered to her from across the plains.

Next, Grandmother approached Rudolfo and Jin Li Tam. "Myth is rooted in truth," she told him, "and though the children of Ahm Y'Zir did their best, their restoration of your son was incomplete. He's been given forty years to do his work, but I can extend it." She looked at Jin Li Tam. "The price of his life has already been paid in full should you choose to apply it to his account." Winters watched the two women and saw the older woman's eyes narrow. "And if you apply it to his account, it will fall to him to return to me and receive the second half of his life before his first half is complete."

Jin looked at Rudolfo, and he nodded. "Yes, apply it," she said.

The old woman inclined her head. "It changes your ending, Great Mother. I will speak with you alone about that—and it must be soon, I'll warrant, for time is indeed of the essence where you are concerned."

The forty-second daughter of Vlad Li Tam inclined her head, dipping it slightly lower than the Grandmother's. And then, the old woman stood before Rudolfo and Chandra. "I bargain with the children through you in trust. For Jakob to see his full allotment of years, he must return to me and he must carry out my final wishes; and for him to reach my heart, he will need to bring his own along."

She glanced to Chandra, but Winters could tell by her tone and the way her eyes locked to Rudolfo's that he was who she truly intended her words for. "And hear my wishes well: He is to use the Firstfall Axe to cut my heart free and he is to plant it in the shadow of the Firsthome Temple. Do you understand?"

She saw the Gypsy King nod his head and saw Amara's mother do the same. The woman stood still for a moment and then inclined her head. When they responded in kind, she moved to Isaak and Marta.

"The People were fragile in their earlier generations," she said, "and they made likenesses of themselves to do the work they themselves could not do. Sometimes that work was for the light, and sometimes it was for the dark." She rested a hand upon Isaak's metal chest. "You are not the first of your kind to be used to destroy, but it was not why you came to Lasthome. You were part of the Home-Shaping Song, along with the Keeper's Hatch and the Seedling's Heart, and down long reaches of time, it fell to your people to hear the Song of Sowing and reignite the Continuity Engine to fulfill the Terms and Conditions of Frederico's Bargain. That you were used by wicked men of dark intentions is secondary to your primary truth: You have been the abacus used to recalculate the worth—and the survival—of a species. And it falls to you, Isaak, to seek one final song with all that you have learned. When the children cut my heart from Lasthome, my crèche will finally fall and the last of my blood will be free to aid you and your Choir of Life in the work ahead."

Her eyes went from Isaak to Marta. "As you go about this work, I beseech you to trust your heart, for it is noble and strong."

Then, the Grandmother Tree inclined her head again. She looked to Neb and then met Winters's eyes, and she saw something in them that lived beyond her words. It was unspeakable love and overpowering weariness. "I have spent myself to give you a home," the old woman finally said. "I will sleep soon, and I will not awaken this time." She smiled. "I'm dreaming again—about home but not this home." She held Winters's eyes for a moment longer, then looked over to Jin Li Tam. "It is the home I left behind. The family I said goodbye to before I made my own bargains and left to serve the Continuity Engine of the People." When the old woman smiled, Winters saw sorrow and memory within it. "I will dream about things I've not remembered since before my heart was planted in Lasthome."

She looked to Winters one last time. "And dreaming," she said, "is a fine, fine thing indeed." Then she took in Neb. "The ghost of your father bargained for the day of your birth, Nebios Whym, and twice before, his seed sprang into our world to prepare a way for this time. You have finished your father's work, and now it falls to you to find your own work and leave behind a better dream to follow for those who come after you."

She inclined her head, and Neb did the same. Then she walked up and down before them, and Winters tried not to notice her wrinkled skin and sagging, empty breasts. She stopped at the administrator and took both her hands. "Your people have served well. The Time of Tending and Gathering is past, and I task you now with finding a new home for your people for this Time of Singing and Sowing."

The old woman walked the line again and stopped in front of each. She looked into each set of eyes for a moment and then continued to the next. Then she walked back to the base of the tree. "The new terms and conditions are executed," she said. "It is finished."

And then Winters blinked her eyes open against red light. The axe was hanging near the heart again, and her mind was quiet in a way that it hadn't been before. *Because she is no longer with me.*

Slowly, she followed the others as they filed out into light that faded, though its position in the sky remained unchanged. The soldiers had finished cleaning up the meadow and had retreated to the tree line. And the quiet in her head seemed to follow into this place as she reached over and took Neb's hand.

It felt warm and strong in hers, and she looked down to be certain she held it now. After so long not, it felt good to intertwine her fingers with his. And yet it felt foreign to her as well.

"I have kin-dragons for you both," Petronus said, "and we'll want to use them again." He was holding a blue stone, and his brows were furrowed. "It seems the Firsthome Temple is . . . singing."

Winters felt her own eyebrows rise. "Singing?"

Petronus sighed. "Never a moment of peace and calm."

She saw a speck of blood and leaned closer. "Your nose is bleeding," she told him.

A dark look washed his face, and he wiped the blood onto the back of his hand. His eyes looked faraway and hard for a moment before they were once more upon her. "We should go soon. I would say any goodbyes that need saying." He glanced at Jin Li Tam where she stood apart with Rudolfo and Jakob when he said it, and she swallowed a lump in her throat. Winters nodded and released Neb's hand.

She approached slowly, feeling a moment of hesitation at interrupting. But Jin Li Tam saw her coming, touched Rudolfo's arm briefly, and passed Jakob over to him. Then she met Winters and took her arm. "Walk with me," the Gypsy Queen said.

They strolled to one of the ponds just out of earshot, and Winters found herself unsure of what to say. There were too many words, too many questions. "She said your ending would be changed," she finally said. "What does that mean? Are you still dying?"

Jin shook her head. "I do not know. But I know she told me to say all of my goodbyes and then come back to her." Now Winters saw the woman's resolve finally break as she wiped a tear from her eye. "And I know that I'm not ready, whatever it is."

Yet Winters could see in those fierce eyes no regret for the choice made. It had been the calculated tactic and accepted sacrifice of a Tam. And behind her, Winters saw Rudolfo standing with their son, watching from afar, his face a mask that she knew concealed heartache.

I must let them have their time together and say my goodbye. She hesitated and then failed utterly at holding back her tears. Her words came out with a sob. "I will miss you," she said. "I've learned more about being a queen and a mother and a wife from you than I could have ever learned from someone else."

Jin's smile was wry. "I'm not as certain of those lessons, Winteria, but I know you can dance the knives with the best of them and hold your own." And her own tears flowed now, making Winters's flow all the more. "And you have taught me," she said, looking over to her husband and her son, "to believe in dreams of home." She pushed the girl away now, holding her apart with firm hands upon her shoulders. "Go build the home you've dreamed of all your life upon the moon, Winteria bat Mardic. Build it with Neb and the others that have followed your dream. Be queen and wife, mother and warrior, seeker and dreamer as you will, but first and always, be Winters and be true."

"I don't know how to say goodbye," Winters said, and her sob became a laugh.

"Just that," Jin Li Tam said, and embraced her again. Then she put her back to Winters and walked away. She did not look over her shoulder as she went, and when she reached Rudolfo, she took back her son and stood with him while Winters watched.

She felt Neb's presence behind her. "It is nearly time to go," he said.

Winters nodded and sniffed as he took her hand. "Do we know what the singing is about?"

"Not yet," he said. "But before we go, there's something we need to do." He tugged at her hand. "Walk with me."

Only as he walked, he did not walk along the edge of the pond. He walked onto it, its surface bearing his feet. "Petronus has a kin-dragon for you waiting at Endicott Station," he said. "One for each of us. But you can't fly it unless we finish your restoration."

My restoration? She looked down and realized she had joined him on the silver pond. "I don't understand," she said.

"I know," he told her, "but you will."

And then Neb kissed her, and as she found herself lost in the kiss, she also found herself descending slowly into the pool, the blood of the earth hot around her as it forced its way into her around the edges of their kiss.

This is our heritage, she heard Neb say into her mind. *Peace, no fear. The blood of the earth will bear you and serve you.*

Yes, she heard the Grandmother Tree whisper.

When she came up from the pool she was still wrapped up in Neb, his mouth still pressed to hers, but now she felt something electric move over her body as a tingling fire came alive within her and the smell of Neb filled her. She felt her eyes grow wide and saw that his nostrils were flaring from the force of it all.

"What is *that*?" It had been a while since those heated, shared dreams when their love was newborn. Those had been steamy enough to keep her blushing, but this was a forest fire compared to that flickering candle.

Neb smiled. "It's the Calling." Then he blushed as he realized what she'd known for a little while now as the evidence pressed firmly into her stomach. He stepped back. "We should go."

Winters blushed now, too, grateful that the evidence of her own arousal was less obvious as she watched his broad shoulders. And beyond the Calling, her body felt alive in a way that it hadn't before. The air was full of smells and tastes, and the colors were more alive than before. She held out a hand to the pond beneath her and furrowed her brow. "Clothe me," she whispered with intent.

She felt it as a mist first as it moved up over her ankles and legs, spinning light until she wore a robe like Neb's. Winters laughed and caught up to Neb.

The last of their goodbyes were a blur—a rush at the end with Petronus calling them to the pond impatiently.

She hugged Marta and Isaak both but couldn't remember what words were passed. Something about visiting on the moon one day. And then she swam the light again and stumbled into a mauve sunrise.to call down her kin-dragon and learn to fly.

Winters could hear the song now, faint, and they followed it out into the sea. The Calling was here, too, only now she had no way to blush as she realized that Petronus stirred a similar reaction. So she focused instead upon the light in the waves and the wind upon her silver skin.

She wasn't certain of how long it was before she saw the massive white arches of the Seaway. As it grew to fill her horizon, she saw the subtle difference in sky and sea within those arches.

And as she passed through them, Winteria bat Mardic thought for the briefest moment that she saw something in the water below. But before she could be certain, the air warmed and the sky became a fiercer blue beneath a bright morning sun.

The sea bubbled and foamed, and at first she thought it was a by-product of the arches and whatever strange science connected the two oceans. But as they moved away and north, she saw that the waters roiled as if being heated.

The song was loud now, too, and she heard within it the familiar notes of Frederico's Canticle for the Fallen Moon. Only now, the canticle had become a hymn that rang out from the white tower that loomed ahead of them and boiled the lunar seas beneath a cobalt sky.

Roaring upon the wind, Winteria bat Mardic gave herself to that new and lunar sky, winging her way homeward at long last.

Chapter 25

Jin Li Tam

Blue-green light flashed within the silver pond as Petronus, Neb and Winters vanished, and Jin Li Tam released her held breath. Already she could tell that things were shifting within her. Gone were the strength and agility she'd had, along with the heightened sense of smell. And with Petronus and Neb now away, she no longer felt that other heat—the one she'd not been prepared for. Whatever the Grandmother Tree's sap had awakened within her was ancient and feral, and she was glad it had finally passed.

She turned to Rudolfo and considered the man as he held their son. He was taking everything in stride given that when he'd woken up that morning, he'd been in the Named Lands meeting with Orius. She didn't know how long it had been since he slept, but she saw the circles beneath his eyes. Still, he smiled at the boy in his arms. Jakob was still waving at the pond and laughing. "Bye," he said, and down the shore, Amara repeated him.

Someday they will swim the light, too. It brought to mind the ghosts that were sometimes sighted in the seas far south—the ones named for those apparitions. They were called the d'jin, and it was from those ghosts that her father had taken her name. And with eyes that moved sometimes between blue and green depending upon her mood, Jin was an apt name. Now, having traveled by lightway and having watched it, she wondered even more if they weren't right to call them ghosts.

Now Isaak and Marta were the last. She'd watched the two of them, and she wasn't sure how she felt about the fierce affection the girl regarded Isaak with. She would've considered it some kind of odd puppy love brought about by bizarre circumstances, but she'd heard the howl of despair in the girl's voice when the Grandmother Tree restrained her and had seen the look upon her face when Jin had finally taken Amylé's head and the others had come out to gather up what they could of Isaak.

She'd seen the metal man after the bomb at the library had nearly killed her and Jakob. The explosion had damaged him badly, but it was nothing compared to what Amylé had done with the axe.

Isaak stood before them whole now, but he'd been in pieces when they'd gathered him up and laid him out in the pond. And Marta had met her grief as one who had met grief before, only she had no shame for her tears and shed them openly. And she'd shed even more when he climbed up from the liquid, shining dimly in the evening light.

She's not left his side since.

"It is time for us to go," Isaak said. "We will meet with Ire Li Tam at Endicott Station, and then Administrator Gras has arranged an airship to bear us back to Behemoth. From there, we sail north beyond the Named Lands and the Dragon's Spine and into the polar regions."

Marta lifted a blue stone from a pouch marked with the insignia of the Expeditionary Force. "They've provided us with communication and recording stones, along with maps."

Jin watched the two of them and saw how easily and eagerly Isaak stepped in to continue. "New Espiran records suggest that P'Andro Whym's scientist-scholars diverted the surviving members of Xhum Y'Zir's Death Choir into the north, where they were buried in a glacier."

Now Marta interrupted. "If we can find them and if Isaak can learn what he needs to and refashion the song—and if they will help us . . ."

Jin had heard it before, and she chuckled. "The world will be healed." They'd said it about her son, too, and about the little girl he'd been betrothed to before his birth, for millennia even according to the Y'Zirite gospels. Then she thought of Winters. "But it is good to follow a dream." She reached out and embraced Isaak. "And it is good to follow your heart."

Isaak inclined his head. "Thank you for your grace, Lady Tam."

She saw him then the way he used to be: fashioned with the best Androfrancine engineering, based on Rufello's Book of Specifications, and shaped with care by Brother Charles. And brought back, without his maker's knowledge, to bear the spell in a bid to defend Windwir from a newly discovered foe. And he'd born it and limped away from Windwir, co-opted by the man whose bed she shared in order to feed her father the best information. She'd met Isaak on the day she'd changed camps, when Rudolfo had sent her and the metal man north and east to take refuge in the Ninefold Forest. It was the first time she'd seen him in a robe. And now, he wore a borrowed robe marked in New Espiran rank she did not comprehend.

So much has happened since that day. She was a mother now. And a wife. And a queen. And through it all, as much as it broke her heart, she was also her father's daughter.

And I am dying.

The tears were there again, but they were never far away. Over the hours, there had been tears of anger, tears of sorrow, tears of regret, tears of hope, and tears of powerlessness.

She forced herself back to Isaak and Marta. "Thank you, Isaak. I know you've been used terribly and that my family was involved both times. But you've also saved lives. Mine and Jakob's, to be certain. You did not choose the ill that befell you, but you did choose to live beyond it. You did not ask for a heart that could break, but you have one." She looked at Marta. "And you have a heart that is full of love." She winked at the girl. "I think you need to listen to her more and guard her less."

Marta inclined her head. "Thank you, Great Mother."

Jin Li Tam let the title move past her and returned the gesture. Then Rudolfo passed Jakob to her.

Rudolfo looked up at Isaak. "You told me not to believe the dark tidings, but it was too compelling."

Isaak nodded. "I'm sorry, Lord Rudolfo. I could not risk the Y'Zirites uncovering Lord Tam's ruse until—"

Rudolfo raised a hand. "I understand, Isaak. And you have seen him into my care. We will leave for the Named Lands in a few days."

She didn't hear the rest of the conversation. She'd lost herself in her son's eyes again, and she feared that it might be the last time. Of course, if anything, she'd learned that she never knew when that last time might be. That every time someone came or went through a doorway, it could be their last.

Of course, that had been the mantra of her family, and the Tams bled lives in the Named Lands as they went about their father's business. But this was different. And she was terrified that she might not be able to name that difference before the time came for her to lay down her life.

It is time, Child. You will fade fast, and you will not want them to see you fading.

She swallowed. Rudolfo was embracing Isaak now. "Come home to me soon, Isaak, and tell me how it has all gone," he said.

"I will, Lord Rudolfo."

He nodded. "I will watch for you." He embraced Marta as well. "And you."

They left, and Jin saw the knowing glance from Administrator Gras as she escorted them toward the edge of the meadow and a waiting wagon. Jin caught Rudolfo's sleeve. "It is time, my love."

Rudolfo pulled her to him, their son between them, and as the boy began to giggle, the Gypsy King began to dance. He held her awkwardly, so much shorter than she and with her hands full of their boy, but they moved together to music that wasn't there.

"You are my sunrise and my sunset," he said, "and I would burn down my forest to keep you."

She laughed. "You would be a fool." But then her tears spilled over. "I've told you how sorry I was, but I have not told you how very much I love you and how proud I am of my husband and the father of my son." She kissed Jakob, and he laughed as she passed him over to his father. Then she looked at Rudolfo, saw the storm of anguish that filled his own eyes, and tucked away any other words. They were not necessary. But leaving was.

She wanted to look back but didn't. She wanted to stop, to throw herself at Rudolfo and her son and beg one last day or even an hour—some better bargain than this.

The Grandmother Tree opened to her, and Jin Li Tam went inside.

It is a hard thing, Great Mother. And you will never forget that you lost something. Now it shifted to a dry whisper. "Come closer to my heart."

"You said my ending would change."

"Yes," the Grandmother Tree said. "It has." *You will never forget that you lost something.* Jin saw shadowy images blurred by tears. *But over time there will be so many other losses. So many. You will lose sight of the ones that shaped your sacrifice and gave you roots for strength, boughs for shelter and sap for life.* But the voice was weaker now. "Come closer to my heart."

Jin moved into the chamber and saw the red pulsing vein. "What is it I'm to do?"

A dry chuckle. "Your body will know. There will be light. And movement. And eventually, sleep. And dreaming." There was a pause. *And then awakening to something new with all of this a distant ache in your heart.*

Branches unfolded again for her, and this time Jin Li Tam stepped into them. They bore her up and pressed her against that heart, and she took the sap into her again and felt it burn from the inside out even as light blossomed within that chamber to a blinding crescendo.

And then she herself was in the vein, feeling the fire all about her as the blood of the earth translated her slowly into light and pushed her through the Grandmother Tree's veins, down into the roots.

She built speed as she went, and she felt the same vertigo that had seized her when she'd used the lightway. Only now, this was no instant flash of arrival. She moved faster and faster and only vaguely became aware of the roots falling away as she raced the deeps of the earth.

When she spilled out into cold water, she experienced a burst of blue-green light and realized it was her.

I am a ghost in the water, Jin Li Tam thought.

Yes, a faraway voice compelled her.

And somewhere ahead of her, a song beckoned and she knew it. Without effort or force of will, her body moved toward that song, and Jin Li Tam poured herself into that forward motion.

She lost all track of time as she raced the ocean, and when she surfaced at last, she saw the white pillars arching against the sky and leaped up, the song pouring out from the waters ahead filling her new body with joy and the need to move.

She swam past a single vessel there in those waters and already could not recall what she'd fled. There had been light there. And there had been love. And so much loss. And she knew she'd left something behind—something vast—but that loss was folded into a larger song, a hymn to light in darkness and life in the midst of death.

Jin Li Tam felt the water shift around her as she moved into the warmer lunar seas. And now she smelled the path of the others who'd gone before her—thousands upon thousands of them—who'd left their scent within the waters. And the scent was enough to guide her the rest of the way.

Jin let the song move through her, let it weigh her as she dove the depths and swam until the light no longer required her to swim. She felt her body shift again in a safe and warm place that waited for her, then felt her roots take hold even as she drifted into the long sleep that would let Jin Li Tam, the forty-second daughter of Vlad Li Tam, grow strong and able to care for her myriad children as only a Great Mother could when at long last she next awakened.

Vlad Li Tam

Spray from the ocean salted his wounds, and Vlad Li Tam strained at the ropes as he screamed.

He'd begged the regent not to cut him anymore once he'd given them the number of screams he thought they might expect, and so, of course, Eliz Xhum cut him more. Vlad did not tell them that the pain in his body—deep in his bones—as he withdrew from the staff was far worse than the Y'Zirite's blades. He'd seen the world go gray enough times of late that he welcomed the knives and the wind.

The hook is set and the line is drawn taut.

And he'd begged them to take him belowdecks when the regent wasn't bent over him with his blades and his constant banter. So they'd left him tied to the table at the bow of the ship with the sky tossing wildly above him and the salt in his wounds.

When he saw the dragons flash past, high in the sky, he knew they were getting close. He'd done his calculations, though there was no way of knowing how long it had been since he'd eaten the fruit and whether or not his body was already too compromised.

Somewhere beneath their knives, Vlad was certain he'd seen his father. The man was the way he was when Vlad was a boy—the summer he'd sent him to Caldus Bay—and he sat at the railing watching in sorrow as they cut his boy. Vlad had met his father's eyes and saw remorse there.

He'd memorized the last word he'd received from his father. *I'm sorry,* the note had read, *I was wrong.* And Vlad knew those words applied so many other places besides his father's complicity with the Y'Zirites.

But he changed paths and created the plan that made me. And Vlad had taken the pain of that making and made it into an army, finishing his father's work.

Because I am my father's son. And there was no escaping that snare. The Tam way was instilled in their children as soon as they were snatched from their mother's breasts too soon and taught to rely upon the lord of House Li Tam for everything.

As Vlad watched his father watching him, he thought about all of the last words he had heard. He'd heard his children's last words—and his siblings' children's—for as long as he'd been the head of the house. And then, there upon that island, under Ria's care, he'd heard so many more. Too many.

He felt the knife twist as it kissed his skin, and he hoped his howl would hide his smile. Ahm was there now, and they'd been asking him questions about the staff.

But he had used it up in his father's work. His father smiled now, too, but it was a sad smile. "It is your work, too, Vlad. And you are nearly finished with it."

Yes, he thought. *It is my work too.* And it was necessary. If they were to survive, they would need time and peace so that they could find their way.

"You can tell us now," the regent said, "or you can tell Sister Elsbet. She is much better with the knife than I am, and she's prepared a place for you near Lord Y'Zir's room." He ran the knife along Vlad's rib lightly where he'd just finished his last Y'Zirite word. "We will have plenty of time to figure out the staff." He leaned forward and smiled. "And our magisters assure me they can keep you alive and feeling pain long enough for your kin-healing to be thorough."

Vlad saw a flash of white from the corner of his eye and stopped screaming. He drew a breath and held it, then released it.

Ahm Y'Zir was there now, leaning forward over him. "Near me, fear me, dear me, hear me," he ranted. A gout of green vapor shot from the exhaust grate in his metal chassis.

Vlad drew another breath. More white—massive and impossible against the sky—and he knew it. He'd seen it before. *The Moon Wizard's Ladder.* That was the name he preferred for it, and he'd never forget the first time he'd seen it in an ocean alive with d'jin, led there by his own ghost in the water.

Now the ocean was dark and the wind was cold.

And suddenly, the moon rose over the bow, blue and green and undulating as it leaped and then fell. And before it dropped beneath the waves, Vlad heard the same song he'd heard so long ago upon the bow of his own ship, only now it was sung by one solitary ghost that swam those waters.

Oh my love, he thought, *swim free of this place and far from me.* As if hearing him, the last d'jin sped away.

He thought about Amal Y'Zir, his ghost in the water, and how she'd found him, guided him, given him the staff. She was the closest thing to love he had ever known, and he was surprised to look up and see her also sitting upon the rail with his father. Her hair was dark and her eyes were darker, and she smiled but it was stern.

"Oh my love," she said to him. And she said nothing else. She inclined her head, and then Vlad's father did the same.

And then he waited in silence while the regent started carving yet another Y'Zirite word into his flesh. At the last, Vlad reached out to the library, but Petronus was not there. But the guard was, and the tower was vibrant with the same song that the ghost had sung alone.

"Are they back yet?" Vlad asked the guard.

Eyes wide, the guard nodded.

Vlad closed his eyes and pushed the library away.

In the end, he faced what needed doing the same way he had expected his children to. And he did it for the same reason he had done everything, without regret but sometimes with remorse: because he was a Tam. Change was the path life took, and House Li Tam shaped and guided that change, moving the rivers to erode the mountains and empty the valleys of life. *I have moved many rivers, and I have been moved myself in more ways than I can ever know.*

"My work is finished," Vlad Li Tam finally said as he met the regent's eyes and smiled.

Then the lord of House Li Tam opened his mouth and began to sing. He sang and kept singing until the ship burst into flames around him, until the ocean boiled and the great stone arches above their heads cracked and trembled and came crashing down. He sang until he was flooded with heat and seawater. And he gave himself fully to his singing until Vlad Li Tam was burned away and nothing remained but motes of light and a song that faded at last into a final gray.

Neb

The song was everywhere, nothing at all like the distant melody that had brought them to the moon in the antiphon, when Neb set foot upon the rooftop and sent his kin-dragon away. This was no ancient metal man bent over a harp. The entire Firsthome Temple was alive with the song, and it emanated from the floor where the library waited.

Petronus led the way. "It's coming from the command pool."

They'd only had a few opportunities to talk since arriving at the Firstfall Forest in New Espira, and all of the new information was a blur. He waited for Winters, and once she staggered onto the rooftop, eyes wide and nostrils flaring from her first flight, he took her by the hand and followed Petronus.

"This is astonishing," she said as they slipped through the doorway and started taking the long winding stairwell down.

Neb thought back to his first experience—starting in the places beneath the tower after Amylé D'Anjite. His pursuit of her up the stairs and finally breaking out into the light on the rooftop when Petronus unsealed the tower and set them free. When he'd first been inside the temple, it had been dark and he'd thought dead. But Petronus had brought it to life, and now something had it singing.

They reached the library, and Petronus paused. "Have we seen him lately?" he asked the guard.

The man shook his head. "I will send for you if I see him."

Petronus nodded, and they kept moving. Nadja Thrall and a handful of officers were waiting at the door when they reached it. Neb was surprised when she took Petronus into her arms and kissed him. Then she held him back from her and looked into his eyes. "How are you feeling?"

Petronus blushed. "I'm fine." He looked over his shoulder at Neb, and Neb saw the embarrassment in his eyes. "May I present Lady Winteria bat Mardic," he said.

Nadja smiled and it set off the dusting of freckles over her nose. "Lady Winteria, the Dreaming Queen. My brother has spoken highly of you."

"He was most helpful. I look forward to treating with you."

Petronus stepped up to the door. "Come with me, Neb," he said. The door opened, and after Petronus stepped in, Neb followed. The door closed quickly behind them.

"What about the others?"

Petronus winked. "Soon enough, Son. But you are the Homeseeker and the Homefinder. The temple was yours to unseal, and the staff was yours to wield. Things haven't gone as planned, but they've still managed to go."

Petronus stopped at the silver rod that jutted up from the floor of the room. Neb felt the room's pulse and saw the pool and vines. "Is that what I think it is?"

Petronus nodded. "When Vlad authorized me, the temple grew this room, and I think it grew a new rod. It's the command pool for the temple. But some things have not grown back; some things have been lost."

They seemed true words to Neb. Much had changed in his life since that day upon the hill. Some things had not grown back—like his awkward, innocent orphan-boy love for Brother Hebda. And all of that innocence lost when he watched the genocide of the only people he'd known, the desolation of the only home he'd ever had, and again when he'd learned of how deeply some of those people had betrayed him.

And so many lives. He forced himself back to the moment.

Petronus placed a hand upon the staff. "Put your hand upon it with me," he said.

Neb did and felt nothing.

Petronus smiled. "*You* are authorized."

Power flooded him. The song upended him and threatened to capsize him. Neb jerked his hand away. "Oh."

"Take it," Petronus said. "You've surely paid for it."

Neb drew out the staff and felt it moving in his hands, pulling like a serpent to the pool. The vines there writhed and waited as the blood of the earth began bubbling in its basin.

Neb let the rod pull him, and he climbed into the basin clutching it to his chest. He felt a binding that held but needed release. He felt a pressure that pulled steady and would not yield. And around all of it, the song roaring, and the Calling hot upon him.

"Oh," Nebios Whym, Homeseeker and Homefinder, said.

Then the temple began to shake, and the song warbled but held. At first he thought it was part of the pool, but then he saw the mottled color of the walls. This shaking was more violent, and he felt his stomach sink even as his heart sang with the temple.

And he didn't fully understand it, but Neb knew that time truly was of the essence. He climbed up from the pool, pulling at the vines as they rushed to release him. And he didn't wait for Petronus. He didn't stop at the door to explain to the curious and fearful looks that met his wide eyes as he rushed past them on his way to the roof.

There was cacophony at the edge of the song now, and it made his pulse race. The staff within his hands sang, too, and Neb suspected that it was the source of the song, augmenting its voice by turning the entire temple into a vast and resonant megaphone.

He took the stairs two and three at a time, and by the time he'd reached the top, the temple had stopped shaking. Far in the south, a white fist of steam rose up in the direction of the Seaway. And all around them, the sea boiled, but it had been boiling even before—or at least had appeared to boil.

Neb stood upon the roof and watched that plume. Petronus reached him first. "It was Vlad," he said. "He appeared just after we left the library."

"The Seaway?" But Neb didn't need to ask Petronus. He moved a thumb over the staff and let the temple tell him. "It's gone."

Neb had no time to ponder that. The song continued to build, and the orphans he and Winters were collecting now came trickling through the doorway to fill the roof of the Firsthome Temple. Y'Zirites, Marshers, Gypsies, mechoservitors and New Espirans all united by a dream that had brought them to the moon.

The song rose, and as it rose, Neb felt the staff grow light within his hand. It pulled upward and he obeyed the impulse, raising it high into the sky.

Now there was a different shaking. A vibration beneath his feet and upon the air as if the world trembled at what followed. The waters foamed, and lightning from a clear sky ran ribbons along the surface of the distant sea.

They were large and dark, oblong and smooth, like seeds the size of a city-state. Neb counted six of them as they slowly lifted from the lunar sea. Water rolled from them, and steam billowed about them as they rose up.

Winters stood beside him, and the wind pulled at her brown hair as her eyes went wide. She took his hand. "The Time of Sowing is at hand," she said in a voice full of awe.

Yes. And Neb watched as those seeds rose into the sky to be light sown in darkness and seeds scattered in hope.

"The Continuity Engine of the People is restored," he said, and his voice boomed out across the jungle and over the lunar sea. Then Nebios Whym watched his people return to the stars in search of their next home.

Chapter
26

Petronus

Petronus looked at what little remained of his life here at the end of it. He'd laid it out upon the mossy bed in his quarters alongside his empty satchel. He had one compact volume of the core precepts of P'Andro Whym, a battered toiletry kit missing half of what was needed, a few scraps of clothing left over from before he could clothe himself with the blood of the earth. And then of course the tiny kin-raven and the blue stone Nadja had given him. He'd lost Vlad's notebook somewhere along the way. Or maybe he'd given it to someone. He couldn't remember. And he'd passed the crescent back to Rudolfo for safekeeping in the library there in the shadow of the Grandmother Tree.

When he looked at what was left, it was very little.

And yet she wants to sail with me and learn to fish.

It baffled him. She had so much more work of much greater importance to do. Cut off now from New Espira with the Seaway collapsed, she was the ranking officer among her people, and they were adjusting to being a more permanent part of the colony.

And I am a tired old man. A backward dream. There was a new dream dawning, and it was vaster than he'd ever imagined. And it was far-reaching, here upon the moon as they found a new life and began slowly relearning what they'd forgotten about themselves. And on Lasthome as they put the Named Lands back together, sorted out the remains of Y'Zir, and started the slow evacuation of the lost crèche to prepare for the death of the Grandmother Tree.

And Isaak and the girl who watched out for him—Marta—sought a choir for a song that Isaak must write to heal a world one final time. All from Windwir and all from a series of dreams left over from a bargain made millennia ago at the center of the world.

And from that bargain, six seeds now sped somewhere, part of a vast machine meant to keep a people with such propensity for self-destruction alive and slowly, slowly learning from their perpetual rising and falling. Rafe said one last d'jin had been spotted in the water just before the Seaway collapsed. The others that had flocked to the lunar seas had vanished some time ago, and their current theory now based on Neb's digging and the New Espiran's Codex was that the d'jin had left with the seeds in search of the people's next home. But Petronus wasn't going to wait for the riddle to be solved. After a lifetime of pursuing knowledge and protecting light, he was finished for whatever days he had left. He would spend those last days doing what he'd done in his youth, how he'd chosen to spend his days after leaving the papacy the first time.

Petronus was going fishing. And Nadja Thrall was coming with him and wouldn't take no for an answer. Not that Petronus had even considered saying it.

He looked at the satchel and finally picked up the toiletry kit and the book. A tap at the door brought his eyes up. "Yes?"

Neb stepped in. "The boat's ready." He looked tired and even had a hint of sorrow in his eyes, but the man glowed. Winters, too, but he'd been careful to say nothing.

Because I'm likely glowing, too. And Petronus was getting ready to leave with her now. As much as he claimed he would spend his last days fishing, he knew that fishing would likely be a secondary preoccupation for at least a few days.

Petronus smiled. "How are you? Are you learning more?"

Neb nodded. "All the time." He held up the staff, and he wore Petronus's library ring now. He'd offered to let him keep it, but Petronus had decided not to. They'd keep a communication stone for emergencies on the boat in case something came up that Nadja needed to be whisked back to the temple by kin-dragon. But the plan was that she take a well-earned leave of absence. Not that enough time had passed to let them reestablish contact effectively for her to request it or have it granted. The relay of communication stones had been dependent upon the Seaway being open and vessels being within proximity to one another. And with it gone, the crescent was now their only link to Last-home until Neb healed the bargaining pool and reconnected the lightways between the temple and the planet they orbited.

So much work ahead, he thought. *But not for me.*

"I'm certain," he said, "that you'll have it all sorted out in no time." He looked around. It hadn't been his room for long, but he had made memories here that he'd never imagined he would make at this age, and he blushed as he looked down at the book in his hand. It had shaped his life, the teachings of P'Andro Whym. It had shaped Neb's life, too, and they'd both found that change indeed was the truest path life took. Life emerged slowly, by accident, in secret hope and terrible fear. And that life changed until it was no longer alive. They'd learned this lesson again and again and had traded their Androfrancine robes for the robes of light fashioned from the blood of the earth. He extended the book to Neb. "I want you to have this."

Neb took it. He brow furrowed and the glow was gone for a moment. "Thank you," he said. "I have something for you, too. Down at the dock. Do you think you can beat me there, or have your diplomacy lessons left you too sore to run?"

His face wasn't cooled off from the last blush, but Neb was gone faster than fast and did not see it. Petronus laughed and left all but the battered toiletry kit behind, racing after Neb out into the wide hallway and then down the stairs.

The temple was busy now all the time, but soon—now that everyone was here and no one new would be coming for some time—life would settle into a rhythm. And at some point, he knew Nadja would return. They'd had one conversation about all of it two nights before, and she'd assured him that she wanted this more than anything and that she would see him to his rest. He'd cried, and it wasn't something he'd done easily or often before. But he did—not just over the shortness of his time remaining but also the sweetness of it because of this dear, beautiful girl who saw things in him he could only hope were true. And she'd held him while he sobbed, quietly but with strength, and he could not ever remember a place of such peace.

They would sail together, and when he was finished, she would bury him in the lunar sea that he had crashed in—a Pope who went to the moon and lived for a time within the Moon Wizard's Tower. And then she would come home and get on with her life and build a home here based upon a dream they'd all had once together.

Petronus smiled and ran. He caught up to Neb as they left the temple and ran into the morning sun side by side, remembering their runs in the jungle not so long ago. At the dock, he saw a small crowd gathered around a yacht that he recognized.

The Sea Gypsy was a boat docked in Caldus Bay when hunting season brought nobles to the forests and hunting estates around the town. Rafe stood by it grinning. "The owner trusts you'll return it in good order when you're finished with it." Then the old pirate glanced at Nadja Thrall with a raised eyebrow. "And you believe you can sail this?"

She was dressed differently now. Breeches and a shirt that was loose and tight in places that complimented her. Her hair was back, and her smile was wide as she winked at him. "I can fly an airship, Captain Merrique. Besides, I have Petronus to show me."

No one else but him knew she was terrified of the ocean, but part of her charm was the way she steered into her fears and took delight in conquering them. She'd spent the vast majority of her life underground, seeing neither stars nor ocean until shortly before her diplomatic mission to the moon.

"And I have this for you," Neb said. "We put it together from what has come in so far."

He pointed to a rod and tackle kit. "There are also nets onboard."

Petronus lifted the rod and weighed it in his hands. It was sturdy, and he wondered how it would hold up against the fish here. "Thank you."

Winters was there as well, now wearing the same silver robes that the rest of them had taken to. And the glow was there as well. The two of them stood near to each other, some part of them touching constantly, and the ache of the Calling was lessened for all of them now that Winters and Neb had taken its lead and begun the work it required of them.

He looked to Nadja Thrall and saw that she was full of light. Neb, too. And Winters. Even Rafe Merrique the pirate.

And I am, too, I reckon.

Petronus smiled. "Are you ready to sail the lunar seas with me in search of great fish and buried treasure?"

Nadja smiled back. "I am, Father Petronus."

It was good, he thought, for them to see one final blush. Then he turned to Neb. "I know you will build something beautiful for the light here, Neb. You've come a long way from that boy who wanted to kill

Sethbert, the boy who helped me bury our family." He paused and looked at Winters as well. "Follow the dream. It's carried you well so far."

They both inclined their heads, and then there was a series of embraces around the dock. His nose started bleeding again as he climbed aboard and cast them off, but Petronus paid it no mind until the sails caught the wind and they were sailing down the canal and toward the sea with the Firsthome Temple vast and towering behind them.

Nadja took a cool, wet cloth to his nose and kissed his cheek as he sat at the rudder. "It seems we're away, darling." She settled into his lap and wriggled.

He chuckled. "Yes, but someone has to sail the boat."

"I think," she said as she adjusted herself slightly, "we could manage to do both." She paused and raised her eyebrows in a menacing way. "Or drown trying."

Petronus closed his eyes and took in the warm, floral air of the jungle that slid by. He could smell the hint of lilacs in her hair and on her skin. And there was the salt of the sea ahead of them. It was a better ending than what he'd expected for himself, between the War for Windwir and the assassin in the night and that cold blade that took his life before Ria restored it to him again and the kin-wolves at the antiphon and the crash landing here on the moon. He'd never thought he would live so long or end so well or see so much.

Or find a love of sorts and someone to share the last of life with. It wasn't bad at all for a fisherman from Caldus Bay.

Then Petronus, the Last Pope of the Androfrancine Order and Lost King of Windwir, opened his eyes and laughed with Nadja Thrall in the light of another brand-new day.

Rudolfo

Summer crept upon the Ninefold Forest like a hunting cat, and Rudolfo welcomed it, savoring the unseasonably warm days and nights after what felt like so long away from home. He'd taken an office at the library now that the Seventh Forest Manor was full of children. It had made more sense to give them the wide-open hallways and so-long-unused rooms rather than build a school or an orphanage, and the manor had never been so full of life.

Or noise or chaos. But they would all be settling down to bed now.

Jakob, Amara and about a dozen Tam children. He smiled as he looked up from his desk and looked out of his window. Below the hill where the library sat, Rachyle's Rest bustled more than it once did of a summer evening. Rudolfo glanced to the metal cage upon the corner of his desk. The golden bird inside slept most of the time, and he didn't wake it now. It carried messages between him and the manor—short ones—and had recently come to tell him that Lysias would be reading to the children tonight at their request. Rudolfo would head back soon so he could catch the old general making faces and voices for the children.

Lynnae and Chandra had already settled the manor into a routine that left its steward with little to do. And Rudolfo suspected that this is what a marriage might feel like once the draw of the flesh lessened from the exhaustion and purpose of children—and with two wives, no less. Chandra had taken up in Jin Li Tam's quarters next to Lynnae's, and the two of them with help from the River Woman and a smattering of others spent each morning teaching the children before letting them scatter off to play on the grounds. His father's Whymer Maze was a favorite, and most of his meditations now were accompanied by children laughing and hiding from one another among the thorny branches.

Lysias had taken a room within the family quarters, too, and now the only time it was quiet was in the wee hours when Rudolfo slipped out of bed to start his day with a walk in the forest. Rudolfo doubted there had ever been a time that the house had been so full.

From the ashes of violence and desolation, this has grown up in our midst. No, he thought, that made it sound like an accident. *From sorrow and loss,* Rudolfo realized, *I have fashioned this.*

And more than that, he had fashioned a different life. Not just for himself but for many. People without homes had come to his forest to find a home. People in need of purpose had come to his forest to make a purpose for themselves alongside his purposes. And the children without mothers and fathers had come to find the best alternative possible. *And now we are a family for each other.*

He took it all in and thought of the many hands that had helped, that had even carried him here. Then he moved off through his library and let himself out the main doors.

The sky was awash with red as the sun set in the west and cast crimson light over the houses and trees. A pair of Gypsy Scouts waited for him, and a guard from the standing army posted at the doors inclined his head as Rudolfo exited into the night.

Rudolfo returned the gesture and took in the sunset.

He'd told her that a sunrise such as her belonged in the east with him. And back then, he'd thought it could be true. But now he knew she was both sunrise and sunset—another hello and goodbye along a path of the same for as long as he could remember. He saw her now at the front and end of the day, a glory of color against a periwinkle sky. And that sunrise and sunset would greet him daily in the child they had made in the midst of so much darkness. Jakob, along with his collection of orphans, had given Rudolfo a different dream.

He would not go to the moon or the deep ice caves in the polar north; he would not sail around the horn again into the Churning Wastes. If he could help it, he would not leave the Named Lands but for to show Jakob the world he would inherit.

Rudolfo's dream now was to live in peace with his orphans and his people and his library. The war was over, and there was a lifetime of rest—and family—ahead.

Rudolfo straightened and looked out over the city and his manor below the hill. Then he took in the building itself. So much of Isaak was in the place. *In all of us,* Rudolfo thought. The metal man had been a mechanism for change in the world—change in Rudolfo specifically—and someday Rudolfo would thank him for it.

He imagined it every now and again, and when he did, he always thought of his father reading to him as a child. It was the Story of the Runaway Prince, one he'd loved nearly as much as Jamal and the Kin-Wolves. And in it, the king's only son—a lonely child—stole his father's crown, sold it and squandered a small fortune upon the pleasures of the flesh thinking it would make him friends before taking ill and returning home. The part he'd always loved most, though he didn't know why, was the part where the king sat alone watching for his son and when he came, threw him a second Firstborn Feast to welcome him.

Rudolfo wasn't sure why that story resonated with him. Maybe it was because as he heard it, he identified with the lonely prince. Still, he loved it, and maybe if there was time he'd keep the children up later and read them that tale. He had a copy of it in his bedroom. He'd lifted it—a collection of children's tales reproduced from the Androfrancine Holdings—from the book-making tent that night so long ago when he'd sat in the sound of their whispering pens and contemplated his choices. It was the night that he'd realized he understood how a lamentation could become a hymn and that he knew what path he must follow to take him there. He'd followed it, and now, beneath a setting sun in the shadow of a new library, Rudolfo embraced the hymn his life had become and the lamentation that had shaped it. And he accepted all of the other points between.

Yes, he thought, *I will go and read them that story.*

And when he read it, he would imagine himself sitting and waiting for his wandering metal orphan like the father of the Runaway Prince. And when he finally one day saw the sunlight glinting from that silver skin, Rudolfo—Lord of the Ninefold Forest Houses, General of the Wandering Army and Protector of the Light—would run to his friend with arms open wide and a grateful psalm upon his lips for the light and love he'd found along that darkened road. And for the life he'd fashioned on the far side of desolation.

Winters

The days had been a blur of people and the nights had been a blur of heat, and both combined with the intoxication of this new place left Winters befuddled and forgetful.

Even that morning, she'd awakened and not realized at first that she was in Neb's room, not her own, and that she was alone. It had taken her a moment to remember she was on the moon and had a long line of things waiting patiently for her to do.

So she'd dressed and she'd gone down to the rooms that had been co-opted for the administration of the temple and the people who lived there. Most stayed within the vast tower, but some opted to build on lands set aside for pilgrims.

Neb's desk was full, but he wasn't at it. She was confident that he'd be in the pool, connected to the library, learning everything he could. Vast sections had been burned away, and he'd found very little reference to the Grandmother Tree or the seeds that had been sown, but he was learning more and more about the People and their long story in the universe.

Our people.

Petronus's desk was empty, and Neb had been quieter since his friend had left. It seemed so long ago now that she had heard the boy Neb used to be proclaiming the old man Petronus Pope there on the plains of Windwir.

They'd been children then, or at least it seemed so. Both had already carried a weight through their lives, but nothing like the path Windwir took them down.

And now here we are. She looked at her desk and everything stacked upon it. She had a meeting with Seamus and the rest of the council first—and there would be at least a few new faces there as they began discussing changes in governance. She looked over to the newest desk and smiled.

Esarov the Democrat sat, his hair flowing and golden around his shoulders and his spectacles down upon his nose as he referenced a battered book and jotted down notes. He looked up at her and smiled. "Lady Winteria," he said. "Good morning. I'm looking forward to our meeting, though I'm sorry to reschedule it at the last minute."

Rescheduled? "I hope everything is okay?"

Esarov smiled. "It's my fault, I'm afraid. I wanted to be thorough in my presentation and begged Nebios for another day. He suggested that you meet him in the portico instead."

Winters looked at her desk again. There was more to do, but it hadn't been scheduled—more debriefings with Sister Elsbet and the other Y'Zirites who had formally come seeking asylum the week before. They'd come with imperial ships stocked with staples enough to supply most of their new colony for a year, establishing themselves initially in an abandoned city until after the Seaway collapsed and they came seeking a truce. And Kember and Ilyna wanted to speak over lunch about establishing a communal farm near the canal. And then of course, there were meetings with the technologists to see some of the new tricks Neb had learned from the library—food, water and tool production built into the temple and waiting for them to use.

"What is happening at the portico?"

Esarov shrugged. "He wouldn't say. But it seemed important."

Winters sighed. On an afterthought, she lifted a blue stone from her desk and slipped it into the pocket of her robe. Then she left and made her way to the stairs.

Few people stirred at this hour, and she reached the main doors and the portico quickly. Neb tossed her a large piece of fruit that looked like an orange but tasted like a plum. "Good morning," he said.

She caught the fruit and closed the distance between them, kissing him hard on the mouth. She could taste the sweetness of breakfast plucked from a tree. "So you let Esarov off the hook for today?"

He smiled. "I did. I told the others. I hope you don't mind." He pointed. "Lasthome is still high in the sky," he said.

She looked to it and then to the twilight jungle that stretched around them, slowly stirring to life with the songs of birds that were new to her ears. "We have a lot of work to do," she said.

Neb took her hand. "We've always had a lot of work to do, Winteria bat Mardic. We will always have more work to do." Then he pulled at her. "But when else will we have a jungle to run before the sun comes up? On the moon?" He grinned.

"Tomorrow, Nebios ben Hebda," she said. His grin faltered at the name, and she winced. Hebda and Renard, along with Tertius and Captain Endrys Thrall, hadn't made the Seaway before Vlad Li Tam collapsed it. She bit her lip and corrected herself. "I'm sorry. Nebios *Whym.*"

He shook his head. "No," he said. "All of it is who I am, for good or otherwise. And we've talked some. They're going to stay with the library, he and Renard and Tertius. Perhaps if I can heal the bargaining pool, we'll see each other again."

He blinked the cloud from his face and forced a smile. "But enough of that. I have something to show you. If you think you can keep up with someone who's run the Churning Wastes."

She heard the challenge in his words. "I've run with the Gray Guard and drawn first blood on a magicked Y'Zirite scout," she said.

Neb kissed her again and then fled, running south along the canal. Winters glanced at the temple and the waiting work behind her one more time and then followed after him.

She caught up, and for a time they took turns running ahead. It was a new trail, and though she'd ventured out into the jungles with him before, they'd never taken this route. As they ran, Winters looked at the flowers and the trees, rainbow shades of color all bordered by a thousand hues of green. Here and there she saw the mounds of foliage with the bits of exposed crystal reflecting back the dim light of Lasthome those few times they were not buried in the jungle canopy.

And finally, as the sun rose, the trail ended at a pool of water fed by a waterfall. Neb dropped to the stretch of long, green grass near the shore and flopped onto his back.

"We're home, Winters," he said as he opened his arms to her.

She went to him and lay beside him in the grass looking up. The Named Lands were above them. She could see the horn and the gray barrens of the Churning Wastes. She could see the rivers and the mountains. The scar where she thought Windwir stood and the nine massive forests set apart in their prairie sea. She saw the Marshlands where she'd dreamed for her people and ridden to war for her kin-clave. And later, she'd found their Homeseeker and he'd found their home. And all of them had found a new dream.

And had lost and found so much along the way. She felt the hollow ache of loss and wondered about her friend, Jin, and how her ending had changed. She remembered Charles, too, and for a moment even thought about the sister she'd never known she'd had. So much loss. So many goodbyes and a handful of hellos, but it was the way of things.

"Yes," she said finally as she kissed Neb's hand. "This dream is of our home." She remembered this place, had dreamed of it before she'd even known it was on the moon.

"I found it while I was running with Petronus," Neb said.

"It's exactly like our dream," she said. Then she reached into her pocket and pulled out the stone. "Speaking of dreams; I have something to show you, as well." She pushed it into his hand.

"What is it?" But as their hands met upon the stone, Neb swallowed his question.

"It's the dream you missed," Winters told him as the plain and its myriad people and its tree white with promise flooded their senses.

He made her take them through the Final Dream three times before he sighed. "Thank you," he finally said. She heard the emotion in his voice and saw the tears in his eyes. And this time as she watched the dream and saw the white seeds upon the air, she thought of those dark seeds rising up from the lunar sea and wondered where they might land and bear fruit. And she wondered about the d'jin who had left and what kind of home they would build for the people there. Alongside that, she wondered what they would build right here. And what Rudolfo and Isaak and the others would build there in the sky above them. Whatever it was, she hoped it would be a home full of light and love.

"This dream," she said again, "is of our home." Then Winters rolled over into Neb and kissed him slowly. She savored him, letting her hands wander his body and delighting as his hands wandered her. The urgency of the Calling that had filled every night they'd spent together since arriving had faded into something assured and constant, and now they made love slowly while she watched Lasthome above them, reflected in his eyes those times that they were open.

When they finished, they swam in the pool and talked quietly and ate fruit until they were sticky and hungry for one another again. And then after, they napped like cats in the sun.

When Winters woke up, she thought at first that she was alone and perhaps dreaming. But the warm breath upon her neck and the hand that gripped hers there flat against her stomach assured her that her dreams had been realized and home had surely and finally been found.

Smiling, Winteria bat Mardic let sleep carry her off again to dream whatever came next.

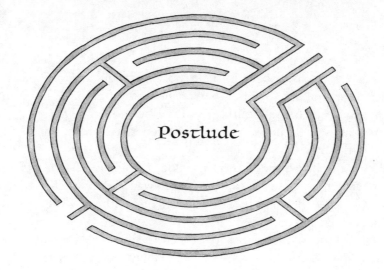

Postlude

When Behemoth began slowing, Marta knew to be quick or be last. And now the vessel that had once felt so large and empty felt crowded and constrained. When Isaak had talked about their quest for Xhum Y'Zir's lost Death Choir, she'd thought it would be the two of them. Or maybe Ire Li Tam would come along.

But when the New Espirans reunited them with the Blood Guard, she had a small group of men and women with her, all covered with the same ritual scarring and all fresh from the New Espiran holding cells where they'd been carefully interrogated. "These are my brothers and sisters," Ire Li Tam had said.

And suddenly they were a family at sea, with Marta in the role of the youngest. Isaak assumed command easily, and the only good thing about the increase in crew was that it meant she could sleep in the corner of Isaak's room now. That and more hands to keep the vessel tidy and everyone fed. Still, she missed the days when they were alone with only the sound of Behemoth's engines and plates clanking.

And so, when they started to slow, she threw on her clothes and grabbed the pack she'd kept waiting. They'd been outfitted thoroughly by the New Espiran Council, including with a type of clothing that she'd never seen that she was told resisted cold, heat and water. The council had also given them blades of Firstfall steel and thorn rifles and tents that could be magicked.

Even now, a few of the Knives of Tam—that's what they'd called themselves—were moving about the corridor prepping to disembark. Isaak had never come back to their room last night after the meeting with Ire Li Tam, but she knew where she would find him.

She could hear the mouth grinding slowly open beyond a round hatch that was slightly ajar; she followed the sound and climbed through the hatch.

The water had drained from the floor of Behemoth's mouth, and she made her way across it to where Isaak waited and watched the line of land beyond the jagged teeth. It was white with snow and specked with dark forms that moved.

Marta stood on her tiptoes to see over the teeth. "What are those?"

Isaak leaned out. "They are people. They are watching us."

"There are people this far north?" She squinted, but they were too far away.

"The New Espirans assure me there's a village nearby where we can double-check our maps and hire a guide." He held up a blue stone to the light and then slipped it into a pouch he wore over his robe.

"Are you ready, then?" she asked. They'd not talked much since they'd left the Grandmother Tree. He'd quietly accepted his part in the final bargain and hadn't discussed what had happened in Y'Zir since. She knew he wasn't finished processing the weight of it all, but she suspected he was done longing for repurposing.

He has found a greater purpose than his sorrow. And now he would some-how fashion a song from the ingredients of desolation and turn it toward life. She didn't understand it, but she didn't need to. She loved him, and so she loved his purpose, too.

Even the darker aspects that accompany it. He looked at her. "I think I am ready, though I am no psalmist."

She felt her brow furrow. "What is a psalmist?"

Isaak chuckled, and it was a musical note in shades of metal. "Some-one who writes psalms," he said.

Marta looked back to the people gathered in the snow and watch-ing them. They were closer now, and she saw they wore bulky furs and held spears. Then she looked to Isaak. "And what's a psalm, then?"

"A sacred song," he said, "or a hymn."

"Like the song we heard in the Final Dream?"

"Yes," he said.

"And the one you heard on the moon?"

"Yes," he said again.

She nodded and thought about it. "Maybe you are already a psalmist, Isaak, and we are the psalms you've written ahead of this time. Maybe this Psalm of Life you seek lives somewhere beneath all of that. Maybe it is more than a song." She didn't know, but she also didn't know why she suddenly felt so strongly about it. "That would make me just one of the psalms of Isaak," she said. "And Rudolfo another. Petronus and Neb, too."

Isaak looked to her. "I do not know, little human. It seems a bit much for a mechoservitor tasked with cataloging and translation." He sighed and corrected himself. "Marta." He looked back to the people gathering upon the shore. "But I know that sometimes you have surprised me with your wisdom. And I also know that we will face danger again soon. Yet I've resisted the urge in my scripting to insist that you return home."

She laughed. "Good. Maybe it means you've finally accepted that my home is with you."

Isaak nodded. "Maybe I have. But I do not know if you are my hymn or my heart for that matter," he said. "And I do not know if I can find the last of the Death Choir or write the Psalm of Life."

"Time will tell," she said, "and I believe that you can, Isaak." She reached and took his cold metal hand to squeeze it. "You can and you will."

The moon was low on the horizon and the sky was an odd twilight cast in tones of blue and green. Stars throbbed in the gray, and the people on shore kept pace with Behemoth as it sailed around a bend and slipped into a natural bay. Squatting at its edges was a village of wooden longhouses, smoke trickling into the sky from mud chimneys. There were more men and women in furs down at rough-hewn docks that were not currently in use.

The Knives had joined them now, two of them taking up positions in the open mouth with thorn rifles as Isaak raised his hands. When he opened his mouth, Marta didn't recognize the words he used, but they did and an exchange ensued.

Within an hour, they were crowded into a longhouse filled with laughter and song and food and drink. The people—dark-skinned and brown-eyed—had never seen anything like Isaak and had never seen anything like the tools and clothing and equipment they'd brought. They'd also never seen anything like Behemoth and made strange symbols in the air when they said its name in their halting tongue.

Within two hours, they'd arranged a guide and some form of pack animal in exchange for some kind of kin-clave ritual involving one of the young Tam men. Marta didn't ask.

Instead, she ate and drank her fill and tried to talk with the chieftain through Isaak, though the old man was too smitten with the metal man to pay her much mind. They spent the night eating and drinking what was before them—Isaak making a great show of pretending to eat and failing to loud guffaws—and at some point, everyone left but the chieftain, who pointed to a pile of furs in the corner before rolling off to his own.

They slept there, and that night she slept close to Isaak and listened to the hum of his inner workings as he did what he insisted wasn't sleeping, eyes closed with red light dancing beneath his metal lids. In the morning, their guide was waiting, along with the bleary-eyed Tam who'd purchased their hospitality and help in some ancient ritual or other.

Behemoth was gone now, sent away to wherever it rested until Isaak called it next. And ahead of them were vast rolling hills of frozen forest and steep mountains of shimmering white.

The guide pointed and said something to Isaak, who nodded.

"He says it will be a long day's walk."

Marta nodded. "Then we should get started."

The guide set out leading a large and hairy oxlike beast with long horns. Isaak followed him.

And for the first time, she noticed the metal man's limp was far less pronounced. Perhaps, Marta thought, he didn't need it anymore to remind him of the wounds that had shaped him. Or perhaps he was simply too focused upon the dream ahead to lose time in the backward dream of pain and regret. Maybe someday, she thought, he would not limp at all. She hoped so. Regardless, she would walk with him wherever he went and be as much his heart and home as she could because she chose to love him—the first and second gifts of the People working hand in hand. And so Marta turned her collar up against the cold to hide her smile as she followed quickly after.

Acknowledgments

A novel—especially the last novel in a five-book series—is an awesome and terrible undertaking, and I want to thank as many as possible for helping me across the finish line.

I wrapped my first draft of *Hymn* in April 2016 and sent the revised manuscript up in August 2016 . . . just a month ahead of the ten-year anniversary of starting *Lamentation*. It's been a long decade in the Psalms of Isaak. If you've been following, you'll know that each volume was dogged by major life events—parents dying, twins born, etc. This final volume was no exception, with the book interrupted at the mid-point by the passing of my close friend, Jay Lake. Jay was one of the two people who talked me into taking on this project. Until that night, I was going to focus on writing short fiction, where I was most comfortable. I will always be grateful to him and to Jen for that dare.

I had a lot of support as I pushed through this final book, especially the second half. I wrote it while adjusting to a New Den of Ken made possible by some wonderful friends who helped me manage more major change. So once more, I thank the Endicotts (and Michelle particularly for being a first reader), along with the Maggis and Jana (also a first reader!). Pam for kid support throughout. Joy and Jerry for moral support and first reading help. Tracy, Rachael, K. C., Tiah, Chaz, and I'm certain to be missing a few others who kept an eye on the book as it grew. Katherine, you came to the table late but the support, encouragement, and care have been invaluable as I've gotten my feet beneath me. Thank you all.

My inner circle worked hard throughout the last few years. Robert, Manny, John, and Alaina all brought wisdom and support to bear as I took the corners of change after change. I don't know what I'd do without you all.

Once more, the fine folks at Tor—with the world's best editor, Beth Meacham, and copy editor, Deanna Hoak—have brought another of my books to life. And Chris, I love the cover with Isaak. Thank you all.

I'd also like to thank my former agent, Jenn Jackson, for her support throughout the project. You are ever the 32nd daughter. And I'd like to thank my current agent, Howard Morhaim, for inviting me to his crew. Now that I'm finished with this project, I can't wait to see what we do together, sir!

I've dedicated the book to Lizzy and Rae and to Dr. Eugene Lipov. My daughters have added more joy to my journey than I could have possibly imagined and Dr. Lipov, with his groundbreaking treatment of Post-Traumatic Stress Disorder, has given me the capacity to experience that joy. My PTSD has now been in remission since January 2015 after a series of treatments with him in Chicago. If you or someone you know suffers from PTSD, learn more about his work at http://globalptsifoundation.org/.

Last, thank YOU, Dear Reader, for coming along for the ride. When I started, a decade ago, I had no idea how much change my life would experience as I wrote my first series about how people faced loss and trauma. It was a bumpy ride, but now we have all five volumes—around 750,000 words all told. And there are more stories to tell—dozens more—if time shows there is a demand for the stories or if the flash of inspiration strikes and I'm compelled to write them. Big thanks to all of you who've written notes, tracked me down on Facebook, come out to see me at events. These books have changed my life most significantly through the amazing people I've met along the way between here and France. So thank you all. If you had fun in my world, tell your friends!

Now, more change is headed my way. In a month, after a decade in the small town of Saint Helens, my daughters and I are moving to Cornelius to see what Story springs out of the Next Den of Ken.

With Gratitude,
Ken Scholes
Saint Helens, OR
May 30, 2017

About the Author

Ken Scholes is the award-winning, critically acclaimed author of five novels and more than fifty short stories. His work has appeared in print since 2000.

Ken's eclectic background includes time spent as a label-gun repairman, a sailor who never sailed, a soldier who commanded a desk, a fundamentalist preacher (he got better), a nonprofit executive, a musician, and a government procurement analyst. He has a degree in history from Western Washington University.

Ken is a native of the Pacific Northwest and makes his home in Cornelius, Oregon, where he lives with his twin daughters. You can learn more about Ken by visiting www.kenscholes.com.